US IN PIECES

Stories of Shattered Souls

BY FELIX I.D. DIMARO

US IN PIECES

Written by FELIX I.D. DIMARO

Cover Artwork and Interior Artwork: Rosco Nischler
Typography: Courtney Swank
Editing: Ally Sztrimbely

ALSO BY FELIX I.D. DIMARO

How To Make A Monster:
The Loveliest Shade of Red

Bug Spray:
A Tale of Madness

Viral Lives:
A Ghost Story

2222

The Fire On Memory Lane

The Corruption of Philip Toles

Black Bloom:
A Story of Survival

Warning

The stories in this collection contain mature subject matter, including coarse language, racist and homophobic slurs, bullying, child abuse, and scenes depicting sex and violence.

Discretion is advised.

For those from broken homes

"Because this city, this city is haunted
by ghosts from broken homes.
Because this city, this city is haunted.
There's no hope left for these souls."

Alexisonfire
(This Could Be Anywhere in the World)

Table of Contents

BENEATH
A WORLD OF
BEASTS

Piece #3

Beneath a World of Beasts

A Novella

PROLOGUE

The baby didn't cry after she had finally pushed it out of her. It made no sound or movement.

She waited to hear it bawl as her previous children had, as all babies should.

There were five people in the room with her and the newborn who hadn't yet decided if it would live or die. An infant who still made no noise, refusing to part its little lips as those all around it waited, silently encouraging.

The only sound she heard was the breathing in the room. And, beneath it, the noise of five hearts pounding, preparing to be broken as they waited to find out if a sixth heart would join their beating.

As she fought to stay conscious, she saw her baby twitch, its tiny limbs beginning to flail in its deliverer's embrace. Then a whimper, a whine, a full-blown wail.

After that came the sound of everyone in the room rejoicing.

She was able to lay back on the birthing bed in relief. Also, in agony.

This was the third child she had given birth to since she had come of childbearing age six years ago.

And it would be the third child she would have to witness being taken away. The third child it was her duty to give up. The third she would see borne out of this place and brought up into a deadly and uncertain world in hopes that it might one day help save it.

At least she hoped she would watch as it was carried up into the world. She wasn't feeling very well. Not very well at all.

The attention of those in the room turned from the baby to its mother. The faces looking down at her – faces belonging to her sisters, her guardian, and her husband – all expressed concern. Worry. Fear.

"Aurora? Are you okay?"

She heard the question, wanted to say 'Yes.' But all at once it seemed like moving her lips would be an extraordinary feat. She tried to nod instead of speaking, but her head felt as heavy as her body. Against her will, it lolled to the side. Her eyes closed.

"Oh, God. She's losing so much blood!"

She wanted to open her eyes, wanted to tell them that it was impolite to speak about her as though she weren't in the room. Then she realized, as she felt herself drift off, that she might not be present for much longer. If the distress in the voices around her was any indicator of things to come, she might soon not be there at all.

PART ONE

LIFE BENEATH

CHAPTER 1

"My, God, Aurora! You nearly scared the skin off me!" Goldy said, her hands at her chest, her breathing heavier than usual. Aurora looked at her, knowing that the woman had a penchant for the dramatic but appreciating that she had genuinely frightened her this time. Goldy never referred to her by her full name unless she was misbehaving. It had been that way since she'd been a child.

Aurora had been waiting for Goldy to return from the Sacred Chamber and one of her many meditations. She had been the first thing the older woman she considered both a mother and a mentor had seen upon exiting the solid metal door. A door to a room forbidden to Aurora and her sisters.

"I'm sorry, Aunty G," Aurora said, doing her best not to laugh. "I've just needed to speak to you badly. And you've been gone a while. Was it a successful session?"

Goldy had been gone an entire day, though this wasn't unusual for her. Aurora knew that what happened in the Sacred Chamber was excruciatingly delicate work that needed Goldy's full concentration. When Goldy entered the Chamber, she could be gone for as little as a few hours, or as many as a few days. There had been occasions when she had been gone for an entire week.

Goldy removed her hands from her chest and used them to smooth the flowing black dress she typically wore. Then ran her hands along her thick, wavy black hair, which was pulled back into a ponytail, as it often was. Her clothes weren't disheveled, and there wasn't a single hair out of place, but this was something she did regularly – the smoothing of her dress, her hair. It was a nervous tick, a calming mechanism.

"It was," Goldy replied, still not looking quite settled. "All is well within the Zone. Your children are safe and growing stronger by the day. The leaders are thrilled to hear of Belle's pregnancy. And that Jasmine's is coming along so smoothly. Two more babies will be a great boon to the Zone, and the prospect of the Rebellion as a whole."

She turned, locked the door leading to the Sacred Chamber, then placed her small ring of keys in the pocket of her dress.

Had that been disappointment Aurora had spotted on Goldy's face? Two babies, she had said. Two babies, when they all knew there should have been a third on the way.

But Aurora hadn't been able to conceive since she had given birth the last time. Since she had nearly bled to death nearly two years prior.

It had been Goldy who had saved her life that day. Now it was Goldy who she sought for permission to change her life. Drastically. In a way that neither she nor her sisters could have imagined might come so soon. But it hadn't come soon enough for Aurora, who had been putting off this conversation for far too long. And, judging by how her sisters had reacted to her plan earlier in the day while Goldy was in the Chamber, she expected this conversation to be a difficult one. Still, she was undeterred.

"The Zone and the Rebellion, that's what I wanted to talk to you about," Aurora said carefully as they both turned from the door of the Sacred Chamber. They walked down the short corridor that led to the main room of the bunker, the place they had been forced to call home for the last sixteen years.

The main room was what the sisters called their den. It consisted of peeling floral-patterned wallpaper, an old brown corduroy couch, a two seater sofa of the same design, an armchair made of cracked leather, and an old table centered roughly between those.

Behind and parallel to the couch was a treadmill. Opposite the couch, against the wall which separated the den from the kitchen, there was an old television set inside of an entertainment center. Beneath the TV was a VCR; surrounding both were dozens of VHS tapes the sisters had been watching for as long as any of them could remember.

Aurora and Goldy stepped onto an area rug in the den which had been tread upon until it was nearly threadbare.

This was the only place Aurora had ever known, though she was aware that, once upon a time, she had lived on the surface. Before they had been driven down beneath it. She could remember a single instance from that time aboveground. It was a fleeting memory, of herself as a toddler being handed from one woman to another. She remembered this only vaguely. But distinctly enough to know that the memory wasn't a pleasant one.

"What is it that you wanted to ask me, dear? Oh! Is that your mushroom soup I smell? *Exactly* what I need after such a long time away."

Aurora stood there, exasperated, as she watched her guardian walk across the den and through the entryway leading to the kitchen and dining area.

In addition to Goldy's retreating back, from where she stood, Aurora could see her sisters, Belle and Jasmine, sitting sullenly at the dining table, nothing on it between them but the burden Aurora had placed there. Dished out and served them. And now she was about to invite Goldy to dine upon it too. That is, if she could ever get the woman to stop and listen to what she had to say.

"Aunty G? We *really* need to talk," she said to her guardian, wanting to broach the topic with her before one of Aurora's sisters beat her to it.

11

"One second, Rory. Hi Belle, hi Jazzy! Did you help with this soup? It smells delish... Jazzy? Why are you crying? What's the matter?"

Too late, Aurora thought. She only had to wonder for a moment whether or not her sister would answer their guardian's question, because Jasmine shot up from the table and raced from the kitchen as quickly as her pregnant feet could carry her, moving through the main room and down the hall that led to the bathroom, the bedroom the sisters shared, and the bedroom belonging to Goldy and Bane, the latter of whom was currently braving the surface on a hunt.

Damn it, Aurora thought. She had hoped it wouldn't be this difficult. Had hoped that her sisters would support her. It was the only way she believed she could convince Goldy that what she wanted had to be done.

"Belle? What's going on with you and your sister?" Goldy asked, her voice spiking with concern. Aurora approached the kitchen slowly, making eye contact with Belle. Aurora could see that her sister's eyes were red rimmed. She had been crying too.

She shook her head at Belle from behind Goldy's back, indicating that it was her news to share. In response, Belle shook her head at Goldy, her short black locks bobbing as she did so. She looked down at the table, unwilling to answer their guardian's question. With no response from Belle, Goldy turned and looked at Aurora, her eyes wide with concern.

"Aurora! What is going on here?"

It was like she was truly seeing Aurora for the first time since returning from the Chamber. Only noticing her because her sisters were upset. Because her sisters were all that mattered now that Aurora was unable to conceive. That was why she had to do this.

"It's what I've been trying to say to you since you returned... I have to... I..." Now that the time to say it had come, she wasn't sure how she would come to say it.

"Spit it out, girl! What's going on with your sisters?"

"It's not about my sisters," Aurora said, finding her voice. "It's about me. It's time, Aunty G... I think it's time for me to leave the bunker."

Goldy only stood there, gawking at Aurora as she tried to process her words. Words she likely never thought she would hear from any of the three sisters. At least not for many years to come.

While Goldy was stunned by what Aurora had said, Belle seemed to take those words as permission to stop holding things together. Consent to fall apart. Like Jasmine before her, Belle, usually the most composed of the sisters, stood and hurried from the kitchen. The sound of her anguish trailed behind her as she followed the same path Jasmine had taken.

Aurora instinctively went to walk after her sister. Her sisters. But stopped. They would be okay, she reminded herself. Right now, she had to convince Goldy that what she wanted was the right thing for everyone.

She turned back to Goldy and saw that the shock had fallen from the face of her guardian. Now her expression was worry, fear, frustration, dismay.

Aurora took a deep breath and prepared to confront every concern evident on Goldy's face.

CHAPTER 2

It took some time for Goldy to speak or to move again. The first thing she did, after she had resumed movement, was to gesture with her head for Aurora to sit down.

Sitting at the table, Aurora watched the woman she called Aunty G, the woman who was the only mother she had ever known, walk across the small kitchen to the stove.

Goldy had rescued Aurora, Belle, and Jasmine from the Beasts Above when they had taken over the world, had saved the lives of the three sisters – three toddlers at the time – with the help of the man who had eventually become Aurora's husband. They had carried Aurora and her sisters into this bunker and kept them safe here ever since.

She watched as Goldy placed two bowls next to the pot on the stove. Bowls which had been left on the counter in preparation for a family lunch that wasn't to be had. The older woman filled them with mushroom soup. She brought the bowls over to the kitchen table before sitting there across from Aurora.

It wasn't until she had spooned and swallowed a hearty amount of the soup that she looked at the girl who was a daughter to her and said,

"So, tell me exactly why it is that you seem to have lost your mind."

Aurora couldn't help but laugh at the request. Goldy could be stern at times, but she knew how to make a tense situation feel better when sternness would provide no solution. She knew how to cheer them all up when cheering up was called for. It had been this way since they'd been old enough to understand that they had been born into a doomed world.

Aurora thought of all that the woman in front of her had done for her, and, mid-laugh, she began to cry. Continued to laugh. Did both.

Goldy smiled sympathetically, placed her hand on one of Aurora's, which had been tapping nervously on the table.

"Tell me why it is you'd want to leave your home, and one of the only safe places left, to risk the dangers of what's above us."

"To go to one of the only other safe places left. At least there I will be of use," Aurora replied.

"What on earth are you talking about, Rory? Not of use? Again, I have to ask you why it is you've lost your mind."

This time there was no laughter.

"Don't humor me, Aunt Goldy. I haven't been able to conceive in two years. You've told me my entire life that my sisters and I were chosen. Chosen by the Oracle at Clouds herself. You've said it was no accident that it was the three of us, girls, young and fertile, who were cut off from the rest of the group who attempted to make it to the Zone of Clouds. Kept safe while many who tried to travel there were slaughtered or enslaved.

"You told me that it was our destiny to survive so we could supply the Zone with children. Soldiers of the Future for the War to Come. We escaped death, you said, in order for us to create life. And to give up that life to save the world. To take it back from the Beasts Above. That is what you said." Aurora paused, let out a breath. She had become increasingly upset the longer she had been speaking. Her frustrations over the last two years were mounting now, but she knew it wasn't right to take them out on Goldy.

She took several deep breaths. Sought calm. Found it. Spoke more evenly though just as intensely.

"Are those not the words you've drilled into my head since the arrival of the Beasts? Is that not the sacred task my sisters and I have been sworn to?" Not waiting for Goldy to answer these questions, Aurora asked another, "How, then, can you ask me why I've lost my mind when you know that the purpose you told me was mine for my entire life – the whole reason for my existence – has been taken away from me by your God?"

Goldy recoiled as if slapped. She looked away from Aurora and focused on her stew. She slowly spooned the hot liquid into her mouth, once, twice, before putting the spoon into the bowl and pushing it away from her.

"It seems I've lost my appetite," Goldy said coldly, not looking Aurora in the eye.

"Aunt Goldy, I'm sorry. I don't mean to insult you. But since giving birth to Chance and nearly dying for the cause you and your Oracle ordained, I haven't been able to conceive. It has been hard for me to believe in the Oracle and God as strongly as you do. Can you not understand that?"

"So, you know better than the Oracle? You know better than me, who saved your life and kept you and your sisters safe for sixteen years? You know more than your husband? All of us want you here. Stay until your sisters can no longer conceive. Then you can all head to the Zone of Clouds together, as was the plan since we were separated from the others."

Aurora wasn't sure how to respond to that. She didn't want to seem disrespectful of Goldy or her Oracle, a woman who was the leader of the Human Rebellion. A psychic who had led several people to safety as the world had fallen.

The Oracle sent messages from the Zone to Goldy, who spent hours, days consulting with her in the Sacred Chamber, receiving communications and visions, instructions on how best they could survive and help the Zone. According to Goldy, the long sessions of silent meditation allowed her to intercept these messages more readily.

This being with a direct link to God had created a safe zone for survivors at the top of a mountain in the thin air near a place called Denver, Colorado, the high altitude making it one of the few places where the Beasts could not live.

They were called Bonkos – Beasts of No Known Origin – or at least that's what they had been called by those who had attempted to warn the world of their arrival. Those such as the Oracle. She had been ignored by most but followed by a few. Those few had made it to the mountain community she had built, the Zone of Clouds.

When the Beasts arrived, they had swarmed the world. From what Aurora had been told, they fed on human beings and other animals. Those they did not eat, they enslaved. The people who had made it to a high enough altitude, such as those in the Zone of Clouds, were safe. As were those who had made it underground.

From all that Goldy had told them, sixteen years ago, when the Beasts had swarmed humanity seemingly overnight and all the nations of the world had been defeated, there had been radio broadcasts from the Zone telling people to head there. Aurora, Belle, and Jasmine had been on their way to safety with their mother and her best friend, Goldy. They were part of a small community of survivors hoping to continue surviving in the safety offered by the Zone.

Most of them had stopped being survivors the day they were attacked, the majority of them killed. Those who had continued to survive did so in two groups, one of which had fled and made it past the marauding Beasts and all the way to the Zone. The other group, the group which had been living inside of this bunker since that day, was saved by the owner of said Bunker.

His name was Sebastian, but they called him Beasts' Bane. They had named him so for his bravery in saving them that day, and for all of the Bonkos he had slain ever since.

From out of woods next to the backroad they had been travelling upon, he had emerged. He'd slain their attackers and taken the children and Goldy underground to the bunker he had built in preparation for some sort of disaster, never imagining that disaster would be an invasion of Beasts of No Known Origin.

The mother of the girls hadn't made it. Not to the Zone nor to the Bunker. Goldy and Beasts' Bane had been taking care of the girls ever since.

And now, Aurora was telling the only mother she had ever known that she would rather face the dangers of the Beasts Above than continue living under her care. At least that was how it was being interpreted.

"I don't think I know better than anyone, especially not the Oracle. It's because of her that I'm bringing this up at all. You have been following her word since you began receiving visions. All these years, you've maintained that her visions have never been wrong. Well, she said I was meant to be a mother, supplying children to the Zone until I'm no longer able to. It seems as though that prophecy has been fulfilled. I'm no longer able to. And now it's time for me to move on to the Zone, reunite with our children, and help prepare for the Rebellion. That was what you said was ordained.... If you've believed in the Oracle all this time, how can you question my choice now? It *is* my choice, isn't it?"

Goldy sighed, stirred her soup with her spoon. Stared into the soup as she stirred as though she were searching for some answer in the bowl.

"We can't be certain you'll never get pregnant again, Rory. You can't give up hope."

"What does your Oracle have to say about that?"

"She says that there are dangers out there between here and the Zone that can kill you. That *will* kill you if you aren't careful. Careful and very, very lucky," Goldy said, looking up from her barely touched soup, her eyes pleading with the young woman she had been guardian of for nearly two decades.

"*He* can take me there safely. He's taken the babies there. And he makes it back each time in one piece."

"He's the greatest warrior the Rebellion has," Goldy replied, letting go of the spoon, giving Aurora a frustrated look. "And he stays here guarding us. He only makes the trip to Clouds when he absolutely must. Taking the babies there is one thing, but the more people who travel to the Zone, the greater the chances are of detection. He can keep a small baby safe in a carrier strapped to him far more easily than he can a young woman who might take a wrong step that will gain the attention of the Beasts."

"I know the logistics. I know I would have to climb and run and fight. But I'm ready. And, if I die, then I know I've served my purpose. I've given three future soldiers of the Rebellion to the ZoC. If I can no longer do that, and if I can't go there and join my children, nieces and nephews, and train as they train in their efforts to overthrow the Beasts, then what am I doing but taking up the limited resources we have here?"

Goldy made a motion to respond, but Aurora could see that something had caught her eye. Something behind Aurora had distracted Goldy. Even before Aurora could turn to see what that something might be, she heard a voice from over her shoulder.

"She's right, Aunty G," said Belle.

Aurora had turned and was looking her sister in the eye by the time she finished the sentence. Both of her sisters were standing in the entryway between the den and kitchen. More accurately, Belle was standing while Jasmine leaned against her. The youngest of the three was still crying as Belle held a supportive arm around her.

"She hasn't been the same since it became clear she could no longer have children," Belle continued. "I've tried to put myself in her position, and I would feel the same. We are ordained to serve the Zone and the Rebellion. We have sworn to it. If I could not bear children, I would want to go and fight. We shouldn't stand in her way if that is what Rory wants to do."

Aurora, relieved, looked thankfully at her younger sister, then at her youngest sister as Jasmine took a moment from crying into Belle's shoulder to glance at Aurora. She attempted a supportive smile.

Goldy sighed. All three sisters turned their attention to her.

"I don't want to stand in your way, Rory. But I can't guarantee that I won't have to. I'll consult with the Oracle immediately. But even then, it will come down to him. If your husband doesn't agree to take you, there's no chance. I can't permit you to go to the Zone alone."

CHAPTER 3

Their normal routine had never felt so abnormal as it did over the next day while they awaited his return.

Typically, they dealt with a great deal of sameness in their lives. Aurora, Belle, and Jasmine only ever saw the same four faces apart from their own. They had watched the same one hundred and thirty-four VHS cassettes over and over in the sixteen years they had been in the Bunker. And though they tracked the hours of each day, there was no discernable difference between morning and night, no changing of the seasons; nothing truly varied from one day to the next. They were aware of shifts in months, the passing of years, but everything was the same as it always was.

Their entire lives had been this two thousand square foot bunker beneath a world of Beasts. Beasts that had reduced human beings to near extinction. It had been this way for sixteen years. For nearly two decades it had been the same.

Now, not long after waking and completing their rarely varying morning chores, the three sisters sat on their same couch, watching one of those same VHS tapes. This time (for possibly the ten thousandth time) it was The Lion King, a movie Goldy had told them had become an instant classic when it had been released prior to the world being brought to a halt.

Most of what they watched were cartoons. When he had built this bunker and stocked it, the man they called the Bane of Beasts had piled it with entertainment that brought a smile to his face. They had grown up watching Fred Flintstone and his friends and family, George Jetson and his brood; the girls had read comic books and graphic novels about heroes and villains, books about magic and monsters. These were the best glimpses of the old world available to the three girls who had grown into young women in Bane's bunker.

As for the actual history of the world, they only knew what they had been told by Bane and Goldy. Goldy, who had been in the Sacred Chamber since abandoning her unfinished soup the afternoon before.

Aurora gave no mind to what communication Goldy might be receiving from the Oracle. She only cared about what Bane would say when he finally returned.

"Ugh. We should have watched something else. I'm going to start crying again if I have to watch Simba talking to Mufasa," said Jasmine. She was between her sisters, her head now on Aurora's shoulder as the three watched the movie playing on their old television. Aurora looked over Jasmine's head at Belle, rolled her eyes. The two older sisters both smiled at Jasmine's statement.

The youngest of the three had spent all of the previous day and night crying in their bedroom as they discussed the real possibility of being separated for the first time in their lives. Her two older sisters had consoled her until they had all fallen asleep in the same bed, despite having three in their room, and having Bane and Goldy's room available in its entirety. Jasmine had been between her two older sisters the night before just as she was now. Had fallen asleep while being reassured that everything would be okay.

"You cry at everything when you're pregnant, Jazz," Belle said bluntly, though not without affection. Aurora laughed and gave her little sister a squeeze. Jasmine had always been the most emotional of the three, and had become an overflowing bag of emotions for most of each of her pregnancies, this one being the third. She was due to deliver in two months, which meant the baby would be transported to the Zone of Clouds shortly after, depending on how healthy and strong it was.

Aurora's last birth, a boy named Chance, had needed to stay in the bunker with them for nearly four months before he was strong enough to transport. He nearly hadn't made it. That had been the only close call of the seven children they had combined to produce and provide for the Zone. Those children destined to be Soldiers of the Future in the War to Come against the Bonkos and their human thralls.

Aurora was desperate to reunite with Chance and her two daughters, her sister's children as well. Her plan was to go along with Bane when he brought Jasmine's baby to the Zone.

This wouldn't be the first time one of the sisters had asked about going to the Zone with him. They had often made this request when they were children, when they had begun to grasp their predicament. And Jasmine had begged to go when she had been forced to part with her first child, missing her dearly after months of separation. Each time, the answer was the same: The Oracle forbade it.

The logic, as far as the sisters could piece together, was that the three of them – the three who had been labeled the Mothers of Humanity – were invaluable. While it was dangerous to take a baby across the two hundred miles to the Zone of Clouds, the Oracle would rather risk tragedy befalling an infant than one of the Mothers. As cold as the logic behind the decision was, the girls were made to understand it. A baby could die and be replaced, one of the handful of women left on Earth who were of childbearing age could not. So, they were to stay in the bunker and produce soldiers for the War to Come. And when they could no longer do this, they would retire to the Zone and join the efforts however they could. Become soldiers themselves. Aurora felt she was ready for this now. It was the only solace she could take in being unable to do the task she had been ordained to do.

"I put this movie on so we could focus on the fun adventure, Jazz. Focus on the stuff with Timon and Pumbaa. Hakuna Matata. No worries, remember?" Aurora said, giving her sister a gentle squeeze. Jasmine pulled away from her, sat up on the couch, looked at her sister with sadness and anger in her eyes, on her face.

"But I *am* worried! Is that what you think you'll be going on when my baby is born? A fun adventure?"

"We agreed, Jazz. We won't be talking about this anymore until he comes back. There's no point. And it's not good for the baby."

Jasmine looked as though she were going to say something, then looked as though she were going to walk away, then as though she had no idea what she wanted to do. All of this was readable on her face over a matter of seconds. After a few more seconds, her choice of action was decided for her. For all of them.

They heard the hatch. The doorway in the ceiling in a corner of the bunker. The only point of entry or exit from their home.

They turned, looked up at the hatch behind them, the entryway located before the corridor leading to the Sacred Chamber. Watched it open, saw daylight shine into the bunker. Felt the chill of the outside air. By then they were all on their feet, still with the couch between them and the open hatch.

There was always nervousness when this happened. Anxiety. Because, each time, it could be the end. Each time, they worried it could be Bonkos or their human thralls who had discovered their hiding hole, shattered the lock, entered their personal safe zone; Beasts Above come below.

It wasn't anyone at first. What came through the hatch was not a person. From the entrance in the ceiling of the bunker fell a carcass, fell a corpse.

It hit the ground with a loud smack. The corpse was covered in burlap, the material red in the places where the dead body had been bleeding.

The three sisters looked at the carcass in the sack for a moment before they exhaled in triplicate. Relief released thrice into the bunker. Then relief turned to joy as the sisters burst into cheer. Hands slapped together, mouths whooped and wooooed as they all looked to the hatch to see the man they expected.

They saw his boots first, then his deer hide trousers. They saw his bow, the quiver of arrows on his back, the puffy jacket he always wore, stuffed with feathers, lined with fur. They looked upon the thick brown mane of hair that his fur-lined hood was supposed to cover.

He rarely had an unsuccessful hunt, almost always bringing them days or weeks of food to prepare upon his return.

This time it looked as though he had dropped a deer into the bunker, wrapping it in burlap before hauling it back from one of the places he had deemed safe to hunt. Places which were hours, if not days, away from the bunker.

He jumped to the floor when he was three quarters of the way down the ladder, landing with a foot on either side of the carcass he had thrown down before him. The slap of his boots against the cement floor resounded all around them.

His face was red from the cold of the outside world, making the long white scar that ran from his hairline to his beard – passing over his right eye and dividing his eyebrow in two as it did so – more pronounced than it usually was.

His name was Sebastian. They called him Beasts' Bane. And what he said, after looking at the three sisters, his three young wives, and flashing them a smile, his hazel eyes gleaming, was:

"Anyone ready for a feast?"

The response they gave him was an uproar of applause.

CHAPTER 4

"Seems like I have to travel further every time I want to get a decent catch," said the Bane of Beasts. "And it's damn cold out there. Colder than I ever remember it being before the Bonkos came."

He paused to cut into his venison steak. Then to dip what he had cut into the gravy on the plate and drag it through the mashed potatoes. Potatoes he'd plucked from the small greenhouse garden he maintained aboveground. He had been speaking about this last hunt since they'd sat down to this feast. And had been met with mostly silence from the girls as well as Goldy, who had returned from her consult in the Sacred Chamber not long after Bane had entered the bunker.

Everyone had been very vocal when he'd first returned. Cheering, crying happily, and singing, the troubles of the previous day seemingly forgotten once they set their eyes upon him. Their husband.

He had returned yet again, and that was worthy of celebration. His return meant survival, not only for him but for the entire family. Their worlds, their purpose, their ability to live, depended upon him surviving his forays to the surface where the Beasts roamed and ruled. Much like Aurora's future and her place in the Rebellion depended on his approval, and his ability to keep them both alive if he decided to transport her to the Zone of Clouds.

That potential expedition, and what it might mean for all of them, was why no one but Bane had done much talking since they'd sat down to eat.

Prior to sitting down to their meal, before coming to the time when they would have to address the terrible topic of Aurora leaving, the bunker had been as lively as it ever got. Not only were they happy to see Bane after he had been gone two days on this most recent hunting and foraging expedition, but his arrival with the deer carcass had given them something to do, and something positive to look forward to. Though the sisters realized they were preparing for a feast that each of them tried not to think of as a goodbye festivity.

As was the norm, Aurora did the majority of the work in the kitchen, though Belle and Jasmine were always happy to help and learn from their elder and more naturally gifted sister when it came to marrying flavors and making minor magic with the few ingredients and spices they had access to.

They had turned on music from the stereo that sat in their living room atop a corner table, choosing a cassette tape labelled "Greatest Hits of the 90s." Aurora and Belle had danced as they prepared their feast, skinning and butchering, pickling some of the meat in jars, putting other portions into their deep freezer for later meals, throwing into pots and pans what they intended to eat that evening.

Jasmine had sat at the table doing her best to stay off her swollen feet. She did sing along, however, even managing to laugh as she diced the onions, chopped the carrots, peeled the potatoes they had all been looking forward to eating.

None of them were eating with much enthusiasm now, however, as they sat at the table waiting for Aurora to deliver her request to the Bane of the Beasts Above.

"Okay," said Bane, his voice taking on a tone that indicated he was approaching a potentially severe situation and didn't know what to expect from it. "What's the matter with you all? You've barely said a word to me since I returned. And not a word to each other since we sat down. Was there a fight?"

"No. No fight," Aurora said quickly. Then, again, wasn't certain what to say. All of the buildup, the conversation with her sisters, her pleading with Goldy, all of it had been practice for this moment.

Her sisters and Goldy were looking at her, curious about how she would continue. Bane, upon seeing them watching her, turned his focus to Aurora as well.

"Rory? Is something the matter?" he asked gently.

"I suppose so," was the only way Aurora could think to respond. She fiddled nervously with the braided leather bracelet she wore on her left wrist.

Each of the sisters had received a bracelet upon reaching maturity and swearing themselves to both Bane and the cause of the Oracle. It was a symbol of their purpose in this world. From it, Aurora was attempting to draw strength.

"Everyone has known for a long time that I can no longer fulfil my purpose to the Zone." This time the eyes which had been watching her – six of the eight of them – turned away. Looked at their food, looked at the air above them, tried not to show how embarrassed for Aurora they had been since she had declared herself barren, knowing that she had labelled herself useless with that same declaration. Only Bane continued to watch her, not yet grasping where she was going with this topic. She aimed to clarify.

"You've told me since I was a child that each of us serves a purpose in the ZoC's plan to retake the world. You told me that it might seem like all we're doing is hiding, but our contributions are going to save humanity. Well, since becoming barren, I have felt purposeless. I've felt like all I am doing now is hiding. I don't want to hide anymore. Not while Aunt Goldy communes with the Oracle to keep us all safe and informed; not while you hunt for us and brave a world of Beasts to keep us alive and get our babies to safety; not while my sisters will continue delivering

Soldiers of the Future to the Zone for years to come. I don't want to sit here doing nothing while you all contribute in some way to the efforts of the Rebellion.

"What I'm saying, Bane", she added when she saw that he still looked confused as to what point she was trying to make. "is that I want to head to the Zone of Clouds with you when you transport Jasmine's baby. I want to go there and help in their efforts. I'm ready to truly prepare for war."

There was silence in response to this. That silence seemed to somehow echo, bouncing back at Aurora until it felt as though she were being assaulted by it. There were still only two eyes on her. Bane's. And they did not look particularly happy.

The silence was broken when he sighed. Then cut another piece of venison. Popped it into his mouth. Chewed it slowly. His face indicated he was considering what he was chewing on, though Aurora wasn't certain if what he was considering was the steak or the request she had just made. Perhaps it was both, because after he swallowed, he said,

"This is the best meal you've prepared for us yet, Aurora. How can I say goodbye to both you and meals like this for the rest of my time here? Is that a fair sacrifice to ask a man to make?" Then he cut into another piece of meat. Gravy. Potatoes. Contemplative chewing.

"I..." Aurora wasn't certain how to respond. Wasn't sure if he was being serious.

"I killed two Beasts before I killed this deer. There are fewer of them now – deer, not Beasts. The creatures feed on them, too, as you know. They feed on the deer just like they feed on us, because we're all animals to them. They grow stronger out there while the Zone prepares a rebellion that might be destined to fail."

30

"With all due respect, Bane, you dishonor the Oracle with those words. The Oracle has saved hundreds of people who would have otherwise been doomed," Goldy interjected. Her time in the Sacred Chamber after Aurora had told her of what she hoped to do had been unsuccessful. The Oracle had not communed with her, Goldy had told them. She had sat in the Chamber meditating for hours without any revelation. It seemed that Aurora's future would truly depend on what Bane would say. Bane, who didn't seem pleased by Goldy's interruption.

"Your Oracle. It's always about your *Oracle*. A person you haven't met for yourself. But I have. And I often think she knows as little as the rest of us. What did she have to tell you about this request of Rory's?"

Goldy looked as though she had been slapped. She only shook her head and stared down at her food.

"It seems the Oracle is leaving this decision up to me," said Bane. "And I say no."

Silence. Then the sound of chewing. A cough. A fork or knife scraping against a dish. All non-confrontational sounds until Aurora cleared her throat.

"So, it seems we're prisoners here after all."

"Stop it, Rory," Belle said. "We've been through this already."

The last time an accusation of imprisonment had been made, it had been made by Belle. This had been when the girls were children. Belle had insisted on seeing the outside world. Both Goldy and Bane had warned her of the dangers and desolate conditions of the surface, but the ten-year-old Belle had insisted that it was all a lie.

After days of tantrums and cries of imprisonment from Belle, Goldy had gone to consult the Oracle. Bane had decided not to wait for advisement. He had taken all three girls up the hatch and out to the surface. Nearly instantly, all of them, Belle especially, had screamed to go back underground.

It had been dark, and it had been cold. A cold unlike any they had ever experienced. The ground was white, piled with snow, a confusing substance that was both frozen and wet.

Because of Belle's days of insolence, Bane had dragged them into that snow, barefoot, onto a path that led into the trees surrounding their bunker.

At the end of the path it had no longer been dark. The glowing eyes of one of the Beasts illuminated the night to the point that they could see each other in the light of its stare.

It had sat there, large but low to the ground, growling at them. A constant rumble that they felt nearly as much as they heard. The creature – as big as all of them combined – had seemed ready to pounce, its large teeth bared between those great glowing eyes.

The sisters, led by Belle, had rapidly retreated to the hatch where Goldy was waiting to guide them back below. They had heard the sound of the Bonko behind them still rumbling on the path as they descended. That sound had haunted them even after Bane had returned to the bunker and closed and locked the hatch after silencing the Beast. That creature, he had warned them, had been only one variety of Bonko. There were many types of them out there.

The sisters had been eleven, ten and eight when that had occurred. Now, nine years later, it seemed as though history might be about to repeat itself.

"*Prisoners?* After we saved your lives and gave you purpose? After we've kept you clothed and fed and *safe*? You ungrateful little..." Goldy censored herself. Paused and seemed to consider her words before continuing.

"Whenever you are ready, I will unlock the hatch for you myself. Feel free to find your way to the Zone. But I will not risk my husband because you don't appreciate what you have here." She said it calmly enough, but this was the angriest the sisters had seen Goldy since Belle's brief rebellion when they had been small girls.

Matching that anger was Aurora, determined, finding confirmation that her decision was the correct one wherever possible.

"You see? She agrees with me! I'm worthless now. She wouldn't care if I left the bunker and was eaten by the Bonkos! But I'm not asking to only be let out of here, Bane. I *need* you to take me along the next time you go to the Zone. I don't want to continue sitting here being so expendable. I want to go to the ZoC. I want to fight!" She glared at Goldy as she said this. This time, Goldy didn't evade her eyes.

"I don't want you to leave, you ungrateful little bitch. Not whatsoever. But that doesn't mean I have to put up with your insolence. Not after all I've done for you, your sisters, and the Zone."

"What *you've* done? What have *you* done, barren as *you* are? My sisters and I have birthed *seven* children. *Seven!* And we've watched each of them be taken out of here to be sent to the Zone of Clouds. We mourn repeatedly for the Rebellion. Don't you dare make it seem as though you've done more for us than we have done for *your* cause! You and your damn Oracle!"

"Enough!" Bane shouted as he slammed a fist onto the table. Dishes rattled, silverware jumped, as did Jasmine. She was crying again, though Aurora couldn't say for certain when her tears had started. Bane continued, "You're no prisoner here. You know that, Rory. I was too quick to dismiss you, and for that I apologize. Tonight,

33

you'll stay in my room. We'll discuss things in private. Now, please, apologize to Goldy. Goldy, you do the same."

"Apologies."

"Apologies."

The same word, the same tone – that of resigned rage – from two different mouths. Their eyes would not connect, both looking at the surface of the table.

"Good," Bane said. "Then we shall continue to feast and treat this as the celebration it ought to be."

He thumbed at his cheek, at the scar that made up a decent portion of his face. It was white and pronounced, though it did not make him ugly. It only seemed to be constant proof of his point. An ever-present reminder of the dangers of the world above. Of what he had endured to drag them into this bunker and save them from the fate that had befallen most of humanity.

There was no retort to his statement. They did as he requested. The sounds of their celebration:

Cutlery against plates.

The hard swallow of a drink of water.

Chewing. Chewing.

Above it all, Jasmine's incessant mourning.

CHAPTER 5

"What do you think he'll say?" Belle asked Aurora.

It was a half hour after Bane had declared they should continue their feast, and they had done so dutifully, wordlessly, finishing their food in short order, no one much in the mood to sit around the table or to speak.

Typically, after Bane returned with a catch and called for a feast, everyone talked and celebrated into the night. They would dance, play games, and chat as a family until it was time to go to sleep, leaving chores and cleanup until the next day.

Currently, Bane and Goldy were in their chamber. Jasmine was in the girls', having complained of her feet, her lower back, and being tired in general. Belle and Aurora were in the kitchen, at the sink, Belle washing the dishes and Aurora towelling them dry before placing each one in the rack on the counter.

"I think he'll say no. I only wish I didn't have to share his bed in order to hear it," Aurora said, looking over her shoulder toward the entryway to make sure no one but them was in the room, whispering regardless of their privacy.

"It's a privilege to share our husband's bed, Rory. And you should count yourself lucky. He favors you. He always has." There was a hint of jealousy in Belle's voice as she said this. It was true, Bane had always seemed to gravitate toward Aurora. She hadn't minded this when their laying together had been an act necessary to fulfil the Oracle's prophecy, their babies the key to taking back the planet from the Bonkos. She had been proud to do it. But it had been nearly two years since she'd been with child, and the act now felt empty and purposeless. It was only during these last two years that she had realized just how little she enjoyed the act of making babies with this man when no babies were made as a result of it.

"It's only because I'm the eldest. I'm the first of us he was told to wed and bed by the Oracle."

"It's more than that and you know it. Your baby weight has always melted right off. And now that you have been without child for so long, you're as thin and beautiful as you have ever been. It's no wonder he won't allow you to leave."

"This has never been about beauty or attraction. It has been about the Oracle's prophecy. About our duty. That is what matters, that is why he should escort me to the Zone. And stop being foolish, Belle. You're twice as pretty as I'll ever be." Aurora meant it, but Belle's words could not be entirely dismissed.

Belle gained more weight than her sisters when with child. Her weight gain was already starting early into this pregnancy. And though Goldy encouraged each of them to make use of the exercise videos and treadmill they had down in the bunker, it was always a struggle for Belle to lose the weight she gained. While Aurora thought her sister no less beautiful because of this, it couldn't be argued that Bane had spent more time with both Aurora and Jasmine than he had with Belle over the last several years. This was especially disheartening to Belle knowing that Aurora could no longer provide the man with children.

"You're kind to say that, Rory, but we both know he doesn't feel that way. You're right, though. It's not about looks or who he lays with more, it's about our duty to the Oracle and the Rebellion. It's about you feeling like you are still a part of the uprising. I can't say I hope he allows you to go, but I want you to be happy. I want you to feel as fulfilled as Jasmine and I do. I'll continue to support you however I can in hopes that you can find that fulfilment, but *please* no more accusations of imprisonment. And no more disrespect toward Goldy or Bane. They saved us and have taken care of us since we were children. Even if he says no, just remember that no matter what you end up doing while we remain here, it's better than being dead. That's the only time you'll truly be useless."

"You're right," Aurora said, placing a dried plate into the rack before taking a wet bowl from her sister and putting her towel to it. "They'll get no more argument from me. It wasn't fair of me to say what I said. I'll do whatever is asked of me."

She meant these words, though she knew how Belle would interpret them. She would interpret them as deceit if things went the way Aurora expected them to. In her mind, doing what was asked of her entailed following what the Oracle had already ordained: the Mothers of Humanity shall arrive at the Zone of Clouds when they are no longer able to bear and birth the Soldiers of the Future.

Aurora would fulfil that prophecy. She was intent upon it. Because, whether or not Bane gave his permission, she planned to head to the Zone with him when he took Jasmine's child. If he wouldn't accept her by his side, then she would find a way to sneak out after him, out of the hatch on her own, and follow him at a distance.

Within two months, one way or another, Aurora would be out of this place and onto fulfilling her destiny.

CHAPTER 6

"Why is it that you choose to continue to lay with me even after knowing that I can't conceive?" Aurora asked nearly immediately after Bane had rolled off of her. It was hard to describe to herself how she felt just then. She had been struggling with feelings of uselessness for years now, but she would never become accustomed to the feeling of being used for something she saw no purpose in.

The act they did together had always been one meant for procreation, the fulfilling of a prophecy, the creation of a soldier that would save humanity. It was said by the Oracle that the hero to reclaim the world would come from Bane's seed and be born from the belly of one of the three sisters he harbored. With her belly barren despite his seed inside of her, she had never enjoyed the act less.

"Is this all duty to you and nothing else?" Bane asked as he lay back on the pillow, sweating faintly and breathing hard after only a few minutes of them engaging in the act. It always seemed to take a great deal out of him, which made her wonder how he managed to make it to and from the ZoC as frequently as he did. It made her believe that the journey must not be as difficult as he made it out to be. That thought was quickly followed by the realization that she was perhaps grasping at straws, looking for ways to convince herself that the journey to the Zone wouldn't be the hellish ordeal it was sure to be. Each time she allowed herself to think that it might be easy, she looked at the scar on his face and was reminded otherwise.

"It is duty *and* it is love, Bane. But..." Aurora began her response before knowing how to finish it "... but it is no longer my purpose. My mind is for the Zone. Have you decided if you'll take me?"

He sighed, took her hand, placed it on his face so that her fingers traced his scar.

"Have you not seen what nearly became of me out there? Do you want this to be your future?"

She looked at the old wound carefully, felt the scar tissue beneath her fingers, then said something she never thought she would say aloud.

"I see the same scar I have always seen, Bane. Each time you return, I see no new wounds. It makes me believe you know your way. That you can keep me safe, and that we can beat these creatures."

He looked at her as though shocked. Then there was something else in his eyes as he and Aurora watched each other in the dim room, the table lamp that he insisted they keep on during the act providing the only light. He was looking at her with a mixture of pride and surprise.

"So observant is our little Rory. You really are the smartest of the three of you. I'll be sad to see you go."

"Wait... Does that mean..."

"I'll take you to the Zone of Clouds," he said, sounding nearly defeated as he did so. He kissed her hand then placed it on his chest. She felt his rapidly beating heart. "But I won't take you when I transport your sister's baby. I'll do so sooner. I can keep a baby safe because it is strapped to me, essentially just another portion of myself. But keeping another grown adult alive is an entirely different matter.

"You'd have to climb and sleep in trees, be able to walk slowly and carefully even when the fear you're feeling is telling you to run. These things out there, they're hypersensitive to movement. And when they detect you, there's little hope in outrunning them. My goal is to never be detected when I travel to the Zone, but I've had to kill far more of them than I like to remember because even I make mistakes. If *you* make a mistake, they'll be on both of us. It's dangerous. And that's an understatement."

"I'll take danger over worthlessness any day," she responded without a moment of hesitation.

"But will you take death?"

"Yes," Aurora said, unflinchingly.

He kissed her hand again.

"Tomorrow we'll do dinner over. Do it properly. And this time it will be a celebration of you joining those at the Zone of Clouds. Then you and I shall leave the following day."

CHAPTER 7

Aurora was surprised to see that Jasmine wasn't crying. It seemed that the youngest of them had somehow come to terms with the fact that she might not see her eldest sister again. Not for decades, perhaps not again in this world.

She had fallen to pieces the day before when Aurora had announced officially that she would be heading to the Zone with Beasts' Bane. Now, as they stood beneath the hatch of the bunker, Jasmine only looked at her sister in an almost contemplative way, as though she were trying to register and remember every detail of her face.

"You'll see me again, Jazzy. I promise," Aurora said as she took her very pregnant sister in her arms, kissing her on the cheek before rubbing her belly. Her words felt like a lie, though she knew she would do her best to make them true. She looked at the rest of them; her entire family standing and watching her prepare to climb up the ladder and face the outside world for the first time in a decade.

She was dressed warmly, covering layers of clothing with a jacket and britches she and her sisters had fashioned of deer skin and rabbit's fur originally for Bane. The outdoor wear had been quickly altered the night before to fit her. It was the warmest she had ever been. And it was the most love she had ever felt as she looked at her guardian and at her sisters, the wives of her husband.

Goldy looked as angry as she looked sad, and Aurora understood why. She was losing someone who had been a daughter to her. Someone she had promised a dying friend to take care of for the remainder of her days. And now that someone was to trek two hundred miles through a world of Beasts. Despite the fact that Goldy was upset about her charge leaving, she walked over and embraced Aurora. Kissed her on the cheek.

"I wish you weren't so headstrong, child."

"I'm a woman now, Aunty G. I have been for some time. And now I can be with our children and help in a way that matters. If you fault my determination, blame yourself. I've learned all I know from you." The words provoked both a smile and a tear from Goldy. She placed her forehead against Aurora's.

"You're too smart for your own good, you know that, *woman?*"

"Again, your fault." They laughed and embraced again. And had barely parted ways before Belle was in front of Aurora saying her parting words.

"You keep everyone safe until you join me in the Zone, okay?" Aurora said in response to Belle's farewell.

"I'll do my best. Take care of our little babies. Raise them to be warriors as brave as you," said Belle.

"I swear it."

There were tears, there were 'I love yous'. There were no goodbyes. Instead, there were many different words that all meant 'I'll see you again'. Then, with Bane leading the way, Aurora climbed out of the bunker and into the cold open air.

CHAPTER 8

"It's been three miles so far. Let's stop and rest here. Pass me the water in your pack, please," Bane said to Aurora as he stopped on the path they had been walking.

They were surrounded by trees – some leafless, some bushy and green – and open sky. Snow was on the ground, but Aurora had been happy to see that it wasn't the mountains of snow she remembered from a decade prior when she and her sisters had witnessed one of the Beasts.

So far, on this brief beginning to their excursion, they hadn't encountered any Beasts. Bane had explained on many occasions that the creatures were more active during the night. Despite it being daytime, she had expected unfathomable terrors. Yet all she had been met with on her three mile walk from the bunker was wonder and marvel.

The feeling of breathing fresh, cold air was unlike anything she had ever experienced. The beauty of the late morning sun shining between the trees was art created right in front of her by nature's hand. She heard birds singing for the first time and nearly cried joyfully at the sound. The surface didn't feel like the dangerous place she had feared her entire life. It was almost enough to cause her to let her guard down, but she knew not to. That was exactly what the Bonkos would want.

"I'm okay to keep going if you are," Aurora responded, but the truth was she was glad to stop. She had run on the treadmill in the bunker all her life but had never physically walked this great a distance. Her feet, which were poorly dressed in deerskin boots, were already beginning to hurt. Looking down at her boots, she wondered how well they would hold up if she had to run. Wondered how she would make it the one hundred and ninety-seven more miles to the ZoC.

"I can tell you need the rest," Bane said. "We have a long journey ahead. It's best we don't wear ourselves out."

Aurora nodded, took her bag off her shoulder and rummaged through it for the water.

"Here it is," she said, grabbing one of three deerskin canteens from the satchel her sisters had made her for the trip. "I just hope we have enough for the entire tr–"

She stopped midsentence as she looked up to hand over the canteen to Bane. He was holding something out to her. But not in a way that suggested it was being offered.

It was something she hadn't seen before. Not in real life. Though she had seen artist's interpretations of it over the years in the many cartoon shows and movies they watched.

"Bane? Is that... Is that a gun?"

"Observant as always, Rory."

It was a gun he held in his hands. She had no idea why he was showing it to her now. Was he hoping to teach her how to use it? Was there something behind her?

She swivelled around, looked through the trees for a giant glowing-eyed Beast like the one she had seen all those years ago, but saw nothing. She turned back to her husband.

"Bane... Why are you showing me that? What's going on? Shouldn't we be on our way? What if the Beasts show up?"

"I'm sorry, Aurora. I'm sorry it had to end this way. I really wish you could still be of use."

"What?" she said, not understanding, wondering why he hadn't answered any of her questions. Though it only took her a moment to figure out that he never would.

She didn't see his finger pull the trigger, but she heard the gun's noise, felt its effect.

There was a bang.

Her body stumbled backward.

Another bang before she even hit the ground.

Then she was on the forest floor, looking up at the clear blue sky she had marvelled at only minutes ago. Now, not knowing why, she looked at it for answers. But the sky provided none. Then the sky was blotted out by the man called Beasts' Bane as he stood above her.

She tried to talk but couldn't. Even if she could have, he would not have given her the chance.

Her aimed the pistol at her. At her head.

"I truly am sorry."

She closed her eyes. Thought of her sisters, all of their children. Thought of her son, Chance, and her two daughters. Thought of the sky.

Heard the sound of the gun for a third time.

CHAPTER 9

Aurora didn't know if a second or a minute or an hour had passed. Every moment was agony.

She was confused, in pain in places while numb in others. She was hurt – her body, her mind – but she was alive. Bleeding too much once again, though this time with no midwife to help her. This time, she thought to herself, she would bleed until she died.

There was a sound near her, coming from her right side. A rustling of leaves, a crunching of snow. A Beast from Above now suddenly beside her.

She wished she would bleed to death faster.

Her eyes were closed. She felt it sniff her, heard its growl. With all the strength she had left, before she could feel its bite, before she could experience being consumed, she willed herself into darkness. And did so successfully.

PART TWO

THE BEASTS ABOVE

CHAPTER 10

Belle had a bad feeling. A terrible feeling. She'd had it since seeing the hatch close behind her older sister. Now she was on the couch, trying to convince her younger sister that everything would be alright.

"Everything's going to be okay, Jazzy. Just try to relax. Focus on the baby. This could be the one who saves the world. You don't want him to come out sick because you've been stressing."

Jasmine had held it together just long enough for the hatch to close, then she had immediately gone to the couch, collapsing there as she cried. Goldy had helped to console her for a few minutes before letting the girls know that she felt she was being summoned to commune with the Oracle.

That had been over three hours ago. Goldy had been locked in the Sacred Chamber ever since while Jasmine alternated between being tolerably upset and being outright hysterical. The television was on, a movie was playing, but neither of them had been paying much attention to it. Nor would they pay attention to the television again. Not this particular movie, not any of the others in their collection.

Because they heard a sound behind them. The sound of the Sacred Chamber being opened and Goldy coming out of it. And that sound, on this day, would signify the end of life as they had always known it.

"Girls!" Goldy yelled as she ran her way down the hallway from the Sacred Chamber to the den. She stopped in front of the sisters, blocking the television they hadn't been paying attention to. She looked upon the girls as though she hadn't been certain they would be there, almost relieved to see them. Her face was plastered with concern, a portrait of things gone wrong.

"Something terrible has happened!"

Both Belle and Jasmine sat up on the couch, neither of them wanting to believe what they were hearing. Belle not wanting her bad feeling to be validated.

"What's going on? What's happened?" Belle asked.

"Is it Rory?" Jasmine inquired.

"It's all of us," Goldy said, her hand to her heart, her face flush, her eyes panicked. "I've been in commune with the Oracle. She has warned me that there is trouble coming. That we are all in danger!"

"From the Beasts Above? How could they have found u–"

Before the question could be asked and answered, they all heard the hatch being unlocked. Jasmine made a squeal of a sound and turned around on the couch to see the opening. Belle stood up, clenching her fists.

Standing side by side with Goldy, Belle wasn't sure whether or not she would have to fight off incoming Beasts and their human thralls within moments, two months pregnant though she was. If that were the case, she was certain it was the end of all three of the women left in the bunker. She took solace in two things; the first being that her sister may have gotten away before the Beasts finally found and invaded them. Rory was likely safe from a fate they'd all feared for years, one that had grown less worrisome with each passing attack-free day but had never fully abated.

The second piece of information that gave her solace was the fact that their children – the seven Soldiers of the Future – were safely in the ZoC, growing, preparing to one day save the world. No danger at their hatch, even if it was Death, could take away from the fact that the women of this bunker had done their duty.

She felt Goldy take hold of her hand as the hatch opened. Cool air and daylight entered in tandem. What followed those was a boot. Another. Deerskin trousers. A thick jacket, a fur-lined hood. The person inside of all these things climbed most of the way down the ladder before jumping down the final quarter of the length.

The Bane of the Beasts Above faced his three remaining wives. The fourth, with whom he had left only hours ago, no longer by his side. On his face was a look Belle had never seen. One she did not like whatsoever. What she liked even less was the fact that her sister was not with him. Bane had closed the hatch as he entered, indicating Aurora would not soon be following behind. Belle's heart sank in her chest as she realized what this meant.

"Aunt Goldy," Belle said to her guardian as she stared at Bane, who was glaring furiously at them. She was struggling to keep her composure, her throat feeling constricted, her chest feeling tight. "What was it exactly that the Oracle communed to you?"

CHAPTER 11

"Your Goddamn Oracle betrayed us!" was the first thing Bane said after dropping into the bunker. He took angry steps toward the three women in the living room. Belle and Goldy took steps back, Jasmine remained on the couch, watching Bane wide-eyed over the back of it as he stormed into the den.

"What do you mean, Bane? The Oracle warned me of danger, but only just now. What has happened? Where is Rory?"

"Your Oracle warned you too late! What good is being in commune with a creature who can only see a 'future' that has already happened?"

"Bane... Where is Aurora?" Belle asked, because he hadn't answered the question when it had come from Goldy.

Bane looked away. It was answer enough.

Belle slumped to her knees right there on the threadbare carpet. Goldy knelt beside her, held her hand. Jasmine was a ball on the couch, crying into herself.

"What happened?" Belle heard Goldy ask, her guardian's voice seeming to float a thousand miles above her.

"Bonkos. More than I could manage. They fell on us. In a blink we were swarmed! Aurora, that beautiful, stubborn girl, she saved me. She threw herself at them before I knew what was happening. She screamed for me to go back as she did it. The last thing she said to me..." He put a fist to his mouth and bit on it, attempting to control his emotions. In his eyes, Belle could see the glimmer of the tears he was fighting against. "...The last thing she said to me was to protect the two of you. Which is what Goldy and I now have to do."

"Has it truly come to this?" Goldy whispered. Belle still wasn't certain what to say. Aurora had promised Jazzy that they would see each other again. That promise had been broken in less than a day. And Belle could never chastise her sister for breaking it, because her sister was gone.

She pulled her hand violently away from Goldy, raised both hands to her face, screaming into them before lowering her head to the ground and weeping, her body taking the position of someone worshiping at the feet of royalty.

"No, Belle. Be strong. Now, more than ever, we need you to be strong." She heard the words as she felt the powerful arms wrap around her, allowed them to lift her until she was kneeling again. And he was there, kneeling beside her. Sebastian Beasts' Bane.

"We have to go. Goldy and I must go and fight. They know we're in the area. If we can head them off, get them to chase us elsewhere, you and Jasmine will have a chance at survival."

Belle looked at Jasmine, who was looking at no one as she burrowed her face into the couch. She turned to her left, where Goldy was standing. Her guardian nodded at her.

It was what they had always feared. The Beasts were here, and now Goldy had to go out and help Bane defend this place. They had discussed this possibility before, but no one had really believed it would happen. Not after so many years of peace.

Belle might have been able to handle the situation better if Aurora were there. But she was not, and there was the possibility that Goldy and Bane might never return. The possibility that his moniker was no longer as fitting as it had been when he'd first saved them all those years ago.

As if reading her mind, or perhaps seeing her doubts written on her face, Bane said,

"If we don't come back, we need you to be brave, Belle." He reached down and removed an object from his gear. Something that had been holstered to his leg. It was metal. It was dangerous. He aimed it in her direction.

"Take this," said Bane as he handed her his unsheathed hunting knife. Eight inches of sharp serrated steel.

"They may come to drag you from here, the Beasts and their thralls. If that's the case..." he looked into her eyes while making sure she had a firm grasp on the handle of the blade. And a firm grasp on what he was about to say. With the blade in both of their hands, he turned the sharp end of it toward her.

"If they try to enter here and take you, do not allow them to. Do you understand me?"

She nodded, though she wasn't certain that she did. As if reading this from her as well, he clarified.

"Being taken by them is a fate worse than death. Remember that. If they come for you and your sister, do not let them take you alive."

With that said, he kissed her on the forehead. Rose. Walked to the couch and rubbed Jasmine's back. Whispered something Belle couldn't hear into Jasmine's ear. Kissed the back of her unturning head.

"We'll be back as soon as we can lead them away from here. But if we can't..." Bane said as he made his way toward the ladder leading to the hatch. Without finishing his sentence, he nodded to the knife in Belle's hands. Belle nodded as well, looking at him through tear-filled eyes. She knew what she had to do.

Without saying goodbye, he sped up the ladder. Before opening the hatch, he turned, looked down, and said,

"Stay safe, my girls. I wish it didn't have to come to this, but we all knew that it would. Stay safe!"

Goldy went up the ladder after him. In her usual black dress, she was clearly unprepared for the cold of the world Belle had been warned of her entire life. Though perhaps the heat of war would give her all the warmth she would need. At least that's what Belle hoped.

Hope? There goes all of our hope, she thought as Goldy waved at them. Said, "May the Oracle bless you both," before heading out the hatch. Belle heard her lock it securely behind her. And just like that, in only a matter of hours, her family of five was reduced to two.

CHAPTER 12

It took hours for Jasmine to cry herself to sleep. She had done so with her head on Belle's lap, her elder sister trying to console her with what felt like many lies.

Each time Belle had said that their guardian and their husband would return soon, she imagined the Beast they had seen in the dark all those years ago. How something that big and ferocious could be defeated, she hadn't a clue. How a world full of them could be overcome, she could not fathom.

Each time she had said to Jasmine that things would be okay, she imagined how many people had told their loved ones those same words when the Beasts had first arrived. Nearly every single one of them had been wrong. Made into liars by the creatures who had swarmed them and turned the world to terror.

Whenever she told Jasmine that they were survivors, ordained to be so, she remembered that Aurora had been included in that 'we', yet she had not survived. Once Jasmine had finally fallen asleep after moistening Belle's lap with her tears, Belle's mind could not escape that last thought. The idea that one of them hadn't survived. She couldn't help but imagine what it must have been like for Aurora, sacrificing herself for Bane, for Goldy, and her sisters. Each time she closed her eyes, she saw her sister being ripped apart, dismembered and devoured. She prayed for the image of her sister's death to leave her mind, prayed to stop picturing Aurora's grisly fate.

Her prayers were answered. Because from the hatch leading to the surface came a noise. A loud sound. One which let her know immediately that she would no longer be burdened with imagining the carnage the Beasts could cause.

It was a banging, several thumps. Then a sound like someone or something trying to manipulate the mechanism that kept the hatch locked. Mixed in with these noises was a muffled, frustrated roar. A beastly shout.

The time for imagining what had happened to Aurora was over. Belle expected that she and Jasmine were about to find out what had happened for themselves.

The Beasts Above, they were here. And they were trying to make their way beneath.

CHAPTER 13

"Jasmine! Wake up!" Belle said, though she hadn't needed to. By the time she had peeled her eyes from the hatch and all the noises coming from it, Jasmine was awake, lifting her head from her sister's lap. She had registered the noises as well.

Belle watched her for a moment, waiting for her to begin to cry again. The youngest of the sisters didn't weep, however, her face only displayed defeat. As though she had been through enough this day, and this new calamity was too much for the world to ask her to deal with.

But to Belle's surprise, Jasmine must not have been as defeated as she appeared, because she reached down to grab the hunting knife from the floor, along with a butcher's knife Belle had gotten from the kitchen to add to their small arsenal before Jasmine had fallen asleep. She handed the hunting knife to Belle as both young women stood up from the couch.

They looked at the hatch as the banging and thumping and shouting from the other side of it continued.

"I guess this is it," Jasmine said, sounding resigned.

"Seven Soldiers of the Future, Jazzy. No matter what happens here today, remember that the three of us served our purpose well," Belle replied, though even as she said this, she was looking around the room, as if some magical portal might open up and give them a way to escape.

She heard the sound of something snapping from the hatch. Pictured, with that vivid imagination of hers, one of them biting off the lock after many of them had worn it down.

Jasmine was hyperventilating beside her as they both watched the hatch rise. Felt the cold air, though no daylight accompanied it on this occasion. It was night, the time these creatures were most active.

With the hatch open, they heard the grumbling of the Beasts. The sound was not as loud as she remembered it from all those years ago on her brief trip to the surface with her sisters, but it was plenty loud enough to break her trance and move her to action.

"Come!" Belle said in a harsh whisper, not interested in waiting to see what would drop down into the bunker. "To Bane's bedroom. They might not find us beneath the bed." It was desperate, but it was the only thing Belle could think of. She grabbed her sister by the wrist and went to pull her along.

"No," Jasmine said staunchly, defiantly. Belle felt her temper flare. She was not in the mood for Jasmine's emotionality. Not when the hatch was open and she could hear the creatures looming outside of it. This might be the only opportunity they would get to hide. When she turned to tell her sister this, she saw that Jasmine didn't need convincing.

"Not Bane's room," Jasmine said, her eyes pleading. "In there!"

She was pointing down the corridor, to something that Belle had never seen in her sixteen years down here in the bunker. She was looking at the door to the Sacred Chamber. And while the door itself wasn't unusual, the fact that it was ajar was.

The Sacred Chamber had never been left unlocked, let alone left open, in all of Belle's life. Goldy must have forgotten to close and lock it behind her in her haste to fight the Beasts. Goldy, who, along with Bane, had undoubtedly failed in her attempt at heroism, Belle realized, feeling a further weight added to the burden she already carried on her heart.

Belle forced herself to push the sadness aside. They were gone, and might be gone forever, but they had left behind for the girls this little bit of hope. Inside the Sacred

Chamber, with that heavy steel door locked behind them, they might have a chance at survival.

"Bless the Oracle. And may the Oracle bless Bane and Aunt Goldy," Belle said as she and Jasmine ran toward the Sacred Chamber. They made it through the corridor and past the heavy metal door just as they heard the Beasts begin to descend into the bunker.

CHAPTER 14

"Whoa! What is *this*?" Jasmine asked from behind Belle after Belle had turned on the lights. For several nerve-wracking seconds until Belle's hand had swept over the switch beside the door, they had thought they would be entirely in the dark. Belle was now facing the door after locking it. Her body weight pressed against it as though that would be the difference between the Beasts being able to break into the room and them being stuck on the outside of it.

Not removing herself from the door, she turned and looked around this room that had always been a mystery to them, to see what could have prompted Jasmine's question.

When she saw it, her surprise was so great that she nearly forgot there was a pack of creatures chasing them, dropping into the bunker one by one to hunt them down. She stopped leaning against the door and walked toward what it was that had baffled her sister.

Belle had expected to see a shrine to the Oracle, a candelabra or two, a comfortable place to meditate. She thought there might even be a toilet, a fridge, and a bed, considering that Goldy sometimes spent days in here communing with the Oracle. But Belle saw none of these things inside the Sacred Chamber. Because she saw no Sacred Chamber at all.

They were not inside a room, but rather a space not much larger than the pantry in the kitchen. At the back of the small space, roughly six feet from the door, was a ladder. It was bolted to the wall just like the one in the main area of the bunker.

"Maybe the Sacred Chamber is outside?" Jasmine said, but she didn't sound like what she was suggesting made much sense to her even as she said it. It didn't make much sense to Belle either.

But there would be no time to stand there and make sense of it because behind her

Thump!

was a sound

Thump!

repeating loudly

Thump!

from the door.

Thump!

And with that sound, a muffled roar.

The Beasts were trying to break in. Suddenly that solid steel door didn't seem like much of an obstacle at all. Didn't sound like it would be an obstacle for long.

"Up, Jazz! Up, up, up!" Belle said, gesturing her pregnant sister toward the ladder.

Thump!

Jasmine looked from the shuddering door to her belly to the ladder. Sighed. She placed the butcher's knife between her teeth, stepped toward the ladder and began to climb.

CHAPTER 15

"Hurry up, Jazz!" Belle said from beneath her sister. She was regretting not going up the ladder first, but she hadn't wanted her sister trailing behind, making it easy for those creatures to get Jasmine if they were able to break into the Sacred Chamber. A place that had turned out to be not much of a chamber at all.

Belle was prepared to fight them off even now as they continued banging on the door behind her. Despite being prepared to give her life for Jasmine and the baby inside of her, she was frustrated with her little sister. Belle believed she could have opened the hatch already if given the chance.

Jasmine, struggling with the hatch, and apparently not appreciating her sister's constant encouragement, mumbled something that sounded like an insult, the knife between her teeth making her words unclear.

"Don't worry about talking, just open it!" Belle urged her.

The thumping behind them had stopped. Belle hoped it meant they had given up.

That hope only lasted for a moment before there was another sound, a terrifying noise unlike anything she had ever heard.

It was a creature that sounded nothing like the others. It must have been a Beast of unbelievable size. And it was screeching incessantly while scratching violently at the door. The sound was loud, piercing, it threatened to penetrate Belle's skull.

"Go! Open it!" Belle shrieked at her sister, though her voice was drowned out by the screeching monster behind them.

Finally, Jasmine did open it. Partially. She pushed up on the hatch. It moved but wouldn't completely lift.

"Get up higher. You have to push it harder!"

Jasmine did. And Jasmine did. Then the hatch was fully open.

She climbed out of the chamber and into the dim light coming from above. Belle followed, only pausing momentarily when she heard, for the second time in minutes, her sister say, "Whoa!"

She scurried up the ladder after Jasmine as quickly as she could.

CHAPTER 16

"None of this makes sense," Belle said. They had closed the hatch behind them, locked it and covered it with the small rug that had been beside it, as though the thin piece of fabric would prevent the Beasts from bursting through.

They were standing inside of a bedroom, not the Sacred Chamber that Belle had still been expecting to find at the top of the ladder. Instead of a shrine or hallowed items, she was looking at a large dresser and the mirror which was on it. On the walls were a clock, pieces of abstract art, and something that Belle believed to be a television. It wasn't like the big box-shaped TV they watched their movies on in the bunker. This one was flat and sleek and seemingly nailed to the wall across from where they were standing.

Where they were standing was at the base of a bed. A bed that rested diagonally on the floor, out of alignment with the walls and the furniture in the room. Belle surmised that the bed had been covering the hatch, and had been pushed out of the way of the entry to the bunker when Goldy had last come down from this place, wherever and whatever this place was.

The door of the room was open, and from the hallway entered the light they had noticed when they'd climbed through the hatch. Jasmine was already headed in the direction of that light.

Before Belle followed, she pushed the bed back over the hatch. It would act as one last bit of security between them and the Beasts Above that were now threatening to get them from below.

"This keeps getting weirder, Belle. Come here and see this!" Jasmine's bewildered voice drifted into the bedroom from the hall. With Bane's hunting knife tightly in her grip, Belle left the room and walked toward her sister.

"Look!" Jasmine whispered, pointing at the wall she was staring at with her butcher's knife, as though Belle could have mistaken what she wanted her to see. Jasmine looked mesmerized by what was on the wall, and Belle quickly saw why.

They were looking at photographs not unlike the few they had of themselves in the bunker which had been taken before their polaroid film had run out. Except these were larger, fancily framed, and not pictures of all five of the residents of the bunker. These were photos of only two of them: Beasts' Bane and Goldy.

In each of the pictures, they didn't quite look like themselves.

In all of the photos, Goldy looked slightly different than the sisters were accustomed to. It took Belle a moment to realize that her guardian's face was painted prettily in each picture. She was wearing makeup like the girls had only seen in the context of their cartoons. Something Goldy had described to them as customary for women in the old world. Before the Beasts.

Goldy was also wearing jewelry; diamonds or small gold hoops hung from her ears, necklaces studded with gemstones decorated a decolletage the girls had never seen. In the bunker, their guardian had always been dressed from head to toe in the same shawls and skirts and long unflattering dresses.

Bane was also dressed absurdly in the photos. He wasn't wearing his furs and skins in any of them. In one, he was wearing a bright floral-patterned short sleeved shirt. It looked so unlike anything he had ever worn that Belle had to triple check to see if it was actually him. But it was. Same face, same scar, same man. In that picture – as in many of them – he and Goldy were together, posing for the camera. Goldy was wearing a bikini that made Belle blush upon seeing it.

What was even stranger than their attire was the backdrop of the photo. Belle recognized, from movies and magazines, that her guardian and husband were standing on a beach. An impossible place, Belle thought. From everything they had ever learned in the bunker, the entire world was supposed to have become cold and snow-filled after the arrival of the Beasts of No Known Origin.

Belle turned her attention from the photo of the pair on the beach to one of them at what she knew was a wedding. Their wedding. In it, Goldy was wearing an ornate white dress, Bane a black tuxedo. They were walking down an aisle, hand in hand; a crowd of people on either side of them smiling, applauding. Goldy and Bane had never appeared happier.

Belle knew of weddings. Had had one of her own at only thirteen years of age when Bane had claimed her as his third wife. Belle, Aurora, and Jasmine had each had the same simple ceremony when they'd wed Bane. At each wedding, they had stood side by side with their husband-to-be while Goldy, on behalf of the Oracle, had prompted them to repeat the sacred vows that would make the marriage legal in the eyes of God. Then, each sister had received a simple bracelet Goldy had fashioned from braided leather. An item that signified their unending devotion, not only to their husband, but to the salvation of humanity. Which, of course, had been the reason for their wedding, and why they'd had to produce so many children so quickly. The sisters still wore their bracelets to this day.

"These must be from before the Beasts," Belle reasoned, nervously fingering her bracelet as her eyes went to other photos of Bane and Goldy's elaborate wedding. It seemed to be the only explanation that made sense. That was until her sister reminded her of a fact that put that notion into question.

"They said they didn't know each other before the Beasts. He saved all of us when we were headed to the Zone with mom, remember?"

It was a story they hadn't heard in years, but one they knew well, for it had defined their lives.

Why would they have lied about not knowing each other before the Beasts?

She didn't get the chance to ask the question aloud, because from the room they had just walked out of came a banging at the hatch.

The Bonkos, they had followed.

There was a sound like a small explosion as they heard the bed lifted from the floor, heard it come crashing down.

The Beasts, they were here.

"Come on. This way," Belle said, taking her sister by the hand and leading her down the hallway, further into this unexpected home atop their bunker.

CHAPTER 17

Belle wasn't sure where she was heading, only that it was away from the sounds of feet – or whatever it was the Beasts carried their bodies on – coming from the bedroom behind them.

She went to turn here or there, but all she saw were bathrooms, bedrooms, what looked to be an office. No escape. Eventually, they turned a corner and found themselves in an open area of the house.

To their left, a kitchen. To their right, a dining room with a cloth-covered table in the middle of it, twice the size and many more times as beautiful as the one inside the bunker.

In front of them, beyond a large living area, was another smaller hallway. At the end of that hallway was a door. A door which stood open.

Cold air entered the house from outside that door, as did light. Not light from the sun, because it was indeed nighttime, but light from the glowing eyes of what looked like dozens of Bonkos outside this house above the bunker.

Shining through the door and the uncovered windows of the large living room, the light was nearly blinding.

In it, Belle could see outlines of what looked to be people, and other smaller creatures which sat low to the ground. The humans and animals the Bonkos had enslaved.

Behind them, they could hear the Beasts making their way from the bedroom atop of what should have been a Sacred Chamber.

Beasts ahead, Beasts behind. What were they to do?

Belle looked at Jasmine as they stood between the kitchen and dining room. Between the exit and the hallway. Between death and death.

Beasts behind, Beasts ahead.

The two stood there in the glow of the large creatures as it bathed the house, making it so that Belle could clearly see the face of her sister. It was a face wet with tears, covered with worry, but somehow resolute. Seeing that resolution there, Belle knew what was going to happen before it occurred. But she couldn't stop it.

"Don't let them take us alive, that's what Bane said." Jasmine seemed to whisper this to no one but herself. Then, only slightly louder. "I love you, Belle. Aurora and I will see you in the next life. We'll meet you in the Promised Place"

"Jasmine, no!" Belle screamed. She dropped the hunting knife she had been holding and lunged toward her sister. But by the time she made her sounds and moved her body it was already too late.

Jasmine had taken the butcher's knife they had gotten from their kitchen, turned it toward herself, and plunged it into her chest.

"Jasmine!" Belle screamed again. Then screamed continuously as Jasmine fell into her arms and slumped to the floor, Belle slumping with her as the strength left her knees. She shouted so loudly that she did not register the noises around her. The noises coming toward her. The Beasts Above – now in front of her, all around her – approaching, loudly and hurriedly. Eager to get at both girls.

It was only when they were already on her that Belle considered taking the knife jutting from Jasmine's chest and turning it on herself. Meeting her sister in the Promised Place, where they had been told they would go when they were done with this life.

"Don't let them take you alive…" That *is* what Bane had said. *"Being taken by them is a fate worse than death…"*

Belle wondered if she would regret not heeding his advice the way Jasmine had.

She heard their roars in her ears, heard and felt the thundering of their feet against the floor as they approached her. Pounced upon her.

She felt them now, pawing, clawing, pulling her away. Wrenching her from the dying body of the only person she had left. Despondently, she watched as a throng of thralls swarmed Jasmine once Belle was clear of her.

She was dragged away, out of the house, thrashing and punching, kicking at the bodies which surrounded her, screaming into the night all the while.

EPILOGUE

Belle found herself standing in a white room, wearing a white gown, trying not to be consumed by dark thoughts.

She was confused, upset, but not unhappy. No matter how badly things had fallen apart, no matter how painful the last day had been, she could not deny feeling a bit of bliss. Because she was not in this white room alone.

In front of her, laying on a white bed, also wearing a white gown, was her sister.

The sister who had unintentionally started this chain of events. The sister who Belle had been certain was dead, a self-sacrifice to a horde of Bonkos while on her way to the Zone of Clouds she had been so determined to get to. Yet here she was. Alive, though not so well.

"Belle," Aurora said, opening her eyes just barely as she lay on her back on the small, strangely designed bed. Complementing Aurora's white gown was a white wrap around her head. A bandage covering up the spot where a bullet had grazed her temple. One of three bandages covering three bullet wounds, the other two on her torso.

Aurora smiled up at her sister. She did so weakly, but in a way that inspired strength.

"They found you," Aurora said, her voice a raspy whisper.

"Yeah, Rory, they found us last night. I wanted to come here as soon as they told us you were alive, but they said I had to let you rest until this morning. Try not to talk. Save your strength," Belle responded. Aurora, hard-headed as she always was, ignored her sister's advice.

"Bane. Shot me," Aurora said, speaking with her eyes half-lidded. Belle could tell that each word was an effort for her. It was amazing that she was alive after having been shot three times. It was a miracle that she was able to talk at all.

"He's no Bane of Beasts," Belle said bitterly. Aurora looked up and smiled again, though this time the expression was both weak and sad.

"They told you everything?" she asked.

"Yes. They let me know what happened to you... to us."

"Jasmine?" Aurora asked, after her eyes had slowly scanned the small white room.

Belle did not answer at first. Her mind went to a memory she wished could be erased but knew would haunt her forever. That of Jasmine plunging a knife into her chest. Then she thought of the reason Jasmine had done so and she began to fill with rage. The same rage she'd felt when she'd been told the truth. A rage which had only dissipated when she'd learned that Aurora was alive and here in a hospital, in a city called Boulder, Colorado.

"Jasmine hurt herself badly because of them. She's in a place called Intensive Care. They say she *should* survive, but it's no guarantee. Same goes for her baby."

Belle went on to explain what had happened to her and Jasmine as she walked over to the window of the hospital room. Looked outside of it at a mostly white world. A world she still couldn't quite believe she was seeing because it wasn't supposed to exist. A world she'd been told had been destroyed sixteen years ago. A lie she had believed for each of the sixteen years since.

Until last night.

The truth of the world was even clearer to Belle this morning as she looked down seven storeys to the streets below. Streets that were brimming with life. No flesh-eating Beasts, no murderous thralls. No halting of society.

Still, it terrified her.

The height, the people, all of that machinery moving among them. It was disorienting. Dizzying. She looked away from the window, turned toward her sister.

"I nearly stabbed myself, too. If the police hadn't grabbed me and pulled me away so that the medical people could save Jasmine, we might both be dead," Belle said. Looking at Aurora and seeing that her eyes were closed, she wondered if her sister had slept through most of the story. But she hadn't. With her eyes still closed, Aurora said,

"What matters is that we all made it. Jasmine *will* survive. So will her baby. He or she is a little Soldier of the Future, after all." Despite the weakness of her voice, the anger in it was clear. As was the hurt, the frustration. Belle didn't have to imagine how Aurora felt, because she felt the same.

Which meant that Aurora also felt embarrassed, also felt foolish. That feeling – foolishness – was one Belle suspected would never fade.

She'd first felt foolish the previous night once she had calmed down enough to listen to those who had dragged her out of the house. Had felt like a fool when it was explained to her that she had been surrounded by authorities and their canine assistants – all there to help her – and not the human and animal thralls of the Beasts of No Known Origin.

That foolish feeling only flourished when she saw that what had been growling and grumbling at them with glowing eyes and great gritted teeth had been cars. Not giant monsters, as she and her sisters had been made to believe on a dark and snowy night when they were children needing proof of an apocalypse. Their big bad Beast on that night had simply been a noisy metal contraption made for transportation.

It had taken Belle a great deal of effort to get inside one of those metal contraptions, despite eventually recognizing them from the animated versions of vehicles she had seen in many cartoons.

She knew of the police, and of what law enforcement was in theory, but still had trouble trusting those who had surrounded her claiming this was what they were.

She hadn't been able to stop thinking that they still might be minions of the Bonkos there to deceive her. That their vehicular contraptions would take the sisters to a fate worse than death, as Bane had warned. She might have run, might have continued fighting them, but they had Jasmine. Had put her on a tiny bed with wheels under it and gently placed her into the back of the biggest of their vehicles, an ambulance.

They had told Belle they were going to try to save her sister from what Bane had made her do. And then they'd told her that Aurora was still alive. No matter her suspicions, she'd had to hope this was true.

It was only when she was in the back of the ambulance being transported to this hospital with Jasmine – observing the medics check on her sister, seeing their equipment being used to keep her alive, watching the world turn to a blur through the windows of the vehicle – that she started to truly doubt everything she had ever known.

"But it's still so hard to believe that he and Goldy tricked us for so long. I feel like such a fool," Aurora said softly, confirming that the two did indeed feel the same.

"We can't be mad at ourselves, Rory. There's no point in giving in to anger," Belle said, trying, for her sister's sake, to sound far more level-headed than she currently felt.

"Not give in to anger? How can you *not* be angry? Do you know what that man did to me? What he *planned* to do to me?" Aurora demanded more than asked.

"I'm angry at everything, Rory. Especially Goldy and Bane... Or Mariam and... what was it? Harrison? God, I don't even know what to call them. But I can't be mad at *us* because we couldn't possibly have known. And yes, I do know what he did to you. I can see it. And if I could, I would kill him with my bare hands just for that alone."

According to one of the officers who had pulled Belle out of the house and away from Jasmine, Bane had lured Aurora out into the woods in order to kill her and bury her there. He likely would have done exactly that if not for a hunter who had been in the area. A hunter and his dog.

The dog's barking and the approach of the hunter had chased Bane off before he could complete his task, causing him to leave Aurora right where he had shot her, which hadn't been his intention. His intention had been made clear when the police had discovered a freshly dug hole in the ground, a shallow open grave, not far from where Aurora's semi-conscious body had been found.

The hunter who had found her had driven Aurora to the closest hospital. Even thrice penetrated by bullets and being in and out of consciousness, Aurora had never stopped whispering about her sisters. Saying, "They're still down there." Begging for them to be helped. With that, a search for other potential victims had been declared.

It hadn't taken long for the police to zero in on Goldy and Bane's home, searching the property around it for signs of the underground entrance a semi-conscious Aurora had described. They had found the locked hatch on the property, surrounded, carefully hidden, by large coniferous trees.. They had acted quickly, saved lives, but hadn't acted quickly enough to prevent the perpetrators from getting away.

When Belle had been told the truth about her guardian and husband, she had immediately thought of Goldy's long communes with the Oracle. About Bane's extended hunting trips, his visits to the ZoC. All an excuse to lead a double life.

Both Belle and Aurora had been given the details of who their captors truly were by this point; the first bits of information in an FBI case being built against the two.

Goldy (who had never provided the girls a name other than that, much as they had never been given last names of their own), had been born Mariam Goldbraithe. She currently went by Mariam Wendelken.

Sebastian Beasts' Bane, slayer of zero Beasts, was really Harrison Wendelken. They were married, and they were also coworkers and business partners.

Mariam owned and operated a foundation for homeless youth called the Future of Youth Initiative. Harrison assisted her in this venture. They were both well-loved, well-respected, upstanding citizens in their community. Their foundation had built several group homes and youth shelters across Colorado, several other states, and even in a few other countries. The two had donated money, food, clothing, to those in need for years.

Why two wealthy, industrious, seemingly caring members of the community would commit an act as heinous as theirs was nearly beyond comprehension to Belle and to the FBI agents who had informed her of all this when she had arrived at the hospital.

And the details only grew stranger, more confusing, with the oddest detail being that Harrison Wendelken was somewhat of a celebrity.

He had invented a popular board game two decades ago called 'A World of Beasts'. The board game had spawned something called an online game, a book, and, years later, a movie that was currently in postproduction, each following the same basic storyline: The world under attack by strange creatures, survivors driven underground or in places of high altitude where the creatures couldn't breathe. And the goal of these survivors? To reach a Safe Zone, a mountain community closer to the sky than the surface, under the guidance of an Oracle in order to help start a rebellion that would save humanity.

The man had designed the story of their lives after this game of his.

"But how could we have known that the only part of their story that was true was the part about us being ripped away from our mother?" Belle said, then, after a moment, added, "I suppose they were telling the truth when they said we were driven underground by Beasts... What I'm saying, Rory, is that it wasn't your fault. It wasn't any of our faults."

"That doesn't bring seven babies back to us, Belle."

The sentence felt like the back of a hand colliding with her cheek. It was the way she felt each time she'd thought of their babies since she had asked the FBI agents if they knew what had become of them.

The agents hadn't answered immediately, had said they couldn't answer at all with any certainty. But eventually, as they sat with Belle in the hospital room she had been led to so she could be looked over, the agents told her what was suspected. Told her that, with the money and connections the couple had, and with Human Trafficking on the rise, it was possible that the babies had been illegally sold to the sorts of people who purchased babies for large sums of money.

The silver lining, according to the agents, was that the babies might have been placed with wealthy families, given wonderful lives with bright futures. But that hypothesis had done little to raise Belle's spirits.

"No," Belle said. "It doesn't."

Aurora, with a great deal of effort, shifted in her bed to face Belle, who was still standing by the window. She extended a shaky hand toward her younger sister.

Belle darted across the room and took Aurora's hand in hers, wanting desperately for her sister to stop expending so much energy. Yet Aurora wasn't done.

Struggling to stay awake, to breath, to live, Aurora spoke with a strength that slowly spread from her to Belle.

"I know the Zone of Clouds and the Oracle aren't real, but it's almost as if her prophecy is being fulfilled. We escaped the bunker and the true Beasts who were a threat to us, but that was just the start. Because as long as Bane and Goldy – or whatever their names are – are out there, as long as they know where our children are, and until the day they are caught and have returned our children to us, we must be soldiers. We must be brave and strong. Finding our children and giving those two what they deserve, *that* has always been the War to Come."

Piece #1

MAKING

GHOSTS

A Novelette

PROLOGUE

Do You Believe In Ghosts?

"Do you believe in ghosts?" Harrison Wendelken asked
Mariam Goldbraithe. The two teenage outcasts were once
again watching the cool kids from a distance. They were
standing within a copse of trees that bordered their high
school's property, a stretch of snow-covered field lay
between where they stood and the parking lot they were
observing.

From here, obscured by pine trees turned white by the
weather, they could see the cool kids doing exactly what
they had expected them to be doing on this night, at this
time. A group of them were sitting inside of the old beat-
up purple Caravan owned by the father of a boy named
Benny 'the Brick'. Inside of that van were Benny, his
girlfriend Laurie, and his two lackeys Gordie and Todd.
They were doing the same thing they did every Friday
night: sitting in their parked van with the engine running,
and lighting up a ton of weed.

They would sit in that same spot for hours with their
windows completely obscured by marijuana smoke,
hotboxing the vehicle. Then Benny would drive everyone
home.

Harrison and Mariam had never engaged in this
activity – the parking, the smoking, the socializing –
before. Had never been invited to do much (other than to
be victimized) by the popular teenagers. The kids everyone
in school either feared or revered. It was the opposite, in
fact. The odd pair was routinely shunned. Pushed to the
periphery by the popular. Cast aside. Cast out. So, it was

unsurprisingly nerve-wracking for these two outcasts to know that Harrison was about to walk toward those teens in that beat-up Caravan in just a matter of moments.

"I think so," Mariam said, responding to Harrison's question of ghosts. Immediately after answering, she paused to contemplate the question more thoroughly. "Yeah, I do," she added after several seconds of silence. "I feel like there are too many people out there with ghost stories for them all to not be true, you know? How about you? You believe in them?"

"I do," Harrison said without hesitation as he looked out at the parking lot which, aside from Benny the Brick's vehicle, was empty at this late hour. He stared at the van, his gaze so intense it seemed as though it could penetrate the smoke shrouding the windows.

He was picturing each member of the group that had made his life a living Hell every single day since he had entered the ninth grade earlier this year. He was imagining the four teenagers who had dragged Mari into that Hell because she had decided to be kind to Harry. Envisioning the four people that he and Mari were not going to let get away with treating them the way those four had treated them. Not anymore.

Harrison turned from the van to Mari, ghosts still on his mind.

"I'm wondering if we're about to make some."

Then, without waiting for a response, pulling the hood of his black jacket onto his head and making sure his backpack was strapped securely to him, Harrison Wendelken walked toward Benny the Brick's beat-up Caravan.

CHAPTER ONE

The Chase

Two months before Harrison Wendelken made his walk toward the lone vehicle in his high school's parking lot on that late Friday night, he had been running on a Monday afternoon.

It was a Monday in late October much like every other school day, each of which involved the bell ringing to signify that school was out, and, seemingly, to alert the bullies that the chase would soon be on.

Harry stayed at least an extra half hour each day in study hall after the bell rang, switching up the time he would head home in an effort to avoid his tormentors. But it made no difference. Each time he left the school at day's end, no matter how late he stayed and tried to outwait them, the result was the same. He would leave by one of the school's several exits, and one of the bullies – Benny the Brick or his boys – would be there. Whichever one of them it was that spotted him would call out to the others. Then Harrison, overweight and awkward, would begin his bumbling run away from them, over the field and toward the fence that separated school property from the shitty little strip of government housing that he called his neighborhood. While this happened, many of the other kids in the yard and on the field would hoot and clap. Cheering on the chase.

If he made it past the fence, they left him alone. Well, they physically left him alone when he made it beyond the chain linked threshold. Rather than chasing him further past the fence in order to beat him up, they taunted him from afar as he walked toward his house. Laughed at him until he reached a range at which his ears could no longer register their mirth.

The thing that troubled Harry most about these chases was that he knew he could never really outrun the older kids who terrorized him. On the occasions when he got away, it was because they wanted him to. On those days, it seemed, the chase alone was enough for the bullies. Just to see him jiggle as he sprinted, the fear seeping out of him in liquid form as he sweat through his clothes, was enough to satisfy whatever urge it was that drove them to do this torturous thing.

On other days, perhaps when one of the bullies wanted to vent their frustrations, they would catch him, topple him over. Beat him.

Last Friday, he had taken a particularly bad beating. Which was why he had told himself that this Monday wouldn't be like every other day. This Monday would be different.

Today, he would do more than run.

There were only two of them chasing him today, as was usually the case on a Monday. It was knowing that he wouldn't be chased by Benny's entire group that had bolstered his decision. On some days – the previous Friday for example – there could be as many as eight aggressors after him. Kids who weren't part of the main group sometimes joined in, inflating the numbers. Usually though, the chase would involve at least one of the core four of bullies: Benny the Brick, his two bosom buddies, and his bitch of a girlfriend.

Today, it was only Benny's boys, Todd and Gordie, who were sprinting after him. Harry supposed that Benny and Laurie had obligations on Monday afternoons, doing whatever it was two sociopaths did after school that took precedence over their usual activity of torturing the fat kid. Whatever it was that kept them away on Mondays – today – he was glad for it. He was still outnumbered, but he knew he wasn't outsmarted by the two teens trailing him.

Today would be his chance to make his stand. Even though he would initially have to do so while on his hands and knees.

Todd – who was currently closing in on Harry as he ran, excitedly calling him several cruel words that equated to overweight, that equaled excrement – was a string bean of a boy, and was called so by other kids behind his back. He was long and lanky, made of skin and wires.

Gordie, slower than the rest of his crew, but always quick to deliver a beating, posed a more intimidating figure. He was squat and square, hard of face and body.

Neither of them on their own scared Harrison, theirs was strictly a strength in numbers type of situation. He had always wondered what his odds would be if their numbers were even. In a few seconds, he expected to find out.

"Got you now, you fat shit!" shouted Stringbean Todd.

Even without the warning, Harry felt the gangly eleventh grader closing in on him.

It was time to make the stand he had been thinking about for nearly seventy-two hours. It was time to do the thing he had been practicing in his small backyard all weekend.

Instead of continuing for the thirty yards toward the gateway in the fence, he stopped abruptly, fell to his hands and knees. And, as expected, he felt a pair of shins collide with his hip and side. Then felt a body flying over him.

"Whoa! Fuuuuuck!" yelled Stringbean Todd as he went sailing over Harry before crashing to the ground. Despite the fact that he landed on grass, it was grass made hard as pavement by the cold Colorado fall.

There was a cracking sound as Todd hit. A noise like a brittle branch breaking. A sound which Harry both relished and regretted. Because, as much as he enjoyed hearing that sound, as much as he felt it was justice to see Todd curled up on the ground clutching what was clearly a broken arm, he had a feeling he would be paying for that in the future.

"Ohhh, you're gonna pay for that, you fat little fucker," said Gordie, still stomping toward Harry.

Gordie had never been fleet of foot. Harry was glad for that now. Not because it would allow for him to get away. But because it gave him a chance to stand up and square off. He did so, facing his approaching bully.

Even as Gordie was making his way straight at him, perhaps expecting him to start running again, Harry gave his angry aggressor something he certainly hadn't been anticipating.

A fist right to the nose.

In the days to come, they would call it a sucker punch. That's how both Gordie and Todd would tell it. They would say they were ambushed and suckered. But that was not at all the case. They just weren't used to someone finally fighting back.

There were gasps, some groans, shouts of surprise from the few students left on school property who were watching the chase take place. None of those sounds were made by Gordie, who fell in silent shock, clutching his nose, the red from inside of it staining his pale skin in a series of streaks and streams as blood seeped through his fingers down the backs of his hands.

"Now leave me the fuck alone!" Harry screamed at the two bullies, who were both writhing in pain on the yellowed October grass. He then walked, not ran, toward the opening in the fence leading to his neighborhood for the first time since the first week of that school year.

CHAPTER TWO

Hard Mari

It was a strange experience for Harry, walking through the opening of that fence instead of sprinting or limping through it. Stranger still was the fact that he wasn't only walking into his neighborhood without the usual slew of slurs hurled at his back, he was doing so with his head held high.

There was a narrow foot-beaten path in front of him. It led to a set of cement steps built into the slight slope of hill leading from the school to the place he called home. Those steps would take whoever descended them to the road which wrapped around and between the rowhouses that made up his block. On either side of the small path was a grassy area where younger kids sometimes hung out, usually playing tag or manhunt. Some of those kids also partook in not-so-innocent activities along the portion of the grassy area which existed around the corner of the back of a strip of houses. It was an area containing a scattering of trees leading toward a creek.

Harry had seen kids playing in this area his whole life. He walked past a few children now. Children not too far removed from heading to high school just as he had at the end of the summer. He only hoped their transition from middle school would go more smoothly than his had. Though, judging by the fact that those who were playing here actually had people to play with, he assumed they wouldn't be treated like he was by the older kids in his school. The way all lonely losers were treated when they were initiated into their high school careers at his educational institution.

Harry had never felt welcome here. Not at his previous school, not in his neighborhood. Certainly not at his high school.

He had hoped to be in an entirely new area of Denver by the time freshman year rolled around. Harry's dad, once upon a time, had talked about moving out and moving up. Leaving this block of government housing behind them. But then Mr. Wendelken had hurt his back at work. After that, it seemed as though they would be stuck here forever.

Harry had begged to at least be allowed to go to a different high school, not the one right beside his home. One he knew had a reputation – almost a tradition – of hazing the new kids. His dad had declined his request to be sent to a different school, not wanting to "waste money on bus tickets and tokens when my son could use the walk to the damn good school that's right fucking there."

That was how his father had put it. And, with that, Harry's fate had been sealed.

With Harry being as roundly shaped, awkward, and unathletic as he was, all through the eighth grade and the summer after it, he understood that he would be an easy target when he got to the ninth grade. Just as he had been in elementary and middle school. But worse. The older kids hadn't proven him wrong.

In this neighborhood, it was common knowledge to eighth graders approaching high school that, every year, a group of bullies chose a fat kid to chase after school for at least the first third of the school year. This year it was Harry who was that fat kid. That easy target.

Between the start of the school year and the previous Friday, he had accepted that role. But that had all changed Friday after school.

He'd gotten a bad grade on his geography test, and had not been looking forward to having to share that news with his dad. So, when he walked out of the side exit of the school and saw Benny the Brick standing there, the tallest and meanest kid in the eleventh grade, he simply said, out of frustration,

"Fuck off, Benny. Just not today, okay?"

Benny, of course, not used to being spoken to that way, had been incensed. He did not fuck off. Harry had barely made it to the field by the time Benny was on him. Then Todd, then Gordie, then others.

Nearly ten kids took turns kicking and punching him for what he had been certain was the duration of his high school years but had only turned out to be three minutes. He had registered the time when he was allowed to get up and retrieve his watch from the ground, the strap having snapped as he blocked his head and face to defend himself.

He had gone home in pain, with bruises and a bad grade to show his dad that Friday afternoon. And experienced a different kind of hurt after doing so.

In their cramped living room, when Mr. Wendelken noticed Harry's limping gait, his dirtied clothes, and his mussed hair after Harry handed him his geography test, he had asked Harry who'd given him a beating. For the first time, Harrison told his father about the chases across the field after school. About the routine torment he endured. His father had responded by letting him know that the kids were doing him a favor.

"No wonder your fat ass looks like it's getting slimmer," had been Mr. Wendelken's response. Then he had said, "Don't think I'm gonna feel sorry for some pussy who ain't do nothing but run. I didn't raise you to be a coward *and* a failure, boy."

The truth was, his dad hadn't really raised him at all. Certainly wasn't raising him at this point. Wasn't raising much these days except for himself when he got off the couch and went to the fridge and got himself a beer. Raised that beer to his mouth and drank it. That was the only raising this man did.

It hadn't always been this way. Harry remembered a time when his father hadn't constantly seemed miserable. But his mother had been in the picture then, and Harry hadn't realized his mother had been taking all the ugliness he was now accustomed to. The consistent verbal abuse. Absorbing it on behalf of both of them. Then it became too much to take, apparently, because she had run off when Harry was in the third grade, leaving him to take the brunt of his father's cruelties. Abuses which had only worsened since Mr. Wendelken had hurt his back at work a few years ago. From that point on, his dad had been either apathetic and indifferent toward him, or angry with him for trivial things like the grade of a geography test he couldn't have cared less about. There wasn't much in between, just as there wasn't much between them.

But last Friday, when his father had said what he had said, Harrison had been determined to prove him wrong. He wasn't just some fat loser. He wasn't some pussy who was going to run forever.

Which is why, on this Monday, he stood up for himself, inadvertently breaking one bully's arm and the other's nose while doing so. And was now walking down the cement steps leading to his neighborhood, not sure if he should be proud or petrified. Either way, he knew payback was coming. He kept telling himself, as the adrenaline pumped through his body and the dopamine flooded his brain from the thrill of fighting back, that it was worth it. Worth it if he had proved his father wrong. Especially worth it if, maybe, possibly, his father would be proud of him as well. These were the thoughts running through his mind as he walked to his block. These thoughts were disrupted only when he felt a set of eyes on him. Watching him.

He looked up at the rowhouses opposite the gateway. There was a girl sitting and reading on the stoop of a house directly facing the fence and field.

She was a Black girl (well, actually, Harry thought to himself, she was more the color of a chestnut). One of the few Black people who lived in the area. She had moved to the neighborhood a few summers ago and had kept to herself ever since. Harry knew that this girl had been subject to alienation by the local kids much as he was, though in a less direct and consistent sort of way.

They called her Hard Mari. Harry thought he had witnessed the day when Mari had earned herself that nickname.

It hadn't been long after she had moved into the neighborhood. Harry had been out on his bike with Eric, his best and only friend. Eric had moved away this past summer, making Harry's transition to high school more difficult than he had already expected it to be.

On that summer afternoon, Harry and Eric had heard some commotion not far from where Mari lived. Following the sound of that ruckus, they saw that a group of neighborhood kids had practically surrounded the new Black girl, calling her names far less flattering than 'Hard'. She had run away, into her house. The group of mostly girls had laughed as though this was a victory. Until Mari came back with a baseball bat and a look on her face that begged for them to repeat the things they had called her. Which, of course, they hadn't. Bullies tend to move on to easier targets when they're stood up to. At least that's how it went in the books and movies.

As Harry recalled this, he hoped his situation with his bullies would be the same. He would much rather be left alone and whispered about, as Hard Mari was, than be chased and openly derided each day.

He might have whispered about her as well if he'd had anyone to whisper to. She was a bit of an odd one from what he could tell. Every day after school, and even on the weekends, she was out there sitting on her stoop, reading one book after the next, apparently never interested in going into her house if she didn't have to. Harry could relate to that. Except, on this afternoon, he was excited to go home. To tell his dad that he had stood up for himself. That he was no pussy.

From Mari's vantage on her porch, he knew she could see a great deal of the school's field. Right until it sloped downward to the school itself. He was sure she had seen him being hounded every single day that semester. Each time he ran or limped through the entryway of the fence, she averted her eyes and focused on whatever book she was reading at the time. But, on this afternoon, she looked at Harrison. He looked back. And Hard Mariam Goldbraithe nodded at him in acknowledgement. He nodded in return, doing his best not to smile, hoping he looked cool for once in his fat life.

He walked past her house and down the strip of road toward his own. He couldn't remember the last time he had felt so alive.

CHAPTER THREE

Fantasy

"You should have seen me, dad! I did what you said. I stopped running. And I kicked the shit out of two of the guys who're always chasing me!" Harrison called from his door before removing his shoes and making the short trip from the entrance of the house to the living area where he knew his dad would be laid up on the couch, the television tuned into Geraldo or Sally Jesse Raphael or The Maury Povitch Show. He could always count on his dad to be ingesting the tabloid topics in TV form.

Harrison also knew a bottle or can of something alcoholic would be on the floor in front of his father, as always. And, as always, Harry was correct.

He saw his father laying there, television on, a can of Coors Light within arm's reach. He thought for a second that the man was sleeping, but he wasn't. His eyes were open, he was watching the television. It was Sally Jesse Raphael today. From what Harry could gather, the topic was survivors of suicide. Sally's studio audience was listening to a woman recount her failed attempt at gassing herself by turning her car on in the garage while she sat in it. Carbon Monoxide poisoning, Harry heard her say.

The grim topic on the television was all he could hear coming from the living room, because his father chose not to respond to his son's good news. Chose not to respond because he really didn't care.

Harry usually would have taken the hint and moved along, but he seemed to be in the mood to push his luck this afternoon. Which was why he said,

"You hear me, dad? They tried to chase me again and I didn't let them. I busted both of them up real bad!"

"You?" his dad finally replied after an exasperated exhale, not bothering to turn away from the television or turn down the volume. He scoffed before adding, "We talking about real life? Or was this in one of those faggy little fantasy games you play in your room? Get me a beer."

Harrison had been struck many times in his life. He had been struck many times the previous week. Despite how many times he had been assaulted physically, somehow, it was always his father's words that hurt the most.

Deflated, he went to their small, dingy kitchen, removed a can of beer from a fridge badly in need of a cleaning. Considered opening it and spitting into it before placing it in front of his dad. Decided otherwise. Instead, he delivered the beer quietly before making his way to his bedroom.

He turned on the light and looked at the small round table he had in the corner of his room beside his dresser. On top of it was a piece of square plywood, four feet by four feet. He had found this board near the dumpster at the back of their block of houses and had used it to create a gameboard.

With some fabric and supplies he had been able to snag from school at the beginning of the year, he'd designed his own fantasy game.

He called it *A World of Beasts*

He was still working out the rules and details. So far, the game involved the world being overrun by strange, inexplicable creatures (maybe from outer space or another dimension, he wasn't sure. For now he called them Bonkos, which stood for Beasts Of No Known Origin), and a mythical mountain where safety could be sought by the humans who survived the invasion. The objective of the game was to evade the invaders and get to that mountain. Once there, the battle to save humanity would begin.

After school, he would usually work on the game for a while before scraping together whatever he could for dinner. Then his focus would turn to any homework he hadn't finished in study hall.

The game was a relief and an escape when the real world was so cruel. In it, he didn't have to be a fat kid running from bullies. Instead, he could be a warrior destined to save the world. He could be brave and true and strong.

He had been thinking of this game since the seventh grade. Now, with his best friend moved away and with no one to play with, working on the game had become his favorite thing in the world. And the only thing that made him feel like his future might be better than his past or present.

He planned to make *A World of Beasts* the next *Dungeons and Dragons*. He was convinced it would be the thing that would make him rich and famous. And maybe, one day, liked. Possibly even loved.

On this afternoon, he didn't bother to go to his beloved game as he usually did. Instead, he did what he always did when he felt truly down. He grabbed a VHS cassette from the collection of Disney movies in his closet – a collection that went well with many of the posters on his walls – and popped it into the VCR on top of the sixteen-inch television that sat on his dresser.

Sleeping Beauty played while Harrison did his best to not think about what his father had just said about "faggy little fantasy games".

While laying in his bed watching Princess Aurora singing to a pair of birds – something that was supposed to comfort him – he tried but failed to not think of what

Benny the Brick would do to him after finding out what Harry had done to Gordie and Todd.

CHAPTER FOUR

Running Again

Harrison was running again the next day – Tuesday – just as he had on that fateful Monday. Just as he had for the previous two months of weekday afternoons.

He had considered not going to school at all, but knew that staying home wasn't an option. Knew that, if he wandered the neighborhood or went to the public library instead of attending classes as he had once before, the school would declare him truant and call his father. Then he would have to hear it from his dad. The insults, admonishments, declarations of disappointment. Mr. Wendelken's lectures often felt worse than the beatings he would get after being chased across the field.

Understanding he had no choice, he'd gone to school. Though before doing so, he had allowed himself to fantasize that things might have changed for him. That the other students would stop him in the hallway to commend him on his bravery. To let him know just how cool they thought he now was. The sort of instant transformation from lame to legend that happens in the movies. But nothing had changed. In fact, things somehow felt worse.

Rather than being ignored, as he usually was until the final bell rang, he thought – perhaps feeling a bit paranoid – that his fellow students were all looking at him as if they knew something was going to happen to him after school. Many of them seemed to gawk and whisper, some of them giggled as he passed by in the hall or from behind him in class. It was as if they were all in on some not-so secret fact that he wasn't aware of.

He did his best to disregard them, just as he did his best, successfully, to avoid the bullies the entire day. He decided to stay for an hour and a half after final period in study hall with a group of kids who were struggling in math class. He hadn't actually needed help with math. He needed, very badly, help with avoiding what he knew was headed his way once he left the building.

Even after staying so late and lingering for so long, he saw them waiting for him through the window of every door.

For one of the few times this school year, he considered going to a teacher or the principal for help. But Benny was the Principal's nephew. Besides, Harry knew that "snitches got stitches." He'd been warned of exactly that on many of the occasions he had been pounded upon by his tormentors.

All day, he had stared at various clocks or at his strapless watch while wanting time to both slow down and speed up. Wanting to both delay what was inevitable and hurry up and face the inexorable. It had been a long and stressful day.

Now, after that long and stressful school day, he was sprinting as fast he could across the field with a half dozen older kids chasing after him. Many others cheering them on.

He was almost at the fence. Didn't think he would get there.

Got there.

Running as fast as he ever had, he arrived at what had always been the demarcation of safety in the form of an opening in the chain link fencing.

Then he was through it.

This was usually where he stopped. Past the gate was where he would slow down and take his time to make his way along the little path and down the steps to his block.

It was typically at this point, while gathering his breath, that he would hear them laughing and taunting but otherwise proceeding to go about their day. But he understood, had known since yesterday evening, that today the game had changed.

He sprinted along the path as he heard them rush into the imaginary safe zone the fence had always signified.

He was feet away from his feet finding the cement steps. They never made it there.

Before he got to the first step, he felt a hand snatch his sweater right at the nape of his neck. It was a strong one, the hand that grabbed him. Likely strong enough to pull him down on its own, yet it was quickly aided by several other hands.

Harrison was dragged around the corner to the area by the creek where kids often played without ever inviting him. Where the kids who were playing there now were excitedly hooting and hollering about what was about to happen. A few chose to leave the area, sprinting away, scared. But most stayed. Most watched.

There was a beating about to take place, and that was always quite the event.

CHAPTER FIVE

Carving

There are two kinds of beatings you can receive when receiving beatings is a regular part of your life. The first, and most common, is a beating you know will remain a beating. Meaning, although you know you're being beat on, you're aware that you'll get out of that thrashing without critical injury or potentially facing death. Then, there's the other kind of beating, where, when you're going through it, you can't help but wonder if it'll be the last beating you'll ever experience in your life. The last experience you'll ever have because it just might result in your death.

The beating Harrison was currently receiving was of the latter variety. It was the first time he had experienced fear of this sort in all his days. Even when these same bullies had surrounded him and stomped him before, he'd always known that it had been part of their sick game. It had been fun to them, nothing they would take too far.

This was something different.

Harrison Wendelken couldn't breathe.

He was gasping for air after having been kicked square in the stomach by big bad Benny the Brick. At least he thought it was Benny who had booted the breath out of him. There were at least eight feet trying to get at him as he lay on the cold hard grass. He'd been having trouble telling which belonged to whom since one of them had stomped his head against the ground.

"Stop!" he yelled. Attempted to yell. Thought he yelled. Though he couldn't tell for sure. Everything, even his own voice, sounded very far away. That was until another voice responded. This voice seemed much closer than every other sound. Seemed closer because of what this voice had to say, and how much it terrified him.

"Hold him still. Give me the knife."

"No! I was only protecting myself! Please!" Harry cried out, then cried tears. Of remorse, of regret. Not because of what he had done to defend himself the day before, but because, at that moment, he was remorseful that he'd had to go to this school. That he had to live in this neighborhood. Presently, as he lay on his side with his arms and legs pressed down by hands, held down by feet, as his torso was sat upon by at least one entire body, he regretted ever having been born into a world like this.

The bodies that weren't holding him down cleared a path for the person who had asked for the weapon.

Harry found himself looking up at Stringbean Todd.

Todd hadn't been at school that day, and Harry could see why. His right arm was in a cast from his forearm to his fingers. Apparently, he had been too injured to make it to classes, but not too injured to make it to these after school festivities. And not too injured to wield the butterfly knife he had requested in the hand belonging to his unharmed left arm.

"So, you like to sneak attack people, huh?" Todd said, crouching down and speaking into Harrison's right ear. The ear was exposed to the air as the left side of his face was pressed into the ground. He could smell something that reminded him of pork rinds on the thin boy's breath.

For a foolish second, Harrison was about to tell Todd that he hadn't sneak attacked anyone, but then thought better of it. Besides, he wasn't sure he was capable of producing a single coherent word, not with how much he was trembling all over. Not with the hand that was pressed down on his cheek, seemingly trying to reset his jaw.

Instead, he mumbled many things that equated to 'I don't want to die today, and you shouldn't want to kill me'. But all the sounds he made were ignored or drowned out by Todd's talking.

"You broke my fucking arm in three places. My doctor said I might never be able to throw a baseball right again. Said you ruined my shot at making it to the Bigs," Todd growled.

From everything Harrison knew of Stringbean Todd, his shot at making it to the Big Leagues of baseball had been over roughly since the day he had been born. Todd was no natural athlete, that was plain to everyone who looked at him. But if he truly believed what he was saying, then Harrison was likely in worse trouble than he already feared.

Would they actually kill him over a broken arm?

He quickly learned that the answer was no. No, they didn't plan to kill him. Yet somehow he wasn't relieved when he heard the alternative.

"If my arm ain't ever gonna be right forever, and I have to think about you every time it hurts, I'm gonna give you something to remind you of me every time you see your fat little fucking face in the mirror."

Then he brought the knife down to Harrison's face, right beneath his hairline, above his right eye. Before Harrison could protest, Todd, a right-handed boy, began to cut Harry's face with the knife in his left hand.

Harry didn't move. He expected pain, but he believed the fear was blocking it out. Because he could feel the knife doing what it was designed to do. He could feel a bead of blood begin to trickle down his face even though the hurt hadn't yet registered. At least not the physical hurt.

He was attempting to form words that might get him out of this situation but couldn't find the right ones.

Couldn't find any. Yet he heard them, those irretrievable words. Not from him, but from an unexpected source.

"Hey! Leave him alone!" someone screamed out.

While Harrison was happy that someone was concerned about him, the interruption didn't do him any favors.

At the sound of the voice, Todd seemed to become startled. He flinched. Badly. And the knife, which had only cut a small portion of Harrison's forehead to that point, suddenly slid down the length of his face, slicing him open. If he hadn't had his eyes closed already, he might have lost the right one.

"What fucking business is it of yours? Get the fuck outta here!" Todd screamed over his shoulder, his body blocking Harrison from seeing who it was that was attempting to rescue him. It sounded like everyone else – the kids who, until now, had been mostly silently watching one of their classmates carving another of their classmates – echoed Todd's sentiment. Each of them, in their own crude way, telling the intruder to leave.

But the person didn't get the fuck outta there as requested. In fact, to Harrison's amazement, they did the opposite.

He heard what he would forever think of as a battle cry. Heard feet – only two of them – stomping toward the crowd he was in the middle and at the bottom of.

And then, all at once, the kids around him let him go. Their hands and feet (and one entire body) releasing his arms and legs and torso. All at once they were running off.

Todd lingered for a moment, looking frantically from the work he'd done on Harrison's face to the person who was charging toward him, as if hoping he'd have a bit more time to finish. Then he said,

"We're not done with you, you little cunt."

After saying that, before running off, he spat in Harry's face. A loogie directly between the eyes.

"You're gonna learn to mind your business, you crazy nigger bitch!" said a voice Harrison could tell was retreating beyond the fence in the direction of the school. It was Benny the Brick's voice. And it let Harrison know who had saved him while his eyes were covered, pasted shut, by blood and saliva.

After sitting up, he used his shirt to wipe the blood and spit from his face until he felt his eyelids were cleared enough to open. Once open, he looked at his savior. Saw who he'd expected to see. He had never been happier to see anyone in all his life.

"Thank you," Harrison Wendelken said to Hard Mari Goldbraithe, understanding immediately why everyone had run away from this lone lean girl.

In her hand, resting upon her shoulder, still in a position to be quickly put to use, was a baseball bat.

CHAPTER SIX

Those Kids Aren't Nice

"Would you really have used that thing?" Harry asked Mari as the two sat on her stoop. Every so often, he looked toward the fence and field to see if his bullies would return. He and Mari had gone to sit on the steps in front of her house not long after she had chased Benny and his gang off with the aluminum bat he was currently questioning her about. It was resting on the ground beside her. Just in case.

When they'd arrived, she had gone into her house briefly before coming back out with rubbing alcohol, gauze, and a variety of bandages.

She had tended to his wound, declaring that he likely needed stitches. He hadn't had to tell her that he couldn't afford them. She'd done her best to keep the cut together with a series of butterfly bandages. And told him, not unsympathetically, that he was likely to "scar something ugly."

Oddly enough, he hadn't been upset about the prospect of a scar. He only hoped it was a cool one. His wild imagination allowing him to envision something that would make him look rough and rugged like Cable or Bishop from the X-Force comics he loved so much. A battle scar that might stop people from being so quick to bully him in the future. He knew that likely wouldn't be the case. Still, he wasn't unhappy in this moment, because, for the first time since his early days in elementary school, he felt as though he had made a new friend.

"I would have used it, yeah," Hard Mari replied to his question, looking down at the ball bat.

"Why? Why would you help me?"

"Because those kids aren't nice. And you didn't deserve what they were doing to you."

Those kids aren't nice. What an understatement. He knew what they called her other than Hard Mari. Epithets that could never be considered nicknames. Words like those Benny had used as she had chased him and his crew away. She was an outcast, just like Harrison, only for an entirely different reason.

"I'm sorry," he said. Not knowing what else to say.

"For what?"

"That you have to go through what they make you go through."

She made a sound that resembled a scoff.

"That's just life. Both of us ought to get used to it. Things aren't going to get any easier after what happened today."

There was nothing to say to that.

Both of them looked at the baseball bat, then at nothing in particular as they contemplated the fact that they were now soldiers in a war they wanted no part of. A war they had not started.

"Why do you sit out here all the time, anyway?" he asked, after the silence had started to feel awkward.

"It's quiet out here," she said. Then proved it by saying no more.

CHAPTER SEVEN

War

The war didn't commence – or continue – immediately. For a few days, there was peace. And there was something else, something that frightened Harrison even more than the prospect of running through fields away from bullies for the rest of time.

There was love.

That was what he felt – or at least what he thought he felt – for Mariam Goldbraithe.

After sitting mostly quietly for some time that Tuesday evening on Mariam's porch, they had agreed to walk to school together the next morning. Then had walked home together after school that day. It was the first time since the first week of the school year that Harrison hadn't hid in study hall to avoid the inevitable. More importantly, to his surprise and delight, it was the first time in months Harrison hadn't been chased. Whether that was because of Mari, or because the bullies had seen the damage they'd done to his face and thought that was enough, Harrison didn't know. Nor did he care. He was only grateful to be able to go home at a steady pace with someone who walked beside him rather than chased after him.

At school that day, when he had been asked by the few people who bothered to ask about his wound, he said he'd slipped in his kitchen and that his face had run down the corner of the counter.

"Yes," he had said, slightly sarcastically, to one of his teachers and to a nosy classmate, "I *am* lucky I didn't lose an eye."

At home, the night before, his father hadn't bothered asking how he'd ended up with such a terrible cut. The man was so often on the couch facing the television that Harrison believed he would be healed before his dad would even notice. But they had run into each other in the hallway when both were headed to the bathroom. Mr. Wendelken had looked his son in the face, looked him up and down, then had shaken his head before entering the lavatory to relieve himself loudly.

That was fine by Harry. After the last few days, his father's opinion didn't matter too much to him anymore. For the first time in a long time, he wasn't rushing home to face that man, even if facing him just meant being aware of his indifference. For the first time since Eric had moved away, he had somewhere else to go after school, someone to play with. He had a friend. One he couldn't help but think of as more than that, though he tried to tell himself not to. There was no way a girl like Hard Mari would be interested in a boy like him, he believed.

She was taller than he was, slender, and pretty despite being a tomboy. She always kept her thick, wavy black hair pulled back into a bun, exposing a sharp jaw that was constantly grinding. She was intense. Or at least she appeared intense. But the more he got to know her, the more he realized she was only shy. It was one of the many things they had in common.

When they left school together the day after his face had been carved, they didn't walk to either of their houses directly. Instead of heading home that Wednesday afternoon when Harrison had slowed down in front of Mari's house, she had said,

"Let's go to the park."

So they did.

They sat side by side on the swings, sometimes speaking, sometimes sitting silently as hours passed. They had the small, heavily graffitied neighborhood park mostly to themselves due to the brisk fall weather.

It was well past his dinnertime when Harrison said he had to go. When he asked her if her family wouldn't wonder where she was, she shrugged and said,

"I don't think they'd notice if I didn't come back at all." She then disclosed to him that she lived in a three-bedroom house with her grandmother, her mother, an uncle who was too old to still be living with his mother, a male cousin who was nearly the same age as her, and another cousin – a girl - who was a toddler.

It had been her and both of her parents for most of Mari's life. But her father had died suddenly of a stroke related to complications from Sickle Cell Disease two summers prior. Mari and her mother had been able to keep their house for a while; however, her mother, barely able to work through the grief of losing a husband, eventually had no choice but to move them in with Mari's grandmother.

She told Harry that it wouldn't be so bad except for her uncle, who was always around, acting like he owned the place. Everyone letting him get away with whatever it was he wanted.

"In a house like that," she said, "it's easy to not get noticed."

It was then he understood her need for quiet. But still decided to ask something that would contradict that need.

"Could we talk on the phone tonight, maybe?" he said timidly, never before having asked a girl for her phone number.

"No. Sorry," she responded abruptly. He felt like he had been cut again for the second day in a row. He flinched visibly, which she couldn't help but notice. And that caused her hard demeanor to soften. She nearly smiled.

"My grandma's always on the phone. And when she's not on the phone, someone else is. I never get to use it. But don't worry, that just gives us more to talk about tomorrow." Then she kissed him on the cheek before asking him to walk her to her door.

He was quiet the entire trek. Mainly because he was too stunned by the kiss on the cheek to have anything coherent to say.

It had gone that way on Thursday as well, and they had met on Friday to do the same. It was only on Friday that things differed.

It was well past dark. Excuses had been made to Harry's father as to why he would be out all evening. Excuses at which his father had grunted and farted as he lay on the couch watching the television. Mari hadn't had to make any excuses at all.

Friday brought with it the first snowfall of the season. As a result, Harry and Mari had the park to themselves again. The two were sitting quietly, this time on one of the park benches. The sitting quietly was much the same as it had been over the previous days. What was different was the reason for their silence on this Friday evening.

They were quiet because they were kissing.

She had started it, and neither of them had felt like letting it end.

Harrison wouldn't have thought it would be so much fun to sit in the cold and push your mouth against someone else's. Yet that's what they had been doing for the last hour. And they would have continued doing so for longer, perhaps all night, except they were interrupted.

"Well, isn't that sweet?" said a chiding voice Harrison recognized at once. This was followed by laughter from voices other than the one belonging to the person who had asked the rhetorical question.

"Looks like we got ourselves a little cookies and cream situation going on here. A little chocolate milk action."

More laughter.

Harrison pulled himself away from Mari. He did so mournfully, not yet ready to be without her touch. Also not yet ready to face what he knew would be facing them once they turned toward those titters.

What he saw when he pulled his lips from Mari's was what he had expected to see: a gang of goons.

Benny the Brick was at the forefront, looking as large and hard and brickish as ever. With him was Gordie, whose face around the nose and eyes was still slightly discolored, and Todd, a demented grin on his long face. Along with those three were Benny's girlfriend Laurie, and two female friends of theirs whose names Harry did not know.

It seemed, in the midst of Harry and Mari's budding love, war had fallen upon them.

CHAPTER EIGHT

Yellow Snow

They were dragged from the bench. Pulled into the playground, to the swings. The goons who had swarmed them shoved a bandana into each of the mouths of the young, smitten pair. They then covered those bandanas with glove-clad hands. Muffling Harry and Mari, nearly muting them.

The bandanas wouldn't be necessary, not for Harrison at least. Because he was sat in front of one of the swings instead of on it. And the chain of the swing was quickly wrapped around his neck.

The bullies ripped the jacket he was wearing off of him, snapping the zipper as they did so. Then ripped his sweater from his torso, the fabric cutting into his skin as they played tug of war with it until it was a large rag on the rubber flooring of the playground. His undershirt was next. Eventually, he was topless under the still falling snow.

A beating took place after that.

Harrison was punched, he was kicked. Each strike delivered many times from the people who had ambushed him and Mari. All the while he was being strangled, the chain constricting around his throat, the sharp seat cutting into his chest and shoulder. Despite these abuses, Harry wasn't worried for himself. Not completely. He was mostly concerned for Mariam. Hoped that she had somehow gotten away.

But when they let him go, when they let him fall to his face in the snow, he saw that Mari hadn't gotten away. Far from it.

As he gasped for air, squinting through a pair of rapidly swelling eyes, he saw that they had Mari on her knees, assailants standing on either side of her, hoisting her up by both arms. She was being held in place by the two girls whose names Harrison didn't know.

Laurie was behind her, looking exceptionally entertained while she held a hand over Mari's mouth and a forearm around her neck.

Todd and Benny, who had just been beating on Harrison with Gordie, entered Harry's field of vision as they made their way to Mari. He saw her eyes track them as they approached her, hard as ever. Hers was a face seemingly prepared for suffering. Unwilling to show any sign of fear.

She thrashed and writhed, attempting to free herself from her captors, looking as though she was ready and willing to take Benny on by herself. He stood in front of her, calmly raised his hand, the back of it facing Mari's direction. He brought it down violently against her cheek.

The sound of skin and bone hitting skin and bone was a sonic boom reverberating in the silence of the park. Mari's body stilled. She stopped struggling. Harry could do nothing to help as he was held down by Gordie. Might have been too weak from the assault to assist Mari even if he wasn't being restrained.

After looking to Harrison with a smile on his face, Benny proceeded to unzip his pants as he stepped even closer to Mariam.

It happened almost too quickly for Harrison to comprehend, his mind groggy and semi-lucid as it was.

He attempted to cry out for them to stop, to leave her alone, but even though the bandana had been beaten out of his mouth, he wasn't able to form the words. What came out was a sound like a wet belch, a bubble of blood popping as he attempted to speak.

He nearly passed out then, but there was a hand, two, both Gordie's, slapping him all over his head, shovelling snow into his mouth, rubbing it on his face. Those hands gripped his hair, pulling his head back as he lay mostly flat on the ground, wrenching his neck in a way it was not supposed to bend, prying open his eyes to make sure he had to watch.

"Next time, you'll mind your own goddamn business," Benny said, as his hands reached into his jeans.

Thirty seconds later, when Benny had done up his pants, and the previously white snow immediately below Mari had been dotted and splashed with yellow, Benny turned to Harrison. Said,

"You're lucky I didn't have to take a shit."

The entire group laughed merrily at that. Then Harrison felt a fist against the back of his head, causing the front of it to crash into and bounce off of the snow-covered rubber surface of the park. Shortly after that, the laughter faded. As did the rest of the world around him.

CHAPTER NINE

Rage

When he woke up, she was there. Hovering above him, kneeling right beside his head. Harrison was relieved to see Mari before he could clearly remember why. Then he did remember why, and his relief turned to rage. Except he was too weak to do anything with that rage. His body badly beaten, he could only look up at her, trying to figure out what he could say. How he could apologize for dragging her into this turmoil.

But he said nothing initially, because the look on her face did something, momentarily, to reduce the rage he felt. She appeared to be as relieved as he had been upon waking up and seeing her, maybe more so. Despite what they had gone through, she looked happy to see him. No one ever looked happy to see him.

"Hey, Sleeping Beauty. I would have kissed you to try to wake you up sooner, but I probably ought to take a shower first," Mariam said. Then she looked away from him – looked up and at the clouds, which were still leaking large lazy flakes of snow onto the world – before she barked out rueful, humorless laughter. How she could joke at a time like this, about a thing like that, he didn't know. It was then he truly began to wonder about what might have gone on in her house and in her life that would contribute to such a hard exterior. Thankfully, temporarily, he saw that exterior soften.

"Are you okay?" she asked, stroking his head tenderly. "Does anything feel broken?"

He patted himself down, realized that she had put his tattered sweater and broken-zippered jacket back on him, both covering his upper body like a blanket. When he was sure nothing of his was broken or fractured, he sat up with great difficulty and, with her help, put the remains of his clothing on the way they were meant to be worn, as best he could in the condition they were in.

"Yeah, I'm okay. Are you?" he said, thinking of what Benny had done to her, feeling the full extent of that rage yet again. Wishing he could do something about it.

"I'm fine. I just... We should have expected that. We have to be more careful."

"Why?" he said sharply. If he'd had his full strength the question would have been shouted. Weak as he was, it was barely a whisper; a rough rasp from a recently throttled throat. "Why should *we* have to be more careful? *We* didn't start this shit. *We* didn't do anything to deserve this!"

"No, we didn't..." she said as she contemplated the situation they were in, her face aimed toward the sky yet again, searching there, catching falling snow that melted as it met her skin. Harry wasn't sure if she was talking to him or to God when she added, "God fucking damnit, I could kill those motherfuckers."

Her voice was colder than the current Colorado conditions.

They knelt there surrounded by that cold, face to face, the snow both beneath them and drifting down from above. They rested in front of the swing set which had just been used to nearly choke Harry to death.

He wasn't certain if she meant what she had just said. But all at once it sounded like the right way to go about things. The only way to go about things.

"So..." he began hesitantly, still trying to gauge her, wanting to know just how serious her last statement had been "...Why don't we?"

EPILOGUE

Making Ghosts

Mari hadn't had an answer to that question. And neither had Harry, despite the fact that they had knelt there in the park and pondered it a while. Contemplated the question of why they didn't murder Benny and his gang.

That had been two months ago. Since then, they had gone from questioning why they shouldn't do it, to planning to make it happen.

Which is why, on this night, two months removed from Harry being beaten to unconsciousness, eight weeks after Mari had been humiliated in a way that neither of them had directly mentioned since, Harrison was walking carefully across a small field toward a parked Caravan in an otherwise empty parking lot, ready to commit murder.

He had waited until their hotbox was going strong, timed his approach to coincide with their car filling with clouds.

Before waiting for the smoke to shield him, he and Mari had waited for weeks to put their plan into action. Weeks during which they had endured more name calling at school, glares, derisive laughter, but no real abuse. Not physically.

They had kept their heads down and acted like meek, defeated dogs, accepting the jeers and slurs, and going on their way without responding or reacting, seemingly admitting defeat in a war they had wanted no part of to begin with. A war they intended to end with multiple murders. Quadruple homicide.

The only question left, after the original question he had posed to her was answered, was 'How?'. How would they exterminate their tormentors?

The first answer was the simplest. Harrison had suggested his father's pistol. It was locked in a box in the old man's barely used bedroom. Harry could easily break into that box, use the gun, and rid the world of people who were destined to help ruin it. But neither Mari nor Harry felt comfortable with that idea. The concept of shooting a bunch of their classmates in cold blood seemed too barbaric, too bloody. And it would cause them to too easily be caught. Captured and vilified. Made into monsters by the media, their peers, their teachers.

Harry imagined the headlines focusing on his and Mari's troubled backgrounds, calling them loners, strange students, ticking timebombs just waiting to explode. All while Benny the Brick and his group would be glorified as innocent victims. He wasn't willing to let that happen.

They needed something that would allow for them to get away with it. This wasn't about throwing away their own lives, it was about saving them. About saving the lives of others who Benny's group was currently bullying, and those they would continue to pick on for as long as they could get away with it. This was about retribution, redemption, not recklessness.

Poison was proposed. But there was no way they could get close enough to a food source that all of Benny's group would share at the same time.

Cutting the brakes of the Caravan was another suggestion. But neither of the two had the mechanical prowess to achieve such a task. Nor did they want to risk the lives of innocents who might be involved in the car crash cutting Benny's brakes would cause.

They looked for inspiration everywhere. And found themselves often talking about murders in the movies

Harry watched, and in the books Mari read. Yet it wasn't the topic of murder that had finally allowed them to find a solution. It was the topic of suicide.

Mariam had just finished reading William Shakespeare's *Romeo and Juliet* in her advanced English class. Since they had met, Mari had begun explaining the books she was reading to Harry in an effort to get him interested in reading something other than comic books. After she explained the events of *Romeo and Juliet* to him one afternoon as they walked from school toward their block, he had laughed uncomfortably, saying,

"At least, no matter what happens, we won't end up like those two dopes." He had expected her to laugh, at least to smile. But when she only looked at him seriously, his discomfort grew, became disquieting. The question she asked him next did nothing to alleviate that feeling.

"Have you considered it, ever? Stopping all the bullshit yourself. Not having to worry about anything anymore?"

He had thought about it, briefly, a time or two. But he didn't want to think about it at the moment. Especially now that Mari was in his life. It wasn't he or her that deserved to die, it was those bullies. But, as he contemplated the question and an appropriate response, he was reminded of something. Something on the topic of suicide he had seen recently. A show his father had been watching on the day he had gotten the best of Gordie and Todd and had briefly felt like he was on top of the world. Far from feeling like he should exit it.

And it was then he realized exactly how they would get rid of the people who could make Mariam contemplate the question she had asked.

Mari had thought the idea was brilliant the moment he suggested it to her. From that point on, it was only a matter of making it happen.

Since that day, they had been observing Benny and his group, had figured out where they went after school when they weren't terrorizing children. Followed them on certain nights when they could. Gathered that, on many nights, including every Friday night, the core members of the group – Benny, Gordie, Todd and Laurie – came to the school parking lot, hotboxed Benny's dad's van, and sat there talking for hours. They had observed this for consecutive Fridays. Watched on each of those nights as Benny would swerve out of the parking lot, somehow getting his group back to where they needed to get to each time.

Once their pattern had been confirmed, it was only a matter of waiting for a cold and snowy Friday night. They needed the cold weather to guarantee two things. The first being that the group of bullies would keep the engine of the van running, the heat on, as they sat and got stoned inside of it. The second reason they needed the cold was to ensure their murder weapon would be the correct temperature.

Now, Harrison was only feet away from the vehicle, stooped low beneath the sightline of the rear window even though the window was opaque with smoke.

He got down on his knees, decided to crawl the rest of the way on the snow-covered grass leading to the back of the van. After getting there, Harry took off his backpack, reached in with gloved hands to withdraw the items he had inside of it. Objects he hoped would be the solution to his and Mari's problems.

Inside of the bag was a collection of snowballs, each of them slightly smaller than a snooker ball. He had been careful to measure and mold them precisely. There were eight of them in total.

He heard laughter from the van, saw it rock. His heart leapt in his throat as he waited, almost expecting one of them to jump out. For all of them to beat him up again, likely to death this time. He shook the thought from his mind, steadied his nerves. When it came to dealing death, he planned to beat them to it right here and now.

One by one, he put the balls of compacted snow into the vehicle's tailpipe. Between each insertion, he placed fresh snow from the ground into the tailpipe, not wanting to leave any space around each snowball. Not wanting to risk this plan not working.

The snow, the cold, would allow the snowballs to stay frozen long enough to block the fumes from the exhaust, keeping those vapors in the car. Adding a bit of variety to their hotbox. Adding something more noxious to the clouds of smoke in there.

With the last ball placed snuggly in the exhaust pipe, and snow packed against the pipe's opening to make it appear as though Benny had backed into a small snowbank, Harry crawled away from the van, as nervous and scared as he had ever been. Though still not feeling the remorse both he and Mari had worried might stop them, might cause them to believe that this was a bad decision. He couldn't feel that way. Not when he pictured Benny unzipping his pants and doing what he'd done.

That had been too far, what Benny had done. That was worth erasing someone from this Earth. Because no one who did that to another person should have the chance to do that again. And the people who encouraged him, cheered him on, were somehow even worse.

No, there would be no remorse. Harrison's only concern was that he and Mari wouldn't be able to get away. Not only with this murder, but from their homes, from this town once this deed was done.

Eventually, when he thought he was out of the range of sight of those in the van, he got to his feet. Got to the treeline and was greeted with a warm, soft hug from Hard

Mari. He kissed her hungrily, longingly, her rapid-fire heartbeat matching his own. He could feel it through the layers they wore. Layers they knew would be necessary, because they planned to watch this entire thing play out.

They stood in the trees for the next two hours, nervous when a car or two pulled into the lot, but relieved when those same cars quickly pulled out of it. The Caravan, however, didn't pull out of that lot. It only sat there, parked, the windows slowly being covered over by snow.

The young couple stood and observed, waiting for the car to move, to rock, for someone to open a door, for that someone to fall out gasping. But none of those things happened. Nothing happened. The car remained still. Just as still as the bodies of the four potential ghosts now inside of it.

When they were sure the act was done, Harry and Mari turned. Hand in hand, they left. Walked over a field of freshly fallen snow, knowing that there would be much more snow to come on this night. Snow that would cover their tracks. Tracks that led away from the van, away from this cluster of trees, away from the school, and, eventually, away from this town.

Where would those tracks lead? Neither of them knew for sure. They only vowed to go somewhere better. Anywhere that wasn't here.

All they knew with certainty was that, wherever they went, whatever the future had in store for them, they would never allow themselves to be bullied or controlled ever again.

Piece #2

MAKING GHOSTS II:

LUNATIC LOVE

A Novel

PROLOGUE

The Meeting

Do you believe in ghosts?

That was the question Harrison Wendelken had asked Mariam Goldbraithe once upon a time, what felt like several lifetimes ago.

Back when she had been a fourteen-year-old girl, she hadn't understood the question. Not completely. Not when she was already scared out of her mind about potentially committing murder. Or at least being an accomplice to the act.

Back then, Mari had taken the question in the literal sense. Ghosts that show up in the dark, ghosts that scare. Unsettled souls, once upon a time alive.

Now, eleven years later, she understood the question in a different way. Understood it, perhaps, in a way Harrison himself hadn't when he had asked it. Now, at the age of twenty-five and looking toward an uncertain but promising future, Mariam Wendelken – formerly known as Hard Mari Goldbraithe – believed that Harrison had been asking about metaphorical ghosts all those years ago.

These ghosts still scared, but they showed up at any time of the day, on any day. And here they were on quite possibly the most important day of her life – of their lives. These ghosts, the memories of all her and her husband had been through since that question had been asked, were haunting her now. She had no idea why, but she couldn't shake them.

"Hey. You okay?" Harrison asked from beside her. At some point he had taken her right hand in his left and given it a squeeze. "You ready?" he added with a smile.

The two stood in front of a high-rise building in the city of Delphi, Washington, only hours away from their home in Seattle. They were at the front entrance of an edifice made of steel and glass, the late winter sun reflecting off it. Shining bright like the future they were set to attain once they stepped inside. If things went according to plan. A plan that had been in development for a decade. A plan toward a future that had, for years, seemed like something not intended for the likes of them.

Mari hadn't realized she had paused in front of the doors until she'd felt Harry's hand, heard his questions. It was only then she understood that she had stopped walking toward their future because she felt dragged back by their past.

Was she okay? Was she ready? She didn't know, but here they were.

"Yes," she said, doing her best to shake off the bad feeling that had been lingering with her all day. The feeling that something was wrong. That something was going to go wrong.

It's all in your head, she said to herself, doing her best not to let the anxiety she had struggled with since her teenage years get to her as it often tried to. *You always think good things are going to go bad. Not today. We've worked too hard for this. Been through too much.*

She gave Harry's hand a squeeze before letting it go, still thinking of the time he had asked that question. Of the time they had walked away from four dead teenagers in a van. Of the four kids they had killed and what had resulted from that night.

With everything that had led them to this moment racing through her mind, Mari and her husband – her partner in life, in crimes she wished she could forget, and in the business they were hoping to get off the ground today – walked into Helping Hand Headquarters. Toward the meeting that would forever change their lives.

PART ONE

No Beds

CHAPTER ONE

Black Mountain

Ten years before The Meeting...

Mariam hated needles. Hated that they had become a regular part of her life. She looked over at Harrison beside her, on her left. He, as always, seemed to be at peace, taking a bite out of the cookie he had just been given and making an expression that indicated he was currently chewing on a portion of Heaven. He noticed her watching him. Gave her the shy smile she loved so much.

"You okay, Goldy?" Goldy as in Goldbraithe, it was his personal nickname for her.

"Yeah," she said with a sigh that she could see as a puff of frozen condensation in the winter air in front of her. The sight of her breath was a reminder of the cold snap they were facing here in Black Mountain, Colorado. She didn't need the visual reminder. She could feel the cold. Despite being only moments removed from the warmth of the indoors, she could barely feel her nose, and her fingers – though gloved – were beginning to tingle with the numbness that near freezing temperatures often bring.

"I just hate this place," she added as she turned back to look at the building they had walked out of moments ago. Looked at the nasty receptionist through the window that made up the front wall of that building. One structure in a stretch of others that made up Bosner Plaza. The one bearing the name Black Mountain Blood Services; one of the two blood clinics in the city. One of the two that she and Harry visited nearly every month.

It wasn't because of the needles that she hated today's experience. It was because of a member of the clinic's staff.

The receptionist, who had made worse an already bad and uncertain day, looked up from whatever she was scrawling on a paper on her desk. As if feeling that Mari's eyes had been on her, she glanced through the glass at the fifteen-year-old and scowled in the same fashion she had at both Mariam and Harrison earlier.

She was new there, the receptionist, and she wasn't used to the two regulars at the blood bank. They had entered to the sight of a chilling glare they could feel despite having just come in from the freezing outdoors.

After filling out the requisite screening form, walking to the receptionist and handing it to her, Mari had watched nervously as the nurse not only looked through the forms, but seemed to read them thoroughly. More thoroughly than the receptionists who were familiar with Mari and Harry.

Mari prayed the woman wouldn't ask for identification to prove they were the appropriate age to sell their blood, which they were not. They were two years too young and gave blood too often. Most of the receptionists they had encountered here didn't seem to care about those details. Understood how desperate teens like them were for money. They also didn't want to turn down the blood.

When this particular receptionist had stopped at a spot on the form, glanced at Mari then stared back at the same spot, Mari had known what the woman was focused on. Had known what question the woman had been fixated with. And it wasn't a question pertaining to age.

When the receptionist – Sharon was her name based on the nametag on her generous bosom – cleared her throat to speak, Mariam had known what was going to be asked.

"You been having any unprotected sex? Any sex with them Africans or Europeans?" she said, looking at Mari, who only shook her head, feeling her face grow hot at the questions and the accusatory look that came with them. The woman had then turned to Harry. "How about you? Any homosexual sex? Orgies?"

"We haven't had sex with anyone," Harry had stated sternly, sounding like he was losing his patience. Sharon, as if searching for the truth written on Mari's face rather than listening to Harry, had stared at the young woman with a look of distrust and distaste. Mari had hoped the hostile woman couldn't see the truth. It was a truth better left unknown. Even to Harry. At least for the time being.

"No, I suppose you haven't," Sharon had said, turning her attention to Harry, disgust taking up space on her face alongside distrust and distaste. Judging from her expression, she'd realized that this wasn't just a pair of kids, but rather two kids who were a pair. A couple. Sharon clearly didn't approve.

"Alright," the receptionist had said, putting away their forms before rising up from her chair with an effort. "We'll get you two ready to bleed."

Now, ten minutes after they had sold their blood, Mari still felt unsettled by the experience.

"I hate it, too. But you know it's just for now. It won't always be this way," Harrison said, cookie crumbs cascading from his mouth onto his coat as he tried to comfort her while chewing. His eagerness to make her feel good always made Mari smile. For her, a rare expression.

They had done their best to make each other smile since they had walked through that snow-covered field a year prior, away from the dead bodies of four teenagers who had tormented her and Harry. Away from four people they had killed.

They had walked away as secret murderers, runaways, Children of No Tomorrow. Wearing the same backpacks they currently wore as they headed from Blood Services to the bus stop, where they would catch the bus that would take them to the mall.

They had boarded a different kind of bus back then; a coach that would take them away from the place that was home to their families, their school, the tortured existence they had led. They had been homeless in the small city of Black Mountain ever since. A city in northwest Colorado that bordered Wyoming and was set many miles from a mountain of the same name.

A city where, despite having no address, no beds to call their own, and no guardians, they had something they'd never previously had. In Black Mountain, over the thirteen months since leaving Denver, they had found something they'd never expected to find: more people like them. A community of unhoused youth. Most importantly, among these, they had found friends.

They were on their way to see those friends now in hopes of having company until tomorrow. People who might help them find somewhere to sleep during what was expected to be one of the coldest nights of the year.

CHAPTER TWO

Food Court

They got to the food court of Black Mountain Mall just as the after-school rush of kids took the place over. Turning the mall from a peaceful place consisting of seniors who considered window shopping a form of exercise to a bustling building full of crowds and chatter, making palpable the excitement and exuberance of unreined youth.

It was that excitement Mariam felt in the air as she took the plastic tray containing what would likely be her one meal for the day (unlike Harry, she was saving her cookie for later) from the counter of the Taco Bell to the pair of tables where she and Harry usually sat and ate.

It was always the same, every Friday afternoon: reams of teens trickling in, talking about how much fun they would have this weekend, where they would go, what they would do, what excuses they would make to their parents.

Mari and Harry ate quietly, observing the food court steadily become full. While Mari wasn't concerned about fun, and had no reason to worry about what she would tell her one remaining parent, she too was wondering where they would go and what they would do this weekend.

That – where to go, what to do – was a constant worry for them. Had been for over a year, especially since this brutal winter had begun. Each day, as evening approached, the thought of how they would survive one more of these cold nights consumed them.

The days were easy enough to handle; there were many places they could spend time without being asked to leave: the library was Mari's favorite, the mall Harry's.

Harry had no problem spending hours in this place, doing only the necessary shopping that would help them avoid being given a ticket and the boot for loitering. What he loved most about the mall was the arcade; going from playing Fatal Fury, to Mortal Kombat, to Street Fighter II. While he could easily get lost in those worlds for long stretches of time, Mari only enjoyed the games in short bursts.

When Harry wasn't at the arcade, he could usually be found in a store called Mountaintop Cards, Comics & Games where he would delve into games of a different sort.

He had made friends with the owner of Mountaintop despite rarely buying a thing there. The owner, by his own admission, loved Harry's passion, indulging the young man's queries about all things game related as Harry attempted to make sure his own game, *A World of Beasts* – the thing he promised Mari would make them rich and take them away from this life – would be a success.

She believed him when he said the game would take them to better places, supported him in his dream. But she had dreams of her own, which is why she loved the library.

Mari was determined to return to school some day. To become a social worker and make a difference to the lives of children like her and Harry. And like the two teenagers who were approaching their table as she chewed on a bite of her taco.

"Hey Harry and Mari!" called a blonde girl as she walked between the rows of tables toward them.

The first thing anyone noticed about Rebecca 'Rebby' Greene was how beautiful she was. The second thing a person might notice was how cheerful she always seemed.

Unreasonably so, especially when considering her circumstances.

Like Mari and Harry, she was homeless, as was the boy who was walking beside her. A thin boy named Brant, dressed head to toe in black, including the eyeliner he wore. The only bit of color on the young man was in his hair and painted on his nails. His hair was a fading fuchsia where the dark brown roots hadn't grown in, his nails were neon, some pink some green.

"Hey Reb. What's up, Brant?" Harry said. Mari gave them both a wave before she, and Harry beside her, shifted their trays on the table to make space for the two to sit in front of them.

"Dirty Harry and Virgin Mari, what are you two doing tonight?" Rebby asked as she removed her backpack and bright purple jacket, putting the former then the latter on the back of the chair before sitting down. She always made a game of their names. Either calling them by the above nicknames she had created for them or using their actual names in an almost singsong manner, emphasizing the fact that they rhymed, as she had when she'd first greeted them moments ago.

The first time they had introduced themselves to her she had laughed out loud at their rhyming names. She hadn't stopped being entertained by that ever since.

Rebby was a larger girl. She described herself as fat because, as she had disclosed to Mari, her mother had described her as fat. But Mari always thought of her as thick, a bit heavy but healthy. Unfortunately, thick and heavy but healthy didn't go very far in the beauty pageants she had been placed in by her mother throughout her childhood.

Her mother, who went by the name of Gorgeous Georgia Greene, had been a beauty pageant star throughout her childhood and into her twenties. She was a woman who had expected the same of her daughter, placing her in the same pageants she had won, even nicknaming Rebby 'Beautiful Becca' the way her own mother had labelled her Gorgeous Georgia. Rebby's mother had wanted Rebby's life to be a carbon copy of her own.

She had done well in the pageants as a young child; however, after it became apparent that her baby fat was staying with her through her early teen years, after many fourth and sixth and tenth place finishes, her mom, in a roundabout and indirect way, had talked the young Rebby into Anorexia Nervosa.

At fourteen, at five-feet-six-inches tall and weighing just ninety-six pounds, she had finished in first place for the first time since she had been nine years old. The way she had told it to Mari, after the win, Rebby had hugged her mother backstage, given her the first-place scepter, the flowers, her sash, the tiara. And then she'd told her mother to fuck off. She said she wanted French fries and freedom. That had been two years ago. She hadn't returned home since.

"Hopefully not freezing to death," Harry said, answering Rebby's question with a chuckle. It was a joke. It was the truth. The temperature was supposed to get down to single digits. With a windchill that would make it feel like it was in the negatives. Skin freezing, fingertips falling off type of weather.

The shelter beds for both adults and youth were filled up not only in Black Mountain but in the entire county.

Mari and Harry had made the trip to the blood services building in order to hustle together enough money for a stay in a motel for a night or two. But after calling around from the payphone by the blood bank, they'd realized that even paid beds were unavailable.

What *would* they be doing tonight? Mari wondered. Would it be huddling together over two cups of coffee at a coffee shop until they were asked to leave? Or would it be riding one of the few buses in this town that went all night, hoping that the driver would have mercy and wouldn't kick them off? Or – and this was a last desperate resort that neither wanted – would they jimmy open a car, hotwire it, and sleep in it all night, just to have heat and shelter against the cold?

It was Rebby who had taught them how to hotwire a car, who had let them know which nights would be best to ride which all-night bus because certain drivers were friendlier than others. It was Rebby who had taught them nearly all they knew about surviving on the street. And it was she who was now offering them a solution for tonight, a way to avoid the bitterest night of the year.

"Hunter is having a few people over at his place tonight, and he's letting me invite some friends. Luckily for the two of you, you're included in that category." She beamed her best beauty pageant smile at Mari and Harry. Then she saw the look on Mari's face. The look of hesitation, of anxiety. Mari hated parties, and Harry wasn't fond of them either.

For Harry, a party was a foreign place he had rarely been invited to. He associated parties with jocks and drinking. With boys like Benny the Brick, now deceased by his hand; with girls like Benny's girlfriend Laurie, now deceased by his hand. The cool kids. And he wanted nothing to do with places where people like that went to gather.

For Mari, she hated parties for a reason she had never told another living soul. Not even Harry. It was a secret she believed she would take to her grave.

"Look, I know you guys don't like parties. But this won't be a party, I swear. It's just a gathering of a few people in a small house. A way to keep people warm while it's freezing balls out. That's the kind of guy Hunter is." She said this with a sycophantic smile, speaking her new boyfriend's name the way a priest might speak of Jesus. It was reverence, it was fawning, it was her latest infatuation.

Although Rebby was technically homeless, she was rarely ever without a home to go to. Not only would her mother always accept her back into her original home, but there was a slew of men, of boys, of both, that would ensure that she had a roof over her head and a place to sleep. Namely, their beds.

While Rebby didn't sleep around, she rarely slept alone. She was a serial monogamist. It was always a new boyfriend. Some (usually older) guy who was the current light of her life. A Chad, a Kevin, a Brian, a Hunter who would save her from the darkness of singledom. More importantly, someone who would save her from the true darkness of the street. And the cold.

"Hunter?" Harry said. "Is that the guy with the Prince Albert piercing?" This was Harry's polite way of asking about her boyfriend's pierced cock. Rebby gave details, way too many details, of all the guys she was with.

"No, that was Robbie. *Such* a fucking asshole. We broke up last month, right around Christmas. Anyway, Hunter is the nice guy who is going to keep your cute little asses from getting frostbite tonight. You in?"

Mari and Harry looked at each other, thinking the same thing: the warmth would be worth the discomfort.

"And you're sure it's not a party?" Mari asked hesitantly, causing both Rebby and Brant to beam at her. The two had been attempting to get Mari and Harry to party with them since they had become friends the previous winter. Now it seemed it might finally happen.

Still smiling, Rebby responded.

146

"A shindig, a gathering, a bit of a hobnob, maybe... But definitely not a party."

CHAPTER THREE

Party

It was a party. That much was clear even as they walked toward the house from the bus stop where they had just been dropped off. As they had turned onto Hunter's street, it was immediately obvious to Mari, Harry, Brant, and a girl named Tammy who had also accepted Rebby's invitation, which house was his.

It was the house with all the lights on in the elsewise dim neighborhood. The house that was bringing sound to an otherwise silent street. Mari recognized 'Jump' by Kriss Kross playing from powerful speakers. The house they were destined for seemed to be bouncing along to the song, following its instructions. It was the house with people standing outside of it – on the porch, in front of the one car garage, smoking and drinking – despite how obnoxiously cold it was.

"So... about this not being a party..." Mari chided Rebby playfully. The two walked side by side, their arms linked, leaning against each other as they walked to generate warmth against the bitter cold.

"I know, I know, I'm sorry. But he said it would only be a few people, I swear."

There was a smile in Rebby's voice; she didn't sound particularly sorry. She had sworn on several occasions that she would get Mari out of her shell and out with her, drinking somewhere, being social. And now she was finally making good on her word.

The two had met at the Center Street Public Library shortly after Mari and Harry had left Denver. They'd decided to take the first coach bus they saw to wherever it was going, and had wound up in Black Mountain. They'd become regulars at the library shortly thereafter.

On the day they'd met Rebby, Harry, as usual, had been working on the rules to his board game while Mari read. She'd heard someone break the silence of the reading room by swearing. Heard them exclaim,

"Why the fuck is he biting his thumb at people? None of this makes sense."

Mari had turned in her chair, surveyed the mostly empty study area, spotted Rebby immediately and known she was the source of the frustrated outburst. Then, she'd seen the book in her hand and had understood the reason for this beautiful girl's exasperation.

Rebby had been reading *Romeo and Juliet*, or attempting to read it anyway. Not being able to resist the chance to discuss one of her favorite stories, she had asked, "Is that Romeo and Juliet?" knowing that it was.

Rebby had seemed surprised to hear someone speaking to her. She'd done a doubletake before locking eyes with Mari, her expression unreadable. For a moment, Mari had wondered if speaking to this lovely looking girl had been a mistake. But then Rebby had smiled and said,

"Can you translate this shit into something I can understand?"

"It's like the middle finger," Mari said after a brief chuckle. To that, Rebby had screwed her face up in confusion, causing Mari to elaborate. "The guy biting his thumb? It's just a crude gesture." She demonstrated by presenting Rebby her middle finger. "Like, when you think about it. Why is *this* offensive? Why is it an insult? It's only bad because we say it is, otherwise it means nothing. Biting their thumb back then was the same as giving someone the finger now."

In response, Rebby had nodded, then raised her own middle finger and aimed it at the book in front of her. Then she had bitten her thumb at it for good measure. The two had shared a laugh, and had shared a friendship ever since.

Unlike Mari and Harry, Rebby could use her mother's address to keep herself enrolled in school despite her not physically living there. And this had a great deal to do with the continued strengthening of the girls' friendship. The two (and Harry, and Brant, and occasionally others) had continued to meet at the library, Mari tutoring Rebby in several subjects despite being a year younger than the former beauty pageant winner and having been out of school for months. Mari relished this second-hand structured learning, the vicarious living of the life of a student.

From the library they had extended the boundaries of their friendship to include the mall, the parks in downtown Black Mountain, the coffee shops, the entire town, with Rebby taking her turn as the tutor, teaching Mari and Harry all she knew of surviving in the street. She had taught them everything but how to loosen up and party, and now here was her chance. Mari, usually the eager student, was already wary of this lesson.

"It's okay that it's a party" she said to Rebby as they walked arm in arm down a street that could be any street in most lower-middle class neighborhoods around the country. "It's better than the alternative." As she said this, as if to illustrate her point, a gust of freezing wind blew the advancing group back, biting at their bodies.

They trudged onward, not taking the wind as a warning that they ought to stay away.

"You hear about the idiots who went up Hellstone Hill?" Brant asked after the group had recovered from the burst of biting breeze. He was referring to the mountain that gave this town its name. Hellstone Hill was what many of the locals called it.

"I thought no one was supposed to go up there," Harry said from Mari's right side, sounding as naïve as Mari could remember. It was one of the things she loved about him, his innocence. But also one of the things she worried about, especially given their circumstances. The streets fed on naivety.

"Ding! Ding!" Brant responded, teasing Harry. "No one is *supposed* to go up there. No one *should* go up there. *And* they have to walk through White Wood Forest first. *Fuck* that. It's suicide."

"You really believe that?" Mari asked, looking over to her left past Rebby at Brant, observing the fear on the young man's wind-reddened face. She had heard all about White Wood Forest and Black Mountain since they had arrived here. About the stony outcrop that gave the town its name, and the woods before the forest that were purported to be haunted. It was as advertised: a small black mountain at the edge of town. Northwest of where they were now. To the left of them currently.

She could sense its presence even though it wasn't visible at the moment. Had it been daytime, she would have been able to see it among the other mountains, its top black while the others were snow-capped. There was something up there that prevented snow from sticking. Something that had been off limits for over a hundred years, something that had been cordoned off with fences and razor wire by the municipality.

The rumors were plentiful: The mountain was actually a volcano that could go off at any moment; there was a series of hot springs at the top keeping it endlessly warm despite the weather around it; an alien asteroid had landed and changed the landscape, creating the small mountain.

Regardless of what the truth was, it was believed that it was warm at the top of Black Mountain. And, according to what Brant was in the middle of saying now, there was a group of teenagers who had gone up there to chase that warmth and play a high stakes version of King of the Mountain. Not only claiming Hellstone Hill, but the building on top of it. Some sort of ancient temple or castle. The rumors that place inspired were plentiful and dark.

"...No matter how cold it gets, there's no fucking way you'd catch me up there," Brant was saying.

"Come on, you can't really believe that Black Mountain is haunted. That's just shit our parents made up to keep us in line," Tammy protested.

"Too many crazy things happen in this town for me *not* to believe that it's haunted. And don't pretend *you* don't believe. I saw your face when Ted and Leigh asked us to go up with them. If nothing's wrong up there, why didn't you say yes?"

"Well... uhh... It's dangerous. And it's stupid," was Tammy's retort. She suddenly didn't sound as confident in her conviction as she had only moments before. The two continued to argue about the rumors of whatever it was at the top of the mountain, why it was cordoned off, if it was haunted.

"Do you believe in ghosts?" The question from immediately beside her caused Mari to stop mid-stride, taking her back to a memory of four dead bodies and a van. Dead bodies that the coroner who had examined them had ruled wound up that way by accident, snow inadvertently clogging the exhaust pipe of the van they had expired in. The van Harry had rigged to be a gas chamber. The bodies that made Mari and Harry murderers four times over.

152

"Mari? You okay? You look like you've *seen* a ghost," Rebby said as her momentum was stalled by Mari stopping.

"Yes... Sorry. I just... I do believe in them. Crazy things happened in our old neighborhood, too. I just... I try not to think about them."

"Ooooo, sounds intense! Maybe you'll loosen up and tell me after a couple of drinks?" Rebby said, testing the waters of a touchy subject for Mari.

"Rebby..." Mari said, turning her friend's name into a warning.

"Hey, hey, no pressure, Virgin Mari," Rebby said. Mari started walking again, but Rebby held her back by their still-linked arms. When they were a few feet behind the rest of the group, Rebby whispered, "I'm just saying. You're here, you might as well make the best of it. A lot of us have bullshit from our past to deal with. I know things haven't been easy for you, but you can't let whatever happened to you before ruin your fun for the rest of your life. Right?" She said this in her usual enthusiastic way, the peppiest of pep talks. Mari was annoyed by it, but that was because she knew, at least partially, that Rebby was correct.

"Right," Mari agreed reluctantly.

They caught up with their friends, walking as a group from the sidewalk to the driveway into the modest little house full of people fleeing from the cold, heading toward fun, a reprieve from the pressures of each day.

Mari tried to adopt their attitude. Tried to forget the ghosts of her past, attempted not to let them haunt her.

They walked into the party that was not a shindig or a gathering or a hobnob, not realizing that their decision to come to this place, on this night, would lead to yet another murder. Another ghost to be made.

CHAPTER FOUR

Just a Kid Being a Kid

It tasted bitter, but not as bad as Mari had expected it to taste. Still, she thought it would take a lot of effort to get used to as she took a second sip from her can of Coors Light.

After they had tossed their coats on the pile of winter wear on the bed in the small guest room and were about to settle down in an area of the den that had recently been vacated by a group of smokers, Mari had been asked what she wanted to drink. She had responded by saying, "Anything but wine." Even the thought of the stuff made her want to vomit.

This – the Coors Light – wasn't the first drink she'd ever had. But it was her first drink since the night of her first drink. Her first since the party four years ago that had made her wary of all parties thereafter. Since the night her life had been changed. Ruined. Since... No, she didn't want to think about that night. She wanted, at least for right now, to be normal. To follow Rebby's advice and make the best of this fucked up transient life she had found herself in. She wanted to be a teenager doing the things teenagers did.

On the coffee table in front of them were empty cans, bottles, and a white residue that reminded her of powdered sugar. She sipped her beer, getting accustomed to the bitter taste of it, feeling herself get a little lightheaded. She was trying not to remember the last time she had felt this way. Instead, she focused on Brant, who was focused on the white substance on the table.

He ran his forefinger across the tabletop, allowing the substance to collect on his digit. He brought the white-tipped finger to his nose. Snorted what was on it. Brought his finger back to the table. Swiped. Returned it to his face, though this time to his gums. He rubbed the area of his gums behind his top lip, then ran his tongue along that area. Sat back, smiled.

Just a kid being a kid.

Mari wondered how she would ever fit in.

Harry seemed to be doing a good job of fitting in. He didn't appear as uncomfortable as she had imagined him being in this sort of scenario. He was drinking a beer as well, sitting on the couch across from her. He was between Tammy and Brant, chatting with them while she sat next to Rebby.

Tammy was a mousey creature; skinny, short. She wore her brown hair in a single pigtail. Had a button nose and an overbite. When Mari had first met her through Rebby at the mall, she had thought the girl looked cute in the way a chipmunk looks cute. Now though, as Harry said something that made both Brant and Tammy laugh, her head back, her mouth open, her overbite exposed, and – something that rubbed Mari the wrong way – her hand touching Harry's arm, Mari saw her as more than just anthropomorphic animal cute. Under the green light of envy, Tammy suddenly looked pretty, alluring, threatening.

Mari took a large swallow of her beer, a sip at a time no longer feeling sufficient.

Have fun, she said to herself. *Stop overthinking everything.*

But she couldn't help overthinking, particularly about her past. That haunted place reached out to her now across the years, a host of ghosts she was unable to exorcise existing within her, possessing her, controlling how she felt, acted, reacted.

She wanted desperately to be like everyone around her. She saw their smiling faces, watched them chatting, laughing, flirting. She couldn't hear most of their words on account of the music. *Smells Like Teen Spirit* by Nirvana blared through the house, the rhythm a living thing, pulsating along with her pulse, pounding in sync with the beating of her heart.

Too fast. Too hard. Her heart, her breathing.

She felt like she was being constricted, like she needed to leave the room. Like it might all start to close in on her.

"Hey! Who invited the faggot? And who told him and his little group of rejects that they could sit where we was sitting?"

Mari heard each and every one of these words, because the owner of them was shouting over the music. And the stereo, somewhere in the house, in reaction to the shouting voice, was lowered by whoever was at its helm. An unseen DJ turning it down upon hearing the sound of drama, trouble, the potential for violence. Something more entertaining than the music he or she was playing.

"You hear me, *faggot*? Who told you you could be here?" And now everyone in sight was looking at their group and at the young man who was accosting them. A man standing beside, in front of, hovering over her group to Mari's right, closest to Rebby.

He was in his late teens, maybe early twenties. He wore denim from neck to ankle. Black jeans, blue jacket, black shirt beneath it. His hair was dirty blond, greasy and stringy like he was a member of the band whose song was playing. The way half the white boys his age had begun to wear it since Seattle grunge had begun taking over the music scene.

As all eyes were on him and the three others – two guys and a girl – who flanked him, his eyes were on Brant.

Brant with his eyeliner, his painted nails, his clothes as tight as most of those worn by the girls around him. His hair a faded fuchsia, an attention attracting beacon, this time attracting the wrong attention.

Brant looked at Rebby pleadingly, desperately. Rebby, in response, got up from her seat, pushed her way past the denim clad aggressor, and ran from the den.

Both Brant and Mari looked, at the same time, from Rebby's fleeing back to each other. They had a conversation at a glance. His eyes, they said: I'm ready if you are. Her eyes said much the same. They knew, always knew, that when they went to public places it could either be her or him. Him being called what he was being called now, her being called darkie, blackie, nigger. Other unflattering names. Aggression, hostility – they were prepared for this and worse.

"Hey! Look at me when I'm talking to you, princess!" Denim Clothing said. Brant responded with a scowl but no words, turning cold eyes to the bully who addressed him.

Mari knew that Brant was used to this sort of thing. Tough guys trying to show other tough guys just how tough they were by picking on someone obviously weaker, smaller. Gay. It would always be the same. The same words, slurs, insults: faggot, sissy, pussy, bitch, cock sucker. Emasculating words. Insults meant to effeminate.

Brant was always ready for these situations to escalate to the worst possible scenario. Always ready for violence because of the one time he hadn't been.

Three boys his age. A rainy afternoon outside of a corner store in downtown Black Mountain. A wrong place wrong time situation as the boys saw Brant with his nails polished and his clothes skin-tight, and his eyelids and lashes made up to make his blue eyes pop.

They had called him many names.

He had told them to fuck off. Or attempted to.

Before the second syllable was said, he realized he had to run. Realized it too late, or ran too slowly, it made no difference. They had set upon him.

The beating had been horrendous.

A fractured forearm, a broken nose, a broken orbital bone, two fractured ribs. A medical bill he couldn't afford. And somehow, with all of that, it was a different kind of pain that had been the worst of the experience. Because, even as they had assaulted him for being gay, at least two of the boys had grabbed him. Down there. Had groped him. Molested him. Had squeezed him until he screamed. And they had enjoyed it. He had never been so confused. Never so hurt. Mentally, physically.

All this, he had shared with Mari and Harry. And they had shared enough of their story – the chasing of Harry, the harassing of Mari, the cause of the scar that ran down Harry's face – for the three of them to come to an understanding. They would never let themselves be victims again. And they would never let each other be victims so long as they could help it.

Since his beating, Brant went nowhere without his switch blade, which he kept in the pocket of his jeans. It was slender, but it was sharp. Harry was much the same. Mari watched him reach beneath his flannel shirt for the fanny pack at his hip. Knew he would be unzipping it, retrieving from it a knife named for a butterfly.

Mari also had items she never walked anywhere without. While the majority of her and Harry's belongings were in a small storage locker in central Black Mountain, she made sure they always had a few essential items handy. In her backpack – a small nylon satchel connected to her by two drawstrings – was a change of underwear for the two of them, a stick of deodorant, toothbrushes, toothpaste, two granola bars, a bottle of water, a bottle of mace, and, most importantly, nine inches of hunting knife, five of those inches blade.

Her bag was on her lap, her hand was in her bag. Denim and his crew moved past her, across her from right to left, entering the living room, shifting the coffee table over so they could have a clear path at Brant. And Tammy and Harry by their proximity to him on the couch.

Her hand was on the handle of the knife, wiggling it out of its small sheath. And, as she readied herself to take it out and change the tone of the party entirely, she understood that she *did* fit in; in a way, and only with a small group, but she wasn't alone.

Brant was blocked from her sight by the bodies eager to confront him, but Mari locked eyes with Harry. There was agreement there. A look that confirmed he was ready. A look she shared.

Expressions that said they were ready to kill or be killed.

She waited, knife in hand, watching to see if the boy in denim everything would put his hands on Brant.

Kill or be killed.

She waited to see which way it would turn out.

There Mariam Goldbraithe was, ready for murder, one way or another. And not for the first time.

There she was, a teenager doing what teenagers do.

Just a kid being a kid.

CHAPTER FIVE

Underwater

Rebby returned right before the boy in denim could place his hands on Brant. On his throat. Right before Mari removed the hunting knife from her bag. Seconds prior to Mari leaping up and plunging it into the kidney of the biggest member of Denim's group, all of whom had their backs to her. She would keep stabbing them from behind while Brant and Harry did the same from the front. Then they would run. From this house, this city, to a better somewhere.

Rebby returned before all of that could happen. And with her she brought peace in the form of Hunter, the owner of this house, thrower of this party. He was in his early twenties, tall, handsome, made of lean muscle. He was exactly the sort of jock type that Harry would have associated with a party like this. But thankfully, he was on their side.

"Leave him alone, Geoff. He's my guest," Hunter said as he stepped into the living room, into the midst of what might have been a bloody, violent scene.

Geoff, the boy in denim, turned in unison with those who had been following him. A gang of goons like all gangs of goons she had encountered; different ages, different faces, but the same. Always the same. Would she ever be rid of these types of people? Mari wondered.

"You're really sticking up for someone like him, Hunter?" Geoff said, sounding truly perplexed.

"If he's a friend of my girl's, he's a friend of mine. Now give it a break before I have to kick you out."

Geoff scoffed. Gave Brant a final glare. He hinted with his head, nodding in the direction of the kitchen, for his friends to follow him. He then gave another indicator with his head. A shake of it, in the direction of Hunter. Body language that said he was ashamed of the owner of the house.

It was tense. Nearly silent. The music was low. Only the drums and bass could be detected, the melody lost, the lyrics indecipherable.

There was that pulsating again; Mari's heart as she watched Geoff leave. Watched his followers follow him.

Suddenly the pounding was all there was. No longer the music, but solely her heart. It was in her ears, taking over her thoughts, making her feel as though her head might explode, her chest following suit if not getting there first.

It was panic, even though the reason everyone else in the room had panicked was walking away.

It was why she hadn't wanted to come to this party in the first place.

Breathe, girl, breathe, she thought to herself, fighting for those thoughts to be heard above the pounding of her heart, her brain.

She was aware of Rebby saying:

"Such a fucking hero you are, babe!" Then practically jumping into her latest boyfriend's arms, kissing him passionately.

Mari was aware that some people in the room responded to that kiss, many clapping, others hissing and booing playfully, crying out for the couple to get a room, doing their best to break the recent tension. Harry was among them, clapping and saying something that Mari couldn't hear. She only saw that his lips were moving.

And what else did she see on his face? Was that jealousy? Of Hunter? Of Rebby? Of both? Is what Rebby had with Hunter what he wanted?

She thought of Tammy touching his arm. Nearly threw up at the idea of his wanting more than Mari was willing to give him, more than she was ready or able to give him. Would he look for that more amongst girls like Tammy?

She saw them clapping, watched them cheering or playfully jeering, but it was as though she was watching the scene play out in slow motion while she was moving at hyper speed. She wanted to run, to get away from there.

She was aware that Harry was calling her name, that Brant was too, both of them asking if she was okay. But she was aware of this as though she were hearing them from underwater. Her ears full, her lungs threatening to match them. She wanted to swim away from this bumping, pulsating, slow motion room before it caused her to drown.

Mari removed her hand from the knife inside of her bag. Took the bag with her as she walked as calmly as she could force herself to walk from the room. From the house entirely.

CHAPTER SIX

Virgin Mari

"Are you okay?" Harry asked. This time she heard it clearly. She had made it outside, the bitter cold going a long way to slapping her back to her senses.

Was she okay? she wondered as she turned on the driveway toward him. She felt like she had just been having a heart attack. This wasn't the first time it had happened. Since they had left Denver being in crowds had become more difficult. Nearly intolerable at times.

"Yes," she huffed, willing it to be the truth.

Breathe, Mari. Breathe.

And this time she could.

"You want to get out of here?" Harry asked her, wrapping his arms around her the moment he was close enough to do so.

She nearly pushed him away. Then remembered the last time she had done that. Remembered the hurt on his face when he had tried to put his hand down her pants not long after they had come to Black Mountain, the first time they had been able to find a motel that would rent a room to two kids, no questions asked.

She had wanted him to, was as curious as he had been, but she couldn't bring herself to take that next step. Her past had been present again. Haunting. Possessing.

She did her best to fight it off now. Instead of pushing him away, she pulled him closer, appreciating his warmth as she raised her shivering lips to his.

They remained in the blistering cold, holding each other, kissing. They might have frozen that way if not for Rebby. Her voice coming from the doorway of the house.

"*Now* look who needs to get a room!" she called out, teasing them. She might have said more, may have asked the question Mari was expecting but didn't want to hear: 'Are you okay?' She might have tried to engage them in small talk, but she never got the chance. Because Mari's mind was on something else. And that something only involved her and Harry.

"Can we?" Mari asked, taking Harry's hand and leading him up the driveway to the door. "Can we get a room? Right now? Just for a little bit."

She could sense Harry's head swivel toward her, felt his body react, grow tense with what she hoped was excitement. But her focus was on Rebby, so she couldn't see the look on Harry's face. If it matched the one Rebby was giving her now, then he was shocked, confused, amazed.

"Do you mean what I think you mean?" Rebby asked, her smile so bright it cut through the night as it went back and forth from Mari to Harry. The former beauty pageant contestant wanted details where others would have avoided prying, would have given an answer and perhaps asked for the breakdown of events afterward. But this was Rebby, and Mari loved her despite her inability to identify and heed a boundary. Sometimes because of it.

"Yes," Mari responded, hoping she didn't sound as scared or nervous as she felt. She tried to match Rebby's happy expression. She smiled, said, "It means I'm finally tired of you calling me Virgin Mari."

CHAPTER SEVEN

Stale Sweat

It was dark. The room smelled a bit like stale sweat. And, despite them laying on top of a blanket, the floor beneath it was uncomfortably hard.

This was not how Mari had pictured their first time together.

Did you picture it at all? Or did you think – hope – it would never happen. Did you expect him to be satisfied with making out forever? Mari asked herself as she remembered Tammy's hand on Harry's forearm; as she reflected on Rebby and her boyfriend, her boyfriends; as she continued to take to heart what Rebby had said earlier, that she needed to grow up. No more living in the past. No more Virgin Mari. All of these thoughts went through her mind as she tried to process what was happening. What was about to happen.

Mari and Harry were in the only room of the house that hadn't been occupied. Hunter's bedroom. After trying to find a place where they could have some privacy for however long this sort of thing lasted, they realized that would be an impossibility anywhere else in the house. Sympathetic to their plight, Rebby had promised them they could have the master bedroom for a bit, lock the door behind them, ignore the chatter, the laughter, the music seeping though it. The only condition was that they use the floor and the blanket she had found for them to lay atop it.

Rebby, with a wink, had said that she needed the bed fresh when she and Hunter used it. Then she had left them in the room, but not before producing a miniature bottle of vodka and a strip of condoms. She had nearly skipped out of the room, giggling the entire while until the door was closed behind her.

Now it was the moment of truth. He was fumbling with her breasts, something she always felt insecure about. She wished they were larger, that he could feel them instead of searching for them. Wished she was more. Wished she was better. At this. In general.

She didn't know what to do with her hands, with herself, and therefore lay there stiffly as he touched her, more bearing it than allowing herself to enjoy it.

Finally, he noticed her discomfort.

"We don't have to do it, Goldy."

"Don't we?" she said darkly, bitterly. Everyone they knew had already done it. Just searching for a place to be private tonight – in the bathroom, in the guest room, in the basement – they had encountered two pairs and a threesome in some stage of 'doing it.'

If *she* didn't do it, *he* would, Mari feared. With somebody else.

Tammy's hand. His arm.

The way Tammy looked at him when she laughed. And not for the first time. How long before she gave him what Mari wasn't willing to?

"Of course not," he answered. "Not if you're not ready. I want you to be sure."

Mari sighed. Thought about this. Understood she would never be ready.

"I love you, Sir Beasts' Bane." It was a nickname she called him. After the main character, Sebastian Beasts' Bane, from the game he was developing. The game he swore would change their lives. "I know that for sure. And I want to be with you in every way, for as long as we can be. That's what I know for sure, too."

"I love you, too, Goldy." He kissed her briefly on the nose.

"That's why we can wait until you're ready."

It was the kiss on the nose that decided her. The chasteness of it, the innocence. It was almost friendly, a gesture of platonic love. Was that where she was pushing him? Because that was not what she wanted.

You can't let whatever happened to you before ruin your fun for the rest of your life. Right? It was Rebby's voice from Mari's memory.

"Right," she inadvertently uttered aloud.

"What?" Harry asked, clearly confused. And there was the concern again. The tension. When did concern transform fully into pity? Was that where they were now?

Her answer to his question was action. Convincing herself it was time. Reminding herself that she had never been ready, so it didn't matter if she was ready now, Mari reached onto the floor beside her. She fumbled for the bottle of vodka, knocked it over, snatched it before it could roll away.

Opened it. First put it to his lips. He sipped.

Then put it to her own. She swallowed.

The vodka, it burned, it soothed. Brought clarity.

Picturing Tammy's hand, she suddenly knew what to do with hers.

Harry gasped, again asked,

"Are you sure you want to?"

"I am. I do," she told him. Told herself.

"Good," he said. Mari could hear the relief in his voice. Already, the concern and tension dissipating. "'Cause I do too."

And, with that, they did.

CHAPTER EIGHT

Bled

Mari hadn't meant to cry. She rarely ever shed a tear, hated herself each time she allowed one to slip. Hated herself now. Because she was crying, and Harry had heard her, and now he was upset. Worried.

The concern and tension – gone for as long as they had been together as they had never been before – was now back.

It hadn't felt bad, more so strange. But even if it had felt good, her mind couldn't possibly have been in it. Her mind was in the past, the past ruining the present. She had tried to push it away, to be there with him in the moment. But each moment it had lasted, she had wanted it to end.

She had been relieved when he had said he'd finished. She'd rolled over. Hoped to sleep, or at least to feign slumber. But everything that she had been holding back, this night, these last few years, came rushing out of her. And now she was crying and hating herself for it.

"Mariam?"

He only called her that when he was truly concerned.

"Are you okay?"

She was tired of the question.

She opened her mouth to say "Yes," but all that came out of her was the sound of her emotion. A sobbing sound, noise that reminded her of an infant. Of her baby cousin, the daughter of her uncle.

Her uncle. All thoughts somehow led to him.

"Did I..." Harry started. Stopped. Seemed to reconsider what he had been planning to say. "Did I do something wrong?"

"She shouldn't have called me Virgin Mari in the first place," Mari said, as though that was a logical response to his question.

"I guess not," Harry agreed, hesitantly, clearly not understanding what the matter with her was, and trying desperately to be supportive. "I mean, it wasn't very nice of her."

"No, it's not that. I just mean... I wasn't a virgin. Not technically, I guess."

His hand had been on her hip. By the end of her sentence, he had removed it, yanked it away from her as though the skin there had caused it to sizzle. As though she had burned him with this truth, with her previous deception.

"I honestly don't know what to say," he said after a few seconds. She wasn't quite sure what to say either but was relieved to find that he returned his hand to her. Not to her hip, but to her shoulder. It sat there limply, its owner not knowing what to do with it. Mari, also not knowing what to do, did the only thing that made sense. The only thing she hadn't done yet to make this terrible thing she carried with her feel lighter. Better. She decided to unburden herself.

Wiping her face in the dark, Mari sniffed, swallowed, took a deep breath, and spoke about the night that changed her forever.

"It was a party to cheer up my mom. It was my grandma's birthday party, but it was really about my mom and giving her something nice after my dad died the year before. She'd been moping since. That's why she lost her job; that's why we had to move in with my grandmother and her son and his kids in the first place." Her words were garbled. Wet. She hoped he understood her because she didn't want to say any of this twice. Clearing her throat, she continued.

"It was a good idea, you know. At first, I remember it was fun. But sad. But not sad in a bad way, if that makes any sense. They told so many stories about my dad; ones I never heard before, ones I'm not sure I was supposed to hear. But everyone was sharing – happy stories, sad stories, they were laughing and crying – and I was part of the group. I remember loving that about that night, too. Even after my cousins went to bed, my mom let me stay up and hang out with the adults. To learn about my dad.

"I just remember I wanted to try some wine, I wanted to fit in with the grownups for real. Because *everyone* was drinking. And I wanted in on it. But no one would let me drink. My mom gave me shit for asking loud enough for the entire house to hear.

"She fell asleep, though... Well, she passed out drunk, but I didn't know that then. I just thought she was tired and decided the couch was just as comfortable as the bed. My grandma put a cover over her and went to sleep in her room. The guests were gone by then. And all of a sudden it was just me and my uncle in the kitchen cleaning up."

She paused her story upon hearing Harry inhale sharply. A sound of realization.

She could see his face if she turned to him. By then their eyes had adjusted to the dark. And there was moonlight, a beam of it coming from the window, its curtain pulled back. But she knew she would have seen anger, hurt, pity on his countenance. And she didn't want to see that last. Didn't want to see sorrow on those features she loved so dearly.

She could have stopped the story, knew that Harry was smart enough to figure out the rest. But she needed to get this off her chest now that she had started it.

"He asked me if I still wanted to try some wine. And I didn't know any better. He's my *fucking uncle*, why would I think I couldn't trust him? I said yes. He said we'd play a game for it. Down at his place. He has this shitty mini little apartment in the basement." She had stopped crying by now, but at this point she felt the tears again, felt her voice getting thicker, her chest getting tighter. She beat it all back, stopped it before it could restart. She wanted to say this once and never again.

"It was fun at first. That's the worst part. It could have been one of the best nights of my life since my dad died. The stories of my dad, seeing my mom finally smiling for real after so long. Even spending time with my uncle... But... But... That fucking *asshole*! We played a trivia game. Every wrong answer and you take a drink. Those were the rules. I didn't realize he was making me read the easy questions while he read the hardest.

"We were laughing. I was sipping the wine and it was fun. He kept telling me that I was cheating, though. He said I had to take bigger drinks. Like a grownup. So I did. And I remember it didn't feel so good anymore, and I was tired. But he said that I should keep playing. He said that it would be the last time in a long time that I could stay up all night and have fun. So, I kept playing. I remember he was still laughing, and I was feeling really tired and dizzy. Then, the next thing I remember was waking up in my bed."

She paused here because this was the hardest part. She also paused because she expected him to say something. To ask questions. But he didn't. He likely still didn't know what to say. However, to her comfort, his hand had rediscovered its purpose. He was gently rubbing her shoulder. Encouraging her to go on. Letting her know she had all the time in the world.

"When I woke up my... my..." Why was she struggling with this word in particular? She had used the word 'pussy' before in front of him. She and Harry were both swearers, as were most kids their age. But right now, in this context, the word sounded incorrect. Sounded far too crude. "When I woke up, my vagina hurt," she finally managed to say. Then added quickly, "And there was blood in my underwear.

"At first, I thought maybe I'd gotten my period. According to my mom, it was supposed to happen soon. But this was different than she'd described it. It wasn't that I *was* bleeding. It was that I *had* bled. And it hurt... The night started to come back to me as the day went on. In pieces, little by little, I remembered what my uncle did to me."

She would say no more about that. Those were details she had no desire to share. Degradations she believed she would take to her grave.

She waited for his response. To hear the judgement in his voice, the disgust. The pity. But when she heard his voice in the darkness, she only heard two things: care and certainty.

His voice was wet and distorted from his own tears, but the words he said were clear, as was the meaning behind them.

"We can't let him get away with that."

CHAPTER NINE

Uncle Rob

"Hello?" came the familiar voice from the pay phone. Mari nearly dropped the receiver upon hearing it. But she held on, held it tight to her ear, breathed into it heavily before saying,

"Uncle Rob."

"Mariam?" her uncle replied, sounding shocked. He obviously hadn't expected that it would be his niece calling in the middle of the night. "Mariam, where the heck have you been? Everyone is worried sick about you. Your mom can barely sleep."

She had heard her mother's voice earlier. Twice. Could confirm that her mother did indeed sound sleepless.

Mari and Harry were currently standing outside of a gas station five minutes from Hunter's house. Mari was inside of a phone booth while Harry waited outside of it. It was one of three payphones standing side by side by side next to a road that was deserted at the moment, two hours after midnight.

She had called on three previous occasions, hoping her uncle would pick up. Once there had been no answer. Twice it had been her mother. Each time she heard her mother's voice, she wanted to say 'Hello,' or 'I'm sorry,' or 'I miss you and love you and wish I could live in your house, but there's a monster there. Your brother. And he's chased me away.'

But she didn't say those things. Couldn't. Instead, she had hung up, placing the phone down carefully both times her mother had said "Hello."

After hanging up, she and Harry had returned to the party, too cold to wait by the phone. They returned again a half hour after every failed call. Each time she picked up the phone to dial her former household, Mari felt more courageous about talking to her uncle, confronting him. It was courage fueled by alcohol.

And now, on the fourth try, she got the person she had been calling for. The person she had been waiting to confront for the last four years.

"*Is* everyone worried about me?" Mari replied coldly, her voice made of contempt. "Are *you* worried about me, too, Rob?"

He said nothing to that. His turn to breathe heavily into the phone. She had never called him by only his first name before. But she wanted to make it clear that she was not the same kid he once knew. The one he had fooled and taken advantage of. This was a different Mariam Goldbraithe. Finally one of the grownups.

"*Of course* I'm worried about you, Mari. I've been over here thinking you were de–"

"Good. If you're really worried, then you'll help me out. I need five thousand dollars."

"What the fu..." His voice lowered. She could picture him in the basement, looking around, crouching into his couch, whispering so his sister, mother, and children didn't hear him. "What are you talking about? I don't have five thousand dollars."

"I know you keep money in the house. I need it. I'm running away to Canada."

"Mariam. *What* is going on? Where've you been? Why are you running away?"

"You know exactly why the fuck I'm running away. And if you want me to stay away, you'll give me the money I'm asking for. Because if I come back, I'm coming back with the police. And I'm telling *everyone* what the *fuck* you did."

Silence from both of them. Her breathing, him breathing. Both thinking.

"Five grand? Okay, no problem," he said, caving more quickly than Mari had expected. "Where and when should I meet you?"

"Meet me at Eastview library at 2 AM tomorrow. So..." she checked her watch. "Twenty-four hours from now. Park at the side parking lot facing the field. Bring what I asked you for. And don't keep me waiting or I swear I will come home. And I won't be alone."

"Fine, fine, Mari. But what is this all about? What's going on with yo–"

His voice faded, receded, as she brought the receiver to its cradle, hanging up on her uncle mid-sentence. Then she walked out of the metal and plastic booth and directly into Harry's arms.

She was telling herself to breathe, forcing herself to do so with great effort, doing her best to stave off that feeling of panic. She was grateful that Harry was there so she didn't have to go through this alone.

They were headed back to a city they had promised they would never set foot in again. And they were going to confront a man she had believed she would never again see. A man who had taken something from her.

A man who owed her.

CHAPTER TEN

Headlights

The field across from the library wasn't quite the field that Mari remembered. A fence had been erected, a combination of plywood and chain-link covering the majority of the property. Inside of it was a construction site that hadn't been there when Mari and Harry had left town the year before. It was being turned into a set of apartment buildings, maybe a community center. She wasn't sure. She didn't care.

Her entire focus was on the empty parking lot across the street from her. It was two minutes past 2 AM. Each second of those two minutes had been slow agony. She waited. Her heart heaving against her breastbone. If each beat prior had been a knock, it was now thrashing against her chest as though it were a door and her heart was eager to be let out.

The pounding in her chest nearly ceased entirely when she saw two headlights appear from around the corner of the library, moving toward the parking spots she was laser focused on. It took a moment to be certain, but beneath the streetlights she could make out the familiar silver Honda Civic, beat to shit just as she remembered.

At the sight of it, she felt her mouth go dry and her palms become wet. Sweaty. Her body, ever so slightly, began to tremble, sending many messages to her brain that each advised her to run. To flee from this person as she had done when she and Harry had left for Black Mountain.

But she stood her ground. Thought of all the cold winter days she had spent on her front porch reading, the hours she had wasted walking around the neighborhood until she was sure he wouldn't be home or would be settled in the basement for the night. She had ignored hunger, thirst, had put off voiding her bladder or bowels for hours on these occasions, all so she could avoid him. No more. She wasn't going to hide or flee from him on this early morning, nor ever again. It was time to confront this demon of hers. This ghost that hadn't stopped haunting her since the day of her grandmother's birthday party.

He parked across the road from where she stood, just where she had told him to park over the phone. It was Harry who had chosen this location for them to meet. It was Harry who had driven them here in a hotwired Ford Explorer, confident this was the right way to go about things and the right place to do so. He knew their old neighborhood better than she did. Said this place would be deserted. The perfect spot for a private conversation. Confrontation. So far, he was right.

Now, Harry was giving her the privacy she needed. Watching safely from a distance. This was something Mari had to do alone.

They had returned to the place they swore they would never return to. Returned to make sure that this man would not get away with what he had done. Were back to make sure he paid.

Mari's uncle Robert exited his car, was walking from the parking lot to the street he would have to cross in order to meet her face to face. Suddenly this thing, this confrontation, was no longer just talk by two buzzed teenagers at a house party. It was real.

He had a duffle bag in his hand. Containing the money she had asked for, she presumed. She hoped.

"Mari? That you?" he said, standing across the road from her.

"You expecting someone else?"

"No... I... You've grown... It's nice to see you again. Can we talk?"

"We're talking now," she said, crossing her arms over her chest, feeling her heart against them. Watching him standing there across the wide road, she wasn't sure what to do. "Is that the money?"

He raised the bag and looked at it as though he'd forgotten it was temporarily connected to his arm.

"It's what you asked for, yeah," he said after a moment's contemplation.

She briefly wondered why he needed such a large bag for such a relatively small amount of money.

"Bring it here."

"Why don't you come here, Mari. Where it's brighter. Let me make sure you're okay."

"I told you no more games, Rob. Bring what I asked for, or I'll start screaming."

He paused at that, and seemed to consider it, apparently finding something funny about what she had just said.

"Is that your plan?" he replied after a chuckle. "To scream? Look around, you little fucking shit, you picked a place to meet where no one can hear you."

He took a step into the road. A menacing step. Ominous. Made more so when he dropped the bag beside him on the curb. With the hand that had been holding it, he reached into his jacket pocket. Kept his hand in that pocket as he took another step toward her.

"You're gonna tell me what this is about, Mari."

"It's about me getting what you owe me," Her voice wavered, but she did not.

"You think I owe you five thousand dollars?"

Another step toward her, a fourth. Mari wanted to run, but knew she had to stand her ground. Had to face him head on.

"I think you owe me your fucking life," she said as she heard a vehicle approaching. Fifty feet away, forty, picking up speed.

"What the fuck did you just say?"

Thirty feet away, the sound of the engine grew louder, the headlights off, helping the black vehicle blend into the night.

Her uncle took another step into the street.

Her heart was more insistent than ever on escaping her body, trying to leave by thrashing against her chest, but also pounding at her ears, her temples, the pulse points at her neck, her wrists.

She held her breath. Waited for impact. Waited for the vehicle to collide with her uncle who was several steps into the road. Right in front of the oncoming SUV.

Twenty feet away.

Her uncle turned to his left. Saw the vehicle after hearing it. Jumped back toward the curb.

Fuck, Mari thought.

The SUV screeched to a stop ten feet away from where her uncle had been standing in the street.

"What the fuck!" Rob yelled to the driver. "Watch where the fuck you're going!"

Mari didn't know what would happen next, because what should have happened hadn't.

To her surprise, the car's headlights turned on. High beams sending their best imitation of daylight down the road in front of them.

"Is this guy serious?" Rob asked no one in particular. "Keep it moving, fuckhead!" he said, gesturing aggressively for the car to drive on.

Mari was amazed by this. That he wasn't looking at her, accusing her.

That he hadn't figured it out.

The driver didn't keep it moving. The driver stayed there, idling, high beams on, shining light between uncle and niece, making it impossible to see who was behind the wheel.

To her further amazement, her uncle – perhaps wanting to see exactly who this was driving so recklessly and acting a fool on top of that – stepped back into the street. Several steps, quickly, in the direction of the car.

She understood his intention. To walk around the front of the car, to the driver's side, to the driver. To perhaps pull him out. To, at the very least, look at him, yell at him, intimidate him into driving off and giving Rob alone time with his niece.

Not for a second did Rob think that this wasn't a random motorist, a stranger simply driving from somewhere to somewhere. He didn't consider that this vehicle had been intending to hit him before he had jumped back toward the curb.

"I said keep it moving, mother fuc–"

He would never finish the sentence because realization stopped it short.

He figured it out too late, Mari knew, as she saw the understanding on his face at the same time she heard the engine rev to life, the SUV accelerate.

She relished watching his expression turn from rage to recognition when the SUV that Harry was driving ran him down.

CHAPTER ELEVEN

Lunatic Love

It was as though her uncle had been replaced. That's what Mari thought as she witnessed it all unfold. One moment, her uncle had been walking in the street, toward the SUV, yelling at the person behind the wheel. The next moment, the vehicle, having come to a screeching halt, was where Rob had been. Idling there.

But Rob hadn't been replaced, he had been repelled.

He had bounced off the grill of the vehicle. Mari heard this more so than saw it. Heard the thud of the car hitting him. A grunt. Another thud of his body hitting the ground.

He was laying on the road five feet from where he had stood, where the car was now.

She looked from her uncle to the SUV, into it. Behind the wheel was Harry. He turned to her. His face was calm determination. He wore the same expression he'd had right after asking her if she believed in ghosts. Right before walking away and murdering four of their schoolmates.

But his eyes, they were crazed in their resolve. In them she saw muted madness.

This frightened her because she knew she had inspired what she was seeing in those eyes. Frightened her because she knew her eyes currently looked the same. His reflected her feelings, her thoughts: *You are someone I will kill for. No one will hurt you again. And no one will get away with having hurt you before.*

His eyes scared her because they were a window into the darkness that was their honesty.

Theirs was insane adoration. Lunatic love.

He nodded.

She nodded back.

They both turned toward her uncle, who was on the ground, not unconscious but trying to gain his feet. He was on his knees reaching out – to her, or at least in her direction – for help. Help she wouldn't give. Help he would never receive.

Mari heard the vehicle react as Harry stepped on the gas. It sped at her uncle, then was on him. Atop him. This time, he was not bounced back. This time, he was run over, the SUV lurching, leaning, its left side lifting as it rolled over his torso.

When it had fully climbed over Rob's body, crushing parts of it in the process, the SUV idled there. Mari could picture Harry looking through his rear-view mirror, surveying the damage. Seeing what she was seeing.

Her uncle was still conscious somehow. He was muttering, moaning and groaning, twitching on the ground. Parts of him were clearly broken, but his eyes were open. They looked at her as he reached out with one hand. Whether he was purposely reaching toward her, or if this was an involuntary movement based on his injuries, she would never know. Because the SUV reversed.

Harry ran over Uncle Rob again. More slowly this time.

Without the acceleration, the impact, she could hear popping noises, a crack, several snaps. The last noises her uncle's body would ever make.

By the time Harry had stopped his reversal of the SUV, the man in the street was a corpse. And a messy one.

She struggled to take her eyes from her uncle's battered body, but did so in time to see that Harry had hopped out of the vehicle.

"Go check the bag he dropped. See if he actually brought any money with him. I'm going to check his pockets," Harry instructed. But she only stood there, looking at the form of her mother's brother. Fixated by the blood leaking from so many different places.

"C'mon, Goldy, let's go. We have to get out of here!" he whispered loudly, putting his hands on her shoulders as he stood in front of her. She was startled by this, as though she hadn't seen him coming or heard him talking before he was right there face to face with her. With an effort, she took her eyes away from the body that had been her uncle. Looked into Harry's.

"Okay. I'll check the bag. You check his pockets. Then we go," she said, talking herself back to reality, to the task at hand, all of this seeming like a lucid dream.

With that, they both went about their tasks. She ran for the bag, he sprinted to the body, both intent on robbing the man they had just murdered.

CHAPTER TWELVE

Kill Him Twice

"Anything?" Harry asked when Mari joined him in the car, her uncle's bag on her lap.

He had already gone through Rob's wallet, finding nothing but fifty dollars in small bills, a debit card, two credit cards (one expired), his driver's licence, two pictures of his children, and a condom that looked like it had been there since his childhood.

Along with the wallet, Harry had found a switchblade in Rob's jacket pocket.

Mari remembered how he had reached into that pocket as he'd made his way across the road. Had he been reaching for the knife? To use it? She might have said no. Might have said that no matter what kind of predator her uncle was, he wouldn't do that kind of physical violence to his sister's daughter. But what she was looking at inside the bag he'd dropped was confirmation that she would have been wrong about Rob. Dead wrong.

"Well?" Harry insisted, leaning from the driver's seat to the passenger side, trying to look into the bag that Mari was wordlessly focused on. She shook her head, as if trying to clear the images that the items in this bag had brought to her imagination.

She tilted the bag toward Harry, opening it wide for him to see.

"Jesus... I wish I could kill him twice," was Harry's response as he gazed into the bag. Reached a hand into it, as if he needed to feel the items to believe that they were real. To comprehend what her uncle had had in store for her.

Inside of the bag: No money.

As Mari watched Harry rummage through it, she remembered what her uncle had said. That in the bag was what she had asked for. But what she was looking at was nothing she wanted. Nothing anyone deserved.

Inside of the bag: Rope, duct tape, a bandana that would undoubtedly have doubled as a blindfold, a sock rolled into a ball that would have acted as a gag. Beside these, a hacksaw. Garbage bags. Among these, a small bottle of something called KY Jelly.

Inside of the bag: Instruments to bind, hold hostage, torture, kill, dissect.

Inside of the bag: What might have been her future if their plan had gone awry; depravities, death, dismemberment. All courtesy of her relation.

She zipped the duffle up, used the hand-crank to roll her window down. Threw the bag into the street. Then turned her attention to Harrison.

She hugged him. Kissed him. Did so fervently, almost feverishly, until he gently pushed her away, back into her seat. Held her by both shoulders.

"Are you okay?" he asked, looking into her eyes intently. Likely wondering if having her witness the murder of her uncle had perhaps been too much for her. Had been ill planned.

But the concern on his face was wasted. Because Mari found that she not only felt better, she felt good.

She looked through the windshield. She could still see the shape of Rob's body on the ground, unmoving. Yes, she felt right. And, oddly, she felt more whole than she had since the night he had asked her, then an eleven-year-old child, to play an adult game.

She felt like something that had been missing was now restored. Like something that had been taken from her had just been taken back.

"I feel like we did the right thing," was her reply. And it was enough to remove some of the concern from his face, the concern for her. What still remained was the worry that they might be caught.

The vehicle sounded rough as Harry maneuvered it around the corpse of Mari's uncle. She worried for a moment that it might break down, but it held steady.

For the second time, they left this neighborhood intending never to return. On this occasion, however, Mari did look behind her, into the rear-view mirror, appreciating the sight of the person who had ruined her life. Until now.

She smiled, ever so slightly, as she gazed at the diminishing body of her uncle.

Smiled as they left behind a murdered mess. A mangled man.

****

Mari and Harry abandoned the Ford Explorer in a Kmart parking lot two miles from the bus terminal. From there they walked hand in hand to the buses, only letting go of each other when they went to pay their fares.

They sat silently during the ride back to Black Mountain.

INTERLUDE

Elevators

Mari wasn't sure why she was thinking of her uncle now as they walked through the lobby and toward the elevators of the Helping Hand building.

The building was the same as most corporate offices. The lobby was large, shiny, and mostly sterile, full of promotional posters. A map of the world made of silver and bronze took up the wall behind the security guard's glass desk, and fancy stone flower beds decorated the floors.

It might have been the Helping Hand Home and Auto Insurance poster that had triggered the memory. The image of the vehicle on the poster bringing back memories of the SUV they had nearly wrecked while running over the body of her uncle, twice, making sure he was roadkill. She had thought of him often in the months immediately following his demise, thought that killing him might lead the authorities to them. But it hadn't. And thoughts of him had become more fleeting as their freedom had become more certain.

Next to the poster of the insurance company owned by Helping Hand was another for Helping Hand Publishing House. Next to that was signage for HH Games. This was followed by several other posters. Helping Hand was a company that had the fingers of its helping hands in many pies.

Mari watched as Harry looked over the poster for HH Games intently. If things went well in this meeting they both hoped to approach the games division with *A World of Beasts* at some point. He had been making and distributing the game independently for years. He'd had some success early on in this endeavor, but things had stagnated recently. They both knew that he'd need the backing or a large company, one such as HH Games, for *A World of Beasts* to make a lasting impact.

But their focus now was on today. On the company called Helping Hand for Humanity, which positioned itself as a corporation for positive change in the world, financing philanthropic projects globally.

A representative of Helping Hand for Humanity, an assistant who hadn't said exactly who she was assisting, had reached out to Mari about the foundation she had started not long after they had left Black Mountain. After they had run to Seattle for yet another fresh start. For the last few years, Mari had been running a foundation for homeless youth, helping place children in group homes, with foster families, in employment. Saving one soul at a time. It was slow work, hard but rewarding when she was actually able to accomplish something. When bureaucratic red tape and a lack of funds didn't stop her.

But Mari had bigger dreams; to save many at once. To house homeless youth all across the country, to give futures to Children of No Tomorrow all around the world.

Only a week ago she would have said those dreams were far from her grasp. Perhaps, if she had been honest, she might have said those dreams were completely unattainable. Then had come the call from The Assistant. And the offer of a helping hand. A French-Canadian philanthropist had gotten wind of the business proposal Mari had sent to several companies like Helping Hand for Humanity. If this meeting went well, he would be the one to make their dreams come true.

"I can't believe this might actually be happening," Mari said when they reached the elevators.

"Same," Harry replied, his hand finding its way around hers again. "It's a bit surreal."

"That's a good way to put it. It's almost too good to be true."

"Hey," Harry said, tugging Mari toward him after she pressed the button to call for the elevator. Once she was facing him, her eyes locked on his, he said, "You have to start believing that we're due some real good our way after everything we've been through. Don't you think?"

"Of course, I ju–" he stopped her sentence with a kiss.

"Don't overthink it, Goldy. We agreed about that, right?"

"Right," she said, feeling flush, looking around the lobby to make sure no one had seen their public display of affection and considered it a sign of unprofessionalism.

"Don't worry, no one saw," he said with a laugh. Then, after doublechecking to make sure there was still no one looking, he playfully slapped her on the behind, bracing himself for a fist to the shoulder after doing so.

She made sure it hurt when he received it, but he shrugged it off because he had gotten his desired result: a laugh out of the woman who was once a girl called Hard Mari. Once a girl who seldom laughed or even smiled. She appreciated it when he was able to draw positive emotion out of her.

Ding!

The elevator arrived. They stepped into it, both of them still smiling. By the time the door closed, however, Mari's smile was gone. It was replaced with the minor anxiety she always felt when riding elevators. An anxiety that was attached to her memories.

Though she hadn't been able to pinpoint exactly why she had started thinking of her uncle when they had entered the building, she knew fully why she was thinking of what she was thinking of now.

Elevators always reminded her of their first condo together after years of living on the street. They reminded her of the man who had taken them from the street and placed them in that fancy apartment. And, most of all, they reminded her of the girl who had briefly lived there with them. The girl who had died there.

PART TWO

Home

CHAPTER THIRTEEN

Squatters

Eight years before The Meeting...

Mariam hated needles. Hated that they had become a regular part of her life again. Hated that she and Harry had to be back here, at the blood services center, getting drained and dripped of blood for a few dollars. This, after a year of not having to rely on this place. a year of having a consistent place to stay.

Now, they were headed toward the bus stop, a ride toward temporary shelter, spending money they barely had to help them avoid another brutally cold night.

Their last couple of weeks had involved all-night bus routes, getting kicked out of coffee shops, sleeping in alleys or on a heated grate in downtown Black Mountain, and, when they were fortunate enough, staying at a shelter.

Unfortunately for Mari and Harry, shelters were becoming increasingly unavailable to the couple. They couldn't often find a place with two open beds, and no place would let a street couple share one bed. For that reason, the pair found themselves on the street more often than they might have if they were solo. They didn't mind though. For three years now their identity had been 'Us against the world.' If they both couldn't enjoy something, they would do without it.

As the bus approached, she looked over at Harrison beside her, on her left. He was eating the cookie they had been given as part of the exchange for their blood, the expression on his face making it seem as though he were tasting something bitter. The cookie, once a special treat and something he had appreciated, was now a reminder of how far they had fallen in the last four months.

Prior to that, they had been staying in an apartment. The bottom unit of a triplex that had belonged to Rebby. Or, rather, it was an apartment that had been gifted to Rebby by the married man she was involved with.

Rebby had broken up with Hunter not long after the night of the party. The night Mari and Harry had been together for the first time. A night she had come to consider as the occasion she had truly lost her virginity. With the erasure of her uncle from this earth, she had also tried to erase the damage he had done to her from her memory.

Rebby and her apartment had helped with that.

The summer after she had broken up with Hunter (and the two other guys she had been seeing after him), she had met a man at a carnival. The carnival had been in town for three weeks, and the three of them and several other teenagers in the area had gotten jobs there.

The man had approached Rebby as she worked at a corndog stand, shamelessly flirting with the teenage girl while ordering food for his seven-year-old son. He would come back later without his child, or the wife Rebby would later find out was there that day as well.

He had asked her out for a drink, not minding that she told him she wasn't quite old enough to have one legally. Legalities, it seemed, weren't this man's concern.

Nor was the thirty-year age gap between he and Rebby.

He courted her clandestinely: hotels, motels, trips out of town. Sometimes pretending to be daddy and daughter to those who raised eyebrows, asked questions.

Eventually, he got her an apartment on Black Mountain's east side to make sure she was off the street, taken care of. And Rebby, being the caring person she was, made sure to take care of her two closest homeless friends.

For one year after that strange summer as carnies, Mari and Harry had lived in the second bedroom of Rebby's apartment. And, for the most part, life had been a one-year party.

Mari hadn't minded the partying. After that first time at Hunter's house, after confronting her uncle and watching his eyes bulge, nearly pop, as an SUV ran over his head, Mari had been eager for the escape of things like music, alcohol, conversations about matters that didn't lead to murder.

Rebby's married man had made it so they rarely had to worry about much at all. Booze was provided, the fridge was always fully stocked. It was a blessing. Seemed like their happily ever after. Or at least an avenue that might help them get there.

Until it wasn't.

Because the rich man with the family who couldn't know about his teenage girlfriend on the side had decided to take a trip with Rebby. She had gone away with him before, but only for a day or two, a weekend here and there. This time, he had suggested that they take an entire week away. A work trip he had to take to San Diego would make for the perfect cover. He promised her beaches and bikinis, sand and surf. Rebby had gone.

Rebby had never returned. And neither had her boyfriend.

Her place was abandoned, other than her two friends-turned-squatters who remained in it.

Mari and Harry had waited there for a while, growing increasingly worried. By the second week of her absence, after calling every mutual friend they had, after searching her favorite hangouts around the city, they came to the conclusion that maybe Rebby had moved on. Had convinced the man to abandon his wife and family, and the two had run off to Mexico. Were probably sipping tequila and eating huevos rancheros right that very moment.

It was better to imagine that than the alternative.

It had taken two months for the first notice to appear. A paper slid beneath the apartment door which read NOTICE OF EVICTION.

A second warning was taped to the door two weeks later. Two weeks after that, the landlord had opened the door with a goon by his side and had politely asked the pair to leave. Which they'd done.

Now, here they were, boarding a bus. Instead of going to Rebby's familiar apartment they were heading to a place called the Sleep Easy Motel, more commonly referred to as the Sleasy Motel by the residents of Black Mountain who were familiar with it. And it lived up to that name. Patchy carpeting, peeling wallpaper, beds like sheet-clad slabs of stone.

For the next two days, the Sleasy would be their home. As bad as the place sounded, looked, was, it would be a five-star resort compared to the alley they had slept in the previous night.

Mari was looking forward to their stay. One of many things she was looking forward to as she sat on the bus, her forehead pressed against the glass of the window as she watched the dowdy old-fashioned homes and low-rise buildings of the ancient-looking city of Black Mountain pass them by on their way to the motel. Though there wasn't a cloud in the sky, the world seemed dulled, gray. Or perhaps that was just Mari's outlook on things. Pessimism perverting her perspective.

She looked out at the world, wondered when it would improve for them, if it would improve at all. Thigh to thigh with Harry, her hand on his lap, his hand on hers, Mari wondered just how dark things would get for them before the world would seem bright again.

CHAPTER FOURTEEN

The Man in the Burgundy Sedan

Harry called it a celebration, spending the little money they had on a motel room so they wouldn't freeze to death; a chance for them to get a bit of a break. And there couldn't be a celebration without booze.

"I hope this doesn't take as long as the last time," Mari grumbled, adjusting her jacket, readjusting to the cold as they walked toward the liquor store. Walked away from the bus stop and the bus they had just departed.

The liquor store was in a plaza, a small strip that included a dollar store, a Blockbuster video, a convenience store, a cash advance, and a Chinese food restaurant. Across the street from the plaza was a McDonald's, a stag shop, and the Sleasy.

"We'll find someone soon enough," Harry said, always more optimistic than Mari. "McDick's or a trip to China?" he asked as they stopped near the convenience store and surveyed the nearly empty parking lot of the plaza. McDonalds or Chinese food, she automatically translated in her mind, familiar with his playful way of speaking. The cookie, apparently, hadn't staved off his hunger.

She wanted to say 'Neither.' For weeks they had been eating McDonald's and other cheap fast food just like it whenever they couldn't get a free meal at one of the soup kitchens in the city. The Chinese food wouldn't be a better alternative. They could only afford the least expensive meal on the menu: sweet and sour chicken balls and fried rice; the balls mostly dough, the rice mostly grease.

"McDonald's," she said, as she watched a car pull into the plaza and park in front of the convenience store, twenty feet from where they stood. It was a burgundy sedan that looked vaguely familiar to her. The man driving it did as well.

He was a white man in his late twenties; long face, dark brown hair, large wire-framed glasses that seemed to be growing in popularity by the day.

Behind those glasses, his eyes caught hers. He flashed her a smile. White, straight teeth. The direct eye contact unnerved her slightly. She looked away from him, still wondering where she might have seen this man before.

"How about we ask him?" Harry said, looking at Mari, nodding discreetly in the direction of the man in the burgundy sedan. "He seems friendly enough."

"Does he look familiar to you?" Mari asked.

"Not really, but he's on his way and I'm gonna ask him," Harry responded.

Harry started in his direction before Mari could tell him not to. Something about the man caused her to feel uneasy.

He stopped in the parking lot as Harry approached him.

"Hi, sir. Would you be okay with..." Harry didn't finish asking the question, never did. As always, he nodded toward the liquor store. Those who were inclined to buy booze for underage kids only needed the hint; those who were against it could at least not accuse the two of directly asking them to break the law.

Sometimes it took them only a few tries to get someone to buy, though the last time they had been here they had stood out in the cold for nearly an hour before someone would help them out, the person insisting on them spending almost as much on his booze as they were on their own.

On at least one occasion they had gone away empty-handed. During days like those, when their moods were determined by whether an adult would buy them alcohol, Mari wondered how they had come to be this way. Remembered the days when they never drank. Now it seemed like alcohol had become almost as important as food and shelter.

"...buying you two kids some booze?" the man inquired, finishing Harry's sentence while looking from him to Mari and back. His voice was slightly accented. French, Mari thought. He was still smiling. Something about the expression unsettled Mari. Made her wish they had waited to ask someone else.

"You can get yourself a couple beers while you're at it," Harry said, removing a ten-dollar bill from his fanny pack. "Just get us a six pack of the strongest, cheapest beer they have, please."

The man looked at the bill in Harry's hand, made no effort to take it. Moving his eyes from the money to Harry, then Mari, lingering on her, he said,

"It's on me. Get yourselves some food with that ten."

Then he turned from them and walked to the liquor store.

CHAPTER FIFTEEN

Brown Paper Bags

Ten minutes after asking the stranger for a favor, Harry and Mari had brown paper bags in their hands. They had just exited the McDonald's and were entering their rundown motel room.

It was a cramped space, barely bigger than Mari's bedroom had been back at home. At the home she had shared with her father and mother, before having to move in with her grandmother and uncle.

There was a twin bed, an end table, a lamp on top of that end table. A dresser across from the foot of the bed, a chair beside it. A small TV/VCR combo on the dresser that they had been told received four channels. The walls had been white once; now they were yellowing, browning, graying with water spots, grime, smoke stains. But it was warm in the room, and Mari was grateful for that.

"That guy was almost too good to be true," Harry said, still sounding amazed by their encounter as he placed his brown bag on the foot of the bed. Mari did the same beside him before taking off her layers as Harry went straight to rummaging through the bags.

She kept glancing at the window, resisting the urge to go to it, part the blinds, and see if the man in the burgundy sedan was still across the road. Still watching. The fact that he and his car looked familiar to her made her wonder if he had been watching them for some time. If he had followed them here.

You're being paranoid, she told herself, though she knew she had reason to be.

It had been over three years since they had killed four teenagers, and two years since they had added one more body to their tally. The last of those five being her uncle. Unlike the first four, whose deaths had immediately been ruled an accident, the police had investigated her uncle's death as a homicide. Which meant there had been an active search for a killer. For them.

The first few months after they had run him down had been the most stressful of her entire life. Everywhere they had gone, she had thought people were looking at them, ready to pounce, to ensnare them, take them to prison to be tried as a pair of murderers. It was a terrifying thought.

Was it possible that someone had found them out after all this time? Could the nice man who had bought them booze (more of it than they had requested) for free be some sort of police officer, private investigator? Someone sent to track them down, finally bring them to justice?

"Jesus, Goldy, this vodka ain't cheap."

The man had returned from the liquor store with a bag that was both too large and too full to have been the sixpack they had asked for. They were astonished to see that he had gotten them two sixpacks of beer that was strong, but certainly not cheap, and a fifth of vodka.

"What if he *was* too good to be true?" Mari asked, going to the bed, retrieving a can of beer, opening it. She gulped down half of it before realizing she had even put it to her lips.

"What do you mean? And hey, what happened to saying 'cheers' and all that?" Harry said.

"My bad," Mari replied. Burped. She chugged when she was nervous. And the man who had provided them with these drinks had given her plenty of reason to feel like chugging. She waited for Harry to open his can, bump it against hers. He said, "cheers." She drank again, this time in a more controlled fashion.

"What if he's a cop or something? What if he's someone who figured out what we've done and is here to arrest us? What if he's just waiting to set us up?" she said after placing a mostly empty can on the dresser. It sounded strange to say it aloud. Like something that didn't quite connect with reality despite it being true.

She was a seventeen-year-old girl. How could she, someone who thought of herself as quiet and kind, just a shy person who liked to read, possibly consider that she might be a fugitive from the law, wanted for murder. Multiple murders, maybe serial, if the truth about the kids in the van ever came to light.

"Why would he wait?" Harry asked, looking at her as though she hadn't just proposed that they might be facing a lifetime in jail. Like what she'd said was no big deal.

"What?" she asked, not knowing what he meant.

"You said that he might be 'waiting to set us up.' If he knows what we did, and he knows who we are and where we are, what is he waiting for?"

The fact that she couldn't think of an answer to this bothered her. Harry's practicality, his ability to immediately turn everything into strategy, sometimes bothered her as well. But he may have been right on this occasion, even if something in her gut told her that it couldn't be that simple.

"You're worrying for no reason, Goldy." He reached into the second bag, the one she had been carrying. Removed from it two Big Macs, two containers of extra-large fries, ten chicken McNuggets. They had been able to upgrade from the usual value menu items they purchased with the money they had saved on booze. Compared to a cheeseburger and small fries this was a veritable feast.

Good booze for free, a large meal. She should have been content. Should have felt the way Harrison looked as he chewed on his burger, his entire face a smile. But she couldn't feel good. Not when she still felt his eyes out there, beyond the blinded window, observing their location, waiting for them to make their next move.

CHAPTER SIXTEEN

Gifts

They barely moved during their stay at the Sleasy Motel. Aside from another trip to McDonald's they didn't move much at all. And it was wonderful. Wonderful not to have to worry about where they would sleep, where they had to spend an entire day, not having to worry about which owner or manager or employee would tell them their time was up while pointing to an always available 'No Loitering' sign.

On each of the occasions they did leave the room, Mari looked out for the burgundy sedan and the man it belonged to. She saw neither.

By the time they were set to check out, the bad feeling she'd had since seeing the man outside of the convenience store was nearly gone. When they gathered their few belongings and made their way to the motel lobby, she didn't even bother looking around the parking lot or across the street for the burgundy car, her concerns nearly forgotten, along with the man himself.

When they got into the lobby, reached the receptionist, handed her the key, they were greeted with a surprise.

"Oh, shoot! Room 8? I was supposed to let you know that your stay has been extended for another night. Sorry to make you pack up..." As she said this, she noticed that they had very few belongings with them. The clothes on their backs, his fanny pack, their backpacks, that was all. 'Packing up' was an exaggeration of what they'd had to do.

"Anyhow," the receptionist, a middle-aged, brown-haired woman named Sally, continued before either of them could question why their stay had been prolonged. "The person who extended your stay also left this for you."

From behind her desk, with some effort, she retrieved two large brown paper bags. One landed on her desk with a soft thud, the other with a clank, a muted rattle.

They looked at each other, looked in the bags.

In one was two six packs of beer, strong, but not cheap. Along with those was a bottle of pricey vodka.

The other bag was from a gourmet sandwich shop. In it was two meals they could never have afforded.

They looked from the bags to the receptionist to each other.

More gifts from the man in the burgundy sedan, Mari understood. He was now at the forefront of her mind again. And Harry no longer seemed so nonchalant about the situation.

CHAPTER SEVENTEEN

Stranger

"Should we get out of here?" Mari asked.

They stood outside of the motel having just exited from the lobby, the few belongings they had now including booze and food.

They had a decision to make.

"I still don't think we have to run. If he was going to do something like hurt us or take us to the police, then why wouldn't he just do that? Why would he go through the trouble of extending our stay and buying us more booze? I don't think he's a cop, or someone after us. I think he wants something. And I think we should wait here and find out what it is."

Mari didn't agree. Mari wanted to flee. Not just this property but this part of the city. Maybe the entire city. Perhaps, she thought, they should head to another state.

"I dunno. What if what he wants is to hurt us? People get murdered in motels like this all the time."

Later, she would regret saying 'I dunno' instead of 'Let's go.' She knew that if she demanded they leave, Harry would follow her. Harry would follow her to the ends of the Earth. She loved him for that. But she didn't want to take advantage of his eagerness to please her, which was why she didn't demand they go. Didn't put her foot down. Gave room for him to negotiate and convince her.

"Can we at least go back to the room and talk about it? No point in us freezing our asses off if we haven't decided yet."

Again, this would have been a good time to say, 'Let's go,' but at that moment a cold breeze bearing a hundred thousand pins blew past, pricking at their exposed skin. Going inside seemed like the only thing in the world that made sense.

"Okay, but that doesn't mean we're staying."

He nodded, they walked toward the room, brown bags in hand, a feeling of déjà vu as they repeated nearly everything that had happened two days prior.

But things weren't exactly as they had been, Mari realized after Harry opened the door and turned on the lights.

What they saw beyond the door differed a great deal from what they had been met with when they'd first arrived. Something in the room had changed even since they'd left it minutes ago.

Inside of the room, on the bed, sitting there, a smile on his face beneath his large wire-framed glasses, was the man who had provided them with the brown bags they were holding. Brown bags which both of them nearly dropped upon seeing him.

"Christ!"

"Jesus!"

"Sorry to alarm you, Goldy. Sebastian," said the man who had been in the burgundy sedan. The man who was now in the middle of their room. "But I'm very glad to see that you decided to stay."

CHAPTER EIGHTEEN

An Offer

Mari was surprised to find that she felt a bit of relief in the midst of her alarm as she looked at the man who was sitting on their bed, his tall frame made enormous by their little room. The relief came from the fact that this wasn't some police officer or agent sent to bring them in.

He had used their aliases, the names they had given to the receptionist when booking this room, the names they used at the shelters, or whenever they'd had to speak to some authority figure since the running down of her uncle. He had no idea who they really were. Hadn't sought them out.

But that relief was miniscule, a drop of rain in the ocean. Even if he wasn't law enforcement, he was here, had followed them, watched them. Wanted something from them.

"What do you want?" Harry asked.

Mari didn't particularly care about the answer, she realized, as she set down her brown bag of gourmet sandwiches. She had been starving just seconds ago, now she couldn't imagine eating. What she cared about more than what this man wanted was how to get rid of him.

Her hand reached into her right coat pocket. Inside of it was the switchblade her uncle had been carrying on the night they had murdered him. An item that had been meant to end her life, now kept as a memento. One that could be put to practical use if the appropriate situation presented itself.

She removed the knife, exposed the blade. Harry, seeing where this was going, dropped the bag of booze and reached into his pocket for a weapon of his own. An expandable baton he had picked up from a friend of Rebby's. With a flick of his wrist, he expanded it to its full twenty-one inches.

They each took a step toward the man. Only stopping when they saw the smile drop from his face, saw him raise his hands, palms open, the universal sign of surrender.

"Whoa! Whoa! I give you food and drink, a place to stay, and your first instinct is to gut me?" His accent was thicker with his upset.

"He *said* 'What do you want?'" Mari reiterated, her knife still exposed, pointed at the man who was only three feet from its tip.

The couple had him flanked, Mari in front of him and to his right, Harry to his left. He was looking back and forth between them. Mari took some pleasure in seeing that unsettling smile gone from his face. But then, to her dismay, there it was again. He smiled at them, took his raised hands, ran them back through his ear length hair.

"I came to make you an offer," he said as his eyes scanned the room, this place that was one step removed from a hovel. "Something that will change your lives."

Mari looked at Harry, briefly, a quick glance, sidelong. *What should we do?* was the question she saw in Harry's eyes. Her eyes, she was sure, provided him with no answer; she hadn't a clue.

Even if they killed him, they couldn't get away with it. Not for long. The receptionist, who was also the motel owner, had seen their faces. She might not know their real names, but she would likely be able to give an accurate description of them to the police.

Mari could imagine the drawings a sketch artist would make. Could picture those drawings posted all over town.

They would officially be wanted. Officially be hunted. She'd watched enough episodes of *America's Most Wanted* to know that, even if they fled, it would only be a matter of time until they were caught.

"May I?" the man on the bed asked. His hands were out of his hair, raised in the air again, though one of them was now pointed to his heart. No, Mari saw, he was gesturing to a pocket by his breast. He wanted permission to reach into it.

"Don't you fucking move!" she cried, taking a step – a lunge – toward him. If there was a gun in there, if he got his hand on it, they were done for.

"What the fuck do you want?" Harry repeated, this time pressing the baton to the man's chest, poking at what he had in that pocket.

"I'd like to show you what *you* want before *I* tell you what I want," he said. "I promise, this whole thing will go quicker if you let me do that."

Harry, seemingly satisfied that whatever he had prodded inside the coat hadn't been weaponry, nodded.

"Hurry up."

Mari tensed as their unwanted visitor – with his left hand still in the air – reached into his breast pocket with his right, removed from it something that made her gasp.

He threw it on the floor in front of them, between them, at their feet.

"Fifteen hundred dollars," the man said, both of his hands back in the air. He nodded at the rubber-banded stack of cash he had casually tossed on the floor. "Fifteen hundred more tomorrow if you are open to my proposition."

Mari and Harry regarded the pile of cash, then each other, then looked over at this increasingly frustrating man.

"What do you want?" they said in unison.

He laughed.

"Look at the two of you, in sync. That is a very good sign of things to come, I think."

He lowered his hands. As he lowered them, he brought them together, interlocked them, placed them on his lap. He looked at Mari meaningfully, leered at Harry. And with that unsettling smile on his face, he said,

"What I want, is to watch."

CHAPTER NINETEEN

Warmth

"Are we really considering doing this?" Harry asked Mari. They were still in the motel room, which in itself was a sign that the proposition was being considered.

When both Mari and Harry had asked the man, who had eventually introduced himself as Nicholas, to elaborate on what he'd meant when he'd said he wanted to watch, the answer was the one they had expected.

He wanted a show. Them starring. A show of the X-Rated variety. His words:

"I want to watch you fuck."

They had all been still and silent for some time before Nicholas broke the stillness by standing. Broke the silence by saying,

"Tomorrow evening. I'll return then with another fifteen hundred dollars. If your answer is yes, then it's yours. And I'll watch."

He had turned to the door before Mari called after him. He looked to her, she looked to the ground, gestured at the pile of cash that was still there.

"What about that?" Mari said. Nicholas had smiled in response.

"Yours either way. Consider it an apology for today's inconvenience. I'll leave you two to figure things out." Then he had gone.

Now, roughly ten hours later, with him sitting at the foot of the bed, and her on the floor to his right, leaning against it, they were still in the motel room trying to figure things out.

They hadn't run with the fifteen hundred dollars. Without even discussing it, they had opened the bags, settled down, made plans for the night. Each knowing the other would want to at least give it some thought. Which is exactly what they were doing while taking advantage of the gifts Nicholas had given them.

Meaning, they were drunk.

They were also warm, also full, not only from the sandwiches they'd had for lunch, but also the pizza they had ordered with the gift certificate that had been at the bottom of the bag with the booze. And that wasn't the only surprise they had found in those two brown bags.

They were currently watching the recently released Beauty and the Beast. They had already seen it in theatres the year before, but Harry had insisted they rent it now that it was out on video. It was one of five movies they had rented that day from Blockbuster thanks to another gift certificate from one of the brown bags; the second such surprise they had found.

The last, and most surprising of the surprises, was the quarter ounce of marijuana they had discovered in a sandwich bag, and the rolling papers that had come with it.

Which meant, currently, they were also high.

They had only smoked up once since Rebby had vanished, both deciding it would be wise to save the money, to keep their wits sharp as they went back to the grind of being legitimately homeless.

They hadn't felt this good, this relaxed, since the time they had spent in Rebby's apartment. And with fifteen hundred dollars, they could feel this good and relaxed for a little while longer. With *three thousand dollars* – Mari's liquor and weed addled mind computed – they could stay feeling this good and relaxed for twice as long.

She took a drink from her plastic cup. Orange juice. Vodka. Much more of the latter than of the former. She needed the liquid courage to say what she had to say. Not only to Harry, but to herself.

"I think we *are* actually considering it. I mean... It's just someone watching. You remember Rebby's last birthday party? We practically had sex on top of her and whoever else was passed out in the living room that night. And I know at least one of them was up, watching and listening."

They chuckled at that. Their laughter, despite being aided by the weed and alcohol, was strained. Prolonged. Perhaps so they could postpone seriously talking about this topic even if only for a few seconds.

"That's true," Harry said eventually, after the laughter had subsided. Then he added, almost whimsically, "Benny the Brick pantsed me once. Pulled down my underwear and everything. In front of about thirty other kids in the middle of the art hallway. That kind of counts as letting people watch, right?" He barked out a short laugh, a single syllable that sounded like it was closely related to a sob.

Mari couldn't join him in his laughter, not even for a second, when it came to Benny. She could count on one hand the number of times they had mentioned Benny in the three years since they had murdered him, his girlfriend and his two closest lackeys. They hadn't made a pact to never mention them, they had just inherently known it was better to leave the past in the past. Dead and buried.

The mention of Benny now was enough to ruin her high.

With that in mind, Mari reached from her spot on the floor to the ashtray on the chair they were using as a makeshift coffee table, grabbed the half-smoked three-paper joint that she had rolled for them earlier that hour...

or two hours ago, she wasn't sure. Time felt funny to Mari just then.

She lit the spliff, dragged, did her best to get her high back to where it had been before the mention of Benny's name.

"I'm glad we did it," she said, knowing that he would understand what she meant. Knowing that that sentence was the end of any conversation about the ghosts of their past. At least for tonight.

"Me too," he said. Then they sat and watched the movie for a while.

When Harry clapped and gave a little yelp of joy, it nearly made Mari jump, snapped her out of her thoughts. Though, for the life of her, she couldn't remember exactly what she had been thinking about.

She looked at him. He was sitting on the edge of the bed, his hands were clasped together in his lap, he had the cutest little smile on his face as he watched the story on the small screen unfold.

She always got a kick out of how much he loved his Disney movies. They turned him into a large child every time.

A large child that someone is willing to pay three thousand dollars to have fuck you while they watch.

This was her conscience speaking to her, swimming up from the pool of vodka she was currently attempting to drown it in, speaking through the haze of weed Mari was using to blot it out. It came unbidden, and came with a bite.

"Take whatever booty you can find. But remember, the Beast is mine!" cried Gaston from the television screen as he led a group of villagers intent on storming the Beast's castle on behalf of Belle.

"He said 'booty'," Harrison said, laughing as though a joke had been told, causing Mari to laugh as well. "The

Beast is gonna kick *his* booty," Harry added before silently staring at the screen in intense anticipation of what he already knew was going to happen.

"Hey, aren't you supposed to be the big bad Bane of Beasts? Shouldn't you be rooting for Gaston?"

Harry laughed again at that. Mari took another sip of her vodka with a splash of orange juice. Took another pull of the joint, passed it to him. He pulled too hard, taking in too much smoke as he tried to contain his laughter. Through his chuckles, around his coughing, he said,

"But *this* Beast is one of the good guys."

Are we good guys? Mari wondered as she played with the smoke in her mouth. Could she and Harry possibly be considered good after all they'd done. And if they were somehow still good now, would they continue to be considered good if they went through with what Nicholas had proposed?

Every bad thing they had done so far had been in the interest of self preservation; justifiable, she thought, maybe even in the eyes of God.

She wasn't sure if she believed in Him the way her mom did, definitely not the way her grandmother did, maybe didn't even believe in Him at all. But some nights she wondered, worried about if what they had done had damned them. If there would be some otherworldly reckoning to contend with even if their crimes never caught up with them in this life.

Her thoughts were too heavy.

She released the smoke thinking it might release the pressure she felt, but it was still there, fuelled by those heavy thoughts. She sank lower to the ground at the base of the bed under the weight of them.

Mari blinked. Blinked again, longer this time, her eyelids as heavy as her thoughts. When her eyes opened, the movie was over. The TV screen was made of dots. Gray, white, black, a million of them each.

Be kind, please rewind, she thought to herself as she looked at the television. Then looked at Harry. He was still sitting up on the end of the bed. He was staring at the screen as if the movie were still playing. But she knew he wasn't watching what was there. She knew that he was really watching something else play out in his head. The potential consequences of them accepting the proposal, as well as the benefits.

Sensing her looking at him in the room lit only by the television, he turned to her, said,

"It's up to you. Your call, Goldy."

He would follow her to the ends of the Earth, she knew. And sometimes that broke her heart even as it made it swell.

She looked at the chair in front of her in the dim light from the TV. Along with the ashtray, she could see the pile of cash Nicholas had given them atop it. But more importantly, she focused her attention on the switchblade beside the money. A reminder of her uncle. A reminder that if she could survive what he had done, she could survive anything.

The thing was, she was tired of just surviving. Of *barely* surviving, clinging to the heel of society's boot.

Three thousand fucking dollars. And maybe more... Hadn't he said there might be more? Yes, if they "performed to his standards," there would be plenty more where that came from. That's what he had said as he told them what they could look forward to. And she did indeed find herself looking forward to it. How could she not when, if she looked backward on the last few years, the last few months especially, she saw nothing but cold discomfort. Being kicked off of the bus at three in the morning when the temperature was freezing, being pitied by pedestrians as they slept on the city grates. Being hopeless as well as homeless. She thought of them lined up at the food bank for bland-tasting portions that filled neither of their bellies.

Looking back on her immediate past, she saw the guilt in Harry's eyes whenever he felt her shiver and could do nothing to prevent it, his arms a meagre shelter.

On the chair beside her uncle's knife, in the gloom, she saw not a pile of cash but reason for optimism.

Looking forward, she thought of the potential for her to go back to school, to really focus and get educated. She thought of new clothes, a better jacket. She thought of Harry, and of him being able to finally develop his game. Her mind went to her future foundation, and all she could one day do to help kids just like her.

She thought of warmth.

A sip. Some smoke. She said,

"I'm in. Let's do it."

His response, around a chuckle,

"Pun intended?"

At that, they both laughed their strained and prolonged laughter.

CHAPTER TWENTY

Jared

When Mari and Harry woke up the next afternoon, still slightly drunk and mostly hungover, they agreed that, despite how much they'd had to drink and smoke the night before, they had made the right decision, and they were going to stick with it.

Nicholas would be there at 6 PM, he had told them. They spent the hours between their waking and Nicholas' appearance mostly laying around, eating greasy food and trying to will away their hangovers.

By 5 PM, Harrison asked if maybe they should smoke something, drink a little, to loosen up. But Mari knew it would be best to have their wits about them until this thing was over. Harrison begrudgingly agreed.

After one of the longest hours of either of their lives there was a knock on the door.

Mari grabbed her uncle's switchblade from the top of the dresser, just in case. When Harrison opened the door, she was glad she'd done so.

Nicholas was not alone.

With him was a bald man even taller than he was. The bald man was heavier as well, barrel chested, broad shouldered. He wore all black and looked like he enjoyed hitting living things for fun.

"What's going on?" Harrison asked as he took a step back from the door. Mari took a step toward him, knife raised. "You said you wanted to... not that there would be a fucking audience."

Again, Nicholas raised his hands, palms out, smiled his smile.

"Calm, Sebastian, Goldy. Calm. This is Jared, my security."

"You need a guy that size because of *us*?" Harry said, disbelieving. Nicholas nodded at Mari, at her knife. Said,

"This one is a firecracker. She looks like she would love to cut me. Besides, fifteen hundred dollars is a lot of money, no? Who is to say you wouldn't try to rob me of it?"

"No one wants to rob you. We just want to make sure things go the way you said. No funny stuff," Mari said, lowering her knife, putting it back on the table. She nodded at the security guard. "Jared there has to go outside. Where's the money? Let's get this thing over with."

Jared made no move to leave. Nicholas lowered his hands, looked around the room as if bewildered, as though he had never seen it before.

"Get it over with... *here*? In a place like *this*?" His smile begat a grin, his grin begat a laugh. "No, no, no, no. Never ever, ever in a place like this." His French accent became thicker as he expressed his surprise. "Pack up your things. We're going for a little ride."

CHAPTER TWENTY-ONE

Mirrors

The ride lasted over half an hour. They headed west, then north to Black Mountain Road and toward the mountain the town and the road were named for. But their destination was miles short of that; a new development past the outskirts of town. It wasn't much – a strip of townhomes, a plaza, and a mid-rise condominium.

Before this new development were long stretches of fields on either side of Black Mountain Road. Miles beyond it was White Wood Forest, the wooded area made of mostly birch trees at the base of Black Mountain itself. Then came the mountain nicknamed Hellstone Hill.

It was the closest Mari had been to the small black mountain. She could barely see it now, the night seeming to absorb it. A part of her was glad for that. With all the strange things she had heard about the mountain, all that had happened on it and in the town named after it, Black Mountain was the last thing she wanted to stare at now. Especially when considering the already strange predicament she and Harry were in.

It was a comfortable half hour ride, though they were uncomfortable during it. Instead of the burgundy sedan, there had been a town car in the small motel parking lot. It was white and chrome all over, gleaming, standing out in the middle of the surrounding squalor. Mari and Harry had looked at each other, half wowed, half terrified. But they were in it now, and they would have to trust Nicholas. Have to hope this wouldn't turn ugly.

The entire ride she thumbed her switchblade, which was back in her jacket pocket. She would be ready if they tried anything.

Jared, apparently, was not only Nicholas' body man but also his driver. After opening doors for Mari and Harry, and then for his boss – them in the back, Nicholas in the front – he had gone to the driver's seat, and they'd been on their way.

Now, he pulled into the driveway of the condo building. Parked. And this was where Jared's part in their adventure ended for the time being.

Instructed by Nicholas to wait there until they finished their business, the security guard did as he'd been bid while the rest of the group walked the short distance from the lot to the front door of the lobby.

The building, from the outside, hadn't been particularly impressive. However, from the inside, the place was like a palace.

They walked on beige marble floors, brown and gold furniture was spread throughout the area, paintings – mostly abstract pieces – hung on each of the walls. Bronze ornamental columns lined the path between the door and the two elevators.

After ascending six floors and stepping out of one of those elevators, after turning left and heading to unit 602, after opening the door, both Mari and Harry spoke for the first time since they had entered the Town Car at the motel. In unison, they exclaimed,

"Wow!"

"And you two wanted to do this in that shithole of a motel," Nicholas said with a laugh. "Come, let's show you the place."

It looked like they had walked into the future. The unit was white and black and chrome, as though the person who had designed the Town Car that had brought them there had extrapolated that design and turned it to a home.

They walked on white marble, between white walls, the ceiling twice their height. There was a black rug in the middle of the living room, black leather seats around it. The tables, the remainder of the furniture, were chrome and glass, both black and clear.

"Here is the master bedroom," Nicholas said, opening the door at the end of a hallway they had entered by way of the living room. They had already been shown a guest room and bathroom before it.

Once again Mari was wowed, though this time it was not by designs or decor. This room did not match the rest of the unit. She couldn't decide if it was the most interesting room she had ever seen, or the worst. Likely both. Neither she nor Harry spoke, each of them awestruck.

"That door there is the closet. It's a walk-in. That one there is the bathroom. The two of you can shower, but no hanky panky. We want to save that for when I come back in an hour. You see there on the bed, those clothes? Put those on after you clean up."

With that, Nicholas left. Mari turned to Harry. She knew he was already looking at her. Knew this because she had seen him looking at her all over the room. Saw him now on the ceiling, on the floor, in several places on each of the walls.

Inside of this condo unit, instead of a master bedroom, they had walked into a house of mirrors.

CHAPTER TWENTY-TWO

Angles

It was about the angles, Mari understood. The mirrors were about Nicholas, their watcher, seeing everything from every angle. Like a porn movie. A live show amplified by options. Endless viewpoints. The idea of it made her cringe. But she would have to endure it. There was no turning back now.

Mari and Harry were standing in front of the bed, which was one of two pieces of furniture in the room; everything else – shelves, wardrobes – was in the walk-in closet that might as well have been an adjoining room.

The bed itself was unlike any Mari had seen before. It was circular, and it was huge. If king size was the biggest bed out there, then this one was made for an emperor. On it was a plush blanket that looked to be made of crushed velvet, its design a swirl of purples and blacks.

Black pillows, four of them. Royal purple sheets. No headboard. And why would there be? It would only serve to obstruct their watcher's view.

Their watcher, who was doing just that, sat on the second piece of furniture in the room – a black leather wide tufted club chair, thronelike, also suitable for an emperor. He wore a robe, his pale and lanky limbs exposed. She was thankful they had convinced him to dim the lights. He had wanted them to do this business in full brightness.

The robe Nicholas wore was along the lines of what Mari had been expecting to wear. She had also expected to be wearing lingerie under it. But what she was dressed in was a beautiful gown, strapless and ruffled; it was a peach color that reminded her of the dolls from her childhood. Harry was wearing a suit, black pants, a purple blazer with black lapels, a white shirt and a black bowtie.

"Prom night," is all Nicholas had said, smiling before sitting down on his throne. Putting his hand under his robe, he provided them with instructions.

"Take your panties off but not your dress."

"Take your trousers off but keep on the blazer. Loosen the tie. Undo the shirt."

"You," to Mari. "Pleasure him with your hand. Aggressively. Faster!" Then he said "Yes," with many Ss.

"You," to Harry. "Pleasure her with your mouth." Eventually, after he had become content with the foreplay, he said, "Mount her."

Three minutes. That's the amount of time Mari and Harry had agreed on. They would give him three minutes of watching them have sex, then Harry would fake it if he had to. Which was what he did.

Mari lay there as Harry did his best to act out an orgasm. Shouted, shuddered, shivered, slid off her.

Three minutes, apparently, was more than enough time for Nicholas. They heard him expressing his enjoyment even as Harry faked his own.

They heard the sound of him taking himself in his hand, whatever lotion or lubricant he had brought into the room being put to use. They heard him mutter something under his breath, then a sigh.

They heard him grunting, groaning.

Breathing.

Breathing.

"Okay. You got to watch. Please leave," Harry said from beside Mari. She was too distraught to form those words.

What did we just do? she asked herself. *What the fuck did we just let happen?*

Mari heard Nicholas rise. Refused to look at him. Wished he was already gone. Wished it more when she heard him say his parting words, a tinge of disappointment in his voice. Or was that anger?

"Next time," Nicholas said. "I want to see the cum."

Then he left. Left the two inside the mirrored room unable to escape seeing themselves, what they had become.

"Next time?" Harry said. "Fuck that."

He didn't sound convinced, though. He sounded like someone saying something in order to gauge the reaction to what he had just said.

Would he really be open to a next time? Mari thought, disgusted. Then she thought of the three thousand dollars. Of how that would change their lives, if only temporarily. She remembered Harry on the edge of the motel room bed, clapping at *Beauty and the Beast*. Three thousand dollars would allow him to be that jubilant on a regular basis. And what if there were thousands more to be had after that? What if this man could permanently change their lives, their status?

"Next time..." she uttered to herself, a whisper. Then louder, for the benefit of Harry, she said, "Let's go."

Even as she thought of the potential for a next time, she felt she had never been as appalled, as repulsed by a man as she was by the Frenchman.

No, that's not true, Mari thought, rising to her feet after she felt sure Nicholas wouldn't pop back into the room. She could remember being this disgusted in the past. Twice. The first time had been by her uncle on the night of her grandmother's birthday party. The second time had been when Benny the Brick had done what he had done to her.

She thought of yellow snow. Was still angered by the memory.

That was when she realized that every man who had repulsed her to this extent was now dead.

Feeling filthy, guilty, low, walking toward the bathroom for a shower and a change of clothes, Mari wondered how all of this – this business with Nicholas – would end.

CHAPTER TWENTY-THREE

Yours

Mari was surprised to see Nicholas fully dressed when they left the bedroom. Not only was he fully dressed but he was standing in the hallway that led to the front door, his boots on, his jacket too.

"Are you escorting us back to the motel?" Mari asked, indicating his clothing. "We'll be fine taking a cab if you don't mind giving us the money you promised."

"You're not going back to that motel," he said, looking revolted by the thought of the place. "Never again."

Mari wasn't sure what that meant, wasn't sure if it was a threat, but she didn't like the sound of it one way or another. Didn't like how he had ignored her request for the money he owed them either.

"So where are you taking us?"

"I'm not taking you anywhere."

"So how are we supposed to get ho–" she caught herself before she said the word 'home,' remembering that she didn't have one. No place like that for her or Harry. But they had an area they were familiar with, spots where they knew they could stay, places nearby where they could get free food, beds in shelters if they were ever available. She wanted to be back in central Black Mountain, away from this man. She wanted to be anywhere in the world but here.

"Home?" Nicholas said with a smile, finishing the sentence she had left incomplete. "I'm glad you asked. Look around you, Ms. Goldy. You *are* home. This place is yours and Sebastian's."

"Are you serious?" Harry said. On his face was disbelief, skepticism and – yes, it was there, Mari recognized it, and couldn't believe she was feeling it herself – hope.

He looked from Nicholas to Mari, then looked around them as the man had suggested. Mari did the same, she couldn't help it. A place she had been eager to leave only seconds ago now looked entirely different. It no longer looked so cold and sterile. It looked warm, welcoming. With the word 'Yours' associated with it, Mari wondered if this place could actually be their home. Then she shook the thought from her mind, turned her head to Nicholas.

"What's the catch? You get to come here and watch us whenever you want?"

"No... Just once a week. And when I come, I will bring five hundred dollars for each of you each time. I will make sure your fridge and pantry are full, give you plenty to smoke, snort, shoot up, whatever your flavor is. And you will never have to stand outside in the cold waiting for someone of legal drinking age to buy you shitty beer again."

She could only stare at him, mouth agape, as much in shock over what was being said as she was about the fact that she was considering it.

Home.

Warmth.

For so long these had been foreign things.

Would she prefer being back on the street? Cold? Would that be a better alternative to putting up with a bit of this man's voyeurism?

They would never be hungry again.

Free booze and drugs, the ability to feel good whenever they wanted.

They could watch TV all the time. No more going days without a shower. No more sleeping in cots in the prison cell sized rooms of the youth shelters. No more sleeping in rooms full of strangers in the adult shelters, or going unsheltered on the heated grates downtown.

No more fucking needles at the blood bank.

She thought of this all in a matter of seconds. Looked at Harry as those thoughts cycled repeatedly through her mind, seeming better, more realistic, more possible each time. She saw that expression on his face again, this time much more clearly: hope.

"Well? Would you like to stay, or shall I return you to that motel after all?" Nicholas asked.

"Once a month, not once a week," Mari said, not believing the words coming out of her own mouth, finding it hard to fathom that she was now negotiating, making a deal that would sell this pervert access to their privacy, their love. Making a deal that would, at least in part, sell him what felt like a portion of their respective souls.

Nicholas smiled. Said,

"Every two weeks. And I will throw in a car, and the identification with which you will need to get away with driving it. That can be in whatever your real names are, or we can stick to these fake names you use now. Goldy Capulet, Sebastian B. Bane." He gave them a knowing wink but didn't pry further. "I trust that one of you knows how to drive."

Mari thought of Harry driving an SUV over her uncle's body, reversing the vehicle over his head. Mangling him.

"Yeah, we can drive."

"Good. So... do we have a deal?" Nicholas asked.

"What happens if we want to leave?" Harry interjected. "We can't live here doing this forever."

"Whenever you want to leave, you can leave. I can't physically keep you here," Nicholas said. He was hoping to sound aloof, amicable, but there was a lie in his words, one that gave them an edge. She thought of Jared who had driven them here. She was sure Nicholas could physically keep them here if he wanted.

"The only thing I must tell you though," Nicholas continued, "is that, if you decide to quit, you will not be able to continue living here. This condo and everything in it will be forfeit. Is that fair? Do we have a deal?"

Mari nodded. Then Harry nodded.

His smile broadening, Nicholas reached into his money pocket and produced a bundle of cash identical to the one he had given them in the motel. He handed it to Mari who put it in her backpack.

They took turns shaking Nicholas' hand. Mari tried not to think of what he had been doing with that hand only minutes prior. While watching them.

The deal was done. If there had been a bill of sale involved, an invoice, it would have read:

Sold. Two souls, for the price of food and shelter.

CHAPTER TWENTY-FOUR

Knock Knock

It started out simply, exactly as they had all agreed. The next two times Nicholas visited Mari and Harry in their home, he had again instructed them to wear the gown and suit as he watched. On the third time, however, things changed.

"Roleplay," Nicholas had said as he sat in his throne, watching them in the mirrored room. Then he had offered instructions:

"You two are going to the prom. You're arriving to pick her up. She answers the door. Go."

"Hey, we said you could watch. No one said anything about roleplay," Mari said. She had always hated roleplay at school in front of a class full of students. She didn't expect to like it any better with this smaller, stranger audience.

Nicholas' response to Mari was to reach into the pocket of his robe, produce another bundle of cash.

"Knock knock," Harry said, turning to Mari upon seeing the wad of cash, "You ready to head to prom, Goldy?"

It went on that way for some time. After prom night they were nurse and patient, house owner and maid, stepsiblings.

When Nicholas grew bored with this, he asked to escalate the situation once more.

"I'd like to join. All three of us in the bed," he had said, producing three thousand dollars from his money pocket even as he asked.

There was humming, hawing, haggling, but in the end, they let him join.

After a couple of months, and the offer of five thousand dollars, Nicholas finally asked the question Mari had been worried he'd been working toward this entire time: Could he have just her? Without Harrison in the bed. Harry could leave the room or stay and watch, but he couldn't be involved.

Nicholas had given them twenty-four hours to decide.

To Mari's surprise, Harry who said yes to this. Told her that he loved her, and that he was thinking of their future. Over drinks, while watching television in their warm condo that had more space than they knew what to do with, they had discussed it. While smoking, they had agreed. They didn't want to leave this lifestyle, didn't want to go back to what they had been doing.

Only a few years ago, they had been a pair of kids who had only known a bedroom each (for Mari that bedroom had to be shared with two cousins who were a constant reminder of the man who had raped her). Now they were young adults with their own place. A palace with a view overlooking the mountains, a view that reminded Mari that not only could this place be theirs, but the world could be as well. One day. If they endured this. Earned enough to start a life that would be both fulfilling and comfortable.

For Harry, what he wanted was enough time to develop his game. He had been working it through in his mind over the last several months as the money continued to pour in. He had worked out all the rules, would find a place that would manufacture his design, then he would promote it himself everywhere he could. Eventually, he was sure, a big game company would hear of his success as an independent game maker, would swoop in and offer him millions for the distribution rights to *A World of Beasts*.

For Mari, the goal was to save enough money to put herself through college and eventually post-graduate school, to get her Masters of Sociology.

She would need a lot of money for school, but she would need even more for what would come afterward: the creation of her foundation. An organization that would help kids avoid situations like those that had befallen her and Harry.

Every time she felt repulsed by Nicholas, by him being inside of her, she reminded herself that she had been through worse in her past, and she had to do this now for their future. To make sure it would be grand. All of this was about ensuring they hadn't struggled and suffered and killed for nothing.

By the time Nicholas made the final escalation – five months into their arrangement – and asked Mari if she would be comfortable sleeping with other men who would pay her handsomely, they had already accrued nearly twenty-five thousand dollars, most of which was hidden in several spots throughout the unit. They figured they would need at least ten times that amount to give themselves a new life and a chance at the goals they wanted to attain. This new level of arrangement would help.

They thought of enduring, surviving, of eventually thriving, as they agreed to the proposition.

And that was how, over the course of less than a year, Mari Goldbraithe went from poor street kid to high end prostitute.

CHAPTER TWENTY-FIVE

A Whole New World

Mari hated roleplay. It was the worst aspect of her job – which was how she thought of what it was she did in exchange for money. Work, employment, sex with strange old men. All simply a means to an end.

She had a small number of repeat clients, half a dozen men, most of them at least thrice her age.

They liked weird things.

It was this that fascinated her most about the direction her life had taken: the strange things the men would ask her to do.

Things that repulsed her as much as they intrigued her. Things they couldn't ask of their wives, girlfriends, the partners in their lives. Things involving beads, strap-ons, all kinds of toys designed for pleasure or for pain.

Often there was violence, perpetrated by her at the request of some of these men. Asphyxiation, whipping, flogging, acts involving clothespins.

She thought of herself as Hard Mari when she was with these men doing these strange things. Hard Mari, the girl who had endured, who had survived, who had saved Harry with a baseball bat and started them down this road. The girl who could face anything. And now, the sex worker, the sometimes dominatrix.

She could put up with all of it, the physical aspects of the job, strange or not, but it was the roleplay that bothered her, because it reduced her to less than what she was. Demeaned her.

Today, with one of her regulars who insisted she call him 'Master' and nothing else, she had once again played the role of slave girl. This time he had driven her to a ranch, had her run through the field behind it, went through the process of chasing her down, directing her to fall, tearing off the rags he had gotten her to change into.

It had been rougher than she was comfortable with. But he had paid her generously to play out this fantasy of his, and she had thought of what that money would mean to her and Harry the entire time.

Now, an hour after that bit of torture had ended, she was standing in front of the door to their apartment having returned from her appointment (which is what she considered her encounters with these men to be). She had been standing there for a full minute, wishing it were nighttime. Unfortunately for her, it was still midday, which meant there would be no sneaking to bed, no avoiding Harrison, no avoiding dealing with what he had become over the last few months of her being paid to have sex with other men.

She knew he would be on the couch, watching something mindless on television; some soap opera, a cartoon, rewatching those Disney movies of his that he had watched a million times.

Sometimes he was still himself, usually when she hadn't had an appointment with anyone for a while. But whenever she would go and do her job, make them money, he would withdraw into himself for days at a time. They would sit in silence, sharing a space but not each other. Drifting apart while side by side.

More and more often this was the case; recently these withdrawals were lasting longer. They barely talked. He looked at her only fleetingly when he looked at her at all. And they almost never had sex anymore.

It was a lot to handle, this drastic change. And it made dealing with her job more difficult than it already was.

Taking a deep breath, she opened the door. Took off her shoes. Made her way to the living room and saw what she had expected to see: Harry on the couch, a drink on the coffee table, the bottle that drink had been poured from on the table beside it. On the television, a scoundrel named Aladdin was promising a princess named Jasmine that he would show her a whole new world as they soared upon a magic carpet.

"Hey," she said. "How's your day been?"

He grunted. "Same as yesterday. Same as every day."

She didn't know what to say to that.

So often she wanted to grab him, shake him by the shoulders, ask him how it was possible that he couldn't see himself turning into his father. But what good would that do?

They were silent, she standing in their large living room, he slouched on the couch.

"How has *your* day been?" he asked. Each word was doused with contempt, dripping with it.

Rather than responding, she walked toward the coffee table, reached down into the ashtray where there was an outed joint. Retrieved the lighter beside it. Lit. Smoked.

"You know I hate every second of what I do, Harry."

"Could have fooled me," he said, still looking at the screen.

She sighed and exhaled smoke at the same time.

"What do you expect from me, Harrison? Do you want me to come home in tears every day? Do you want me to act as miserable as doing this makes me feel? I'm just trying to make the best of it."

He looked at her. She was so unaccustomed to having his eyes on hers these days that she flinched. He looked her up and down, taking in her skin-tight jeans, her lowcut shirt. With his face nearly blank, he looked away again. Said,

"The best of it. Right."

His attitude frustrated her. Especially because she had offered to quit several times. They had survived before with nothing, and now they had money, a lot of it. They could do without the condo, find a small apartment. They would have to get regular jobs, which would make attaining their dreams difficult, maybe impossible, but that wouldn't stop them from trying. Because struggling with Harry was better than fighting with him, growing distant from him. No amount of money would make her want to lose him. But whenever she brought up quitting, he wouldn't hear of it. Said that they had to think of their futures, had to keep this thing going for now until it was the right time to get out.

Whenever she asked him when that time would be, he had no answer, became agitated, withdrew further. Harrison hated when he couldn't figure out the solution to something. When his strategies didn't pan out.

Mari took another deep inhale of smoke, hoping it would mellow her, wishing it would calm her down. But her blood was boiling, she was ready to explode with her frustrations. The frustration of having to deal with what she had dealt with earlier, having to come home to someone who could only look at her and speak to her contemptuously. She was tired of feeling guilty for something they had both agreed to. Something she wanted to quit but wouldn't because he didn't think she should. She was tired of it all.

"Do you think I *like* this?" The sentence started as a near whisper and increased in volume with each word. "An hour ago, some sixty-year-old fucking pervert was choking me until I nearly blacked out. Want to know what he said? He said, and I quote, 'Ain't no nigger cunt ever escaped my plantation, and you ain't 'bout to be the first.' He said this while his dick was in me." By the time she finished speaking, her joint was out. She flicked the roach in the general direction of the coffee table, not caring where it landed.

The outed bit of joint bounced off the table, hit Harry on the knee. He flinched as though a grenade had landed at his feet. He looked up at her, shocked to hear her words, softened by them. On his face, the expression of contempt turned to remorse, sorrow.

"I go through that, and then I come home to you acting like I like it. And what have *you* done? What?" As she spoke, as her voice elevated, she reached into her purse, pulled out the wad of cash she had been paid for today's degradation and hurled it at Harrison, hitting him in the chest. "I do this for both of us. For *both* of us! For *our* dreams. And what have *you* done to help? When's the last time you even *thought* about your game?"

He didn't answer. She didn't give him much of a chance to.

"You know that's how I think I'll die, sometimes. Being choked to death while someone insults me. I risk that for us... just so I can come home and see how much you hate me now."

"Hate you? Goldy... I could never..."

But she wasn't listening. Didn't care about his words, only cared about the way he had behaved these last few months.

She could feel tears coming; a rarity. Another thing she hated, to be seen crying. To be seen as being weak.

Not wanting to be seen by him at all, Mari turned from Harry, back to the hallway, back into her shoes. She grabbed the car keys in the bowl on the credenza by the door.

She left the apartment, the door closing behind her, cutting off the sound of Harry calling out her name, begging her to come back.

She ran down the seven flights of steps to the parking garage. Got into the car that Nicholas had provided them. Drove.

For the first time in a long time, she had no idea where she was headed.

CHAPTER TWENTY-SIX

Shelves

Mari only realized she was driving to the library when she saw the building approaching.

Makes sense, she thought, as she pulled up to the Center Street Library in central Black Mountain. It was the building she and Harry had gone to nearly daily when they had first arrived in this town, freshly homeless.

This had once been her happy place. This and anywhere she could get her hands on a book, jump into another world, leave this one behind. It had been that way since childhood, her reading becoming more intense as life revealed itself to be the bastard that it was.

When she had learned that her father was seriously ill, his Sickle Cell Disease worsening, she had turned to reading every day, often reading through the night in order to avoid her worrisome thoughts. When she found out that he'd had a stroke and wasn't expected to recover, there was rarely a minute when her nose wasn't in a book. That remained the case after he died, Mari reading a novel even to and from his funeral.

When her uncle had raped her, it had been books she had turned to for help, sitting on her porch with a novel regardless of the weather, perusing pages for answers on how to cope, even if those answers came from fictional characters.

Now she felt alone again; this world felt too dark. It made sense that she would come here seeking some escape. Searching for illumination.

When's the last time you read anything? she asked herself. She couldn't remember, and that saddened her.

Both she and Harry had changed. Even when they had been on the streets, destitute, they had always kept their goals in mind. Spending hours in this library, learning, working, making themselves better.

Then there had been that party at Rebby's ex boyfriend's house. The murder of her uncle. That was when the change had begun. They had started to party consistently, drinking regularly, taking drugs, telling themselves they were just living, not realizing they were trying to escape life itself. An escape from the world that not even books could compete with.

She wondered, as she always did when memories of that party and all the parties that followed it came back to her, just where in the world Rebby Greene was. Wondered what had happened to her old best friend, and if she would ever find out. Wondered, maybe, if it was better that she didn't know.

Terrible things happened to young women lost in the world, she knew that firsthand.

Despite her dark thoughts, she smiled as she entered the library. The place smelled familiar. It was the smell of old books. The smell of a hundred thousand adventures all within her reach.

Instinctively, she went right back into the routine she'd had in every library she had ever entered. Going to the shelves in order of genres she loved most to least. Horror first, then sci-fi, then fantasy, eventually ending at romance. After nearly an hour of going through the shelves, she had a pile of books in her arms.

Her plan was to sit there and read until the place closed, just like the old days. Then she would maybe go to the Center Street Cinema. The cheap, run-down old theater that only charged two bucks for a movie and fifty cents for a bag of popcorn. A quarter for a drink of watered-down soda.

The theater had been an escape for her and Harry on the days they could afford it. She hoped it was still there.

Mari understood the irony of doing all the things she had done while homeless in an effort to avoid returning to her current home. Knew she was practicing avoidance behavior but didn't care. She couldn't spend an entire day looking at Harry, seeing what and who he was slowly turning into, not understanding how he couldn't recognize it himself.

She would start her return to reading with *Gerald's Game*, a Stephen King book she had been meaning to read since its release two years ago. She would see if she could finish it before the place closed. Then she would have to check out the rest.

As she entered the study area, she wondered if her library card was still in her purse. She would have to get a new one if it wasn't.

These were Mari's thoughts in the moment before her life would once again be irrevocably changed. Her mind filled with mundane things: what book she would read, the movie she would watch, the potential of a fee for a new library card.

One moment it was occupied with mundanity. The next moment, a second later, her mind was a blank. Because, in the study area she had just walked into, she was seeing something, someone, she had never expected to see again.

She dropped her books, felt her eyes welling up once more. Crying twice in the same afternoon, this was a record for Mari. But she couldn't help it because who she was seeing made her feel restored.

Sitting at a table looking at Mari, unsurprised, as though she had been waiting for her, a tentative smile on her face, was Beautiful Rebecca Greene.

CHAPTER TWENTY-SEVEN

Rebby

"Rebby!" Mari cried as she ran toward the best friend she hadn't seen in a year. Someone she had many times thought was dead, by now a ghost. Yet here she was.

There were a few people sitting in the study area, looking quizzically at Mari as she broke the sacred silence of the library with her dropping of the books and screaming of a name. But she didn't care. Didn't care if they judged her or if her noise got her kicked out. The only thing she cared about right now was the person who was in front of her.

Rebby. Rising from the table, tears of her own running down her face, approaching Mari. Hugging her.

At that point the silence returned. The two embraced without words, quietly crying into one another's shoulders.

"I never thought I would see you again," Mari finally said, breaking the embrace, taking a step back and looking at Rebby.

She was still as pretty as ever, but in a worn-down way. Her mother might have been proud to look at her now because Rebby was as thin as Mari had ever seen her. She had bags under her eyes, and her hair, once thick and lustrous, had a thinning quality to it. It was cut short, jaw length, where previously it had always gone past Rebby's shoulders.

It still worked though, the hair, the entire beatdown look; Rebby had a face that made any look work.

"I wasn't sure I would see you either," Rebby said, guiding them to where Mari's dropped books sat on the floor. They began to pick them up, to place them on the nearest table.

"What happened to you?" Mari asked, still not sure if she wanted to know.

And she wouldn't know, because Rebby simply shook her head. The girl who loved to divulge and digest details would offer none. And Mari wouldn't pry. She understood that something awful had happened to Rebby in the time she had been gone. Understood how hard it was to talk about the awful things. She hoped, in time, that Rebby would feel comfortable opening up, sharing her experience, and Mari might share her own.

With the books picked up and placed on the table, Mari and Rebby sat across from each other, Mari still not believing she was seeing her old friend.

"You look fucking great, Not-So-Virgin Mari," Rebby said, after looking at Mari's formfitting clothes, a far cry from the baggy jeans and sweatshirts she had worn even while partying with Rebby. "You look so grown up. So *sexy*," she added with a hint of her usual flare.

"Thanks. I kinda have to look this way. I'm a prostitute now." She didn't know why she said it, but the words had just slipped out. Rebby had a way of extracting details even when she didn't badger. She laughed at this detail, though, not taking Mari seriously.

Rebby's laughter soon transformed to something close to sobs. A combination of laughter and crying that left Mari feeling mixed emotions of her own.

"I'm so glad you finally showed up," Rebby whispered.

"Finally? What do you mean?"

"I've been... I've been coming here every day for the last month, just hoping, you know, that you were still around. I didn't know how else to get in touch with you after I found out I'd lost the apartment and you and Harry got kicked out. I figured you'd be back on the street. And back on the street meant back in here. I hoped I was wrong but... Either way, I'm glad I waited. It's good to see you, Mari. Where's that boyfriend of yours?

Mari, unsure how to tell Rebby that she was far from being back on the street, and not particularly wanting to discuss Harry, asked,

"Where have you been staying? How long have you been back?"

Rebby shook her head, picked up one of the books and began thumbing through it absentmindedly.

"I went back home. To my mom's house. She was happy to see me, until I told her what I'd been up to the last year. I reached out to her for help, you know. I figured if I laid it all out, then we could start over. But she couldn't even look at me." She was worrying the book now, nearly wringing it in her hands. And Mari understood why Rebby wouldn't share the details with her. Rebby believed Mari would judge her the way her mother had. "So, I left again. I've been staying anywhere I can. Got a regular bed at St. Jude's"

St. Jude's, Mari recalled. Named after St. Jude Thaddeus, the patron saint of impossible causes. It was supposed to be a place where kids believed to be lost could be found, could have a second chance. Mari remembered staying there once, watching a boy be stabbed, his attacker arrested; police, ambulances. It wasn't exactly the best place for a fresh start.

"Stay with us," Mari heard herself saying before even registering the thought.

"Where are you staying?"

Mari pondered the question, knowing that her answer would likely lead to many more.

"Oh," she said. "Just a little place on the way to Hellstone Hill."

CHAPTER TWENTY-EIGHT

Bacon

"Wow. You really are a prostitute," Rebby said as they walked along the hallway, heading toward Mari and Harry's unit.

Mari flinched at the word despite having used it herself earlier. It was the first time she had been described as such by someone else. It would take some getting used to, though she didn't want to be doing this job long enough to allow that to actually happen.

Rebby had been saying "Wow" since they had walked to Mari's and Harry's car, despite it being nothing fancy. Was wowed by the drive to this building, by the building itself, the foyer, and now by the hallway approaching their door.

"I feel like I'm fucking dreaming. Like I'm friends with Julia Roberts in *Pretty Woman*, you know. Jesus, you guys made it big."

Had that been what Rebby had been trying to do when she'd been hopping from boyfriend to boyfriend? Trying to 'make it big'? And is that what Mari and Harry had done? She felt as though they were a long way from making it. Still had money to earn and save, an education to get, plans to execute. They couldn't be under Nicholas' thumb forever. She couldn't subject herself to what she had gone through earlier that day for much longer.

But she didn't say any of this. She only smiled, opened the door, and was greeted by the second surprise of the day.

The place smelled like eggs and bacon, her favorite food no matter the hour. And – she took several quick paces to the living room to make sure her inkling was correct, and it was – Harry wasn't on the couch. He was in the kitchen, cooking.

More accurately, he was coming out of the kitchen. Had just exited it with a spatula in his hand after hearing her enter the apartment. He was turning toward her, talking before looking at her, speaking without seeing who had accompanied Mari there.

"Look, Mariam, I'm sorry about earlier. I know I have to be more supportive, it's just... it's just... it's just... Holy fuck! *Rebby?* Rebby! Is that you?"

"Hey, Dirty Harry," Rebby said, seeming to be wowed by Harrison as well as their apartment. He had grown since they'd last seen Rebby. He had grown immensely since they'd left Denver. He was nearly six feet tall now, and though he was still heavy, no one would call him fat.

It was only then, seeing how Rebby looked at him, that Mari realized just how different this version of Harry was from the short, pudgy boy she had left Denver with. How different the two of them were, both physically and mentally.

Hearing his nickname as confirmation that this was indeed Rebby, Harry sprinted to her, the spatula raised to the roof because both of his hands were in the air. Then both of his hands were extended as far as they could get from his sides before they found their way to Rebby's back, his arms wrapping around her. Mari stepped back, watching the two embrace, fighting off tears. A battle she lost for the third time that day when she saw that Rebby was crying.

Mari was looking at the two people who had most drastically changed her life. The young man who had helped her escape a broken home, and the young woman who had saved her from the street, giving her shelter, showing her how to survive in a world that seemed eager to destroy her.

They had been kids then, Mari thought, astonished at all they had been through, all they had survived, over the last few years. And she knew, with the three of them together, they could survive whatever would next come their way.

She placed an arm around both of their shoulders. Both of them wrapped an arm around her waist. She and Harry held the only person who they had ever mutually loved, and were held by the only person who knew and loved them both.

And, to Mari, in that moment, with the three of them huddled together in the hallway of their home, things finally felt right.

CHAPTER TWENTY-NINE

I Want In

That feeling of completion, of things being right, lasted for less than forty-eight hours.

Rebby agreed to stay with them. She would be moving into the Room of Mirrors. Neither Mari nor Harry had any interest in staying in there. Since their first night in this apartment, they had made the spacious guestroom their own. Though Harry, these days, spent most nights sleeping on the couch. The room Rebby chose made no difference to him.

They began to pamper Rebby nearly as soon as her shoes were off. She took a two-hour long bath, received a fresh change of clothing – having to settle for wearing Harry's sweatpants and shirt because Mari's clothes were still too small for her.

They had ordered the food of her choice that first evening (a deluxe pizza which they dressed with the bacon Harry had made. The eggs, unfortunately, had burned while the three were reuniting), then they'd all sat in the living room and watched whatever she had wanted to watch.

With the television on but no one paying much attention to it, they did what they had always enjoyed doing best: sat, smoked, drank, talked. And repeat and repeat throughout those first two days of being back together.

They talked about everything except for the things that mattered most. Reminisced about their time living together, the parties, the things they'd had to do to survive, the friends they'd had. Friends, like Tammy, who they'd lost contact with; friends whose lives had improved, like Brant, who had moved in with his grandmother in California not long after Rebby had vanished. They spoke about the group of kids who had gone to the top of Hellstone Hill during the winter of Hunter's party and either never returned or never returned the same. What they didn't talk about were topics such as multiple murders, vehicular homicide, the explicit details of Mari's new profession, or the fact that Rebby had disappeared for a year and was not quite the same as she had been before.

Harry had asked where she had been after they'd parted from their initial group hug. Rebby had all but dismissed the question, saying only, "It was bad," before changing the subject.

Mari noticed differences in Rebby. She had always been relaxed and almost nonchalant, constantly laughing, excited and optimistic despite her circumstances. Now, as they sat in the living room still talking, still with the television being ignored in the background, she seemed tense, almost jittery, smiled tentatively when she smiled at all. And while Mari and Harry were headed toward drunk, Rebby was racing to wasted. She never let her cup stay empty for more than a few seconds.

She was also chain-smoking, not only marijuana but cigarettes. This was especially shocking to see. Rebby had told them, years ago, that her mother had forced her to smoke cigarettes to get thin back in her pageant days. Had force-fed cigarettes and black coffee to a little girl, and not much food to go with them.

When they had first met Rebby, she had wanted nothing to do with either of those things, couldn't even stand the smells. Now their apartment reeked like the smoking section of a restaurant thanks to her new, old habit.

Who am I to judge? Mari thought, reflecting on all the new habits she had formed since meeting Rebby.

She took a swallow of her beer.

Harry passed her a freshly rolled joint.

She puffed on it, coughing up smoke when she heard the knock on the front door.

"You expecting someone?" Rebby asked. Mari and Harry both shook their heads.

They never had visitors here, other than Nicholas or the occasional client of Mari's. But she only had one more appointment this week; one set for the weekend, which she was planning to cancel. She intended to tell Nicholas she wasn't feeling well. Spend more time with Rebby and Harry, perhaps make it the first step toward pulling back entirely. Quitting for good. Harry would argue, but maybe, with three of them together and the money they'd already earned, it would be easier to build a future without Nicholas' help.

When they didn't move to answer the door, Rebby, concerned, said,

"Oh my God, you guys aren't like squatting in some rich guy's condo, are you? The police aren't gonna bust in here, are they?"

"No, it's nothing like that," Mari said.

"Sebastian? Goldy? Is everything alright in there?" came a slightly accented male voice from beyond the door.

"Shit..." Mari said under her breath, then aloud, "Yeah, we're fine! One second!"

"Sebastian?" Rebby asked, glancing skeptically at Harrison. Then she turned her attention to Mariam. "And since when does anyone but him call you Goldy?" She gave them both a quizzical, slightly suspicious look.

"Aliases, you know, just in case," Mari answered. Rebby replied to this with an expression that said, 'Just in

256

case of what?' But Mari turned from her before she could ask the question, got up and walked toward the door.

"It's her boss... and our landlord, I guess you'd call him," Mari heard Harry explaining to Rebby behind her as she got to the door.

Was 'boss' the right word? she wondered. Was it 'pimp'? Was it 'client'? The lines between she and Nicholas were blurred. What she knew clearly was that she didn't want to see him just then. Didn't like the idea of him randomly popping in.

She opened the door. Before she could greet him, Nicholas, not looking pleased to have been kept waiting, said, "You have a guest," as he looked over Mari's head into the apartment.

Mari turned around, expecting to see Rebby standing there with Harry, but no one was behind her. They were still in the part of the living room that couldn't be seen from the vantage of the front door, wanting to give Mari privacy with her 'boss' without being too far away. But, if Nicholas hadn't seen her...

"How did you know?" Mari asked.

"I know everything that happens in this building," he said stonily.

"Ah, one of the concierges told you," Mari said, giving him a knowing look, which he responded to with a smile.

"You catch on quickly. One of them found it odd that a young woman came in here with you and still hasn't left two days later. I find it odd as well."

"Are they keeping tabs on us?"

"No. Only taking note of the unusual. I have a lot invested in you, Ms. Goldy. You are one of my most popular girls. I have to make sure you're making safe and sound decisions so we can keep it that way. Which is why I can't have someone who is not involved with our business staying here with you."

"She's an old friend. Like a sister, really. She just needs some time to get on her feet. She won't be here long."

"No, Goldy. If she isn't part of our business, she cannot stay here. I can't risk outsiders knowing where I operate, and with whom."

Mari was about to plead again, or perhaps to give an ultimatum: Rebby stays, or you can kiss one of your most popular girls goodbye. But a voice from behind her spoke before she could.

"I want in," said Rebby Greene. Mari whirled to face her friend.

"No."

"Well… what do we have here?" Nicholas said, his voice full of longing, lust, reactions Mari had seen Rebby inspire in many men and women over the years.

"No," Mari repeated.

"Do you know what it is you want in to?" Nicholas asked, giving Mari a look that said, 'I hope you haven't been talking about what we do here.' For a moment she thought they were about to be in trouble, but Rebby was a street kid, the best of them, and sharp.

"No, I don't. But I haven't seen my best friend in a year and all of a sudden she's living in a mini palace? Having a strange man – no offense – who she said is her landlord telling her she can't have people stay over. I know whatever you have her and… Sebastian doing might not be legal, but I've never really given much of a shit about legal. Drugs? I want in. Sex? I want in. Whatever it is, I don't care. I want in. I want in on some money and I want in on a place like this… If I can't stay here that is," Rebby said the last sentence while looking at Mari, as if wanting acceptance even though she had not asked for permission.

This time Mari mouthed the word, 'No,' shaking her head, but knowing it didn't matter. The deal was nearly done. Might have been done from the moment Nicholas had learned that a beautiful young woman had been spotted coming to this apartment.

"Ohhh, I *like* this one," Nicholas said, nearly clapping in his excitement.

Rebby forced herself to smile, and Mari could see, in that strained expression, how lost the girl was. Her eyes were red, nearly glazed over from drink, from smoke, from the ways she had already been trying to escape her issues before adding this new way out.

"Just so we're clear," Nicholas said, making his 'I want to watch' face, "we're not talking about drugs."

"Even better," Rebby said without hesitation.

"Would you be open for an interview? Immediately?" Nicholas asked, nodding toward the interior of the unit, indicating they should enter, perhaps head to the Room of Mirrors.

Mari looked back and forth between them as this interaction went on, not believing it was happening. Again astonished by how quickly life could veer off course.

She saw something in Rebby's face. Almost a faltering, a flinch, her false bravado fading. But only for an instant.

Then Mari watched her jaw clench, saw Rebby do her best to focus, a look of determination on her face. Then a smile, a seductive smile, a well practiced expression.

"A paid interview, I hope."

"Of course." He reached into his money pocket, withdrew from it a stack of bills, counted out five of them, each one adorned with Benjamin Franklin's face.

By the time the money was in the pocket of the sweatpants Rebby wore, Nicholas was already in the house, walking side by side with her as they headed toward her newly acquired room.

"No," Mari whispered, not wanting Rebby to be subjected to the sorts of things Mari had been subjected to. Not when she was clearly as fragile as she was.

But she didn't stop it. Didn't believe she could.

Mari only watched guiltily as the two of them walked into the condo, vanished around a corner. She wondered if she had just witnessed her best friend take the first steps toward what might be her destruction.

And Mari couldn't help but feel responsible for being the one who had set her on that path.

CHAPTER THIRTY

Sinking

Rebby never detoured, never strayed. Never once veered off the path toward destruction she had set on when Nicholas had shown up at the apartment offering her a new life (or a twisted extension of the life she already knew). She also never slowed, going from not involved in this business of theirs to fully in, full throttle, accepting her first appointment only days after she had been 'interviewed' by Nicholas.

He had taken her picture after the interview, just as he had taken Mari's when she had started. Had used the photos in whatever underground marketing was involved in the prostitution of young women, old girls. The same marketing that had led to Mari meeting men with warped fantasies, men who liked to roleplay seemingly for the sake of mental cruelty as much as physical pleasure.

Then there were the guys Mari had said no to regardless of the amount they offered her. Because these men wanted violence more than sex. Offering thousands of dollars for the right to punch her in the face. To lay her on the ground and kick her ("Only once or twice, no big deal," Nicholas had said) while she was naked. Men who wanted to cut her. Negotiating through Nicholas ("Just a slice with a sanitized razor here or there, no big deal."), letting her know it would only be a small slit, a simple parting of the skin that would barely scar.

And, of course, there was the offer she was most inflamed by: urination. Even the suggestion made her blood boil. Made her think of Benny. Made her think of murder.

But would Rebby turn down these requests when they were made? Could she say no when she was presented with money in amounts she hadn't earned since her early beauty pageant days? It was money she couldn't imagine earning again in her lifetime. Not with the way things had been going for her.

Rebby had been propositioned before, as many kids on the street are. By men who wanted her to climb into their cars for ten minutes, and perhaps the same amount of dollars. By guys at parties who offered her whatever was in their wallet just to see her flash her breasts.

Both Rebby and Mari had met lifelong street walkers, their days filled with ten-dollar blowjobs, twenty-dollar lays, all in an effort to pay rent on hovels they could call home, and to obtain the substances they could abuse within those places.

Rebby knew it could be worse, and used this as her reasoning when Mari tried to steer her away from the path she was on. When that rationale didn't land with Mari, Rebby called her a hypocrite, reminded Mari that she was doing the same thing she was trying to warn Rebby away from. Reminded Mari that Rebby had been a prostitute for years, whoring herself out for her mother, for judges, for people who wanted to look and leer and label.

And there were her ex-boyfriends to consider. Hadn't she lived with over half a dozen men before running off with one who was married? Hadn't she always been trading her body and her company for sustenance and shelter? This would be no different. Except, this time, she would have more control. Thanks to Nicholas, she could accept or deny whoever she wanted.

Mari couldn't convincingly argue with the logic of this. Eventually, after hours of attempting to, she relented, allowing Rebby to do as she pleased. Even invited Rebby to join in on the fantasies that she and Harry shared with each other. About what they would do with their money once this part of their lives was over. The dreams they would attain, the lives they would change.

They would be millionaires one day, the three of them agreed, and this would be the fast-track there.

Rebby seemed to take the goal of millionairedom as a personal challenge, working once a week, then twice a week, then nearly nightly almost immediately.

"Are you okay?" Mari would ask her. "You sure you're not doing too much?"

And Rebby would always smile and say she was fine.

But she wasn't.

Over the next few weeks, Mari noticed several things about Rebby. The chain-smoking and nonstop drinking weren't her only new habits. There were others. Habits Nicholas helped her indulge in.

Pain killers, tranquilizers, sedatives, cocaine, a buffet of drugs that Rebby might have only dabbled in before.

Mari noticed that she would often mix and match many of those drugs, washing them down with alcohol, often detaching from Mari and Harry after doing so. Rebby would go to her room, to the bathroom, would spend hours in her bathtub sinking into her thoughts.

And Mari noticed, most of all, the night that Rebby Greene once again didn't come home.

CHAPTER THIRTY-ONE

Where Is She?

"Where is she?" Mari said, nearly screaming into the phone at Nicholas. She was pacing back and forth in the kitchen as she talked to him, twice nearly ripping the phone from the wall as the cord attached to it stretched to its limits, telling her she had paced too far. Harry watched, leaning against the wall, as Mari waited for an answer from her boss.

"She's with a client," Nicholas said, yawning. It was seven in the morning, and Mari had likely woken the man of leisure up. But she didn't care. She'd been up all night listening for the door, looking at the mouth of the hallway, waiting for Rebby to step from it and into the living room, to look at the two and call them Virgin Mari and Dirty Harry as she still sometimes did. Mari had been worried sick for hours.

"He paid her extra to stay the night. I assure you she is fine."

"Okay... But if *anything* bad happened to her, I'll..." What would she do? What could she do to a man like this, so obviously connected, so clearly in control? "...I'll quit," she finished, not sounding as confident as she had hoped.

"There won't be any need for that," Nicholas said, then hung up the phone. Mari looked at the receiver before returning it to its cradle, wanting to slam it but restraining herself.

She'll be fine, she told herself. *You're worried over nothing.*

"What did he say?" Harry asked.

"That she's with a client who paid for her to stay overnight. But I dunno, I just have a feeling that something bad happened."

It was at that moment they heard the lock; a key sliding into it, turning, the door opening.

"So much for you being a psychic, huh?" Harry said snidely. "Sounds like she's fine to me."

He walked from the kitchen and returned to the couch.

Since Rebby had started working regularly, Harry had withdrawn again. Had gone back to barely talking, to being short with Mari when he did talk, to laying on the couch, drinking all day, and paying little attention to what was going on around him unless it seemed like an emergency. But she couldn't worry about him and his issues now. She was still concerned about Rebby.

When Mari entered the main hall and saw her best friend, she knew that she had been right to be worried.

"Fuck, Rebby. What did they do to you?"

They had hurt her is what they had done. That was clear.

Her left cheekbone was swollen and bruised, her lip was cut, her neck discolored.

"Nothing I can't handle," Rebby responded, her words sounding slurred. She reached into her purse, removed a rubber-banded roll of cash. Tossed it to Mari, who let it drop to the floor, roll away until it was stopped by the baseboard of the wall. "We're gonna be millionaires, remember?"

Rebby walked past Mari, who was still stunned by what she was seeing of her friend. Rebby wore a short sundress, exposing arms and legs that were too pale where they weren't purple. At her wrists were rope burns, bruises on her biceps, her thighs polka dotted black and blue with thumb sized spots.

Mari followed her into the kitchen. Watched Rebby go immediately for the cabinet where they kept their pills. Take out what looked to be a bottle of pain pills. Unlid it, tip out two. Just as she seemed to be about to close the bottle, she reconsidered, tipped out two more. Tossed them all in her mouth before walking to the liquor cabinet.

"Rebby... Don't you think that's enough?"

Apparently, she didn't. Because she ignored Mari, grabbed a bottle of gin, a tumbler. Poured the contents of the first into the latter. Poured the contents from the glass down her throat.

She shivered, feeling the burn of the hard liquor, her back to Mari, her face to the cabinet as if contemplating whether to drink more or return the bottle. After a few seconds of this, she left the bottle on the counter, closed the cabinet, turned to Mari.

"It feels like so many guys who call you beautiful can't wait for the chance to turn you ugly, don't you think?"

Without waiting for a response from Mari, Rebby walked past her, around the corner, and toward the Room of Mirrors.

CHAPTER THIRTY-TWO

A Thousand Reflections of Her

"She's been in there for a while," Mari said to Harry. She had come to the living room from their bedroom, hoping that Rebby would be there. But she was nowhere to be found. It had been at least three hours since she'd arrived home, bruised and beaten.

"Of course she's been in there for a while. Did you see her? She looks like she just went to war."

Harry was laying on the couch, watching one of his afternoon talk shows. His eyes didn't leave the screen as he spoke to Mari.

He was clearly bothered by what was going on with Rebby, but, as usual of late, when he was bothered by something, he shut down. Mari, from the entrance of the living room, wanted to go to him, to get him to sit up, to look at her, talk to her. But she only stood there watching him watch the screen, his clothes stained, the coffee table and the area around him a disaster zone. She had no idea what to say to get him to open up to her.

"I'm going to go check on her," Mari said, after several uncomfortable seconds. Harry grunted in response.

Mari turned, walked slowly, almost woozily to the main bedroom. She knew she shouldn't be as worried as she was. She was aware that Rebby often spent hours in the tub, thinking, or perhaps not thinking, maybe just letting her mind drift away. But Mari had a bad feeling. Hadn't liked the look in Rebby's eye when she had said that thing about the men in the world who tried to turn beautiful things ugly.

She was going to talk to her again, sternly this time, about quitting. Rebby had only been at this for over a month but had made nearly twenty-thousand dollars. Mari had made over thrice that amount in less than a year.

They had enough. They could take it, go.

Sure, they would lose the condo, but they could rent another, or stay in a hotel until they figured out a plan.

This place, the money, it wasn't worth what Rebby was putting herself through, or what Harry was turning into. Wasn't worth the anguish Mari constantly felt.

She took a deep breath when she got to the bedroom door.

Knocked on it. Waited.

Knocked again. Received no response.

She opened the door.

Inside of the room was a thousand reflections of her, and an empty bed. Across the room, she could see that the bathroom door was ajar.

Something told her to stop there. To leave well enough alone. Turn back, go to the living room and work on Harry instead. Something told her not to continue forward into the bathroom. She ignored that something.

She walked across the room, entered the lavatory.

At first, she thought it was empty. The bathroom was large, the bathtub opposite the door. She looked at the clawfoot tub but couldn't see anyone in it. She almost turned away, nearly left to look for Rebby elsewhere, but she saw the water on the floor, noticed it dripping from the edge of the tub.

She approached the basin slowly, delaying seeing this thing she already knew had occurred. Hoping that, if she barely moved, didn't breathe, it might somehow change what had already happened. That she might not be walking toward the dead body of her best friend.

"No..." Mari whispered.

The first thing she noticed was the hair, floating in the water, looking dark brown even though it was blond, obscuring Rebby's face and parts of her upper body.

"No..."

Then it was the bruising, the cuts, the scars. All over her body she was battered. But that didn't matter now.

"No... No..."

But it couldn't be denied. In front of her was Beautiful Rebecca Greene, underwater, not breathing. Dead.

Mari heard the screams before it registered with her that she was the one responsible for them.

CHAPTER THIRTY-THREE

The Body

Before Mari knew what was happening, Harry was there, attempting to pull Rebby out of the tub, slipping, falling, submerging her again. Recovering his feet, he finally dragged her out.

"Oh fuck, oh fuck, oh fuck, oh fuck..." he said as he lay her on the cold, wet tiles, attempted to administer CPR to a corpse. They both knew it was pointless, but he tried. He breathed into her mouth, pounded on her chest, crying, nearly wailing, repeating, "Oh fuck, oh fuck." Alternating that with "C'mon, Reb, c'mon Reb."

After five minutes, he gave up. Mari, standing there watching him, saw him fall back, slump against the tub. It didn't seem real, didn't make sense. She had *just* been alive. Mari fell to her knees.

She fell asleep, Mari thought, wanting to believe that. Not wanting to think that her friend could have overdosed intentionally. *She just fell asleep, and now she's gone...*

They remained that way, Mari on her knees, Harry against the tub, the corpse of Rebecca Greene between them.

There was sobbing, then there was silence.

For five minutes, ten. Fifteen minutes, longer.

Until Harry, ever practical, always looking for a solution, said,

"We have to figure out what to do with the body."

CHAPTER THIRTY-FOUR

Bad Meat

"We can't tell him. That's not an option," Harry said. They were in the living room, the television was off, Harry was alert and focused for the first time in a long time. Stumbling upon a dead body has a way of doing that to a person.

They were arguing. Had been arguing since they'd left the bathroom, about what to do with Rebby's body.

"Why can't we tell him? Nicholas knows people. He can help us figure a way out of this without involving the police."

Oh, God, Mari thought to herself. *Are we really talking about getting rid of Rebby? Like she's some piece of bad meat.*

Mari was struggling to hold back tears while Harry was struggling with words he had been holding back for some time now.

"He's going to kill us," he said, his voice flat, a notch above a whisper.

"What?"

"Nicholas... If you quit, he's going to kill us."

"No... he said he would just take back the condo..."

"...'And everything in it.' That's what he said. He knows we can't keep your money in the bank. When you quit, he's going to take it back, and we're going to be right back where we were. And that's the best-case scenario. What I think is more likely to happen is that he'll kill us. You've seen too much. We both have. He can't have us walking around knowing what we know. So, once you say you're ready to quit, that's the end of it for us… That's why I've been encouraging you to stay on. I've been trying to figure out a way out of this. Think about it, Mariam. Why would I want to live this way?"

She did think about it. Wondered why she hadn't thought about it more intently before. She also considered something he hadn't mentioned: running away. But immediately knew that it was out of the question, and that Harry had already realized this. Her clients, the men Nicholas connected her with, were all rich, all powerful. With those resources, Mari and Harry wouldn't be able to escape him for long.

Harry was right, she knew. They would be stuck, or destitute, or dead. These were the options for their future. After all they had done. All she had endured.

"But he doesn't *want* to kill us, or at least not you. He would love to have you working for him until you die of natural causes. Or until he doesn't think you're useful anymore. If he finds out about Rebby, he'll hold that over us forever. You'll be his property for good."

What she said in response, she said before fully thinking it through. When she heard her own statement, she knew it was the only recourse they had.

"He has to die," Mari said.

Harry only nodded, as if their need to murder someone was simply a fact to quickly acknowledge. A trivial concern affirmed and moved on from. She could see that there was something else he needed to say. Something he did not want to say, but something he had to.

"We have to get rid… take care of Rebby's body first."

"And how exactly can we do that from the sixth floor when his concierges monitor our every move and there's security patrolling the area?"

She saw it on his face then. He was working himself toward saying what he didn't want to say, what he was worried about her hearing. Harry took a deep breath, avoided her eyes. Said,

"We have to take her out of here in pieces."

CHAPTER THIRTY-FIVE

Stained

Mari argued, of course. But in the end, she saw Harry's logic. Understood there was no way around this part of his plan. Not if they didn't want to be found out. Blackmailed.

Controlled. Something they had promised themselves they would never allow to happen again. Not after leaving their lives behind in Denver to chase freedom, an opportunity at a happy future.

It was freedom they thought of when the two returned to the bathroom after their difficult conversation. Harry brought with him towels, as well as an item which he placed on the counter next to the sink. There were things they had to do before he would need it.

They drained the tub of water before they stood at opposite ends of Rebby's body – he at her head, she at Rebby's feet – and grabbed her, lifting her back into the tub.

It was the idea of freedom that continued to roll through Mari's mind as she saw Harry lay the towels down around the tub, then take the chef's knife he had brought to the bathroom from the counter and walk back to Rebby's body.

Mari turned, couldn't watch as Harry began the process of letting Rebby's body bleed out.

Even though she couldn't bring herself to look, she knew exactly what he was doing. Couldn't stop picturing it in her mind. She knew he would take that knife and put it to Rebby's major arteries and veins – carotid, jugular, femoral, each of her radials – and slice and cut and allow any blood that hadn't already begun to coagulate to spill from her, down the drain.

Like a stuck pig, Mari thought. *Like some fucking farm animal.*

It was a painful thought. She tried to replace it with others. Thoughts of them no longer being in this apartment. Of them no longer being under Nicholas' thumb. Most importantly, thoughts of what she had to do right now.

"I'll be back as soon as I can," she said to Harry as she walked toward the door.

"Wait," he called from behind her. She turned to him, saw him get up from a knee next to the tub, wipe the red from his latex-gloved hands with one of the towels that had been on the floor.

He walked to her, the white gloves he wore stained pink.

"We'll be okay," he said, stopping inches in front of her. "I love you. Please don't forget that."

Then, careful not to touch her with his stained gloves, he kissed her on the lips.

Sometimes she did forget that he loved her. They shared the words so infrequently these days, shared kisses such as these infrequently as well.

When they parted, she nodded, said, "I love you, too."

Then she turned and went about her task. Left the apartment to go purchase the supplies they would need to dismember the body of their best friend.

CHAPTER THIRTY-SIX

Polyethylene

When she saw Rebby's body upon returning, Mari gasped. She knew what Harry had been doing while she was gone, but it was jarring to see her friend cut open in so many places.

At her neck were gashes like gills; her forearms were split open from elbow to wrist, the flesh visible, puffy and pink. At her torso were smaller wounds, slashes between her breast, cuts running from her sternum to her waist. Dissection lines, Mari realized. He hadn't only cut her to bleed her out, he had scored her skin where he would later hack and saw.

The body sat in a shallow pool of pinkish water, globs of darker reds floated in it here and there – coagulated blood, bits of flesh that had fallen from her gashes.

"You don't have to be here for the rest of this," Harry said from beside her, both of them having entered the bathroom with the supplies she had purchased.

"I would never let you go through this alone," Mari replied quickly, though she badly wanted to turn and run from the room. Clenching her jaw, steeling herself, she set to help Harry handle this task.

Those words were the last that were said between the two for a while. Each of them quietly contemplating what they had to do next, then working silently as they did it.

With their silence, the sounds that filled the room were those of their supplies and the tasks they were needed for:

There was the sound of a hacksaw meeting skin, sawing through it. Meeting bone, working its way through that as well.

The sound of tendons being snipped, of bones being twisted and wrenched from sockets, hammered in half when the saw was not enough.

Of body parts being removed from an ever-decreasing torso and wrapped with strips of polyethylene cut from the heavy-duty garbage bags Mari had gone to obtain.

Of strips of duct tape being ripped from its roll, sealing and securing those polyethylene-wrapped parts.

There was the sound of those packaged parts being placed in piles – in the sink, on the towels they had laid out on the floor.

The noises that filled the bathroom were of barbarism, of butchery.

These were the sounds of two people working desperately to save their futures.

CHAPTER THIRTY-SEVEN

Many Places

They buried her in many places. Between their little complex on the outskirts of the city of Black Mountain and the city itself there were expanses of fields that were rarely touched, rarely even driven past. North of their condo, before Hellstone Hill, there was White Wood Forest.

They could have chosen either location to dispose of the body. The forest would likely have been the more prudent choice of the two, considering all the shelter the trees would provide. But the word around town was that White Wood Forest was haunted and they worried that burying Rebby there might curse her bones. Curse her soul into being forced to wander this Earth.

So, they chose the fields; walking deep into the bushes and tall grasses, they dug a new hole in a new spot each time they brought those polyethylene-wrapped body parts down several pieces at a time.

A head in her backpack, two arms in his duffle, hands and a ribcage inside of her purse.

The parts that couldn't be taken immediately were stored in their freezer, in their fridge, in a bathtub full of ice.

In the end, they removed her from their unit in twenty-five pieces, including the bag of innards they had extracted from her core.

In five trips over four days, they buried Rebby in five holes, falling to pieces as they left pieces of her all over a high-grassed field along Black Mountain Road.

Then they cleaned. For a day, they cleaned. Not only the bathroom, but everywhere. Removed from their apartment all traces of Rebby, of her death, of the time she had spent there while alive. It was like the girl had never been there at all.

But they weren't erasing her completely. They carried her in their hearts, in their minds, even as they removed all evidence of her from their lives.

And they understood that what they had to do next, they would do in her name.

CHAPTER THIRTY-EIGHT

Let Me Out

"What are you doing here?" Nicholas asked upon seeing Mari standing beside his burgundy sedan. Leaning against it. Nearly slumped.

They were in the parking lot outside of the Sleep Easy Motel, the place where he had first propositioned them, manipulated them into this lifestyle Mari regretted. Where he had first pushed them toward all that had happened, and what was going to happen next.

"I told you on the phone," Mari said as Nicholas walked – faster now than he had before noticing her – toward the vehicle. "Rebby hasn't come back. And I think you know why."

She had called him a day after Rebby had died, then a day after that, then three days hence. Each day she had asked him, pleadingly, to tell her if he had any idea where Rebby might have gone.

"And I told you, Goldy, I have no idea. It has been an extremely busy week for me, and I've had to take time from my schedule to do damage control with clients who were looking forward to her. Not exactly a great use of my time. What are you doing here?" he repeated the question.

"I figured you'd be getting yourself more whores here at the Sleasy. I knew I'd find you here."

Her words were slurred, she gesticulated wildly to the motel he had just walked out of, nearly falling over as she did so, hanging onto the vehicle to keep her balance.

Mari had been waiting for him for hours. For days if you counted the fact that she had been there twenty-four hours earlier, staking the place out, hoping he would show up.

Then she had seen the young Asian woman; beautiful, sad, down on her luck. And knew it would only be a matter of time before Nicholas made an appearance, the receptionist likely tipping him off. He probably paid the desk clerk and owner to let him know when there was a fresh young life available for him to corrupt.

He had proved Mari correct, emerging now from the room the young woman was currently in. Mari couldn't help but wonder what he had offered her, what words and payment she had accepted in exchange for a ruined future.

"You're drunk," he said, taking in her slurred words, the uncoordinated motion of her limbs, her vertiginous movement. He looked her in the eyes, and she knew that even in the dark he could see how reddened they were. "You're high, too," he added.

She only stood and stared at him. Swayed slightly as she did so.

"How did you get here?" he asked, looking around for the car he had given them.

"I ditched my car and took a cab. I can afford that now, you know. And I wouldn't want to risk being hurt and slowing down your fucking business!" She hadn't shouted it, but it was close enough to a yell for him to flinch in his spot. He looked around again, this time not for a car but for potential witnesses.

"Get in the car, Goldy. You're not yourself."

"You don't fucking know who I am!" Even louder this time.

"Get. In. The. Car." As he said this, he speed-walked around the front of the vehicle, opened the passenger door for her, and half guided, half shoved her inside of it.

"Hey! Why so rough? It's not like you're paying me for this!"

"Christ, can you be quiet?" he whispered harshly. Bending down, he grabbed her legs, which were still dangling outside of the vehicle. He lifted and pushed them into the car. Then helped get Mari from a slouch into a proper sitting position. He strapped her in with the seatbelt, his hands brushing against her breasts in the process.

"Is this what you did to Rebby? Huh? Did you kidnap her and feel her up? Did you rape her before you killed her? Where is my friend?" Mari rambled as the door was closed.

Nicholas ran to the driver's side, quickly entered, and started the car. Mari heard all of this while the side of her head was pressed against the passenger side window as she slumped over in her seat.

"Goldy, I don't know what's gotten into you, but I have no idea what has happened to Rebecca... I'm going to take you home."

"I have no home," Mari whispered.

Nicholas reached over, put his hand on her lap, let it linger there squeezing at her thigh.

"Have you forgotten the home that I put you in?" he asked as he drove out of the parking lot and onto the road headed in the direction of the condo he was referring to.

"That's not a home. Especially not without Rebby and Sebastian."

"Rebby *and...* What's going on, Goldy? What happened?"

"Rebby, she came home all fucked up that first morning that I called you to ask you where she was. One of your fucking clients. He beat the shit out of her."

"Come on now. You know that's not how it went. Whatever happened with her was agreed upon in advance. And she was paid well for it."

Mari raised her head from the glass of the window, turned to look at Nicholas who alternated his glances between her and the road.

"They don't always stick to what's agreed to. Don't act like you don't know that."

"What happened to Sebastian?" he said, ignoring Mari's accusation.

"Nothing... yet... But he'll be gone soon, too. We've been fighting for a while."

"What about?"

"About *you*! About whether you'll ever let me quit."

Nicholas said nothing to that. He seemed to ponder her words as they turned north onto Black Mountain Road.

After several wordless minutes during which neither of the occupants of the car saw another vehicle travelling in either direction, Nicholas finally asked:

"Is quitting what you want to do?"

"Yes," Mari said without pause. She was surprised by the question and leapt upon it as though worried that if she didn't the opportunity to address it would scamper away. "After seeing Rebby the way she was... I can't do this anymore."

Another wordless minute passed. No music played in the car; the only sounds that filled it were their breathing and Mari's beating heart. A heart that sank – a feeling of bitter confirmation – when she heard Nicholas' response.

"It's not that I won't let you quit. I don't own you, Goldy. It isn't like that. But I need you to stay on. Not forever, just for a bit longer. I have clients who cannot wait to see you. And with Rebby now gone – if she *is* actually gone – I can't risk having my clients believe that I can't hang on to my employees. Especially two of their favorites."

"How long?" Mari whispered as she looked out at the unlit road. They were halfway to the condo, though she knew they would never reach there. She could already see the point where they would stop. "How long will I have to keep doing this?"

"How about we revisit this in... three months? I have appointments booked for you all the way until October. We can see if you still feel this way then. Just not quite yet, okay?" He patted her on the lap, then let his hand linger there again, his fingers first caressing her, then groping, treating her thigh like dough in need of kneading. He was unable to resist touching her, taking advantage of her, even in her apparent drunken distress.

And there it was, the proof they needed. He wouldn't simply let her quit. It would be "Not quite yet" and requests to "Revisit this" in the future each time she asked. And when he finally tired of her asking, he would retire her himself. Permanently. Harrison had been right.

Ahead of them were two blinking lights along the east side of the road. The lights were obvious to Mari, who had been looking out for them, but not so clear to someone who was only partially concentrating as he drove.

"Let me out," Mari said, her voice still sounding thick and slurred.

"I told you, three months, then we revisit the issue, okay?"

"No, I mean let me out now. Right here. That's my car up there."

"Your car?" Only then did he take his focus – and his hand – from her and look ahead into the darkness at the two flashing lights growing larger with each revolution of his wheels. Wheels that began to revolve less frequently as they slowed, crawled, eventually stopped twenty feet behind the vehicle with its hazard lights on as Nicholas pulled over to the shoulder of the road. "Why on Earth would you leave your car here? Goldy, did you drive this thing, drunk as you are?"

She sat upright in her seat for the first time since entering the burgundy sedan. Her voice, when she spoke, was crystal clear.

"I didn't drive it. I'm not drunk. And I'm not working for you anymore."

Before he could react, she reached across him, grabbed the key in the ignition, twisted, turned the car off, pulled the keys out, then flew back in her seat away from him until her body was against the door.

"Goldy? What the f–"

From behind him, hands.

Two of them.

The two hands, covered in latex, were moonlight white, contrasting against the gloom of the car, the gloom of the outside world. Between those two hands was a mundane thing. Ordinarily. But, on this night, for this purpose, between those hands was a thing of great consequence.

Normally, it was only the drawstring of a hooded sweater. Tonight, removed from that sweater, repurposed, wrapped around those two gloved fists, stretched between them as taut as was possible without it tearing in two, it was a garrotte. A murder weapon.

Mari watched as those hands, with that rope, reached from the back seat to the front. Watched, her hands at her mouth, as the rope came up and over the driver's seat, the driver's head, in front of the driver's face, beneath his chin.

Then those two hands wrenched back, went to wrap the rope around Nicholas' throat.

But he was quick.

Before the makeshift garrotte could make contact with his Adam's apple, he managed to get five fingers – three on his right hand, two on his left – between the rope and the flesh of his neck.

He was thrashing against the hands which were attempting to snuff his life. Bucking wildly in the driver's seat, his thighs crashing against the steering wheel. This might have been their saving grace, the fact that he was constricted. Because, if not for the confines of the vehicle, this grown man would surely have reached behind him, grabbed Harry, and made short work of the young man barely out of boyhood.

Mari could see him twisting in his seat, his legs making their way from beneath the wheel, his body turning in an attempt to get to the backseat, to get to Harry.

But Mari's part in this plan wasn't only to lure Nicholas to this place and witness what was occurring. She was there to help in case things got out of hand, as they were about to.

"Hold on, Harry!"

She reached into her pocket, felt her uncle's switch blade, an item once meant to end her, now one that she hoped would save her and Harry. Harry who was currently playing the role of a desperate rodeo rider struggling to stay astride a bucking bull.

"No," Nicholas said, the word a muffled grunt as a rope and five of his fingers all converged on his throat.

She pulled the knife out.

"You don't want to do this!" he insisted, looking at her as he struggled, panic in his eyes.

Yes, I do.

"It doesn't have to be this way!" he protested. Begged.

She flipped the knife open.

"I know powerful people! They won't let you get away with this!" The words were a series of desperate gasps.

"If they were so powerful, you wouldn't be about to die," Mari replied, then she plunged the knife into his chest.

His hands went to stop her, moving from the rope at his neck. Seeing his opportunity, Harry wrenched back harder on the string. Turned those gasps into groans, those words into meaningless noise.

Nicholas looked frantically at Mari, spittle on his lips and chin, his eyes bulging, the whites of them cutting through the dark. The whites of them turning red as tears emerged, as blood vessels burst, as life left him.

She pulled the knife out of him with an effort. Blood left him as the blade did. Spurts of it wetting her hand, wetting the steering wheel and dashboard; spatter reddening the windshield.

She stabbed him again, stabbed him several more times, turning everything directly in front of the man being murdered red. All the while Harrison continued to pull as hard as he could on the rope. They did this – the stabbing, the strangling – until there was no more awareness in those eyes. No more life left inside that body.

Whether he died from the rope or the knife, neither of them could know, they were simply content with the fact that he was dead.

His eyes stared sightlessly, soullessly at Mari. While there was no longer life in them, she still saw in those eyes Nicholas' final warning:

I know powerful people. They won't let you get away with this.

"Do you think he was telling the truth? Do you think whoever he knows will come after us?" Mari asked Harry. Both of them were breathing heavily, Harry was still strangling a bleeding corpse, making sure every ounce of soul was squeezed out of it. After hearing her question, he loosened his grip on the rope. Fell backward in his seat, exasperated. Panting out the words, he said,

"Nothing we can do about that now. All we can do is stick to the plan."

CHAPTER THIRTY-NINE

Beautiful

"It's kind of beautiful, don't you think?" Harry said to Mari as they stood and watched the burgundy sedan burn from twenty feet away. His hand in hers, hers entwined with his, both hands drenched in blood.

"Not just kind of, it is," she replied, feeling the heat of the inferno they had started even at this distance.

After murdering her former boss, they had raced to their car, gotten a Jerry can of gasoline from the trunk, doused the corpse, and doused his car. Mari had been the one to light the match.

"I think Rebby would have appreciated it," Harry said.

"I think so too," was Mari's reply.

She gently let go of his hand, indication that it was time to go. After cleaning up with a towel in the trunk, the two walked toward their respective seats, Harrison the driver.

Before Mari entered the vehicle, she turned and bit her thumb as she looked at the burning sedan. She thought Rebby would have appreciated that, too.

They drove, first west, then north. Where would the roads they travelled lead? Neither of them knew for sure. They only vowed to go somewhere better. Anywhere that wasn't here.

All they knew with certainty was that, wherever they went, whatever the future had in store for them, they would never allow themselves to be manipulated or controlled ever again.

EPILOGUE

The Meeting

Everything they had gone through had brought them here. To Helping Hand Headquarters. To these doors, to this moment.

"Here we go," Mari said after a deep breath and a long exhale. She looked over at Harry, who was still smiling encouragingly but was giving off that air of nervousness he got when he had to speak to more than one person at a time.

She reached out her hand, grabbed his, gave it a squeeze. Then, for reasons she couldn't explain, she said,

"You think Rebby would be proud of us?"

Harry looked surprised. They didn't talk about Rebby often, hadn't brought up her name in years.

"Of course. I only wish she was still around to share this with us."

They parted hands and took a step toward the large oak double doors leading to the ninth-floor conference room. Mari raised her hand to knock but never did her knuckles meet the door. Because it opened, as though the people on the other side had been watching them and knew they were ready to enter. Ready to start the meeting.

"Good morning, Wendelkens!" said the person holding the door open for them, a slender woman who Mari would have guessed was Hispanic. She wore a gray pantsuit, had black hair, wore glasses with thick black frames. A black clipboard sat in the crook of her left arm as she hugged it against her chest. "Nice to finally meet you! I'm Santana Tenn, The Assistant."

She gestured them into a sterile looking board room. Beige walls surrounded a large, dark conference table around which four people sat; behind which one person stood.

Santana Tenn didn't say whose assistant she was, and never had any of the times they had spoken to her over the phone. But that didn't matter now, because she was introducing them to the people around the table, any of whom could be her employer, all of whom were likely higher on the Helping Hand totem pole than she was.

"This is Dr. Sundra Lucroy, clinical psychiatrist..."

The Assistant went on to list Dr. Lucroy's accolades. Her education in child and adolescent psychiatry, her years of clinical practice with both children and adults, her dedication to ensuring that the children they were set to save would wind up in the right hands. Helping Hands.

The woman herself looked kindly enough. She was approaching middle age, had blue eyes, and her blonde curls were piled atop her head in a high bun. She wore a purple blazer with thick shoulder pads that had gone out of style over a decade prior. She smiled at Mari and Harry as the two stood in front of the room while Santana, The Assistant, continued her introductions.

She next turned to the two men at the table. The man closest to them was tall with dark blond hair slicked back from his forehead. He wore a white shirt with a tie that was two tones of blue.

"This is Turner Shaw, he is chairman of the board of Helping Hand for Humanity's Child and Youth division. He'll be overseeing this project along with ..." She turned to the man at the head of the table, extended her hand toward him, "...Mr. Raynaud Bedard, our primary investor."

He had thick brown hair that was a mix between wavy and curly, his face was lightly bearded. He appeared to be in his early forties and wore the odd combination of a leather jacket and sunglasses while indoors.

"...And this is our intern, Elareen."

Mari nodded curtly at Mr. Bedard then at the young woman to his right who had been introduced to them with a single name. She was much younger than the rest of them, perhaps in her early twenties, had pale brown skin, and was attractive in an unconventional way, her features sharp and pointed. Thick, black hair framed her face, falling past her shoulders. Shoulders which were covered with a floral-patterned scarf.

While Raynaud smiled and nodded enthusiastically, the young Elareen did not return Mari's gesture. She only watched and observed, her thin lips pressed together, the expression on her face a mix between rage and resignation. She didn't look happy to be there, and that caused disquiet within Mari.

It made sense that the young woman was there, Mari reasoned to herself. Elareen the intern might have been a street youth once upon a time, now volunteering to make sure this program would help girls like her avoid walking around with expressions on their faces such as the one she currently sported.

"Everyone, these are the Wendelkens."

But everyone hadn't been introduced to them. There remained the man standing behind the conference table, not quite leaning against the wall. Mari looked at him; a white man, tall with a bald head. His expression was stoic, unreadable. But the familiarity of his face, now that she focused on it, was unmistakable.

She turned to Harry to see if there was recognition in his eyes. And there was. It was written all over his countenance. Worry was there as well. She tried to hide her expression more carefully.

It might have been a coincidence. He might not have recognized them. He had only seen them a handful of times.

Standing against the back wall was the man who had been introduced to them nearly a decade ago simply as Jared, Nicholas' personal security guard.

293

It couldn't actually be him, Mari told herself. Just another tall white guy with a shaved head. There were thousands of men who looked like him all over the place.

When The Assistant noticed Mari's focus on the man, she said, almost dismissively, "Oh, that is Jared, Mr. Bedard's security."

"Do your business proposal meetings always require security?" Harry asked The Assistant, locking eyes with Jared. Jared showed no sign that he recognized the two of them. It had been years since they had last seen him. They'd only been children then. And each time they had encountered him, it was briefly.

It was Mr. Bedard and not Santana who answered Harry's question. And when he did, his voice chilled Mari to her core.

"These meetings tend to get a bit excitable from my experience," Raynaud said with a chuckle. Turner Shaw, Dr. Lucroy and The Assistant all laughed as well. Elareen and the security guard behind Bedard made no effort to join them.

Mari was as far from laughter as she could get. Because that voice, Mr. Bedard's French accent, reminded her of Nicholas. But while Nicholas' accent had been faint, Raynaud's was thick, English clearly being his second language. Each of his words seemed to be carefully thought of and selected before being said.

A coincidence. Only a coincidence.

"Do you have your presentation material? I'll get the computer and projector set up for you," The Assistant said, extending her hand toward Mari. Mari looked at her carefully, suddenly wondering if she could trust the smile on that face.

Mari nodded, gave Harry another quick, worried glance, which he returned. He noticed it, too. There was something odd about this. Something unsettling. She handed the CD with her PowerPoint presentation on it to Santana Tenn nonetheless. They were here, they might as well put their best foot forward. If there was something untoward going on here, they would find out eventually.

"Finally, the Wendelkens! I have heard so much about you, it feels as if I know you!" said Raynaud Bedard when the room had gone quiet.

"Thank you for the warm welcome, Mr. Bedard," Mari said, trying to refocus on the meeting while doing her best to ignore the fact that there was someone in the room who might recognize them as the people who had vanished immediately after his boss was found dead, burned to a crisp in a vehicle that had been headed toward their apartment.

They had been lazy then, she knew now. They should have gotten rid of Nicholas' body entirely. The same way they had Rebby's. But they had been angry, and had wanted to do what? Make a point? Express their fury? She rued their decision now, though deep down she knew that it wouldn't have mattered. Whether he had vanished or was found burned, his being gone would have raised suspicions. The two still would have had to flee.

She wished she had heard as much about Raynaud Bedard as he seemed to have heard about them. Intimate knowledge of his past would have helped with her present paranoia. All she knew of the man was that he was a business magnate and philanthropist who hailed from Montreal, Quebec, Canada, but had interests all over the globe. He was on the board of directors of Helping Hand, and – through The Assistant – had been the one to reach out to connect the Wendelkens with Helping Hand for Humanity. To offer the generous amount that would help to bring their dreams into reality.

"Okay, your presentation is up and running. Start whenever you're ready!" The Assistant said cheerfully from

Mari's left, outside her field of vision, before she came around and sat at the board table to the right of Dr. Lucroy.

Mari saw that all eyes had shifted from her and Harry to the projector screen behind them. She turned to look as well, saw that the logo Harry had designed for their foundation was there; orange and blue bubble letters – almost comic-like – spelling *FYI* with a little exclamation point after it.

She turned from the projector and began her speech. As she did so, she saw The Assistant raise a small remote control in her hand and point it in the direction of the computer her presentation was playing from. Mari would have liked to have the clicker to control the pace of her slides, but she supposed it didn't matter. The Santana woman had the air of someone who very much enjoyed being in control as much as possible.

"Thank you for having us here. As you know from our proposal, Harry and I would like to expand our foundation, the Future of Youth Initiative. Currently we are..."

Mari started the presentation. The two went on to explain their five-year plan, ten-year plan, their goal to perpetually help children all over the country, then the continent, and, hopefully, one day, the world. After ten minutes of talking and signalling to Santana to switch each slide when needed, Mari finished with a summary.

"... in the end, it will be a multi-pronged approach to helping curb the problem of youth homelessness. Not only through group homes, foster homes, and shelters, but through access to opportunities like the businesses we plan to open that will employ youth without a stable home, the first of which will be Foster's Family Restaurant. Each of these businesses will be essential in sustainably financing several scholarship funds for the youth in perpetuity while still producing a healthy profit for our investors and board members." She made sure to look each person in the room in the eye as she came to the conclusion of their presentation. "Thank you all for your time, and for the opportunity."

She expected immediate applause, then waited for it. Then looked over at Harry when it didn't happen at all. Did they do something wrong?

"Your presentation, Wendelkens, it doesn't appear to be over," said Raynaud Bedard. It was then that Mari saw The Assistant raise the remote in her hand and click it once more, despite the fact that there were no more slides to be shown.

"Ah yes, these are the behind the scenes details I wish we could get with every proposal," the French Canadian said, a smile on his face that Mari didn't like the look of.

Just like Nicholas'.

She saw similar expressions on the faces of Santana Tenn and Dr. Sundra Lucroy.

"Oh fuck," she heard Harry whisper from beside her. And even then she didn't want to turn, didn't want to see something she already understood would be their undoing. But she did. She turned. And, as she expected, on the screen was their personal apocalypse.

On the screen, playing, was a colorless video.

A bathroom.

A perspective from the ceiling, as if a hidden camera had been placed there. Which, of course, it had.

In the bathroom, on the video, were two people. And one corpse.

What they were looking at was a bird's eye view of a young man sawing pieces from a headless body in a tub. A young woman taking those pieces and wrapping them in portions of garbage bag before taping them up, placing them gently on towels which were laid out on the floor.

Mari's mouth was open, it was moving soundlessly. There were words in her mind she might have said aloud if not for the severity of her shock, two of them on repeat:

How? How? How?

No. No. No.

This was supposed to be a great day. It was supposed to be *the* day. The day they would get the break they had been waiting for and working toward for all these years.

"Next slide please, Ms. Tenn."

Mari nearly jumped at the sound of the accented voice. The room had been so quiet, she had been so stunned, that Mr. Bedard's sentence accelerated a heart that already felt as though it was heading toward bursting.

The next slide was the head of Rebby Greene. Not as it was when they had removed it from her torso, but a headshot, from picture day at her high school. It looked like it might have been taken the year they'd met her. In the photo, she was as beautiful as she had ever been, and Mari nearly wept at the sight of her. In all the years since her death, when Mari thought of Rebby, she pictured bruises and scars, bits and pieces. Had nearly forgotten the face of this perfect looking person pictured in the projection.

Above Rebby's smiling face was the word **MISSING**. Beneath it was her name, big and bold. Beneath that was information on who to contact if she was found.

Mari had never seen this poster. By the time anyone would have even realized Rebby was missing, they had been in Seattle, nearly a hundred thousand dollars richer, their new lives already begun.

"Next slide please, Ms. Tenn."

This time she didn't flinch at the sound of his voice, but she had begun to shake, to tremor at the thought of more. She felt Harry's hand take hers as she stared at the projector screen.

The next image was of the two of them and Rebby embracing in the condo hallway on the day Mari had found their old friend waiting at the library.

Another slide appeared. This one was of the three of them watching TV on the couch. Then a photo of them on the balcony. The entire condo had been under surveillance. Because Nicholas had liked to watch.

As she looked at these images, Mari's stomach sank with the realization of what this meant. This group, they had videos of Mari with the clients who had come to their apartment to use both her and the Room of Mirrors. Not to mention those of her and Harry. Dozens of amateur porn films was what those amounted to.

How long had Nicholas been spreading videos of her, still a teenager at the time, to his clients? The internet hadn't yet caught on back in those days, but it would only take minutes for those videos to be put all over the web now, if that's what this group of people in the room with them wanted. Even without the evidence of their disposal of Rebby's body, this group that was not a helping hand at all had the power to ruin them.

"Next slide..."

Mariam grimaced at the sight of the next image. It was of her Uncle Rob. A photo of him in the top left corner of a news article. The headline: **DENVER MAN VICTIM OF FATAL HIT AND RUN, POLICE STILL WITHOUT SUSPECTS**.

"The police may not have suspects, but we do," Bedard said. This was followed by laughter from most of the people who flanked him. "Next slide, Ms. Tenn."

It was a photo of Nicholas. But that wasn't what made Mariam's eyes bulge. It wasn't seeing her former boss that made her hands go to her face to cover her open mouth. What caused her reaction was the fact that Nicholas wasn't alone in the photo. Beside him, an arm wrapped round his waist as the two men embraced, posing for the camera, was Raynaud Bedard.

The slide changed. On the screen was another news article, this one from the city of Black Mountain, detailing the discovery of the burnt remains of a business owner in his smoldering car at the side of Black Mountain Road. Police suspected foul play, according to the article.

Mari whirled around to face the conference table and those sitting around it. She could sense that Harry had done the same beside her. Before either of them could ask, Raynaud answered.

"My nephew, Niko." Then he said no more.

The Assistant put the remote down on the table. Everyone in the room simply sat there and watched the Wendelkens.

"What do you want?" It was Harry who finally spoke.

"The same thing you want," replied Bedard. "We want you to have your foundation, your businesses, especially that family restaurant. They all sound like wonderful ideas. We want you to take youth off the street and bring focus to their lives. Give them a different Lifestyle. All we ask is that you allow us to have certain... influences over each of your ventures. And that you assist us in a project of our own."

Mari looked over at Harry. His face was pink except for his scar, which was white. He wore a skeptical expression. Trepidation and fear were there on his face as well.

She desperately wished she had her old switchblade. But when she looked over at Jared, now standing at attention behind his boss, she had a feeling that using a knife, or any other attempt at violence, would do them no good here.

"What's the catch? You tell us that you think we... we had something to do with whatever it is you just showed us... with your nephew... And you still want to go ahead with our proposal?"

"Of course! Business is business. And we have waited for some time for *you* to be ready to hear *our* proposal."

How long had they known? If they had the surveillance of what Mari and Harry had done to Rebby, then they must have known for years. But something wasn't adding up.

"W-why?" Mari asked, struggling to find her voice. "Why did he let me in his car if he knew what happened to Rebby?"

"He must not have known." This time it was The Assistant who spoke. "We imagine that he didn't check the surveillance regularly. We only happened upon it when we learned the news of his death and began investigating what might have happened to him."

"So, you've known for years..." Harry stated, sounding mystified. A whisper from a winded man.

"We tracked you down in Seattle within weeks of my nephew's death. I went for you myself. But the two of you, you impressed us. We expected a pair of junkies we would have no use for. But she had already enrolled in school, and he was already promoting his board game.

"I wanted to see what would become of you. How you could be useful to us one day in the future. And now you are, with your beautiful little foundation and bright ideas that will no doubt make a great deal of money. Money that your calculations do not come close to predicting. This business we will do outweighs the ugly business you did to Niko," Bedard stated. Then added, almost as an afterthought, "My nephew was not particularly careful, I must admit. His operation in Black Mountain, much of it was rogue. On his own without permission." Bedard shrugged as though being murdered and burned to a crisp was the inevitable outcome of his nephew's transgressions.

"But we are not only interested in your business, Mrs. Wendelken," Bedard went on. "Mr. Wendelken, your game, we will back it. HH Games will take care of everything. We will distribute and promote it worldwide. Not only that, but we will develop a... how do you say?... *online* game to go along with it. And haven't you written a book based on the characters of your game? Helping Hand Publishing will take care of that. And, who knows, perhaps a movie some day!"

"What do you want from us, really?" Mari said, not enjoying the desperate tone her voice was taking. In all their time together, after all they had done, she had never felt this way. Trapped. As though they were at an end. She had felt worried each time they'd run to a new city, but that worry had dissipated over months and years, until she eventually truly believed they would never be found out.

Now, here they were, two fish on the end of one massive hook, their dreams the bait that had caused them to be caught. Their chasing of a better future what had brought them to this present doom.

"Next slide, Ms. Tenn."

Mari and Harry turned to see a sprawling modern farmhouse surrounded by an expanse of woodland.

"Your headquarters," said Bedard. "Property we acquired in Colorado, not too far from Black Mountain. An absolutely gorgeous state of the art home where you will run all of your businesses from. And beneath it..." he pointed to Santana Tenn. She clicked to the next slide "...is where you will operate *our* business."

"And what business is that?" Harry asked sounding as confused as Mari felt as she looked at an image of a living room.

At first, she thought it was the interior of the farmhouse. And in a sense, it was. After giving the couple the chance to look at the furniture, the treadmill, the television and VCR, and the cabinet which enclosed them, Santana clicked to a picture of a different perspective that made things clear to Mari. One that showed the ladder which was drilled into the wall, the hatch it led to. Mari understood she was looking at what was beneath the house that was being offered to them.

She was looking at a bunker.

"Think of it as a social experiment." Bedard called for another slide and one appeared.

In this latest photo were three little white girls, two brunettes and a blond. The eldest couldn't have been more than three years old. The youngest looked as though she had only recently escaped the womb.

"No. We had nothing to do with them," Mari blurted out before realizing that denying any connection to whoever these children were meant she acknowledged having knowledge of what happened to everyone else who had shown up on the screen before them. Not that it mattered. With the video of them disposing of Rebby, this group had Mari and Harry dead to rights.

"We know," replied Bedard. "It's what we want you to do with them that matters."

"We're not hurting children," Harrison said sternly. Mari nodded in agreement.

"Good! We wouldn't want you to hurt them, valuable as they are. What we are asking is that you keep them healthy, keep them fit, and keep them away from the world... Previous slide please."

The image of the bunker reappeared on the screen.

"Down there. That is where you will raise them."

"Why?" Mari asked. "To what end?"

Bedard answered, though it wasn't Mari who he spoke to when he did so. Because it wasn't Mari who would play the largest role in the madness this group had planned.

"When they are old enough, Mr. Wendelken. We want you to breed them. And we will pay you handsomely for each child that you produce."

Piece #4

Rope

A Novella

PART ONE

BANG
BANG
BANG

CHAPTER 1

Harrison pulled the trigger even as she spoke.

Bang!

She wasn't expecting it. Had no idea what was happening to her.

Bang!

A second shot as she was falling onto the snowy forest floor.

He was standing over her by the time she hit the ground. He looked down at her and was surprised to find that she was not dead but was looking up at him.

Her eyes seemed far too alert. He saw too much awareness in them. What he also saw in her eyes was confusion, uncertainty, a question:

Why are you doing this to me?

He couldn't give her an answer, not one she would understand. Not one that would matter at this point.

He aimed the gun at the young woman he had named Aurora. Saw a wife, a daughter, a mother to children he had never claimed as his own. He saw a young woman who would not have needed to be murdered had she not been so headstrong. So insistent. He saw, as he pointed his gun at a person who hadn't had a clue she was going to be shot before it happened, someone who was at fault.

In his mind, he was looking down at the person who was to blame for all of this.

He aimed at her chest, went to pull the trigger.

Reconsidered when he saw the fire still in her eyes. Instead of her torso, he aimed the gun at her head. He did not want to have to take a fourth shot.

"I truly am sorry."

He pulled the trigger.

Bang!

But did so at the exact moment he heard the barking of a dog. A sound that threw him off slightly. He didn't hit her in the middle of the face as he had intended, but he didn't miss either. He saw the blood leaking from the side of her head, saw that her eyes had closed and remained that way. He considered taking a fourth shot just in case, but by then the dog sounded like it was growing more aggressive.

Worse, it sounded like the dog was getting closer.

Worst, it sounded like there was a human calling for this animal, both of them coming his way.

He looked at the body in front of him. Below him. It was now no longer *her*. It was *it*. And it was still and motionless, eyes which had begged and pleaded and questioned still closed. He considered the hole in the ground several yards away, a makeshift grave behind a large spruce tree to his right. In the direction the dog and the man were coming from. In the direction opposite his home.

Fuck, he thought. *No time to bury the body.*

He wondered if he should wait here for the man, ambush him, ambush the dog. Two more bangs before he buried all three. But the only people who travelled these woods were hunters, and he did not want a firefight. Especially after it had taken him three shots to do away with a clueless girl he had shot at point-blank range.

He looked down at the bleeding body. He thought of the life he had been forced to share with this person-who-once-was, the life he and Mari had given her and her sisters. A life he felt he'd had no choice but to take away.

And he resented her for it.

Resented her because she'd made him do this. Begrudged her because he wouldn't have the chance to bury her and go on living as they were. A double life that wasn't ideal, but kept all of them safe. And now that life, much like hers, was over.

He resented her because he would have to flee.

Not only from this body, not only to his home, but from it. He would have to flee from it all. From his life, from everything he had ever known. All because of this bloodied body who had once been someone he'd cared for deeply.

Harrison Wendelken – a man who, along with his only true wife, Mariam, had convinced three young girls to think of him as a warrior, a savior called Beasts' Bane – ran.

He fled from the body, from the approaching hunter and dog. Ran to his home. All the while knowing that he might now be running for years to come.

Might not be able to stop running for the rest of his days.

CHAPTER 2

He had barely made it through the door of his farmhouse before Mariam was in front of him, saying, "Harrison, you're back so soon!" Asking, "How did it go?" Opining aloud, "I really wish we didn't have to do that."

"It might not be the only thing we have to do," he said grimly, gently pushing her by her shoulders further into the house before closing the door behind him.

She had been standing here, looking through the glass portion of the front door, anxiously waiting for him to come back from committing a killing for the last half hour. During that wait, she had realized that it was the first time he'd murdered someone without her being right there with him.

Mariam Wendelken (formerly Mariam Goldbraithe, and Aunt Goldy to those other wives of his) was the first of his four wives. Three wives, if you considered the bloody divorce he had just gone through in the woods.

She was the first, and the only one he was legally wed to. The only one of the four he planned to take with him from this beautiful house that had not only been their home but had been the location of one of the strangest projects ever undertaken. A project they would have to abandon along with their home.

She looked at the man she had wed over twenty years prior, when they were barely adults. The two had married not long after murdering a man and leaving his corpse and car to burn on the side of the road in a town called Black Mountain.

They had known each other since they were both fourteen-year-old kids, lost in the world. They had watched each other age over the years, allowed time to run its course, but never had Mari felt as old as she did on this day, right now, after losing sleep over what they had decided must be done with Aurora, his other wife. The one bleeding on the forest floor.

"What do you mean?" she responded, nervously, uncertainly. She wasn't sure how to gauge this man freshly returned from murder. It had been so long since they'd had to kill. She'd thought those days were behind them. Had hoped desperately for that to be the case. But Aurora just hadn't been able to let go of the idea of leaving the safety of the bunker. Of living out the illusion they had built for her and her sisters. Of heading to some mythical safe zone in order to save a world not in need of saving.

Mariam had loved the girl because she was headstrong. And a part of her hated the girl now for that same reason. Hated more the fact that they'd had to hurt her.

They had promised each other that wouldn't be the case. Had declared to their employers that they wouldn't hurt the kids they had been put in charge of. Now Aurora had made liars of them both.

Mariam's main concern at the moment was to make sure they didn't fail the other two girls. To keep them safe for as long as this project she and Harrison had been placed in charge of lasted. She couldn't bear the idea of going through this again.

"We have to go. There was a hunter and a dog. An–"

"Jesus! Did someone see you?" she asked, clutching at her rose-colored robe, tightening it around her chest as though she had suddenly realized she was partially exposed and in the midst of strangers.

"They didn't see me, thankfully. But they heard me. And I had to take off before I could bury the body. They'll see her there and it won't take long before the police come knocking. This is the only house within miles. If they start snooping around and find the hatch..."

"My God..."

315

"I think... I think we have to kill the other two. Then leave," he said, referring to his other surviving wives, Aurora's bunker sisters. He spoke of their execution matter-of-factly, though not eagerly. He spoke of two more murders like a man tasked with doing his least favorite chore.

"No! Jesus, Harrison! They're both pregnant!"

"Don't I fucking know it. You think I haven't thought about what will happen if we don't produce those babies? And who do you think's going to have to break that piece of bad news to *her*? She's expecting Jazzy's baby in two fucking months!"

This new concern winded her, the fear of it like a fist crashing into her solar plexus. She leaned against the hallway wall contemplating what this would mean for them.

She hadn't thought about having to deal with their business associate if things went wrong, because she hadn't thought things would go wrong. Not after nearly two decades of this operation running so smoothly. So profitably.

"She'll understand. She has to understand."

"You think someone with the nickname she has is understanding?" he said, referring again to their business associate. More accurately, their handler. The person they would have to call and explain their predicament to. Because, while they could flee from their home and life and the police, there would be no running from this person. Hunting down those who needed to be hunted was part of what she did.

"Whether or not she understands," Harrison continued, "we have an issue downstairs. The police *will* find them. The more they say to the police, the worse things will be for us."

"We've gotten away with quadruple homicide before. This time it'll be quintuple. And this time, you want to do it in a house full of evidence, and proof that we've been here? They'll lock us up for Aurora. They'll gas us if we do what you're saying we should do to her sisters." She looked at him defiantly, an expression somewhere short of anger. Her full lips were pursed, her brow furrowed, her jaw clenched, her eyes searching for reason within his eyes. What she saw there was confusion.

"*Quintuple* homicide? What are you talking about?"

"We killed Aurora; you want to kill Jasmine and Belle, who are both pregnant. They'll count those babies with the rest of them. That's *five people*. They haven't given anyone the chamber in Colorado in a long time, but they'll put us to death once the media hears about the murder of two pregnant teenage girls. We can survive everything else we've done up until now. We can't survive that."

"We won't get caught," he snapped.

"Says everyone who has ever been caught," she retorted instantly.

They both stood there in their foyer, glaring at each other. Both shaky, both unsure. Both angry at the situation they found themselves in, just as they had been when originally forced to live this lie nearly twenty years ago.

After a few seconds she stepped toward him, put her left hand to his right cheek, caressed the scar that ran from that cheek nearly to his hairline.

"Even if we don't get caught, baby, I don't want their blood on my hands. I know we had to do what we had to do with Aurora. She would have stirred up trouble down there and eventually made them doubt everything with all her talk of *imprisonment*. But I still think of those girls as my nieces; my daughters, really. And I don't want to kill them. Not if it's not necessary. And not if it'll only make things worse for us."

Harrison only looked at her, clearly taken aback by her statement. Although the girls called her aunty down in the bunker, and thought of her as their guardian, she never referred to them as her nieces or daughters when speaking to him in private. But that's how she felt about them. She loved those girls deeply even though she had helped to hold them captive for all these years, lying to them the entire time. She knew he cared about them as well, despite having just shot one of them in the woods, and his talk of murdering the others.

How had it come to this?

Everything had been perfectly fine just days ago. As perfectly fine as things could be for two people living double lives. Now each of those lives, all four of them, were over. And they could only hope to have a chance to live once more.

"Okay," Harrison said, "I know what we have to do."

CHAPTER 3

Fifteen minutes after telling Mariam his plan, Harrison was descending the bunker ladder. Mariam was already down there.

From his view into the open living area, he could see that Mariam was holding Belle's hand while Jasmine cowered on the couch. He wouldn't miss hearing that one sniveling all the time, he thought as he jumped down from the ladder.

He could tell from the looks on their faces that Mari had done her part, had come in here crying about her imaginary Oracle showing her a vision of something terrible.

She had changed out of her robe and back into one of her bunker outfits. A shapeless dress that made her look like something out of the 1800s. He had already been wearing what he thought of as his bunker gear – one of the animal-everything outfits that his wives had made him. The clothing was all part of the illusion, part of making sure it all felt genuine and realistic to the girls he and his wife kept underground. He needed their act to feel genuine and realistic now more than ever. Needed for the two surviving sisters to believe, to accept another tall tale. One last little show before he and Mariam left.

Mariam had convinced him that it was best not to murder the girls and their unborn babies. She didn't want their blood on her hands, and neither did he. But, to Harrison, it was an Us or Them sort of situation. And hands, at some point, would have to get bloody, if only to prevent his remaining bunker wives from ever testifying against them. He only hoped to make it so those bloody hands wouldn't be his and Mariam's.

As soon as he landed in the bunker, Belle and Mariam began asking him questions – about what was going on up there, about what had happened to their fellow wife.

"Bonkos," he said. It was the made-up acronym he had used to describe the made-up creatures they had been telling these girls had taken over the Earth for the last sixteen years. It stood for Beasts of No Known Origin, and it was also the name he had given to the evil creatures in his board game *A World of Beasts*. He had been able to live out his game, his lifelong fantasy, for years, using the details from it to control the girls. To keep them prisoners without them realizing they were imprisoned. That was until those same details had caused Aurora to want to leave and had subsequently ruined all their lives.

"There were more of them than I could manage," Harry continued. "They fell on us. In a blink we were swarmed! Aurora, that beautiful, stubborn girl, she saved me. She threw herself at them before I knew what was happening. She screamed for me go back as she did it. The last thing she said to me…" He put a fist to his mouth and bit on it, wanting to clearly display his emotions. Wanted the sisters – Belle especially – to see that he was despondent and truly desperate due to what had happened on the surface. "…The last thing she said to me was to protect the two of you. Which is what Goldy and I now have to do."

"Has it truly come to this?" Mariam asked forlornly, playing her role of the worried guardian.

Along with the made-up world above, the husband and wife had given themselves made up names and back stories. She was Marigold Capulet, though she was only referred to as Goldy, the semi-psychic in constant communication with the Oracle who was meant to help them save the world. He was Sebastian Beasts' Bane, a great warrior and slayer of Bonkos. The man responsible for building this place and saving them all from the Beastly invasion.

Mariam was a great actress, Harrison thought as he watched the woman he had been with for twenty-seven of his forty-one years. It was Mariam who had done the majority of the work taking care of the girls in the bunker. Mariam who had fielded most of their questions about this grand illusion they had been fed since they were babies. But on this occasion, he could tell she wasn't acting. And, other than the lies he was telling, he wasn't doing much acting either. He was just as worried as Mariam and the girls were about the world crumbling down around them all.

Everything had been going smoothly for so long. Now their lives were ruined all because Aurora hadn't left well enough alone. He almost wished he could have shot her a fourth time just then with how angry he still was at her. At her disobedience. But what he really wished was that he hadn't had to shoot her at all.

All three girls could have lived down here happily for decades to come. It could have been so peaceful, so easy, so profitable. But now they were going to have to take their stash of emergency cash and run, leaving the millions of dollars they had in the banks and tied up in several investments to the authorities. And – he looked at Jasmine there on the couch – they would have to leave behind a baby that was two months away from adding another two hundred and fifty thousand dollars to their coffers.

There was a baby in Belle as well. She wasn't nearly as far along as her younger sister, but that was still another quarter million they would be leaving behind.

It was this he thought of – the loss of money and the potential loss of freedom that would accompany it – when he approached Belle and embraced her as she knelt there on the ground believing that Beasts that didn't exist other than in their imaginations were coming to claim her and her sister. To destroy everyone she had ever cared about.

He knelt beside her and caringly, lovingly, told her more lies meant to scare her and her sister further.

"If we don't come back, we need you to be brave, Belle." He reached down and removed an object from his gear. Something that had been holstered to his leg. It was metal. It was dangerous. He aimed his hunting knife in her direction.

And for a moment he considered plunging it into her neck. It would be messy, but it would be quick.

Then he imagined turning the blade on Jasmine, whose sniveling was annoying him even now. He could slit her throat, and he and Mariam could cut the baby out of her. People did it all the time with babies that weren't as far along as hers was. It could work. And it would help soften the blow of having to inform their business partner that their operation was over. The baby would be a parting gift. One that might diminish the backlash they were due to face. One that might prevent the punishment he was worried he and Mari would inevitably have to deal with.

Or forever run from.

But his wife was right. Even if he truly were capable of committing these acts, there was no time, and it would only bring them more trouble. Their business partner and her associates would like that even less.

Instead of committing quadruple murder here in the bunker, he said, "Take this," handing Belle the unsheathed hunting knife. Eight inches of sharp serrated steel.

"They may come to drag you from here, the Beasts and their human thralls. If that's the case... If they try to enter here and take you, do not allow them to. Do you understand me?"

She nodded, but he wasn't convinced that she would do it. He had to make sure she understood how high the stakes were. Perhaps not for her, but for him and his true wife.

"Being taken by them is a fate worse than death. Remember that. If they come for you and your sister, *do not* let them take you alive."

And with that he kissed her on the forehead. Rose. Walked to the couch and rubbed Jasmine's back. The girl flinched beneath his touch, then moaned mournfully, refusing to turn her head from the nest she had made for it with her arms. While her theatrics usually aggravated him, Harry appreciated how emotionally erratic she was right now. He thought it might be something that could benefit he and Mariam if the police actually did show up.

Into her ear, he whispered,

"Don't fret, Jazzy. If we don't return, it means we have gone to the Promised Place where so many of our loved ones are. A better world than this. If the Beasts come for you and you have to... put an end to things, just remember that we will be waiting there. We'll see you again one way or another." Then he kissed the back of her unturning head.

He said goodbye to the two girls as he followed Mariam to the ladder. With her leading the way, they scaled it. The two of them climbed up and out into a world which was as uncertain as ever. They left their double life behind, preparing to start an entirely new life. One they hoped wouldn't involve capture, incarceration. Execution.

CHAPTER 4

"I'm going to miss them. Can you believe that?" Mariam said to Harrison as he drove their truck down the long stretch of country road leading from their house toward what he hoped would be a life of anonymity.

He wanted to tell her to stop being ridiculous. He wanted to admonish her because they had far more important things to think about than missing the girls they hadn't wanted anything to do with in the first place. But the truth was, he would miss them too, which was something he wouldn't have thought possible sixteen years ago in the meeting that had changed their lives. When they had been blackmailed into the life – a life full of lies – they had been living since.

He would miss the feeling of having a family, as odd as theirs was. He would miss the feasts they'd had when he would bring rabbits, game birds, or even a deer carcass that he had paid someone to kill and wrap for him into the bunker. He would miss how happy they were each time he descended that bunker ladder. He would miss their innocence, how content they had been with the simple lives they'd led.

But he would also miss them for more selfish reasons.

It wasn't very many men who could say they had four wives, three of whom believed him to be one of the last men on Earth. He had been worshipped in that bunker. He had been Sebastian Beasts' Bane, practically a king. He would certainly miss that.

Now, he was going to have to get used to being a nobody. In fact, his highest hopes were to be a nobody, to find a nothing place where no one would recognize him and Mariam. He looked into the rearview mirror at the scar that ran down his face from his forehead to his beard, passing over his right eye. He was far too recognizable to feel optimistic. Once the police raided their home, his scarred face would be all over the news.

"Yeah, I can believe it. There's a lot I'm going to miss. Including our freedom if we aren't careful."

"What if we didn't have to run?" Mari asked.

It wasn't a question he wanted to ponder. After all they had been through and done, after each time they had successfully run from one tragedy or the next, he wasn't fond of questions that began with "What if…" Things were as they were. All they could do was improve their circumstances going forward. All they could do was sort out a plan and stick to it.

He ignored the question. His attention was turned to the afternoon traffic. He was looking for police cars, listening for sirens, wondering if he was already being chased. But there was no evidence that was the case. "Maybe you overreacted," Mariam pressed on. "Maybe we could have talked to the police if they showed up."

"And said what?" This time he couldn't ignore it. What she was saying was preposterous. And he wanted the conversation she was attempting to have to end. "Should we have said that all the footprints in the snow leading straight from where the body was found back to our house aren't direct evidence of our involvement? Or maybe I could have told them that the hunter who saw me running away from the girl I had just shot was mistaken? 'No officer, you can't search the house. Oh, you'll be back with a warrant? Okay, we'll wait right here…' We'd be arrested within days, if not hours, Mariam. I fucked up, I know it. But don't make it worse by thinking this could've been avoided. We had no choice but to run."

For a few moments, as they made their way through the slowly building traffic, there were no more words between them. The sun was a few hours from setting, and Harrison had no idea just where he was driving to.

"Where are we going?" Mariam asked him.

He seemed to consider the question for the first time.

"I don't know. I just..." He didn't know where he was going, but he knew what he was avoiding. *Who* he was avoiding. And his wife knew it too.

"We have to call her, Harry. The longer we drive around aimlessly, the more likely it is we're going to get caught. We can't just run away; we have to run *to* somewhere and start over. And we can't do that on our own. Not this time."

He didn't want to call their business partner, their handler. He ignored his wife again, continued to drive, his jaw set, his knuckles turning white as he squeezed the wheel. But she would not relent.

"No matter where we go to, they'll find us. She'll make sure to find us personally, you know that! Don't you understand? It's not the police I'm worried about here. If *she* finds us... She'll do to us whatever it is that made people give her that awful nickname."

He continued to drive. Ahead of him was the sign for the freeway onramp heading south. He could stay on the main road or hop on the freeway and keep driving south until he hit the border. Then what? Hide out in Mexico, live in fear of capture and extradition for the rest of their lives?

Or they could head north to Canada and do the same exact thing, only while being considerably colder in the process. Neither sounded ideal, neither sounded like the right choice. He slapped the steering wheel in frustration, causing Mariam to flinch beside him.

"Fuck!" he said. "We got comfortable. We should have planned this out."

"Sixteen years and no problems, baby. Not a single issue. We couldn't have known it would fall apart so quickly. But we can still get out of this. We always have before. Just call her. We've given her and her people seven healthy babies. We've done everything they've asked of us this entire time. All we'd be asking is that they protect us. And really, they'd be protecting themselves."

"You want to tell *her* that? That sounds like a threat to me. And I can't imagine how she would respond to that." The onramp to head south on the freeway approached. He drove past it. Ignored the onramp heading north as well.

"No. We don't have to say that at all. Of course not. But she'll know. It's just common sense. Us getting caught by the police wouldn't benefit anyone. And she'll appreciate us calling rather than trying to run off. We have no choice, Harrison. You know that. They've owned us since we took that fucking meeting all those years ago. And they won't like having to chase after something they own."

He wanted to scream, but he didn't. He turned right instead, down a residential street. Turned right again. A left after that. Drove until he pulled into a small plaza.

From where he was parked, he could see a convenience store, a fried chicken restaurant, and a tailor.

They had driven from their farm and bunker at the northern edge of Boulder, Colorado, and were now in Longmont. They had driven for nearly half an hour without even realizing how much time had passed.

They came to this city often enough, but now Harry found himself in a part of it he didn't recognize. In a world that seemed more unrecognizable with each passing minute.

As he sat back in his seat and prepared to do something that terrified him, he understood that he would likely never get the chance to become more familiar with this town, with the surrounding state. He and Mari might have to part with the country entirely. If things went as they hoped, the person he was about to reach out to would keep them hidden somewhere they would never again be found. Somewhere there would be no returning from.

Mariam watched him anxiously and wordlessly as he sighed, pulled out his mobile phone, connected it to the car's speaker so both of them would be part of the conversation.

Then, on this ruinous afternoon, Harrison Wendelken, the self-styled Bane of Beasts, placed a phone call to their business partner and handler.

A woman named Elareen.

A woman called The Beast in the Night.

CHAPTER 5

"Wendelken," said the calm voice with the accent Harrison had never been able to place. She had answered after one ring. This was how she always greeted them when they called. A statement of their last name followed by, "What can I do for you?"

For a moment they both sat in the truck, not certain how to respond to the voice which had just come through the speakers. They had expected her to pick up their call; she always did. They had expected the question; she always asked it. Yet they were not prepared at all to answer it.

How do you tell someone like this that you not only need help running away from potential murder charges, but that an operation which had been running smoothly and profitably for years was now about to come to a crashing halt.

In the seconds it took for them to think of what to say, Elareen had already figured out something was amiss.

"What has gone wrong?" she asked. Then waited again for them to answer either this question or the last. Mariam answered both.

"We need your help relocating... We had to leave our house, and the bunker. The oldest of the three girls, Aurora, she... she tried to escape, and we had to kill her."

She looked at her husband and potential co-defendant when she said these words. He arched his eyebrows at her when he heard the lie. But he appreciated it. It was far better than the truth he had been ready to divulge. It made them sound less incompetent, even if only slightly.

If Aurora had actually tried to run away, this would have been easier to take. But he couldn't stop kicking himself, internally beating himself up because he hadn't planned things out well enough. Hadn't planned much of anything at all, including the operation they had helped run for most of the last two decades.

He had always told himself he was just a cog, a gear in the machine they had been forced to be a part of, to keep operational. But that mentality had caused them to become complacent, lazy, careless over the years. Had made them feel invincible because of who it was they worked for. They hadn't thought there could be an emergency these people couldn't handle. He had never imagined a scenario such as this.

If they had imagined this, or something even close to this, they would have tried harder to keep Aurora in the bunker when she had asked to leave for the imaginary safe zone they had promised the sisters they would go to once they stopped being able to produce children. Even if she had continued to insist on leaving, they could have said it was forbidden. They could have tried to convince her that the made-up Oracle who lived in the imaginary safe zone and gave them their non-existent directives would not allow it. But Aurora had been agitated since it had become clear she couldn't bear any more children for their cause. She had been a hassle even before she had declared her intent to leave. And he knew she would have become unbearable if she hadn't gotten her way.

He hadn't wanted to deal with it. Hadn't wanted to be bothered by a potentially angry Aurora for another three decades until the others became menopausal or barren for other reasons. He hadn't wanted Aurora to be a corrupting influence in the bunker, causing the other two to perhaps want to leave as well. To question the illusion that he and Mariam had carefully crafted for them.

Harry and Mari had told the girls, as soon as they were old enough to comprehend, that the world outside the bunker had fallen to a Beastly apocalypse. That they were all victims of the end of the world, but that the girls could save the future if only they produced a child that might one day do so. They were made to believe that each child they produced was then taken by Harrison, the man they knew as Sebastian Beasts' Bane, to the safe zone to train to be a Soldier of the Future for the War to Come.

In reality, each child had been given to Elareen and taken God knows where. For purposes Harrison had always been afraid to even ponder.

Now, Harrison felt as though he was going from an imagined apocalypse to a real one. Felt like the world was about to end if it hadn't already. They were currently waiting for words from a beast, real and true. Someone deadlier than any of the imaginary Beasts they had described to the three sisters they had been guardians of.

That someone was currently not responding. Neither Harrison nor Mariam repeated what she had said. Neither checked to see if the call was still connected. They simply sat there, his right hand intwined with her left, and they waited.

This was what Elareen did. Whenever they asked a question she was not fond of answering, she responded with extended silence before anything else. He was certain that she took joy in making people feel discomfort. Though, if she took joy or rage or any other emotion, he had no way of knowing. Her voice, it never changed in tone or inflection. Elareen's face, if he could have seen it as Mariam had made her statement, would not have changed in expression despite the severity of the situation.

She was calm to the point that she inspired the opposite in others.

Eventually, when Mari had begun to tremble and it looked like Harry was on the verge of tears, Elareen's cold, toneless voice came through the speakers.

"The other two girls. What became of them?"

"We left them there. They think the bunker may come under attack. Which it might, if the police show up. But, if the police do show up, the girls will think the war has been lost, and they'll take their own lives the moment they hear that hatch open and see it isn't us."

Silence. Growing discomfort by the second. Mariam squeezed his hand. Harrison began to sweat in at least three places. Thankfully, because the situation was pressing, the silence didn't last as long as it might have otherwise.

"You killed their escaping sister and the girls still believe your lies?"

Damn it, Harrison thought. Now he wished they had told the truth, because he didn't know how to explain how they could have shot a girl trying to get away without arousing suspicion in the others.

He began to speak but stammered. Luckily, Mari was much better at deception than he was. Years of lying in response to the questions of inquisitive children had made her able to think creatively, and quickly.

"She ran out. I got the rifle we keep in the shed not far from the hatch, and I chased her. The two girls stayed in the bunker. They didn't see or hear me chase her down and shoot her. I took my time getting back to them. I made myself look roughed up, like I'd been attacked before going back down there. I told them that both Aurora and I had been attacked by the Beasts, and that she had been killed. They believed it. Then I told them that our location had been compromised because of Aurora, and that Ba– I mean Harrison and I would have to leave to fight off the approaching Beasts. I thought we would just get rid of the body and regroup, and then go on running the operation. But when we got to the body we saw that someone was right there standing over it. A hunter more than likely.

"We figured we'd best leave because the police could have already been on the way by that point. We grabbed what we could and took off... Now we need your help."

There was a pause – only a brief one – before Elareen said,

"Write this down, or commit it to memory. From where you are now, head to..." She proceeded to give them directions to where they had to go. When he realized where she was sending them, Harry fought the urge to decline. He looked at Mari. What he saw on her face was disbelief, hesitation, fear. An expression that said, 'Anywhere in the world but there.'

Elareen was sending them to a location neither of them wanted to go to. A place that terrified them almost as much as she did. But what choice did they have?

"I'm currently in Seattle on business," Elareen said in her cool, detached way of speaking. She almost sounded bored. One would never suspect she had just been informed that her multimillion-dollar operation had come to an abrupt end. Harrison didn't want to imagine what sort of business she might be on.

"I will meet you at the cabin in two days with new passports and identification. I will let you know where you will be moving to when I get there. I'm sure you understand there will be many details to iron out between now and then."

They both nodded to acknowledge that they understood, then looked at each other in mutual embarrassment before they said, "Yes," out loud.

"Good. Go there now. I'll see you as soon as I can. Destroy your phones after this call."

The call disconnected. Elareen had hung up.

Their instructions had been given. If they followed them they would be okay. Or so he hoped.

Finally glad to be able to express a little bit of rage, he took his phone and twisted it in his hands until it shattered. Mariam handed him her phone and he did the same to that device.

"How long do you think she's been tracking us?" he asked.

"What do you mean?" Mariam responded as he began to drive, following the directions that he had committed to memory as Elareen had requested. They now had two damaged cell phones that they would no longer be able to rely on to guide them to where they needed to go. But there was a roadmap in the glove compartment he was now immensely glad he hadn't gotten rid of.

"You didn't notice what Elareen said?" he replied to his wife. "She said, 'From where you are now...' But neither of us told her where we were."

She had no response to that. Harrison was relieved he had listened to his wife and called The Beast in the Night instead of running. Because, from a person like that, there was no escaping.

CHAPTER 6

Harrison couldn't believe they were back on this road again, headed in this direction. A road and a path he and Mari hadn't taken in over twenty years.

"Not much has changed," Mariam said as she looked out of the car. The side of her head was against the windshield of the window, a sign that she was nervous, worried. It was something she had always done whenever she was stressed out.

What Harry saw beyond the windshield was fields, the road they travelled cutting through expanses of snow-covered land.

What he saw beyond the glass, more so than the fields, was a graveyard. One they had created. Somewhere in this stretch of mostly untouched land was a body. In pieces. The corpse of a girl they had both loved, a girl they'd had to cut apart and bury.

They were on Black Mountain Road. On the road to Black Mountain.

They had already passed through the city where they had spent their formative years as homeless youths just trying to survive. And now they were headed north, to a cabin in White Wood Forest at the base of the mountain itself.

It was a place they weren't eager to get to, yet they rushed there nonetheless because it was their only place of refuge.

"I think you spoke too soon," Harry said, astounded by what he was seeing ahead of him. He would have agreed with Mari before spotting it in the distance, miles beyond the edge of the city of Black Mountain.

The road past the outskirts of the town was still sparsely driven, and the fields that shouldered it largely empty. Now though, they were approaching a familiar area made less familiar over the years.

"Wow. It's an entire town now," Mari said, lifting her head from the window and looking straight ahead for the first time in miles.

"Apparently, it's a village," Harry responded, pointing to his right at a sign they were approaching. A sign that read:

WELCOME TO BLACK MOUNTAIN VILLAGE

They could still see the building they had once lived in, not tall, but towering over most of the structures around it. Near it were townhomes, other edifices, entire streets that hadn't been there over twenty years ago when this place had been their home.

The strip of stores was still there, but those few stores had been enveloped by an entire shopping complex. What had been grass and trees and mud, a condo, a few homes, and a small strip mall, was now a community.

It didn't take long for them to drive past the still expanding village. When they were several miles beyond it, they were met by another surprise.

Another new street branched off to the west, to their left. Harry just managed to read the two signs on the post at the top of that new street. One read:

NEW HORIZONS ROAD

The other, larger sign, read:

BETTER BALANCE
MENTAL HEALTH CENTER
2 MILES

Rope

"You know what," Mariam said after they had passed New Horizons Road, "I think I remember hearing something about an asylum being built up here." She shuddered at the thought of a facility like that being so close to the purportedly haunted stretch of woods surrounding the mountain that was still a mystery to most who looked upon it. "You'd have to be crazy to build anything this close to that forest and Hellstone Hill."

Yet they were heading straight toward that forest. In the distance, they could see Black Mountain, Hellstone Hill. A behemoth of a black boulder surrounded by white mountains, the top of it seemingly untouched by the snow that blanketed the rest of the world around it.

They both looked at it, looming, the sun nearly fully set behind it.

Harry fought the urge to make a U-turn, to drive as far away from their destination as they could. Mari resisted the urge to tell him to do exactly that.

Against their better judgement, knowing they had no choice, the two made their way to White Wood Forest at the base of Black Mountain.

CHAPTER 7

"She really undersold it when she said it was a cabin in the woods," Mariam said, looking appreciatively at the lodgings in front of them.

They were now officially on the property of a two-story cottage home, driving down a stretch of road that cut through the birch trees that gave White Wood Forest its name. It was a sight to behold, white trees, white snow. A world that seemed pure and peaceful. And, in the midst of all that white, was their destination. Their little hideaway until Elareen sorted out their escape and relocated them to a new life.

The structure they drove toward was designed in the fashion of a log cabin. A porch made of varnished wood ran across the front of the log and timber frame house. Mariam couldn't help but think of what a wonderful place this would be for a summer gathering. The porch had standing room for two dozen adults with space between them.

Evergreen shrubs topped with snow surrounded the house. From the roof emerged a stone chimney. She was looking forward to the fireplace inside after such a long and dreary drive.

This was far from the cabin she had been expecting. But she should have known their accommodations would be lavish. They had been treated to the best of everything since being coerced into this business partnership with Elareen and her associates.

Since they had been forced to become part of an organization called The Fold.

It was an organization that existed in the shadows of the Helping Hand corporation. Everything Helping Hand was involved with, The Fold was too, conducting their illegal and immoral dealings. Making it so that almost everything Helping Hand touched became corrupt.

Mari and Harry had gone to them as naïve young adults wanting to change the world. Two people whose goal was to save other youth from the dangers they had experienced.

Mariam had brought them many ideas that she had thought would be both profitable and philanthropic. And they had used them. Her series of Mariam's Mission homeless shelters and the FYI – Future of Youth Initiative – group homes were now in half the states in the country, as well as in a few Canadian cities.

Then there was Foster's Family Restaurant, another idea of hers, which was now franchised in five countries, a place that was meant to give teenagers who had been on the street or in the system a chance to make a living, to earn scholarships, to better themselves. Helping Hand had made all of that a reality. And The Fold had bastardized them all.

The shelters, the homes, the restaurants, all of it a front to traffic young boys and girls, to direct children into what members of The Fold referred to simply as The Lifestyle. The exact lifestyle that Mari and Harry had hoped to save these children from. The Lifestyle that had killed their friend and had nearly ruined them entirely.

It burned her to be involved with The Fold. The fact that her name was attached to the places they used to traffic children was a torch to her soul.

At first.

Then, along the way, at some point, Mariam had accepted it. Grown cold to what the reality of the world was. Told herself that, if it hadn't been her ideas used to harm children, it would have been someone else's. She had talked herself into believing that what The Fold was doing to the kids they took from the street was inevitable.

Above all though, she took solace in the fact that, while some of the children who made their way through her organizations were trafficked, most of them were genuinely helped. It wasn't all bad, Mariam had convinced herself over the years.

And, with that rationale in mind, she had begun to enjoy The Lifestyle The Fold had provided her and Harry with. They had become millionaires, just as they had set out to be as teenagers; they had a beautiful home, were well loved by the public. Harry had created a game that brought joy to millions around the world. And a book, and soon, a movie. All about the fictional world of Beasts they had convinced three little girls was real.

It had been tough going at first, being tethered to the bunker for so long while the girls were growing up. Rarely being able to spend time together unless it was down there in their underground shelter. But over the last several years, once the girls had been old enough to take care of themselves, Mari and Harry had made the best of it. Sneaking away for the occasional weekend in Aruba, the South of France, an island or two in the Caribbean. Going to galas, award shows, parties, places where they were often the toast of the town.

It hadn't been an ideal life, but it had been a good one. One where they had wanted for nothing. Now nothing was all they had.

But maybe not, Mari thought, looking at the gorgeous cottage home they were driving toward, knowing it would look even more beautiful in the light of day.

Maybe this was just a brief chapter of their story. If this lovely place was what the hideaway looked like, then their future might not be lacking any of the luxury they had grown accustomed to.

She was deep in thought, thinking about what was next even as they approached what was now, which was why she didn't see what Harry was currently telling her to pay attention to.

"We may not be the only people here," Harry said, his voice a whisper, as though whoever he suspected was around might hear him.

When she looked at him, he gestured to the long driveway in front of them as he stopped two car lengths away from the elaborate porch of their hideaway cabin.

In the beam of the truck's headlights, she looked at what he had gestured to, what he was looking at with an expression of deep concern on his face.

Tire tracks.

Not only were there tire tracks leading all the way to the house but Mariam could see footprints going from those tire tracks up the porch and to the front door.

It had snowed the night before. The footprints must have been made by someone who was here this day.

"Do you think..." Mariam started.

"Someone's waiting to ambush us." Harrison completed her sentence, answered her question.

They both stared ahead at the footprints, not quite knowing what to do. Not knowing if Elareen had lied when she had said she would meet them here in two days. Not knowing if, perhaps, she had sent an associate to meet them right away.

An associate who might be waiting for them, not with any documents, passports, new identities for a new life, but with instruments that would end the lives they were living presently.

CHAPTER 8

"Be careful, Harrison," Mariam said as he went to leave the vehicle, the gun he had used to shoot Aurora and subsequently ruin their lives in his hand.

He nodded. Went to leave the car. Reconsidered. Turned back and kissed her on the lips.

"I love you. I'll be back."

Her eyes shimmered. She nodded.

"You better be. I love you, too," she said. He pecked her again quickly. Before he left the truck, he looked at her, looked at the key in the ignition of the still running vehicle. Said,

"If you hear trouble, if I'm not back... you drive away from here as fast as you can. Drive to Canada before they start looking for us at the border."

Then he turned and hopped out of the truck. He slipped on a slick spot created by the tires of the vehicle which had been there before them. A vehicle which might have left mercenaries here waiting for Harrison and his wife.

He scrambled to find his footing. Found it. Stayed vertical. Even though he was facing potential danger, his first thought was to hope his wife hadn't noticed him nearly fall.

Not a great start at trying to play hero, he told himself before taking a deep breath of cold winter air. He moved toward the porch and front door. Held his gun in front of him the way he had always seen brave people on television do. People on television who he had very little in common with, whether they be cops or criminals. Bravery had never been his strong suit.

Even when he had killed the people he had killed, he had done so from a distance, or from behind the wheel of a car, or from behind the driver's seat inside of a vehicle.

Like he had done with Aurora, he preferred to attack when people weren't looking or when they weren't expecting it. Never had he behaved as the brave warrior he'd pretended to be down in the bunker.

If he had been braver when The Fold had first approached them to run their sick project, he would have said no, even if that likely would have been the end of them.

If he were half the hero he had pretended to be in a bunker full of girls who didn't know any better, he would have accepted the consequences of what he and Mariam had done prior to the meeting.

They could have gone to the police when they'd discovered Rebby's body. They wouldn't have had to dismember their best friend, bury her in several small, unmarked graves in a field in the middle of nowhere. And he wouldn't be walking toward a potential surprise attack now.

Both he and his wife would have been in trouble. They likely would have been locked away for a long while, shunned by society when they were released, but at least they wouldn't have been put in the situation they had found themselves in for the last sixteen years; namely, having to lead double lives. Having to become kidnappers, false imprisoners, traffickers of little human beings.

He wouldn't have had to shoot to death a girl he had cared for as both a wife and a ward.

And now he was having to play hero, a role that seemed foreign to him.

In truth, Mari was the braver of them. Had always been. She was the one who had saved him when Stringbean Todd had been about to carve something foul onto his face. Ever since then, she had been his hero.

She had insisted on coming with him now to inspect for an ambush. Had asked to carry the gun and lead the way, but he had insisted she stay behind in the car. She argued, but he had demanded it of her.

This was his fault. That was what he couldn't stop telling himself. Not only being spotted by the hunter and being forced to run, but their entire situation, the strange and unsettling lives they had wound up living.

It was he who had introduced murder to their lives in the first place. He who had steered them into danger each time Mari had tried to veer away from it. If not for him, they would have left the Sleasy Motel in Central Black Mountain when the man in the burgundy sedan had approached them with his gifts. Mari had wanted to go, Harry had wanted the gifts, not knowing that one of them had been a ruined future.

Now, he was hoping this out of character act of bravery could make up for some of that. Those life altering mistakes. If there was an ambush, if this was the end, then at least Mariam could get away. At least she could have the chance at a happy future she hadn't had since the moment she'd met Harry.

He reached the porch steps, pistol raised and pointed ahead of him as he looked from the door to the footprints in the snow leading to it. Footprints that didn't stop until they seemed to lead through the door and directly into the house.

He went to take a step toward the entrance, but what he saw on the door made him pause. Made him grip the grip of his gun even tighter.

Whoever had tread on the path and up to the doorstep and potentially into the cottage had left something on the door for the newly arrived couple.

It was a piece of paper, a palm-sized white square affixed to the door by a strip of tape across the top of it.

He approached the paper with his gun aimed at it, as though it might somehow loose itself from the door and cause him physical harm. Like this paper itself was a dangerous thing. And perhaps it was, depending on what was written upon it.

He saw words, a message, blurry letters that became less blurry the closer he came to the door.

He walked up a step. Two. Three. All six.

He stood in front of the door and pointed the gun at the note as he read it. Didn't lower the gun until he was finished reading it, until he was feeling more relaxed, less like he was about to be taken by surprise, gangland murdered. He was able to relax because of what was written on the note:

We hope you arrived safely. The pantry and fridge have been filled to accommodate your stay. Hopefully everything is to your liking.

It was addressed to no one, signed by no one. But Harrison knew who it was for and who it was from.

After folding the note and putting it in his pocket, the adrenaline that had fueled his approach to the door all at once seemed to leave his system. He had to lean against the cottage to stay upright, his legs shaking badly, his entire body a quivering mass.

After he felt steady enough, he almost ran back to the truck to tell Mariam that all was fine, but he decided it would be best to check things out further. Explore the house. Just in case.

He opened the door with a small, tentative smile on his face, looking forward to seeing what the inside of the place was like, what had been stocked in the fridge and pantry, not thinking they would have any further issues after seeing the friendly note. A note that had indicated they would be okay, that, even now when things seemed to be at their worst, they would be taken care of.

He entered the cottage letting the friendly nature of the note lead him. This buoy to his spirits quickly sunk when he saw what was waiting for him. What was hanging there from the light fixture in the middle of the foyer.

What he saw was a rope.

It was white, and it hung from the elaborate fixture, dangling down from the ceiling into the hall.

What he saw was not simply a rope, he realized after looking at it longer, staring at it in disbelief.

It had once been such, but, as he adjusted the words in his mind, as he replaced one with another in order to find the correct term, he understood that this was a sign, a warning, a notice of caution. No longer just a rope.

What he saw was a noose.

Hanging there from the light fixture in the hallway, it swayed slightly, as though subject to a gentle breeze he could not feel.

It screamed at him to go.

It dared him to enter.

He stood in the open doorway, not knowing what to do.

PART TWO

WHITE ROPE

CHAPTER 9

"You think it's a warning?"

Harrison wasn't entirely sure how to answer the question his wife had asked. Why would they be warned moments after being warmly welcomed? That was the question on his mind as he and Mariam sat at the kitchen table, a round table meant for six. At the moment, it was only the two of them sitting there. Between them was the rope Harrison had ripped down from the light fixture in the hallway.

After a moment's hesitation, after standing there not knowing what to do, he had ripped the rope down, bringing the fixture it had been attached to down with it.

It had crashed. Shattered. Provided him with a release. Catharsis.

It had made him feel good to watch it break. It provided Harrison solace to know that he wasn't the only thing falling to pieces.

After bringing down the rope and fixture, he had held himself together long enough to check the rest of the house before going back outside and telling Mari it was safe to enter. He had kept his emotions in check long enough to put the rope on the table and allow his first and only love to debate with him what it might mean for their futures, their lives.

Along with the rope, on the table was a cellular phone; a simple Motorola flip phone unlike any he had seen in nearly a decade. Like the rope, it had been waiting there for them.

Harry had opened it and checked the contacts. There was only one. The only contact he had expected to see. The single name in the phone, next to the single number in the phone, was made up of a single letter.

E.

For Elareen.

"I would have thought it was a warning, but what about the note? And the fact that the fridge and pantry are full. Why would The Beast get her lackies to leave a noose that threatened us at the same time they left a heap of supplies that would help us out? It doesn't make sense. And it doesn't seem like something she would do. From everything I've ever seen and heard of her, she doesn't play games. Neither does her employer."

"I don't know about that," Mari responded tersely, her fingers tapping on the table near the end of the rope, though not daring to touch it. "They made a game of our entire lives. I wouldn't be surprised if they just wanted to keep fucking with us until the end."

Harrison got up and walked through the kitchen to the fridge in order to get a beer. As he looked around the elaborate kitchen, the words rustic and bucolic came to mind. He had the absurd feeling that he was walking through the inside of a tree. With the exception of marble countertops and stainless-steel appliances, everything, including the floors and ceiling, was made of wood.

"Yeah, well, game or not, at least back then their message was clear. This just doesn't make much sense," he said as he looked into the fridge. "You want anything?"

The fridge was as fully stocked as it could possibly be. He was grateful to see all of the freshly purchased groceries waiting for them. But there was something unsettling about what was in the fridge as well.

It all looked too familiar.

Every item in the fridge, right down to the brand of beer he had reached in to grab, was something that would have been on their grocery list or inside of their fridge back at home.

"Harry? Did you hear me? I asked if there was any liquor in the cabinets."

"Oh… Sorry. I'll check." He had been so focused on the grocery items, many of them his favorites, that he hadn't heard his wife the first time.

He opened up a few cabinets. In one of them was canned goods including Italian Wedding soup, tinned sardines, his favorite brand of canned chili, his wife's favorite brand of chicken noodle soup.

In the next he saw the gummy bears he would likely have been craving after dinner, saw the Doritos his wife had been a sucker for since they were both outcast teenagers.

In the third cabinet he opened was the booze. There was vodka, gin, white rum, and not a single dark liquor in sight. Mariam had always reacted adversely to dark liquor.

"Everything you would want to drink is here… This is unbelievable," said Harrison, sounding like he truly was in a state of disbelief.

"*Everything?* Tanqueray gin, tonic water and mandarin slices with a splash of lime?" Sometimes when he exaggerated, she challenged him. It was a quality of hers that had irked him early on in their relationship, decades ago. But he had learned to love it as he loved just about everything else about her. One thing he especially loved, whenever she got to sounding all high and mighty, was having the chance to deflate her. This was one of those times. But he didn't take the same joy he usually did in letting her know he hadn't been exaggerating. He was too scared.

"All of that is here, Goldy. Jesus, it's like they know everything about us," he said as he used shaky hands to prepare her drink of choice.

He placed the gin and tonic in front of her when he got to the table, not far from the white noose that was still in the center of it.

He sat, swallowed half of the bottle of Coors Banquet he had taken from the fridge.

"I think they've been watching every step we've made since we got to Seattle after dealing with Nicholas. And watching us even more closely since the day of the meeting. I just can't tell if this…" He indicated their drinks, the fridge, the cabinets "…is treatment for a job well done since then. Or…" He used his free hand to lift then drop the noose. "…if this is a threat because we fucked up and ended their little project so much earlier than we should have."

Mari took a drink of her gin and tonic, two ice cubes and two mandarin segments in it, a splash of lime to pull it all together. She went to set the drink down, changed her mind, took another gulp. Then a tiny sip after those two big swallows. The drink was nearly finished by the time she put it down.

"That fucking meeting," was all she said.

They both sat there for a moment, contemplating how their lives had spiraled out of control nearly twenty years prior, and how their lives had been out of their control ever since.

"Fuck. We were just kids," he said mournfully, regrettably. "We shouldn't have to suffer for the rest of our lives because of what we did back then."

"Would you take it back? Everything we did?" Mariam asked, finishing her drink.

He contemplated this for a while. The four kids they had killed in a van, her uncle who he had run over, what had happened to Rebecca Greene, what they had done to Nicholas Bedard.

"Only Rebby," he said after some time. "I wish she had never gotten mixed up with Nicholas. Everything else, we had to do."

Did he really believe that? Over the years he had convinced himself this was so, and now he clung to what he had convinced himself of, not wanting to make room for any more regret than he already felt. But, at that moment, he had a thought that filled him with the additional regret he had been hoping to avoid.

"Fuck!" he said, so suddenly and loudly that Mariam pushed her chair back from the table, looking as though she was ready to jump up and sprint. Or to fight, if it came to that.

"What?" she asked, looking around the room, as if expecting assailants to come pouring into it from around the corner.

"The shelters and the group homes," Harry replied after tempering his voice and tone.

"What about them?" Mari said, her body relaxing. She picked up her empty glass and went to the cabinets to refill it.

"They're all attached to us and the FYI foundation. After the police investigate our house and find the girls, dead or alive, they're going to go straight for the shelters. Everything Mr. Bedard, Elareen, and The Fold were running through there is going to be in jeopardy. Or at least under scrutiny. The sort of scrutiny that's going to slow their business down and cost them money. So that means we've cost them their three cash cows in the bunker *and* we're going to make them lose out on traffic from the shelters and homes. How can they *not* want us dead?"

Leaning against the kitchen counter, looking at her husband, Mari sighed.

"You didn't think about that before now?" she asked.

Harry felt himself become angered by the question. Felt his eyes flare and his nostrils do the same. He hated overlooking things, always felt foolish when he did. He was as angry about the way she had asked the question as he was about the fact that his lack of forethought had inspired it.

Before he could say anything that might start an argument, he saw Mariam set her tumbler on the counter and raise both hands – palms out – as if indicating surrender.

"I'm sorry. I've just been worried about that for a while now. But you know what? There's no point in us sitting here looking at that rope and worrying. She left us that phone for a reason, we know that for sure. And she's expecting our call. Let's just ask her what it is she meant by the rope, feel her out if she doesn't answer directly. And if it feels like this is just a trap, we'll go. Even if we're on our own, at least we'll still have a chance."

A pause. Heavy silence. They both stared at the ancient looking cell phone.

"Yeah," Harrison said after nearly a minute had passed. "I'll do that. At least we'll know." He was trying his best not to sound as utterly defeated as he felt. He would make the call and hope it went well. But if it didn't, there would be no running. His wife had said they would have a chance, but Harrison knew that if they had to run from the police *and* The Fold, they would have no chance at all.

CHAPTER 10

"Okay," Harrison said into the phone, relieved the call was coming to an end. It had gotten colder and darker since they'd arrived.

He and Mariam were standing on the expansive porch of their hideaway cabin. They had headed out there after attempting to call Elareen unsuccessfully a few times in the kitchen and realizing that service inside of the cabin was dodgy on a phone like this.

"Thank you, Madame. We'll be waiting. Thank you. Thanks."

Then he hung up the phone.

"Christ, did you win an award? What was with all the 'thank yous'?" Mari said impatiently, but not without some humor, which he was glad to hear. Although not gladder than he had been to hear Elareen tell him that they had nothing to worry about. That she had no idea where the rope might have come from, and that she would ask the people she had sent to prepare the house for their arrival.

"She said she had nothing to do with the rope, and I believe her. Her exact words were, 'Wendelken... do you know how many times I could have had you and your wife killed since you called me from that plaza?'" He did his best impression of Elareen's cold, breezy, sightly accented voice.

Harry and Mari laughed at that momentarily, then realized exactly what they were laughing about and looked at each other in the way that people only do when they're not certain how much longer they'll be able to look at each other for.

"At least we can count on that woman never sugarcoating anything," Mariam said. "She does raise a good point though. If she wanted us dead, we'd be dead by now." Harry could hear a bit of optimism in his wife's voice. Something that had been absent from it since the incident with Aurora.

"Yeah," Harry agreed. "She said her people's objective is to keep us safe, not to frighten us or harm us. *Keep* us safe, present tense... I don't think we're quite as alone in these woods as it seems. I think whoever got this place ready for us is still nearby, probably watching us right now, making sure we don't run." He said this in a tone just barely above a whisper.

"I don't think so," she replied after a moment of contemplation. "I mean, unless they're hanging out in the trees in these woods at night in the middle of the winter, I can't imagine they would have stuck around. There's nothing but trees out here for miles. Besides, Elareen obviously has a tracking device on our truck. If we leave, they'll be able to find us wherever we try to go." What she said sounded logical enough, but there was a waver to her voice that said she wasn't as confident about her statement as she wished to seem.

He wondered if she felt it, too. The feeling of being watched.

They both looked out into the darkness around them; the woods, the world suddenly feeling even colder.

For years – their entire time as teenagers living in the city of Black Mountain – they had heard of this place. White Wood Forest. The supposedly haunted stretch of woods at the base of Black Mountain.

There had been a town here once. A town devoted to the temple that was purported to be at the top of the mountain.

The Holy House on Hellstone Hill.

From all Harry had heard, terrible things had happened at that temple, and in the town that had worshipped it. Terrible things that had led to the town being destroyed.

Rope

The government had cordoned off the mountain, making it off limits. They had razed what remained of the village around the place nicknamed Hellstone Hill, imported the birch trees Harry and Mari were currently surrounded by, built this forest on top of the fallen town as a buffer between the mountain and the world around it.

As far as Harrison knew, no one should have legally been able to build a cabin such as the one they were staying in here in the White Wood. But The Fold was rarely troubled by what was legal and what wasn't. If they wanted something, it was done.

He looked out at the forest, trying to picture it as it might have been before: a small town, innocent people not realizing their demise was near. Not knowing that when they died their existence would be leveled – their homes, their shops, their graveyards – built atop of, this entire area revamped to make it as though they had never been.

"Do you believe in ghosts?" Mari asked. Her voice, after a stretch of silence, startled him.

It was a question he had asked her twenty-seven years ago. Right before they had become murderers. Right before they had become runaways.

He had been worried about two things when he had asked the question then. Two things that were the same thing but slightly different:

He'd worried that what they had been about to do might haunt them figuratively.

He'd worried that what they had been about to do might haunt them literally.

The first had happened, their haunted past had chased them to this place. Looking out into the woods, he wondered about the second.

"No," he said, sounding more convinced than he felt.

"No?" she repeated. "The stories about this place don't scare you?"

"They do," he admitted. "But some stories are meant to scare. And that's all they are, scary stories. I mean... if ghosts were real, don't you think they would have come back for us by now?"

Mariam didn't answer that. He sensed she didn't want to.

"C'mon. Let's head in," she said eventually, hugging herself to indicate that the cold was getting to her. She turned toward the door and Harrison followed, changing the subject, filling her in on further details of his call to The Beast in the Night.

"Elareen said she'll be here in a little over twenty-four hours. They've already set up our new home, prepared two lifetimes worth of backstory and all the documents we need to start over. And she said she'd find a way for us to still be useful to them, if possible. I'm not sure if that's a good thing or a bad thing, but I'm just glad they're taking care of us. We've made them a hell of a lot of money over the years. Besides, this was bound to come to an end someday," Harrison said, trying to talk himself into completely believing they were safe even though there was a part of him that wasn't entirely convinced. Still, he felt much better than he had before leaving the house to make the call.

As odd as the hanging rope was, there must have been an explanation for it. Some practical reason. The cronies who had set the cabin up for them might have needed it for something. They likely just forgot to take it down when they'd left.

They entered the house. Harrison removed Mariam's jacket for her, opened the closet near the front door intending to hang it up before doing the same with his own. But, in that moment, he forgot to hang up either jacket. Forgot he was wearing a coat at all, dropped Mari's on the floor.

She was walking toward the living room, but he was stuck to his spot, staring into the closet.

"Where did you put that noose when we went to call Elareen?" he asked, his voice atremble, his body the same. He heard his wife stop. Looked at her as she turned to meet his eye.

"I left it in on the kitchen table. I didn't touch it. Why?"

He didn't answer, his pulse accelerating. He only looked back into the closet, wondering how the white rope that was hanging inside of it – the noose that seemed to be staring back at him – had gotten there.

CHAPTER 11

They were in the living room, watching the television. The rope, which should have been on the kitchen table but had somehow wound up hanging in the closet, had since been tossed out the back door into the back yard.

Every so often, Harrison looked to his right, from the television to the sliding glass doors that led to the yard. The doors were currently covered over by blinds so he couldn't see what was out there. On more than a few occasions, he had considered pulling those blinds aside to check if the rope was still there, laying where he had tossed it in a mound of snow beyond the railing of the large back deck.

Mariam had told him not to worry about it, that even throwing it out there was an overreaction. One of them must have carried it to the closet when they had originally gone to get their coats in order to head outside. Then they'd simply forgotten they had done it. They'd been panicked, scared, and a little bit drunk. It wasn't impossible that one of them had done something so absentminded.

He had accepted this explanation but had pushed aside the notion of not worrying. Even if they didn't have to worry about the rope specifically, they had plenty to worry about in general.

And their worries were only growing worse by the moment, it seemed. At least according to the newscaster on the television who was currently talking about them.

"... in addition to multiple charges of felony counts of kidnapping, false imprisonment, child abuse and sexual assault, according to the District Attorney's office, new charges of manslaughter have been levied against Harrison Wendelken and his wife Mariam Wendelken in connection with the strange case of the three girls kidnapped, held in a bunker, and made to believe for sixteen years that they were hiding beneath a post-apocalyptic world. The girls are believed to be sisters; DNA tests are being done to confirm this, and to potentially locate their parents or any living relatives.

"The youngest of those three girls, fighting for her life after suffering from a self-inflicted knife wound, went into labor prematurely earlier today. The baby – a little girl – unfortunately did not survive, prompting the District Attorney to charge the couple with the unborn baby's death, a decision that has people around the city and the country debating..."

Mariam changed the channel from the two newscasters on NBC to a panel of talking heads on CNN. And those heads, too, were talking about the couple that America had dubbed the Bunker Baby Bandits.

"These people kidnapped three young girls, who may or may not actually be sisters, lied to them about every single aspect of their lives, *and* stole their babies. *Of course* they should be charged with manslaughter in the case of this newborn who sadly didn't make it. And, God forbid, if that young mother dies, they should be charged with that too. Throw the book at those sickos," said one of the panelists. No one seemed to have an opposing view.

Mariam turned off the television. They had been watching news reports about themselves for hours.

The only bit of good news they had heard from the television so far was that Aurora had survived being shot by Harrison and was expected to make a full recovery. He was happy about her being alive while also wishing he could have done the job of killing her better. Of actually accomplishing and getting away with it. But now that they were on the run and the girls were no longer part of The Fold's insane project, having Aurora die on top of that, for no reason, would have been a tragedy.

"Sickos. That's officially how the world is going to remember us. A pair of child abusing sickos. We should have just gone to the police after that meeting with Bedard and the rest of them," Mariam said from her side of the sofa.

They were on either end of the couch they were sat upon despite needing each other's comfort. On the couch between them, currently, was the weight of the world.

"You really think we had a choice at the end of that meeting? Harrison responded.

"I think we might have gone to jail. I think we would have had to struggle when we got out, but at least we wouldn't have wound up being hunted down like dogs, having to rely on someone who could kill us just as easily as she could save us with no difference to her."

Harry leaned over, reached for the ashtray on the table in front of him. From it he plucked a freshly rolled joint. From beside it, a lighter. Elareen had been kind enough to provide them with weed as well as food and booze.

This, the drinking, the smoking, they still indulged after all these years, but not as much and not as frequently. Now, with Harrison nearly a dozen beers in and about to start on their third joint, it almost felt like they were on vacation. A vacation that had sent them back in time.

He thought of the Sleasy motel, where they had met Nicholas, the man who had lured them into all of this with promises of money. Who had kept them in his web by fulfilling those promises. The man Harrison had been certain would have killed them if they'd tried to escape his grasp. So they had killed him because of that.

He lit up, took a hit. Passed the spliff to Mariam. Around a cloud of smoke, he said,

"I think it would have been just how it was with Nicholas. I think that if we said no to their proposition at that meeting, we wouldn't have even made it back to our car... The police?" This time it was Harry's turn to scoff at Mari's naïveté. "We didn't have a chance, Aunty G. We were theirs the second we got rid of Rebby's body."

"It wasn't all bad," she said. "Our lives since the meeting have been an adventure. I can't pretend I've hated it all. But... I dunno. Do you think it was all worth it? Would you really change it? Would you have given up everything we had?"

Had it been worth it? Harrison was surprised to find that he hadn't asked himself that question yet. He pondered it as he took a swallow of the tenth beer he'd had since they'd arrived.

He thought back to the adoration and recognition they'd received when they had opened their first shelter for homeless youth in Seattle, then the subsequent acclaim as they expanded; the awards, the applause. He reflected on all of the philanthropic ventures that had gotten them hailed as heroes, no one understanding that they were only figureheads for an organization running a highly efficient human trafficking operation through their causes.

People noticed when you helped a whole heap of children at the same time, they didn't notice – and often didn't care – what happened to every individual child in that heap. Didn't notice or care that not all – or even most – of the children they rescued from the streets in bulk wound up having bright futures.

The acclaim they'd received had made it worth it at the time. The millions of dollars they had accrued over the years had also seemed to make it worth it. Now, most of that money would be seized by the authorities. Made worthless.

But what had really made the experience with The Fold feel, at times, like an amazing blessing were the perks.

The huge house, the short, exotic trips, the money, the best of everything that money could provide.

And the stroking of his ego.

For so long, Harry had been nothing. A victim, a loser, a bum. In that bunker, he had been a king. A man with four wives. A man who was depended upon by all of them. Worshiped as a savior.

And, on the surface, in his other life, he had also been revered. Lauded for his philanthropic ventures, loved for the joy his game and its many iterations had brought to his fans.

Fans! He'd actually had fans! For a former fat kid who had been beaten and bullied just for existing, few things could have felt better.

But was it worth it now?

"It honestly depends on how things go with Elareen. If she keeps her word, then yes, I do think it was worth it. The world might think Harrison and Mariam Wendelken are sickos, but soon we won't be those people anymore. Just like we aren't Sebastian Beasts' Bane and Aunt Goldy, the Voice of the Oracle, anymore. We'll have new identities and new lives. And none of Harry or Mari's worries," he said. Then he closed the gap between him and his wife on the couch, momentarily pushing the weight of the world aside. He placed his head on her lap and she stroked his hair as he stared up at her.

"They don't know what we've been through, Goldy. They have no idea what we had to do to survive and make it here. The world has never given a fuck about us, and it has never done us any favors. You remember that, okay? These same fuckers who claim they care about those girls and their babies didn't give two shits about us back then. It was only me and you. And it's still only me and you. We can't care about what they think of us. The entire world is full of sickos."

Rope

She smiled down at him. Sadly. Lowered her head, he raised his, they met halfway. Kissed tenderly.

"Let's go to bed," she said. "The faster tomorrow comes, the faster we'll be out of here."

"You go ahead. I'll catch up when I get tired. Right now, I feel like I'll never be able to sleep again."

He had no idea how prophetic those words would turn out to be.

CHAPTER 12

Harrison had successfully gone from drunk to hammered in the two hours between his wife going upstairs and him deciding to join her.

He didn't quite feel tired, more so ready to black out. He saw that it was 2:06 AM as he stood in the kitchen looking at the green numbers on the microwave above the stove. He had switched from beer to gin and was taking one last drink to put him over the top.

For the last two hours of drinking and smoking, he had been watching cartoons. Something he and the girls had often done when they were living underground. He'd found himself missing the bunker, missing the girls. It wasn't a feeling he had expected to experience. At least not as strongly as he did.

As a result, he'd turned to the collection of DVDs in a tower next to the television. Hadn't been shocked to find all of his and his wife's favorite films.

He'd ended up watching several of them, skipping to his favorite parts. To the parts that had always made the girls laugh hardest, to the moments that had caused them to cry.

He'd checked in on Aurora, the Sleeping Beauty. Watched beautiful Belle and her Beast. He'd broken down in tears by the time he saw Princess Jasmine being promised that she would get to see a whole new world with Aladdin. Something Harrison had promised his Jasmine she would experience one day.

All a fiction. All a lie.

One of many lies he had been made to tell them. A lie, if he was honest with himself, that he had whole heartedly embraced. One that had made him Prince Charming, had transformed him from Beast to Beasts' Bane. Had turned him from the wayward child he had been to the kingly figure that he was each time he descended into the bunker and was greeted by grateful girls whose entire lives were an illusion created by The Fold. A deception abetted by him and Mariam.

In that bunker, he had gotten to experience the fairy tale he'd wanted to live for the majority of his life. For the fat, awkward, lonely child he once was – neglected and verbally abused by his father, abandoned by his mother – Disney movies had been one of his only sources of comfort.

As he watched them on this night, he wasn't quite as comforted as he had hoped he would be. But when he'd broken down at the sight of Princess Jasmine's wonder, he'd gotten the measure of catharsis he'd sorely needed.

Lying on the couch, Harrison had sung softly along with the movies as he wept and drank his drinks, hopeful of attaining the happy ending all of his favorite characters seemed to get.

Eventually, he had turned off the television and gone to the kitchen for this last swig of gin.

Swallowing it, he left the kitchen and walked toward the front of the house, to the stairwell that would take him up to the second floor to join his own sleeping beauty. But, before ascending those stairs, he decided, had a feeling, almost felt like he was being urged, to head back to the living room. To part the blinds covering the glass doors leading to the back yard. To look outside and make sure the rope was still where they had left it this time.

Which was what he did.

He stumbled toward the back door. He nearly tripped over the wide mahogany center table in the lush living room of this place that felt more like a getaway to a cabin than a cabin they were using to make a getaway.

Getting away was the first thing he wanted to do when he turned on the lights in the back yard. Parted the blinds. Looked out.

Instead of turning and running when he saw what he saw, he let the blinds fall back into place, covering his view to the outside world, his body reacting without him giving it permission.

He had instinctively jumped back, had made a little croaking sound in his throat. Contemplated what he had seen. And, with a great deal of effort, he went to the blinds again. Parted them shakily. Looked out.

No, he hadn't been mistaken. What had made him jump and recoil was still there.

It was the rope.

It was still in the backyard. But it was no longer in the middle of the yard in the pile of snow he had tossed it in. Now, the white rope swung from a large white tree.

And from that tree, from that rope, hanging there, swaying in the breeze, was what looked to be a body.

The dead body of a child.

CHAPTER 13

Harrison scrambled to open the back door. Struggled in his attempts to get to the child and let them down. Free them from the noose they were hanging from.

Once he finally opened the door, he ran outside onto the snow-covered deck, not caring or feeling that his feet were bare; his adrenaline warming him all over.

It wasn't until he was fully out the door and looking at the tree that he felt the cold again. And it had nothing to do with the temperature, the snow, or the wintery world around him.

There was no child hanging from the tree he was staring at. The tree he was staring at was one of many that divided this property from the rest of White Wood Forest. He looked at each of those many trees, searching for the person he was sure he had seen, searching for a white rope he was confident he had witnessed swaying there. Looking desperately for the hanged child that had been swinging from that rope's end.

But all he saw was forest, snow.

No child.

No rope.

He took a hesitant step toward the railing that separated the deck from the yard itself, ignoring the snow surrounding his bare feet, freezing them. He wanted to see what was in the snow on the other side of the railing. Wanted to look at the spot he had hurled the noose to earlier that day.

Cold, slippery step after cold, slippery step, he made it to the railing. Peered over it.

He saw what he had expected to see. Saw what he had feared he would.

Where he was confident the rope had landed earlier that day, there was no rope. But he could clearly see, by the bright light beaming from the back of the house, the imprint of the rope that had landed there. And the footprints in the snow leading both to and away from where the rope had been.

CHAPTER 14

Harrison chose not to wake Mariam when he entered the master bedroom. She looked at peace while sound asleep, and he wished for her not to share in his disquiet.

He had convinced himself that he'd simply had too much to drink, to smoke, and that was why he had seen the child hanging from the tree out there. The footprints must have belonged to the operatives who had been here setting the place up for the Wendelkens' arrival. Perhaps it was a coincidence that they seemed to be leading to and from the exact spot the rope had landed.

He had convinced himself of these things after he had run back into the house and to their room, his feet both freezing and burning.

He had slipped into bed quietly, not wanting to bother Mariam, wondering how he would relax his mind enough to go to sleep. Wondering how he would sleep at all.

It wasn't until he was in bed that he realized the room wasn't as dark as it should have been.

There was a light coming from the doorway. A single line, white and dim. For a moment, he thought he had left the door open and the hallway light on, but neither was the case.

He could see that the line was in the middle of the door, and it only went a small part of the way down. He squinted across the large room and saw that it wasn't a light, but a white object hanging from the hooks on the back of the door.

It was the rope, shorter than it had been, but it was the same rope, nearly glowing in the dark.

Seeing it here was bad enough, but seeing what was beneath it made him clench the sheets and pull them up against his chin like a kid expecting the boogey man to jump out of his closet. Like a kid watching that closet open and witnessing his worst fears emerge.

At the end of the short, glowing line of rope, just as he had seen outside, was the hanging child.

He could barely see the figure hanging there. It was a faint form, darkness outlined by darkness. He would have dismissed it outright, if not for the fact that the child's eyes were open, and they stared straight at Harrison.

Looking at him through the gloom were two bright spots against the back of the door, both Bunsen burner blue. Twin flames ablaze in the darkness of the room. Burning into Harrison's very soul.

He closed his eyes, took one long blink. And hoped, much like earlier, that when he opened his eyes again the child would be gone.

But the child was still there when Harrison's eyes opened. He considered waking Mariam, considered the both of them jumping out the window and continuing to run. But then he thought of the child climbing down from its noose and giving chase. The idea of it made him freeze to the spot.

He clutched his blanket, forced the back of his head against the pillow, and watched the child for movement.

It never moved. It never blinked.

And for nearly the entire night, while wishing his uninvited guest away from his room, Harrison found himself in a staring contest with what he now believed to be a ghost.

CHAPTER 15

When Harrison woke up the next morning, he did it with a start. Nearly jumping out of bed, terrified but not quite remembering why. He looked over to Mariam's side of the bed and saw that she wasn't there. He looked at the door and saw it was ajar. There were sounds coming from the kitchen downstairs.

His eyes lingered on the door as he remembered why he should feel scared. Remembered why he was surprised that he had fallen asleep at all. Those memories allowed him to realize now, as he felt the cold dampness of the sheet and mattress beneath him, why it was that he had wet the bed.

He had wanted to go to the bathroom but hadn't risked moving with those burning blue eyes watching him throughout the night. He recalled feeling equal parts shame and relief as he released his bladder into this bed, careful to aim toward his side of the mattress so he wouldn't soak his wife.

Now, he got out of bed and tore the sheets from it in frustration. With the light entering the room from the slightly open curtains as well as the hallway, he felt ridiculous.

"It was a nightmare. You drank too much and smoked too much and thought too much and scared yourself silly."

The boy hanging from the back of the door hadn't been the only nightmare he'd had, he recalled now as he bunched up the sheets and threw them toward the door. If Mariam asked, he would tell his wife that he had sweat excessively throughout the night and the sheets needed to be changed, washed and dried.

It was the need to do laundry that had reminded him of his nightmare. Because, in his nightmare, there had been bloody sheets.

It played in his head hazily now, the ill dream. He had been back in the bunker. Standing at the foot of the bed the girls had all used to delivery their babies.

Beside the bed had been Mariam, on the bed had been Aurora, and they were scared. Because Aurora was bleeding to death.

It had been part nightmare, part memory of the living nightmare that had set this all into motion.

It was a memory from nearly two years prior, when Aurora had nearly bled to death after the complicated pregnancy and delivery that had caused her to no longer be able to conceive. Caused her to want to leave, and him to believe he had to kill her because of that.

In real life, she had eventually stopped bleeding. The baby had come out weak and sickly, but more or less okay.

In his nightmare, what had come out of her was more blood. Waves of it. Filling up the room. It was hot, and the copper scent of it was cloying, nearly clogging Harrison's senses.

Somewhere in the sea of red had been a baby, which Harrison kept diving beneath the surface of the rising blood to attempt to find. If he didn't find the newborn, if he failed, he knew everyone would drown.

Eventually, he had found the baby, picked it up and coddled it. It cried but refused to open its blood covered eyes. He had wiped at the blood. Continued wiping it, hoping to see pink beneath all that red. But the blood would not come off, and the room would not stop filling with it.

In the dream, he'd turned to the birthing bed, had seen that Mari was no longer standing next to it, and it was no longer Aurora on it. It was Belle.

When he blinked, it was Jasmine. And she was reaching for her baby as her blood filled the room. Her dead baby, he recalled. *His* dead baby. The baby whose blood would eternally stain his hands.

If there had been more to the dream, he couldn't remember it. Even as he thought over the details he could recall, they began to fade.

Exasperated and feeling as though he hadn't slept at all, Harrison put the sheets in the washing machine in the laundry room next door to the master bedroom before heading to the shower. To hopefully wash away the ill feelings the dream had left him with.

It was two dreams, he reminded himself. *There was no child hanging from the door.*

After his shower, he went to the closet to find a change of clothes. He and Mari had taken many important things with them when they had fled – their emergency stash of cash, Mari's medication, Harry's gun – but they hadn't taken much in terms of a change of attire. Luckily, Elareen had informed them that there were clothes for them in the bedroom. In the closet.

He found himself standing in front of the closet wondering if he might not be better served going about his day naked. He was afraid to open it, expecting to see a white rope. Or, worse yet, a white rope fashioned to form a noose. A noose with a child hanging from it, swaying from the rod.

Taking a deep breath, reminding himself that he had to be brave, could no longer be a coward, he pulled the closet door open and jumped back from it at the same time.

There was nothing inside of it but clothes.

Feeling equal parts relieved and foolish, he pulled out a pair of jeans and a sweater, put them on. Wasn't surprised to find they fit him perfectly. Then he headed downstairs to see his wife.

He was already counting down the minutes until Elareen would come to whisk them away to their new lives.

CHAPTER 16

"Is that bacon I smell?" Harrison asked as he was halfway down the stairs. Nothing improved a person's mood like unexpected bacon, he had always believed.

Despite his rough night and the day which had preceded it, he was smiling as he made his way to the first floor, feeling like he was leaving his nightmares behind him with each downward step.

"Good morning to you, too!" Mariam called back from the kitchen. "Welcome back to the land of the living. I was just putting your food on the table. I thought you'd never get out of the shower."

"I would have been here sooner if I'd known you were cooking bacon!" he said, turning the corner to the kitchen.

As soon as he entered the kitchen, the first thing he wanted to do was leave. Turn. Sprint away.

Mariam was placing a plate of bacon in the middle of the table, but Harrison no longer had any interest in breakfast of any sort.

He was far more concerned with what was above the bacon, above the kitchen table, what had caused his appetite to flee the way he soon expected to.

Hovering there, in the air, he saw red high-top shoes. Above those he saw black jean-clad legs, an open black button up shirt with a red t-shirt beneath it.

His eyes trailed up and he saw a young face, ashen, that of a boy.

The boy's eyes were closed, his head, which was covered by a bloodred hat, sat askew upon his shoulders, his chin touching his clavicle.

His head was askew on account of the noose around his neck. A noose made of bright white rope.

Above the plate of bacon on the table, Harrison saw a boy, the same boy he had convinced himself had been a nightmare, hanging from the light fixture.

CHAPTER 17

It was a very long and troubling day for Harrison. For he and Mariam both.

He had called for her to step away from the kitchen table when he'd recovered from his shock at seeing the dead boy hanging there. Asked her why she was still in the kitchen at all.

She had only looked at him, perplexed.

Does she not see this? he had asked himself.

He could see the boy more clearly than the previous two times. Could observe what he hadn't been able to see the night before when he had looked at the boy in the darkness of the backyard and the darkness of his room. With the light – which the child was hanging from – on in the kitchen, as well as daylight beaming through the uncovered windows, Harrison could see that the boy was not emptyhanded.

In the hanging child's arms, almost cradled there, was something wrapped inside of a black blanket. Something Harrison strongly hoped he would never ever see unwrapped.

"Don't you see him?" Harrison had said, starting to feel more and more like he might still be dreaming. Having a nightmare. Or, perhaps, maybe had lost his mind and was bouncing off the walls of some rubber room, imagining this all. Because, to his horror, his wife had only continued to look from him to the spot in the air he was staring at. The spot in the air occupied by a hanging child who looked to be about thirteen years old. "Do I see who?" Mariam had asked, slowly, cautiously, as though she too feared he might have lost his mind.

Harrison had fallen then, his legs simply no longer capable of doing the task of their design.

He had slumped to the floor and had begun to sob. He crawled out of the kitchen, toward the front door, wanting to escape. But Mari was on him shortly, stroking his hair, whispering in his ear that it was okay. That they were under a lot of stress, and people responded to stress in strange ways sometimes. She let him know that Elareen would be there soon, and then they wouldn't have to deal with any stress at all.

She had guided him further away from the front door, toward the living room, Harrison still crawling, she stooped over and scooting along with him, like an owner and their dog.

She had led him to the couch. He had crawled onto it and curled up into a ball, his face burrowed in the back of the sofa. For a while, he refused to say a word. Did not respond to her questions.

He had been on the couch ever since.

It was approaching 8 PM. For the last ten hours, other than for five brief minutes when he had gone to the bathroom, Harrison had been on that couch.

He hadn't wanted to leave it, not even to void his bladder, but he wasn't going to shame himself again by wetting yet another piece of furniture in this cabin that didn't belong to them.

His wife had cautiously followed him, not knowing what he might do but thankful that he was up and moving.

After using the bathroom, he'd headed straight back to the couch. Had been halfway there when he'd decided to check the kitchen again. He'd hoped to see nothing there so he could tell himself that what he had seen earlier was a figment of his imagination. But when he'd checked, the boy in the bloodred cap was still hanging there by the light fixture, his eyes closed, the bundle wrapped in a black blanket securely in his arms.

Harrison had sprinted back to the couch, jumping onto it like a child leaping into their parents' bed after having their first true nightmare.

That was what it was like to him. A nightmare. A bad dream that had him feeling all alone. The first time he had felt this way since meeting Mariam nearly three decades prior.

"Come on, Harry! You have to eat something. Elareen is going to be here in *tonight*. We need to be ready. Who knows how long we're going to be travelling for. You need to keep your strength up."

"What I need is for you to believe me when I tell you what I'm seeing," he had said, his voice sounding too petulant for his liking. He hadn't felt this low or helpless since he had been a teenager being pushed around by Benny the Brick and his brood of bullies.

"I believe you *are* seeing something, Harry. I didn't say I didn't believe you. I just… I don't know if I believe that it's a ghost. You told me just yesterday that *you* don't even believe in them. I think… Look, like I said, we've both been under a lot of pressure. You said it yourself. You never got much sleep last night. People see things that aren't there all the time when they're going through immense pressure and not getting enough sleep. You know that." She sounded like someone who was trying, with great difficulty, to sound like someone who was patient.

She had been comforting, even soothing, when he had first told her that he thought he was seeing a ghost. He described to her first seeing the boy hanging from the tree, then seeing him with his eyes open on the back of the bedroom door, and finally in the kitchen.

In response, she had told him what she would go on to continue saying all day: stress, mental health, so much pressure, blah blah blah.

"The rope. You saw me throw it outside. Someone walked right up to it, picked it up and walked toward the tree. I saw the prints." This had been the best thing he could think to say that might prove to her he wasn't going insane.

Either humoring him, or genuinely wanting to see this bit of proof, she had gone out there and checked the evidence in the back yard. After a few minutes she had come back in, first complaining of how cold it was out there, then saying,

"I can see where the rope landed. And you're right, it's gone. Something dragged it away. And you're right again, it wasn't anything human. But I don't think it was a ghost either. There are only animal prints out there. Except for a pair of prints that belong to someone crazy enough to have gone out in the snow barefoot." She had meant that last bit as a joke, though the world 'crazy' had been taken by Harrison as an insult.

He had again stopped talking for some time after that, had curled up on the couch and watched the television.

All day, they had alternated between watching the news – which had informed them that there was now a hundred-thousand-dollar bounty on their heads – and watching more Disney movies, which was an overall more pleasant viewing experience.

Both Harry and Mari had hoped the movies would give him a boost, but he had only sunk further into the couch as the day progressed.

Now, she seemed anxious to get him back on his feet. After letting him know that she had made his favorite meal – ribeye steak, buttery asparagus, and garlic mashed red potatoes with the skin left on – she reminded him again that Elareen was coming soon. And that Elareen would not respond well to seeing him so out of sorts. It would erode whatever faith The Fold might still have in them.

Rope

"I've been in and out of the kitchen all day, Harrison," Mariam reminded him. "If there was some sort of evil spirit in there, don't you think I would have noticed it? You *have* to get it together. There is no ghost here."

Harrison finally looked from the television (upon which Pocahontas was asking John Smith, in singsong fashion, if he could paint with the colors of the wind) to Mariam, one of the few times he had done so during the ten hours he had been laying there.

"I know what I said yesterday, but once upon a time you told me you believed in ghosts. Now, I'm telling you to believe me when I say that I'm seeing one. I was staring at the fucking thing all night. And now he's in the kitchen, hanging there. How can you dismiss the fact that there might be something wrong with this house when you know where it's been built?"

"And I'm telling you..." Mari began after taking a couple of deep, patience-inducing breaths, "...that I don't doubt what you're seeing. All I want you to consider is that this could be a mental health thing after everything we've been through. I may not have really been communing psychically with an oracle for all those years down in the bunker, but don't you think I would have felt or sensed something by now if some evil spirit wanted us out of here? What I've sensed all day is that you've been getting lost again. I've been thinking about how lost you used to get when we were living in Nicholas' condo. You would barely talk to me for days, lost in your movies or shows, or just staring at a blank screen, lost in your mind.

"And for a while in the bunker, on more than a few occasions, I was starting to think that you really believed you were Sebastian Beasts' Bane, hero and survivor of an apocalypse... Sometimes you get lost, Harry, I've always known that. But this is the only time I've been worried that I might not be able to find you."

It hurt him to hear those words despite the fact that, deep down, he knew them to be true. His mental health had begun to deteriorate even before they had met Nicholas, the man who had turned Mari into a prostitute before the two had even realized what was happening. The man who they blamed for Rebby's death. The man they had murdered.

Before Nicholas, what had started Harry's mental deterioration had been his mother's leaving, his father's neglect, the many murders he was responsible for. Murders he had worried would haunt him even before he had committed them.

Worry about being caught for the deaths of the four teens they'd gassed in a van and Uncle Rob, who they had turned to roadkill, had taken its toll. Add to that Rebby's dismemberment and the brutal way they had decided to rid themselves of Nicholas, and Harrison, for a time, had become outright paranoid. Jumping at shadows, worried about anyone who looked at him or Mariam for more than a few seconds.

After some time that had dissipated, and he'd felt normal again. As normal as one could feel after doing and seeing all that they had done and seen. Then, when The Fold had first entered their lives, his mental health had worsened dramatically. He'd had thoughts of suicide to get out from under their thumb. He had promised himself, had promised Mari so often, that no one would control or manipulate them again, and he felt that he'd broken that promise, would never be able to keep it.

If not for Mariam, he might have ended things.

But he hadn't, and their lives had improved, The Fold had even set the two of them up with mental health help in the form of Dr. Sundra Lucroy, one of the organization's top psychiatrists.

They had spoken to her over the phone once a week, and she had flown from Daphnis, Washington, to Boulder, Colorado, several times a year in order to visit them in their home above the bunker. To assess them, to prescribe Mari the anti-depressants and anti-anxiety pills she had likely needed since her teens, since what her uncle had done to her. Pills which Harry had refused.

Dr. Lucroy had listened to them talk about their worries concerning the situation they were in. And even though the Scandinavian shrink had been there to spy on them just as much as help them, she had helped them, nonetheless.

Everything Mari was bringing up now was ancient history as far as Harry was concerned, and just because he might have been a bit off before, a long time ago, didn't mean she should discount what he was saying now.

"That was a long time ago. That was all different. I haven't been that way for years," he said, sitting up, making sure to make eye contact with her.

She looked at him with an expression too close to pity for his liking.

"There's no expiration date on mental illness, Harry. It doesn't matter how long ago it was when you were at your worst. You know that better than anyone. And you haven't properly dealt with any of your trauma. Even when we talked to Dr. Lucroy you held things back. We both did, because we didn't trust her. But you did especially. You just didn't ever want to fully deal.

"Now the media is saying we're responsible for the death of Jasmine's baby. On top of that, you had to point-blank shoot a girl who we'd both grown to love. I think you're just manifesting a lifetime full of undealt-with guilt in the form of this hanging boy. All I'm asking is that you at least consider this. And let me try to help you get it together before Elareen shows up and thinks we might not be worth saving."

He could tell she was expecting a battle after those words. She tensed, sat up straight in her seat; her eyes were focused, her jaw was set, nearly grinding, as it always was when she was uncomfortable, when there was the potential for confrontation.

He almost enjoyed watching that tough demeanor fall apart when he simply said,

"Okay. Let's go have dinner. You should know by now I'll always listen to what you have to say."

And he meant it.

CHAPTER 18

Dinner wasn't quite ready to be served, according to Mariam. Not until Harrison was fed an appetizer of more discussion as well as a decision. Which was fine with him, he still wasn't quite hungry. Couldn't imagine ever being hungry again considering what his wife was saying to him now as they sat at the kitchen table.

"I think it'll be worth a try. I've been taking them for years and they work. You've been trying to tough so much out for so long, and you've helped so many people through our foundation, partially because you gave them the same advice I'm giving you now. Maybe it's time you just accept that you can't do it on your own."

On the table in front of her, in addition to the placemats and cutlery, was a small bottle of pills.

"I don't suffer from Depression, Mariam," was all he could think to say in response to her request that he take the medication she had been using to treat the Chronic Depression she'd been battling for over half her life.

"They're anti-depressants, but they're also anti-psychotics. They might help you with the episodes you've been having. Obviously, it won't happen right away, but start with these now and when we get settled we'll speak to Dr. Lucroy or whichever doctor The Fold sets us up with about what's next."

Mariam hadn't wanted to use the term 'anti-psychotic,' and had flinched after saying it when she'd seen his body tense and his face tighten into a look of sheer defiance.

Harry, after hearing that dreaded 'p' word, was considering going the cantankerous route and challenging her on the issue, telling her that he wasn't psychotic. But, he also had to consider that, at that moment, he was looking at her around a pair of shoes belonging to the dead boy who was still hanging from the light fixture above and between them.

He wanted to say, 'I'm fine without them,' except he was shaking and sweating, hoping she didn't notice his discomfort as much as he felt it. So, instead of arguing, he simply said, "Okay."

She looked as though she were about to cry. Her head lowered slightly, her shoulders relaxed, her lips trembled. But no tears came from her. Not from Hard Mari, Goldy, the voice of the Oracle, the toughest girl he had ever known.

"Thank you," Mariam said. Instead of crying like a part of her wanted to, she stood up and walked around the table to where her husband sat. She placed the bottle of pills and a glass of water in front of him. Watched him take both from her, watched him remove and ingest a pill. She laughed when he swallowed in exaggerated fashion, opening his mouth and lifting his tongue as though she were a nurse in an asylum making sure he wasn't avoiding his medication.

"All gone, ma'am," he said in an exaggerated country accent. They both enjoyed the moment of levity, laughing together despite the peril they were in.

She put her hand on the back of his neck and ruffled the hair there. Leaned over and kissed him on the forehead, right where the knife had scarred him on the first day she had come to his defense. The same spot she always kissed since the wound had healed when they were fourteen.

"I love you," she said. Kissed his lips. "We're going to make it through this. Just like we've made it through everything else."

He nodded, lowered his head, a tear ran down his face. He said, "I love you, too," but quickly and quietly, knowing that if he tried to speak for any extended period of time, he would start to blubber.

He looked at her and nodded. They would make it through this. They always had. At least that's what he wanted her to interpret from his nod. But the motion, it felt like a lie. One she seemed to swallow.

"Good. Now, dinner time. Elareen really went all out with the groceries. Prepare to have the best ribeye steak you've ever tasted."

But he didn't expect to have that ribeye, didn't expect to eat at all. Because, as Mariam had begun kissing him, loving him, telling him that things would be okay, the boy hanging from the fixture had opened his eyes.

Harrison had looked into those eyes. Abysmal blue. And had understood from what he saw there that his wife was sure to be proven wrong. They wouldn't make it out of this. Not both of them.

The boy was no longer still, no longer simply hanging.

Harrison was watching the rope unfurl itself from the light fixture like a snake slithering over grass. The boy was lowered slowly to the table until he was standing on its center.

He took a step forward, and at the same time extended to Harrison the bundle in his arms. Offered what it was he had wrapped inside of that black blanket.

Whatever it was, Harrison did not want it.

He stood. Pushed back his chair.

Mariam heard those sounds. Turned to ask her husband where he thought he was going when dinner was nearly served. But, by the time she went to say those words, Harrison was already gone.

CHAPTER 19

Harrison only stopped to open the closet and grab his jacket before heading out the door. Paused again to put on a pair of shoes. Then he fled, knowing the dead boy – The Boy With The Hangman's Noose – was chasing him. Chasing him and trying to give him whatever was wrapped inside that blanket.

He jumped into their vehicle, took the keys from their place in his coat pocket, started the car and drove down the snow-covered path.

He travelled as quickly as he could without risking skidding off this poor excuse for a road and finding himself in a ditch. In his rear-view mirror, on the porch, he saw the dead boy standing, the white rope of his noose hovering behind him, above him; his arms were outstretched ahead of him, offering the blanketed bundle to Harrison.

Before he looked away, he thought he saw his wife step outside and stand right beside the boy.

Harrison convinced himself that he was doing the right thing. That the dead boy would follow. That the little demon would leave his wife alone.

He drove until he was off the obscure road that led to the cabin, taking lefts and rights down a few other little used paths until he found himself back on Black Mountain Road.

It didn't take him long to get confirmation that he had done the right thing. Because the boy had chased him. Chased him without moving a step.

Each time Harrison looked into his rear-view mirror, the boy was there, twenty feet behind, hanging in the air, his feet hovering a few yards above the snowy surface, his arms outstretched, offering his bundle.

Rope

The noose was still around his neck, though the length of the rope defied logic, floating above and behind the boy into the sky, making it seem as though he had been hanged from the cosmos. It trailed the ghostly child in the air. Shining in the dark like a bolt of lightning which had struck and become stuck. A flash frozen forever.

Harrison drove, his eyes going back and forth from the road to the boy giving him chase, feeling like he was attempting to outrun the Devil.

When he turned his eyes from the road to his rear view this most recent time, he understood that running from the Devil was futile. Even if he got away from The Boy With The Hangman's Noose, he would never escape his fate, never outrun the demons of his past. Because this creature, this ghost, whatever it was, had not come alone. He was here with friends.

Beneath The Hanging Child, on the road, behind Harrison, was a vehicle he recognized.

"Impossible," he said to himself, his eyes bulging, his hands trembling so hard the entire truck was shaking as he drove it unsteadily along.

It *should* have been impossible, yet, according to his eyes, it wasn't.

But what if he couldn't believe his eyes?

Right now, he didn't want to. Right now, he wanted the anti-psychotic pill to kick in, even if it was long before it could possibly work. Because, right now, he was looking at a van he had last seen twenty-seven years ago.

A purple Dodge Caravan.

"Just your imagination," he whispered to himself, gripping the steering wheel so hard, his arms so rigid, he thought he would push the wheel into the car's engine. "It's impossible, it's impossible."

But there it was.

A Caravan filled with smoke.

He couldn't see inside of it, the windows were too clouded. But he knew who drove it, knew who the passengers were as well.

Benny the Brick, his girlfriend Laurie, Gord, Stringbean Todd.

The four teenagers, the four schoolmates he had murdered when he and Mari had been fourteen. The same van he had placed snowballs into the exhaust pipe of to gas to death those teens.

The purple Caravan still blazed behind him, though it didn't seem to be gaining ground. It stayed at the same distance from him, its windows shrouded by smoke, The Hanging Child above it.

All in your mind. All in your mind.

Trying to convince himself of this, Harrison took his attention from the rear-view mirror and placed it back on the road in front of him.

This time, what he saw caused him to swerve. To nearly lose control.

All in your mind. All in your mind.

But in his field of vision was something he couldn't deny.

In the beams of his headlights, he could see a shape, something in his path.

Something moving, but barely, shakily. Something struggling. Twitching.

At first, he told himself it was an animal; a moose, a deer, some road-killed corpse.

He turned on his high beams as he got closer.

Saw the thing in his path for what it was.

A corpse, but not of any animal. Not in the literal sense.

On the road in front of him was a monster who had, for years, dressed himself in human skin. A monster of a creature he had put down for its misbehavior.

Rope

On the road in front of him was a murdered mess. A mangled man.

On the road in front of Harrison, stretched across both lanes, was the shattered corpse of Mari's uncle Rob.

And it was reaching.

Its hand, erratically, convulsively, stretched from its body, disfigured fingers aimed in the direction of Harrison.

Pointing. Accusing.

He was staring at Harrison. From the road, through the glass. Staring as he lay there with his limbs akimbo, his mouth drooling saliva, drooling blood. The back of his head concave where Harry's stolen vehicle had once upon a time run over it. One of his eyes bulged ludicrously from its socket, making it appear twice the size of the other. From both of those uneven eyes, he stared. He questioned. He blamed.

His hand continued to waver in the air, not only blaming but begging, just as he had the night Harry had run him over. The first time. Before Harry had seen these signs of life and had reversed, running him over a second time. Making sure the mangled man had stilled entirely. Making sure he had, without doubt, murdered Mari's uncle.

Would a third time be the charm?

Harry considered running over uncle Rob again here and now, seeing if he could cease his movement one final time. But something told him that he shouldn't. Something told him that if he tried to crush the mangled man with this truck, Mari's uncle would reach up, somehow reach through the bottom of the vehicle, and climb in. Then, his hand wouldn't only point, it would grab. It would reap.

Hallucinations, the stress. It's not real, it's not real.

But his eyes disagreed with his mind. The body in front of him looked real. In his rear view, the smoke-clouded

393

van, still exactly the same distance behind him, seemed all too real as well. As did the boy hovering above it.

Here he was, being cornered, being chased once more. The way he had been as a boy, the way he had vowed never to be again.

Pain consuming his mind, madness threatening to overtake him, a dead man in his road, dead children behind him, not knowing what to do, Harry twisted the wheel to the right. Violently. Narrowly avoiding rolling over the murdered mess. He turned the wheel so violently that he was now heading toward the side of the road, veering in the direction of a snowy ditch.

He attempted to twist the wheel back in the opposite direction, to regain his bearings, but it was too late.

Harry closed his eyes. He thought of Mari, hoped she would be okay as he felt his truck begin to roll.

CHAPTER 20

Fretting was the best way to describe what Mariam had been doing for the past hour while her husband had been gone. Feeling despondent would be another fitting phrase.

She had been pacing the house, from the living room to the kitchen and back. The television in the living room was on, the volume was low. She had no idea what was playing on it because her mind was elsewhere. Her mind was outside with her husband, with the twenty-seven-year love of her life. She was willing him to return. Praying he hadn't truly had the psychotic break that she suspected. Wishing the pill she had given him could be an instantaneous cure.

As she paced toward the kitchen, she heard tires crunching over snow before she saw lights beam into the house through the open blinds of the kitchen window.

Harrison!

Her prayers had been answered, she thought.

She ran.

Through the hallway.

Sprinted.

Into her shoes and then out the front door.

Slipped.

Steadied herself on the railing of the steps leading down from the porch to the driveway.

Paused.

Stopped entirely.

Sighed.

Because it wasn't their truck in the driveway. It wasn't a truck at all. It was a dark-colored SUV.

The windows were too tinted to see who the driver was, but that didn't make a difference. Because it was the door behind the driver that opened. And the person who emerged from that door was all that mattered.

In the light of the front porch, Mariam could see her clearly. She reflected back to the time they had seen her first.

She had been introduced as an intern back then. Someone The Fold had been training. Someone they had apparently trained well.

Over the years, she had risen in the ranks, taking over from Raynaud Bedard – the man who had set them up in the bunker – as their handler nearly a decade prior.

She had always been stern, cold, but always fair.

Mariam hoped she would remain that way now after the Wendelkens had dragged her from her business, altered her routine, risked finding out the reason people called her what they did.

Black hair that blended with the air around her. Green eyes that seemed to stab into the night. Eyes that hurled daggers at Mariam as she stood, still gripping the railing of the porch, her heart thrashing against her breastbone like a prisoner in a cage.

The approaching person's facial features were an amalgamation of ninety-degree angles, everything about her hard and sharp and squared.

She was dressed head to toe in black save for the tawny fur which lined the hood of her coat. Fur which reminded Mari of the mane of a lion. Reminded her that she was dealing with a creature just as deadly. Likely more.

In the darkness, stalking towards the entrance of the cabin, was Elareen, The Beast in the Night.

CHAPTER 21

Harrison's head hurt. He was dazed, confused. For a moment, he wasn't quite sure where he was. He looked out of the driver's side window of his truck and was glad to see the world was right side up.

His memory came back to him in reverse: the truck rolling, the mangled man in the road, the smoke-filled van that had been chasing him, the dead boy that had seemingly initiated this all.

He searched for them now, from his stalled and ruined vehicle, and saw nothing. Outside of the truck, the world was a black sky, a white surface. From where he had stopped in the ditch beside the highway, he saw field and road and field.

He didn't see a corpse in that road, nor a clouded Caravan. Most importantly to him, he didn't see a boy hanging from a rope, floating in the sky.

He rested his throbbing head against the steering wheel. Closed his eyes.

"Maybe Goldy was right. Maybe I am losing it."

"I always knew you were a lucky fuck. With that chocolate piece of yours."

Harry heard the voice beside him but didn't react. Didn't move.

It's all in your head, it's all in your head.

But the voice, which sounded very much like it was coming from outside of his head, continued to speak from the passenger seat as he kept his eyes closed, his forehead on the wheel.

"That's what I always liked about you, Sebastian," said the voice with the almost undetectable French accent from beside him. "You never made a peep. You never got in the way while all those old men turned your woman to a whore."

Harrison hit his head against the steering wheel. Once, twice, three times, harder with every hit, the horn honking in response to his violence.

"Fuck you. Fuck you! FUCK YOU!" Harrison screamed, unsurprised by who was there speaking at his side.

"YOU RUINED OUR FUCKING LIVES!" His voice was a pistol, each word a bullet. A barrage of which he had been holding in for days, for years, the entirety of his life.

Not caring if he was speaking to a shade or to his own bad psychology, he turned to face the person beside him, to continue to lash out. But his words stalled in his throat when he got a look at who was there.

Nicholas, two decades dead, looked calmly back at Harrison, smiling a rotted version of his slimy smile.

"I saved you from the streets. I gave you shelter, money, food, everything you could ask for. And this is how you repaid me."

His face was gray, the skin there loose, sloughy. His mouth was agape, open and contorted. His eyes were dull, glazed over, vacant. Yet they stared at Harry with a bright intensity that contradicted their state of decay.

As awful as it was to gaze upon that face – frozen as it had been in the moment he had died – what was below his face was somehow worse.

His chest, his stomach, his entire torso where Mari had stabbed him all those years ago was still bleeding now. Perpetually so. The white shirt he wore was soaked with it, his blue jeans were red, the car seat below his body was filling up with a thick liquid of that latter color. So much so that it reminded Harrison of the nightmare he'd had of the baby that had filled a room with its mother's blood.

But it was Nicholas' neck that really brought it all back for Harry. The sight of it like a memory-rattling blow to his skull.

Rope

His neck, red. His neck, purple. The skin of it black and blue all at once. Peeling in places, rubbed raw in spots where the rope had made contact, been pulled on, twisted and constricted by the hands of a teenager desperate to stop a grown man from killing his love, from ending both of their lives.

What he had thought would be a quick strangling – that had been how he'd imagined it, how he'd explained it to Mari when they had planned things out – had turned out to be a struggle with three lives on the line. A tug of war with the chance to murder as the prize.

And Harry had won, with help from Mari. They had ended this creature, this exploiter of hopeless children.

Then they had burned him. Yes, they had burned him in his car. Had hoped to burn all evidence of him from this plan–

It was during this reverie that Harry smelled gas. Right there in his truck.

The dead man wheezed, spoke, every word a choking noise. Still, he said it. Expelled a reminder of what he had mentioned right before he'd died. Previously it had been a threat, now it was a taunt.

"I told you I know powerful people."

Then Nicholas began to burn.

The flames started from inside of him as Harry watched this woeful wonder in his passenger seat. The man's skin turning pink, turning red, turning black, then afire.

Harrison panicked in his urge to flee.

He went to open the door before he had unlocked it. Fumbled to unlock it. Unlocked it. Opened the door.

The strength with which he pushed it open, in combination with the wind, caused the door to bounce back, nearly hitting him in the face.

The burning corpse beside him continued to chide him. To choke out words that brought him back to a time and place he had tried desperately to forget. To get over.

He jumped out of the truck. Or at least attempted to. But he didn't get very far.

At first, he thought the burning man beside him had reached over and held him in place. But it turned out, just as he had forgotten to unlock the door before attempting to open it, so too had he tried to exit the truck before undoing his seatbelt.

The belt did its job, securing Harry to his seat.

"It didn't have to be this way. I told you you wouldn't get away with it." croaked the burning corpse of Nicholas Bedard, each word intensifying the temperature inside the truck, and in Harrison's mind.

His side searing, sweat pouring from the singeing heat, he fumbled to undo his seatbelt, he stumbled into the snowy ditch.

He sprinted into the field, leaving the man burning in the vehicle as he and Mari had done over twenty years before.

CHAPTER 22

"He thinks he's seeing the ghost of a dead boy in a red hat hanging around this house?" Elareen asked as she sat across the table from Mariam. In the same chair Harrison had been sitting in an hour ago.

Mariam hadn't known what to do but to tell the woman the entire truth. There was no logical or believable excuse for why her husband had run away right before they were set to be rescued. She only hoped that The Beast in the Night didn't consider him a flight risk. She prayed this creature wouldn't make prey of her husband.

"Yes... It's... I'm sorry, Madame. I know you wanted us to be ready and for this to go smoothly, but he's been under a lot of pressure..." the moment she said those words she wished she could retract them. She was looking at a person who represented the reason for their pressure. "I mean, I know it's our fault... I'm sorry... We're sorry..."

She stuttered and stammered for some time, and Elareen simply watched her for a while, not offering a word that would alleviate her discomfort. It was only when Mari stopped talking and hung her head that Elareen decided to speak again. And she said the last thing Mariam had expected to hear.

"It's okay. I understand."

Mariam's head snapped up and her face expressed the question on her mind, 'You do?'

Elareen read the question and answered without Mariam having to verbally ask.

"I do understand. Of course. I know what they call me. I understand my reputation. But I am a human being, Mrs. Wendelken. And I know that this job brings a lot of pressure. I've seen people crumble under that pressure. Even strong people like your husband. I can track his truck, as I am sure you two have figured out by now. In fact..." She reached into her pocket and removed her phone. Typed quickly into it what Mari assumed to be a message. "I've just told Jared, my driver, to track and retrieve Mr. Wendelken right now. We'll find him. And you two will be on your way."

Before Elareen finished that last sentence, Mariam heard the sound of the SUV she had arrived in pulling out of the driveway. Mariam was immensely relieved to know that someone would be able to track and locate her husband.

Elareen patted a large manilla envelope sitting on the table in front of her, bringing Mari's attention back to the situation in the room.

She explained that the envelope contained the details of where Mari and Harry were headed, what they could expect, the future they could look forward to.

"Remember, your future is in here, Mrs. Wendelken. This is all you should be focused on. Leave everything else to me." Then came another unexpected occurrence. Something that nearly sent Mariam falling backward out of her chair.

Elareen, The Beast in the Night, smiled.

It was not a grin, there were no teeth involved, but the corners of her lips curled upward slightly. Her high cheekbones rose higher, and she looked, for a moment, not like someone who was constantly in the mood for bare-handed murder.

Elareen adjusted the scarf she wore on her neck. She had previously removed her jacket, hanging it on the chair behind her, revealing an elaborate floral scarf which rested on her shoulders and covered half of her torso. It was pink and white and red, adding the only color to Elareen's black attire. Her dark clothes and dark hair emphasizing her sharp features and sand-hued skin.

"Thank you, Madame Elareen. I just... I guess I'm surprised because I didn't expect you to be so understanding."

"No, understanding is not what most people expect from me. But I do understand. Few of us want to be doing this thing we are doing, but circumstances sometimes make it necessary, as I'm sure you can appreciate. It's all a matter of finding a way to exorcise our stressors and work out our frustrations so that the pressure does not damage us."

She said this as she unwrapped the scarf from around her neck entirely, letting it hang over her shoulders like a towel. Mariam had only seen Elareen a handful of times since she had taken over their handling from Raynaud Bedard. This was the first time she had seen the woman without one of her many scarves wrapped around her throat and chest.

She had revealed a long, elegant neck, around it a necklace. A gold, heart-shaped locket rested on a moderate bosom. This was another surprise for Mariam. From all they had seen and been told, she hadn't believed Elareen had a heart inside her chest, so the last thing she expected was to see her wearing one outside of it.

It was seeing this locket and experiencing the less than murderous expression on Elareen's usually stone-hard face that inspired Mariam to ask something she had never believed she would ask.

"How do you exorcise your stress and work out your frustrations?"

Elareen looked into Mariam's eyes, seeming to search for something there. Perhaps something she could trust, a sign that Mariam was worth further opening up to.

"That's a good question, Mrs. Wendelken. And a difficult one to answer. But I will. But first, tea?" Elareen asked, pushing back from the table and rising up, her scarf still dangling from her shoulders. "Or would you prefer something stronger?"

For a moment, Mariam didn't know how to respond. She had been terrified to see Elareen at her doorstep this night. Had thought, with Harrison nowhere to be found, that The Beast would be furious. That they had experienced the last of the kindnesses extended by The Fold.

But Elareen was being excessively kind, reassuring, even offering to serve her a drink. If only Harrison were here. She was certain that seeing Elareen this way – open and kind, contradicting the rumors they had heard about her – would do a great deal to help put his mind at ease.

"I wouldn't say no to tea with something stronger in it," she said hesitantly, wondering if she was asking for too much. But Elareen shared her slight smirk again, nodded and moved from the table to the cabinets full of supplies she had provided them, and the tea kettle on the counter behind Mariam.

Mariam's eyes immediately fell to the envelope on the table in front of her. She was desperate to know where they would be sent to live the remainder of their lives.

The day before, she and Harrison had discussed where they thought they might wind up. His guess had been somewhere in Northern Canada, maybe the Yukon or Northwest Territories where life was mostly cold and isolated from the rest of the continent. No one would look for them up there.

But Mariam had been hoping for somewhere in Central or South America. Maybe Panama or Venezuela, somewhere infinitely warmer than Harrison's guess.

"Feel free to look in the envelope, Mrs. Wendelken," Elareen said from behind her, as if reading her thoughts. Mariam could hear her fussing with the cabinets, filling and turning on the kettle.

"Thank you. I've been dying to find out this entire time," Mariam said with a nervous chuckle. She didn't need any further encouragement.

She reached across the table, grabbed the envelope, and was surprised by how light it was. She opened it and gasped when she saw what was inside of it.

Was stunned by what wasn't inside of it.

There wasn't a single document in the envelope. No passports, no papers, no false identification or carefully crafted background stories.

The envelope was empty.

"But..." Mariam began, before remembering what Elareen had explained earlier. She had said that this envelope contained the details of:

Where they were headed.

What they could expect.

The future they could look forward to...

Nowhere.

Nothing.

None.

Now, despite feeling betrayed, Mariam understood that Elareen had been honest all along. Their future would be as empty as the envelope in her suddenly shaking hands.

"Elareen, *pleas–*"

But she never got to complete that sentence. Because, by the time she started it, she felt Elareen's scarf around her neck. Except it didn't feel like a scarf. It felt like a rope.

And it was choking her.

"*This* is how I exorcise my stressors and frustrations," Elareen said, her voice a cold-winded whisper in Mariam's ear as she strangled her. "I could have had you killed a thousand times between when you ruined this operation and now, but I took time away from my schedule to make sure to do it myself. Because people like you make me sick. People like you *disgust* me. And if I have a chance to eliminate people like you, I take it. And I feel slightly better for doing so. Did you like the look of your future, Mrs. Wendelken? Maybe not. But rest assured, you won't be alone. Your husband will be joining you soon enough."

It didn't take long, Mariam marveled, as her legs bucked and she reached behind her and tried to claw and slap at Elareen, for a person to go from believing they had a hopeful future to understanding they were about to die. It didn't take long at all.

Her clawing and slapping turned to pawing. Then, she could not even manage that as the oxygen was cut off from her brain, as her life was removed from her body.

Her hands fell to the table, then slid off it and hung limply at her sides. Her legs stopped kicking.

As she understood that life for her was over, Mariam's final thought, her last hope, was that her husband, her only love, had somehow gotten away.

CHAPTER 23

Harrison was running again. He was making his way across the field. To either side of him the world was white, ahead of him the same. He had no idea where he was running, only that he was running away. All he knew was that he couldn't look back. Was terrified to see what might be giving chase. Which one of his regrets would be running there behind him.

He was attempting to sprint, but the further he got into the field, the deeper he got as well. The snow reached to his knees, causing his attempt at a run to become a plod.

He struggled on, head down, whipped by the winter wind. The more slowly he went, the more tempted he was to turn, to see if the things that had been chasing him were currently closing in. If they were there at all.

It was all in your mind, he kept telling himself. But the words rang hollow, felt like untruths.

So he plodded on until his plodding turned to trudging. Then he trudged until he tripped.

He lurched as he felt something bump his leg. An object that threw him off balance. He attempted to regain his footing. Failed. Fell.

His panic made him feel as though he were swimming in the snow, nearly drowning in it. By the time he got his wits about him, his balance returning as he raised himself to his knees, he saw the object that had felled him. And all at once he was religious.

"God... help me."

It was a head.

"God, please, no."

A human head.

"This can't be real, this can't be..."

It was the head of Beautiful Rebecca Greene.

"Reb..."

He looked around him. They had buried them, all of her pieces, in a field just like this.

"Rebby, I'm sorry," he said as he stared at the head. Its skin too pale, hanging from the skull almost soggily.

It extended him no solace, would provide no absolution.

Rebby's head only rested there, eyes shut to the cold world, offering no closure.

"I'm sorry," he repeated, then he reached for her. Perhaps to stroke her hair, to touch her one more time, to see if she was real.

But as he reached, she receded, her head sinking into the snow. He watched as she gradually disappeared, his face growing colder as the wind froze his tears.

When he looked up from the snow where Rebby's head had been, he saw that he had gotten turned around after tripping. He was now facing the road, the direction he had run from.

He hadn't made it nearly as far as he had thought. He knelt there, only forty yards from the stretch of road that led to and from Black Mountain.

What he saw on the side of that road froze him to the spot, chilling him in a way the snow around him never could. What he saw there made him understand there would be no more running, plodding, attempting to escape.

Do you believe in ghosts?

The question echoed in his mind, his words from the past.

I'm wondering if we're about to make some.

He had said this almost flippantly. Chattering to stave off his nerves. Not really knowing what he was talking about or why exactly he had posed the question to his future wife.

And when Mari had repeated the same question yesterday, he had been honest in his reply. His 'no' had been sincere. He'd thought phantoms only existed in one's psyche.

But now, at the edge of the road, he saw a vehicle ablaze, beside it was a van, its windows opaque with haze.

Between them, on the ground, was a man Harrison had taken pleasure in running down. A man that still stared, stretched his hand out to Harrison as though Harrison owed him something.

Perhaps a pound of flesh.

Above them all was The Hanging Child, his white rope flowing into the open sky above him.

Do you believe in ghosts?

He had said no, but now his mind was changed.

Because after all these years, here they were, the ghosts they'd made.

But not The Hanging Child. All except The Hanging Child.

This was no mere ghost, Harrison was beginning to understand.

This was a demon and these were his damned.

Only once Harrison understood this did the boy begin to move toward him. No longer slowly making his way after Harrison but seemingly flying at him. His downturned toes skimmed the snow as he was dragged by the rope to Harrison, his feet creating runnels in its surface.

In his arms he held his bundle, the package wrapped in a black blanket.

Harrison, still on his knees, had his hands open in front of him, to protest, to tell this thing to stop. To beg the demon child to turn, to please leave him alone.

But the closer he got, the more Harrison realized he was reaching out to the boy. Not to stop this demon but *to* this demon. This thing he had prayed wasn't real but a ghost made of guilt.

His hands were out of his control, going from gestures of protest to those of invitation.

His arms ignored his commands as they extended, his hands moving forward. Against his will, he was being forced to take the bundle.

Ten feet away. Then five feet. Then no space between them at all as The Boy With The Hangman's Noose placed the bundle in Harrison's waiting and unwillingly welcoming arms.

Then the dead boy spoke, eyes like cobalt coals boring into Harry's skull. He said, in a voice that was the sound of ten thousand broken children, ten thousand shattered souls,

"For you. Your burden."

Hearing that voice – those many voices – caused Harrison to weep.

He looked down at the blanketed burden that had been placed into his arms. And saw what he had feared he would see all along.

Inside of that black blanket, Harrison saw a baby bathed in blood. A red-skinned little girl just opening her eyes. Eyes that Harrison did not want to see. Eyes that he had no choice but to look into as they opened.

Harrison met the stare of this dead child of his. As he gazed down at his baby, he felt everything – his will, his mind, the world – shatter to pieces.

POST-MORTEM

Jesse Williams-White was a psychiatric nurse at Better Balance Mental Health Center – known to those familiar with it as Black Mountain Asylum.

His job had never been busier, nor had the mental hospital ever been under such close scrutiny as it had been over the last two weeks.

That was because, for the last two weeks, the asylum had been home to a genuine celebrity and short-term outlaw.

"They say he never sleeps. The crew's got a pool going. We're wagerin' to see when he manages to finally conk out," Garrett LeMahieu said from beside Jesse.

Garrett was one of his closest friends, and head of security at Black Mountain Asylum. The two men were currently making their rounds in the quiet early morning hours and had stopped to look in on their local celebrity.

"Poor bastard," Garrett added with a smile that contradicted his words.

Not many people felt sorry for their current guest. Jesse certainly didn't. Not after all he was suspected of having done. Not after he had held those three young girls captive, raped and impregnated them, stolen and potentially sold their babies. Or worse. And now he was suspected to have murdered his wife whose whereabouts still weren't accounted for.

The patient had been questioned extensively for the last two weeks since he'd been discovered by a trucker, wandering along the side of Black Mountain Road while looking down into his hands and weeping as he walked through the wintery night.

The trucker had been a good Samaritan who had simply been trying to help a man in distress. When he'd stopped to offer that distressed man a helping hand, he had recognized him from the reports all over the internet, in the newspapers, and dominating nearly every television station since word of the Bunker Girls had broken – the story of the three girls who had been found after being kidnapped as toddlers and unknowingly held hostage for nearly twenty years.

The police were called. And, in short order, Harrison Wendelken had no longer been a fugitive.

But the capture hadn't brought about the celebration the police, the city, and the world had wanted. Because, by the time Harrison had been found, he was no longer in his right mind. And seemed incapable of answering or even understanding anything that was asked of him.

He had been bawling, babbling incoherently and looking down at his hands or to the corner of his cell ever since he'd been found walking along the road. Refusing, or legitimately unable, to answer any questions about where he had been, about where his wife might still be, and about the reason he and Mariam Wendelken had decided to hold those girls for so long.

Worse yet, he hadn't shed light on what everyone was most concerned about. He wouldn't – couldn't – answer questions pertaining to where the seven babies the Bunker Girls had birthed may have gone to.

He had been taken to Black Mountain Asylum not long after his capture, periodically being fruitlessly interviewed, being treated with no promising response. The general consensus, after two weeks of nearly constant prodding and observation, was that the man wasn't faking the state of his mind. Most believed that he had truly lost it.

Some said it was the guilt over all he had done. Others thought it was the pressure of knowing he would be in prison for the rest of his life, or perhaps might get the needle, that had cracked him.

And there were those who refused to believe he was truly experiencing a psychotic break. Those who demanded he be released from the more comfortable confines of this hospital and thrown into a maximum-security prison where rapists and predators like him belonged.

Jesse knew, however, as he looked through the bulletproof glass into the padded cell which contained this famous criminal, that there was no comfort for this man here. There would be no comfort for him no matter where he was caged and stored.

"Nothing poor about it," Jesse responded to Garrett. "You know what he did to those girls."

"True. Poor was a poor choice of word. Let's just stick with bastard," Garrett said. Then the two men walked down the hall to continue their rounds, neither wanting to think for too long about the amount of evil that existed in that padded room in the form of a relatively mild-mannered looking man named Harrison Wendelken.

****

Inside the padded cell, Harrison sat with his back against a wall, babbling softly as he rocked from side to side, his hands bound to his body by a straitjacket. A precaution thought to be necessary after he had attempted to claw out his ears and eyes shortly following his capture.

It had been difficult for Harrison over these last couple of weeks. If he were still capable of understanding and keeping track of a thing such as time, he would not have been surprised to hear that he hadn't slept in half a month. What he did understand, one of the few things he could still comprehend, was the fact that he would likely not get sleep any time soon.

He might never sleep again.

How could he? Every time he closed his eyes, the bloody baby in the corner of his cell began to cry.

Thanks For Reading!

This entire anthology was started because I needed a few paragraphs of backstory for a character in a future project of mine. A series called *The Women of the Woven Womb* that centers around a post apocalyptic world where over 90% of humanity has disappeared from the planet seemingly overnight (for real this time). Some of those who remain, a small society of women, have decided to enslave the remaining men they encounter while using these men in their goal of repopulating the planet in their image. In the image of their society, the New Womb of the World.

The character from that project who inspired *Us in Pieces* is named Aurora Rose.

When I started thinking of Aurora's story, it blossomed into *Beneath a World of Beasts*. When I finished that, I needed to know what happened to the people who held her and her "sisters" captive, and why they had done such a thing. So, I wrote *Rope*.

And when that was finished, I wanted to know more about what would cause Harry and Mari to take the route they took. Then came *Making Ghosts*. And finally, a short story called *The Meeting*, which eventually became the novel *Making Ghosts II: Lunatic Love*.

The Meeting was a 3000-word short story. About 2994 of those words were pretty bad (other than names, the only words that made it from *The Meeting* to *Lunatic Love* were: "A whisper from a winded man").

Lunatic Love turned out to be the most important story in this book. Not only because I think it is the story that binds the four tales in this collection together, but because it introduces the city of Black Mountain and a place called Hellstone Hill. I hope to revisit Hellstone Hill and show you its origins, why the original Black Mountain Village was destroyed, and how it all ties into Greek mythology.

More important than all of that, though, are the topics of human trafficking and youth homelessness throughout *Lunatic Love* and the rest of this collection. Some of the most horrifying stories I've ever heard have been told to me by homeless youth. Stories I heard from unhoused friends when I was a kid, and from those I interacted with professionally as a Child and Youth Worker and Youth Counselor. Situations described that make much of the events that happened in the *Making Ghosts* stories tame by comparison (other than the murders). These kids I used to know are never far from my mind, which is why I write much of what I write.

As for the project that inspired this anthology, we'll be reuniting with several characters mentioned in *Us in Pieces* when *The Women of the Woven Womb* series is completed. Including Aurora, Jesse Williams-White and Garrett LeMahieu (the asylum employees at the end of Rope), and Gorgeous Georgia Greene (the mother of Rebby). I'm expecting to have at least the first book out by the end of 2023. I really hope you'll be along for the ride. It'll be a wild one.

Thanks to those of you who have been reading my work so far. Your support and encouragement keep me going (your reviews help a lot as well). And a special thank you, as always, to the people who help me with the publishing process: Courtney Swank for putting my books together, Ally Sztrimbely for her editing and opinions, and Rosco Nischler for the amazing art you see in this and most of my other books.

I dedicated *Us in Pieces* to those from broken homes. But this book (much like everything I write) is also dedicated to my older brother, Fred, whose death when I was a child broke my home. But his brief life continues to inspire me even now.

Thanks again for reading. Stick with me. We have MANY more crazy adventures ahead.

DIMARO
(August 23, 2022)

If you would like to read more about The Fold and
Elareen 'The Beast in the Night,' check out
Bug Spray: A Tale of (Love and) Madness
and
The Corruption of Philip Toles

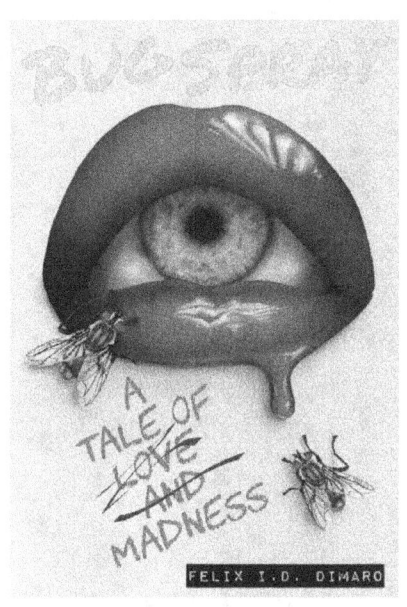 

Available at Amazon

www.thingsthatkeepmeupatnight.com